Concetta was born on the Island of Sicily in 1939. She was the sixth child in a family of nine children. Married in 1957, she moved to England with her husband and son in 1960 and was later blessed with two daughters to add to her family.

She has lived in the picturesque university town of Cambridge for the past fifty-four years, and although England is her home, Sicily is never far from her thoughts and she visits every year.

Concetta enjoys reading action adventure books and writing her stories. But most of all, she enjoys the company of her seven grandchildren.

The Return of Rosita

To Doctor Annabel Wood
My best wishes i Hope
you enjoy as i Have writing
Concetta
Cannavino   16-02-2017

Also by the same Author

A Difficult Situation

Volcanic Destiny

Concetta Coppolino

The Return of Rosita

Vanguard Press

A CIP catalogue record for this title is
available from the British Library.

ISBN 978 184386 987 0

Vanguard Press is an imprint of
Pegasus Elliot MacKenzie Publishers Ltd.
www.pegasuspublishers.com

First Published in 2016

Vanguard Press
Sheraton House Castle Park
Cambridge England

Printed & Bound in Great Britain

I would like to dedicate this book to Saverio, my late brother, the eldest of my siblings, who moved to Argentina when he was a young man and died there tragically and inexplicably soon after arriving. Our family never really recovered from the shock of losing him. I remember my father saying to my mother, 'If we let him go, we will never see him again.' And I am convinced my father died of a broken heart because he never wanted Saverio to leave Sicily.

I would also like to thank my son, whom we named after my brother, for the time he has spent helping me get this book to publication.

CHAPTER ONE

Today was one of the hottest days they had ever experienced in the village of Las-Cejias, Argentina. Joe Onanusi, a 58-year-old black man, affectionately known as Papa Joe, was resting under a large leafy tree in front of his squalid house, snoring away in a deep sleep. As usual after lunch he was having a rest in the shade. He had already been working from dawn to the middle of the day, under the hot sun. His wife, Bimpe, was lying on their bed' also having a rest for a while. She could not sleep well though because she was too hot and sticky, but the heat was not her only problem. Bimpe Onanusi could not stand the flies that incessantly buzzed around her head. Their house was old, and below its sombre grey wooden roof the window to the front stared blankly into wide-open fields.

Their three children, Vittorio, Felicia and Anna also lived in this hovel. Vittorio had been married for nearly ten years to Tope but they have no children. Times were mostly hard and dangerous for Negroes in this area of Argentina in the 1940s. Joe Onanusi and his wife Bimpe worked for a wealthy landowner called Don Camillo Ferrero on his ranch called Hacienda Antigua. He worked them very hard for a meagre wage, just enough to eat. They were all mistreated by Don Camillo's men, especially the women and children who were constantly physically and mentally tormented mercilessly. They were all afraid to defend themselves because of the heavy repercussions they would face.

Fifteen years before, life was not so miserable for the people working on the Hacienda Antigua. Back then, they were happy in their lives and hearts, they had everything and were respected by their boss, Don Sebastian Miserendino, and they in turn respected him like a king.

Joe Onanusi slowly woke from his lazy afternoon nap, stretching his arms. He yawned and rubbed his eyes. He was still feeling tired and confused. He remembered the dream he had had, about a little girl who was screaming and running toward him. He had just put his arms around her when he woke up suddenly. His attention went to a lizard that was scurrying around looking for water and a breeze. In the distance he heard the sound of approaching horse hooves. He wondered who it could be at this time of day, when the sun was scorching hot. He could not see very far these days and the sound was now getting closer.

Joe Onanusi could now see a white horse, but he could not see the rider's face, still the horse came closer, he was suddenly surprised. He held his breath for a slight moment, and it seemed as if an angel was astride this stunning horse in front of him. It was a young woman with long dark brown hair, wearing a wide rimmed hat to protect her from the sun. She came towards him and smiled, greeting him as if she knew him well.

'Good afternoon, my good man,' she said, as she dismounted, her face bright red from the heat. 'My horse and I are tired and thirsty. Could we have some water, and do you mind if we stop to rest for a while?'

Joe Onanusi looked at her still slightly confused. And without speaking nodded his consent, wondering at the same time what a white girl was doing in this part of the hacienda, and in this hot weather. She must be lost, he thought, and then he remembered his dream, when the little girl was running toward him for help. After a few seconds, he turned his head and called to his wife, Bimpe.

'What is it Joe?' she answered.

'Can you bring a jug of water for this girl, please?' Then he called his son Vittorio and asked him to bring a bucket of water for the horse.

The beautiful brunette drank and sighed as she carried on looking at Papa Joe in an almost affectionate way. Her face was tired and her eyes were glazed over as if she was going to cry. She felt like flinging her arms around him and telling him who she really was. The little girl he used to love so much. She wanted to ask him if he remembered when he used to play the guitar and sing songs for her, when she used to sit on the steps listening to him playing until she fell asleep. She wanted to tell him that she knew that he was one of the few best friends her father used to have.

Papa Joe and Vittorio just looked at the beautiful brunette in silence, but suddenly she seemed to waver and then fainted. Joe Onanusi and his son saved her just in time from toppling on to the floor. It was not only the heat and exhaustion, but also the emotion of remembering the past. Now that she was finally back in her true homeland, the overwhelming concoction of emotion, anxiety, dread and relief that she had found her past again had made her feel this way. She was afraid of what the future held for her now and the extent of what she had to do to regain control of this hacienda, to free the people and to avenge her father's death. Anna and Felicia, Joe's daughters ran out to see what the commotion was about. They saw the girl lying in between her parents and brother, who were trying to revive her by tapping her hands and wetting her forehead and neck. The two sisters exchanged puzzled looks. Mrs Onanusi was now using a paper fan to cool down the girl. She was worried for her, and looked at her husband questioningly. What was the white girl doing here? If anything serious happened to her, they would all be in great trouble. Then, the brunette girl opened her eyes and looked up to find five concerned people looking at her.

'My goodness! I'm so sorry for putting you to so much trouble,' she exclaimed, and pulled herself up. 'I feel much better now, thank you.'

All at once there was another voice, directed at Vittorio.

'Are you all ready? We have to go back to work.' It was Tope, Vittorio's wife.

'You rest here until you have recovered. We have to go back to work, please help yourself to any food you find if you are hungry,' said Joe Onanusi, to the girl. 'There isn't much, but you are welcome to it.' His eyes were kind, yet sad. The Onanusis grabbed their tools, hats and water containers and went back to work leaving her under the shade of the tree.

While working in the field, Joe Onanusi and his family could not put the white girl out of their minds. They did not know who she could be and what she had been doing there. They all had that odd feeling that something was wrong. When the time came to return home, they set off for their house, wearily. To their surprise when they arrived home the girl was still waiting there. She was sitting on a bench playing the guitar and singing an old song. Joe stood in front of the girl shocked, his old heart started to beat faster. He recognised this song, a song he had not heard for many years. The song he used to sing, long ago to a little girl, a girl who he thought had been dead for fifteen years. Tears began to roll down his face as the realisation hit him.

'Oh dear God, is it really you? Rosita?' he cried. He had always prayed to God that she had been playing safely in the garden when the assault on the hacienda had occurred and that someone had rescued her. Fifteen years before, bandits had led an attack on the hacienda. Tragically, during the fighting and the ensuing fire in the out houses and servants quarters, many of the occupants, most of them servants, were killed. Little Rosita, the daughter of the very rich boss of the hacienda, had disappeared and everyone thought she had perished with the others in the fire.

As Joe was reliving all of this in his mind's eye, Rosita jumped up from the stone bench and flung her arms around him, embracing him with all her might. Bimpe Onanusi and her two daughters were crying with joy.

'This must be a dream, how can it be true?' exclaimed Bimpe. When Rosita had finished embracing everyone, she began with her long story, explaining to her dear friends what had happened that night fifteen years ago and how she was able to escape, and why she had returned.

'Papa Joe. Mama Bimpe. I have come home to avenge my father, and all those who lost their lives defending this hacienda, and get back what was mine.' Then looking at Joe's tear filled eyes, she said, 'I used to call you Papa Joe; may I still call you that? It would give me not only joy, but strength as well.'

The old Negro consented with a simple nod of his head; he was still too emotional to talk.

'I will need your help and also that of any other people who knew me and are still here. Please, tell them that I'm still alive, and I have come back to claim what truly belongs to me and restore peace to the people and my hacienda.' She hesitated, trying to stop herself from shivering, not from the cold, but because she was remembering the way she had escaped from the hacienda, and the dark scary tunnel she had to be in at such a tender age. Lucky for her, that day before her father had been killed he had shown her, and Nunziato Curro, a Sicilian man who worked for her father, a secret tunnel in his study. She continued, 'Also, let everybody know, that I know it will not be easy, and that many of you will suffer for a while, I know it will be dangerous and some of us may even get hurt. Papa Joe, Vittorio, you know the people we can trust. Please inform them of the situation, and please, take care.'

Joe Onanusi and his family were listening to what she was saying as if she were a teacher, as they were all sitting round the table eating what Vittorio's wife had prepared. After the meal, they all insisted she relaxed and freshen up before she carried on with her story. Meanwhile the rest of them cleared away the dishes and washed up. Rosita strip washed at the back of the house, but she didn't change her clothes. They all met under the large tree out front, in the fresh evening air. The crickets were singing away as if they were welcoming Rosita as well. She looked at her friends, a beautiful black family, she used to think the world of them and she still did.

Rosita, a very beautiful twenty-three year old, with long dark brown hair, hazel eyes, and lovely golden brown sun kissed skin, attained by helping her adoptive parents on their small farm. A very good-natured girl, who knew how to look after herself, both mentally and physically.

'Papa Joe,' she began. 'How is Vincenzo Curro? He was one of my father's best friends. Do you remember, I used to call him uncle when I was a little girl. I thought then, he was related to us.'

'Yes, my child, how could I forget, he and his son are fine people and they are our best friends, they in fact respect us like family. We always talk about the past.' said Papa Joe, nodding his head pensively.

'Tonight,' began Rosita. 'I'll surprise them and I hope Vincenzo will allow me to stay at his house. I don't know if you remember, but when this hacienda was attacked he was away, as my father had sent him on a job. I assumed to the town on farm business.'

'Yes, Rosita,' answered Papa Joe Onanusi. 'I am sure that he will be very pleased to have you there at his house, it will be a great joy for him. One thing that I have never understood over all these years is why he remained here? We have never seen him happy since your father died. Maybe he felt the need to stay here out of respect for your father. So he carried on working for your mother, even though he knew that her new husband was a bad person. And, it seems, by the way, that she is happy with him.'

Joe Onanusi's last words hurt Rosita, she felt as if she had been punched in the stomach. She closed her eyes and breathed in deeply. She remembered her father's handsome face, his beautiful smile and the way his eyes used to light up with joy each time he saw her.

'Why, dear God, why did he have to die so young, he was such a good man?' thought Rosita, aloud. Then she burst into tears. She cried her heart out, the emotion of all those years that had been consumed with anger, all those years of praying to God to give her strength, to live and avenge her father. Also, to punish her mother for letting all this happen, for her selfishness, for never having loved Rosita as a mother should love a daughter. The only beautiful thing she remembered was the love from her father and all his close friends.

Rosita Miserendino had been born in 1922 at her parents' mansion in Las-Cejias-Argentina. Her childhood was not always a happy one as she was an only child; she'd spend lots of time playing alone making pretend she was a princess. Her father, although he cherished her and worshipped the ground she walked on, had always surrounded her with expensive presents, but was out running the hacienda most of the time.

Rosita's father, Don Sebastiano Miserendino had been born in January 1880, a descendant of an old Spanish family, established in and around Argentina since the late 1700s. Unfortunately, he was the only child in the family. He grew up to be a very courteous and handsome man, he was tall and he had dark curly hair. On his boyish face he wore a small moustache outlining his sensuous lips. He was fifty years old when he had died and had been married to Teresa for ten years, a beautiful, but fickle woman. Yes, Rosita's mother was a stunning woman, tall, blonde, fair skin, but she was vain and only interested in herself. The only reason she had married Don Sebastiano was because of his wealth, so she could live a luxurious lifestyle.

Before the assault on his hacienda, his life had been hell for him. A group of bandits had made off with hundreds of his livestock and they kept returning to frighten his employees. And unfortunately that wasn't his only problem; an old acquaintance of his wife has been visiting his home regularly. It was obvious to him what was going on, but he hadn't done anything about it straightaway and for that, it cost him his life.

'Don't worry, Papa Joe,' answered Rosita. 'Her day of judgement will come I promise you that, one by one Don Camillo Ferrero and his men will pay for what they have done to my father and my people.'

Joe's dark face looked concerned. He asked Rosita what she intended to do next; the poor old man still had vivid memories of the horrible scene he and lots of other people had witnessed fifteen years ago.

'Well,' she proceeded. 'At this time of the year Don Camillo Ferreros employs extra people, surely there is a job that I can do.'

'Come on, Rosita, be reasonable. Your life would be in terrible danger, you shouldn't even be here without somebody looking after you twenty-four hours a day,' Bimpe Onanusi said with her husband's approval. Joe was still looking at Rosita with his searching eyes. He was not sure, if what he had in front of him was real or just a dream. And even though what Rosita had in mind, was definitely the right thing to do, a rebellion against the evil Don Camillo would be very, very, dangerous. And many good people could be hurt, including their Rosita.

'Please, Papa Joe, Mama Bimpe. Nunziato and his wife taught me a lot and I'm prepared to work hard.'

The old Negro, looked at his wife, as if for an answer, then, shaking his head he asked Rosita if she wanted to stay the night and visit her uncle in the morning.

'No, I'd better not!' she replied. 'Thank you all the same, but I should see my uncle tonight, because on my way through many people saw me, and if I go to the hacienda tomorrow, Don Camillo Ferrero could ask questions about where I stayed.'

Papa Joe nodded his head to show his agreement and then Rosita continued.

'I don't want to raise any suspicion as to my purpose here. The villagers don't know me, except for Uncle Vincenzo and I'm not sure if Vincenzo's son, Angelo, would recognise me,'

'And what will your name be, when you meet everybody in the village? If you don't mind me asking?' Papa Joe politely interrupted.

'Francesca Curro, of course. As it has been for the past fifteen years.'

'What?' exclaimed Bimpe.

'Oh, don't worry,' reassured Rosita. 'Like I said, for fifteen years I have been known as Francesca Curro, and it has served me well. So that's what I'll be called as long as I need it. After all it's a good name.' Rosita hesitated for a few seconds then she proceeded. 'I have to thank them for the rest of my life. If Nunziato and his wife hadn't taken me away the day the assault took place, I would have died along with my father. I may as well tell you the entire story now.' said Rosita quite suddenly. The expression on her face changed, as the recollection of what had happened became vivid in her mind's eye.

'The day the assault took place, Nunziato, his wife and his young daughter, Francesca, who you all knew was very ill, were at the hacienda. The doctor had told them that their daughter only had a few months to live. That day I saw Nunziato Curro in my father's study, he had come to say goodbye and to thank him for the kindness he had shown him and his family.' Rosita stopped, and began to massage her forehead. Her eyes were closed as if she was trying to remember something precisely. 'I saw them shaking hands and my father told him he was pleased to have a good man and good worker like him on his hacienda, and that he hoped the doctors were wrong about little Francesca. Then, they said goodbye to one another and that they hoped to see each other the following year. Suddenly we heard shots. People were screaming inside and outside the mansion. My father ran into the hall and saw one of the men servants fatally wounded, coming towards him. He was crying out for help, saying that Don Camillo Ferrero and his men were killing everybody.'

Rosita stopped. Tears were tumbling down her flushed face, even after all these years it was still very painful to remember this tragic event in her life. She could never forgive the people who killed her father and many of his people.

'Rosita!' interrupted Papa Joe trying to console her.

'No, Papa Joe, please, let me finish. My father came back towards us and told us to be quick. We went back into his study with him. He then went to his desk and took out a wooden box from one of the drawers and gave it to Nunziato. Then my father turned and gave me a quick embrace, then grabbed my hand and dragged me towards the bookshelf. He pulled out a lever disguised as a book and the wall opened to reveal a secret passage, which led down into a dark tunnel and eventually far away from the house. My father told us he was the only one in the family who knew about the passage. He told Nunziato Curro, that if anything should happen to him he should take me far away from the hacienda and out of danger.' She took a deep breath, dried her eyes, but hot tears were still running down her face like a stubborn dripping tap. Sniffling away her nasal fluid, she began again.

'Then, he told us to go quickly and he returned out into the corridor closing the door behind him. My heart started to thump heavily in my chest; I was so confused and frightened, that I ran after him and opened the study door wanting to call him back. Then I saw Don Camillo Ferrero walking towards him with the look of the evil on his face. I remember my father asking him what was happening, but he didn't have time to finish what he was saying, because Don Camillo stabbed him in his belly, right in front of my eyes. Suddenly I was aware of being pulled away by Nunziato. He rushed me into the secret passage and immediately found the lever to close the false wall. Then he struck a match and lit a wooden torch that he found nearby and we started to walk. A walk that seemed never ending. All I could think of, was the man who murdered my father in cold blood. I do not remember when we got out of that tunnel, but when we finally did, we made our way to where he had left his family and belongings on a cart. We found his wife crying inconsolably.

I hadn't realised at the time, but their only child Francesca had just died. They hid me in the cart, which started to move away immediately, and they told me not to come out unless they called me. I understood that it was for my own good. Then Nunziato told me that they loved me and I had to trust them. Shortly after we left I fell asleep in my living nightmare. I didn't know for how long I slept, but when I eventually woke up I just laid completely still, listening for any sound other than the horse and cart. Suddenly the cart stopped, I remembered that they told me not to move from my hiding place so I waited still for what seemed like an hour.

Gradually fear was enveloping me and I began to sweat underneath the blanket and very soon I felt as if I was going to suffocate. I lifted the cover a little and peeped out, but I couldn't see anyone on the cart, as by now it was pitch dark.' Rosita sighed, she began to feel lighter, as if a heavy load was lifted off of her chest, then she continued.

'As I was saying, I raised myself a little and looked out and saw Nunziato and his wife holding each other, and they were both sobbing. A lantern hanging on a nearby tree illuminated them. Beside them in the ground stood a wooden cross signifying their little daughter Francesca's grave. Moments later, we began to move along again, we travelled for a couple of days and every time we passed through a village, Nunziato and his wife hid me. They would tell me to stay under the cover so that if anybody they knew enquired about Francesca, they would just say that she was asleep in the back. At the time I was too young to understand what Nunziato and his wife Battistina were doing for me. All I knew was that I should obey everything they told me to do. I knew my father trusted them and they would do everything in their power to protect me.'

Rosita looked up at Bimpe; tears were sliding down her wrinkled face too. And she wasn't the only one who was crying, Rosita dried her tears with the back of her hand, then she proceeded, taking Mama Bimpe's hands into hers.

'They raised me as if I was their own daughter, maybe even better than that.

'After what I thought at the time was about four days' travelling, we reached Bella Vista village. It was almost dawn as we crossed the village to their home. We saw the small glow of paraffin lamps in some of the windows. Those people were already up, and having their breakfast before going to work, long before the sun had risen. We drew up to their house. We all got down from the cart and

Mrs Curro took hold of my hands and led me to the front of their home.'

'Come Rosita, we're here and from now on, this is your home too.' Mrs Curro hesitated at the front door for a few seconds. Tears began to cascade down her cheeks, she embraced me, and then she said. 'You're very welcome here; I hope we can make you as happy as our daughter was.'

'God knows what was going through her mind. But at that very moment, I suddenly realised that I was to take the place of their daughter, Francesca, and I hoped that I could fill them with as much pride as their daughter had done. Then Mrs Curro retrieved the door key from under a stone and we entered. First of all she lit a paraffin lamp and then she asked me if I would like to sit down.

'Nunziato will be going to fetch some milk for us soon; you must be very hungry Rosita?' she asked me.

'No thank you;' I replied looking around the room. Everything seemed so small; I had been used to living in a very large house. Here at Nunziato's house the furniture was basic, sparse and meagre. Downstairs one room served as a kitchen, dining room and sitting room. The wood in the fireplace was all prepared ready for a fire. It didn't seem as if they had been away for four months as everything was tidy and clean. Mrs Curro lit the fire and sighed, obviously she was unhappy to be back. She had lost her only daughter just a few days ago; only God knows how she was suffering.

The only obstacle on their minds now was how Nunziato Curro and his wife were going to tell their friends, and their doctor, of all these tragic events as well as convince them and keep up the pretence that I was Francesca. They could easily fool the villagers, because Francesca had always been sick and so hardly ever went out. She had also been away with her family for the last four months; consequently they didn't know her that well. As I was the same age as Francesca and I had the same colour hair, I could easily pass for her. But even so, they decided they would tell the truth to their close friends, one at a time as time went by. After a while I would be able to go out to play without fear, and people would assume I was Francesca Curro.

Their best friends were a Chinese family who lived nearby, it was they who had looked after the house and animals while the Curro's had been away. Nunziato and Battistina owned a small piece of land behind their house where they grew crops and there was also a stable for the horse. Nunziato unloaded the cart and brought in a few things. He told his wife he was going to see their neighbours and at the same time, he would fetch some milk.

Nunziato walked to his neighbour's place, as he needed to stretch his legs after the long journey. The moment Nunziato left he knew of course, he shouldn't be leaving his wife and Rosita alone straight away, but he felt he had to tell someone what had happen. The four days of hell he had just been through. He was so desperate to talk to Jon Chian, who he considered not only his best friend, but also his confidant. He trusted him with his life. Nunziato still felt a bit shaken from what had happened four days ago before his very eyes. He felt guilty for not being able to help his friend and master.

'Come with me dear' said Mrs Curro, laying her hand on my shoulder, I followed her upstairs and at the top we entered the first room. 'This is my bedroom' she announced. 'Come I will show you yours' she said, accompanying me to the room that from that moment on was to be mine. It was simple and clean, I got the feeling that there had been a lot of love and affection there. I lay on the bed and she come to me and touched my forehead.

'I hope you like this room,' she said simply. Then she turned and left me alone. I lay on my back staring at the ceiling, thinking about the past few days, replaying every detail and feeling all the pain and anguish again. I eventually fell into a deep sleep. I dreamed that I was at my home in my mother's kitchen, and she was there with me, along with her lover, Don Camillo Ferrero. But before I started to panic, I suddenly woke up. I could hear voices and I smelt food cooking. It must have been at least midday, I got up slowly and went to the window. The first thing I saw was a chicken coop and lots of chopped wood piled up, ready for the winter. Nearby I saw two children playing. There was a boy who looked to be near my age and a girl who I thought was probably four or five years old. I was hungry, my stomach had begun to rumble and in my heart I felt happy at seeing the two children enjoying themselves and I decided to go down. As I got to the kitchen, I could hear voices. Gingerly I opened the kitchen door and stepped inside. At once everybody stopped talking and turned to stare at me. One of them, a Chinese man stood up and came to greet me, he was not very much taller than I was.

'Hello Francesca, how are you? Did you have a good journey? My name is Jon Chian. And this lady here, is my wife Giovanna,' he said.

I looked at Mrs Curro, who came and put her arm around me, and then she lent forward and kissed my forehead.

'Francesca,' she said, smiling to reassure me not to be afraid of her friends. 'These are my very good friends and neighbours. Now, will you come outside with me, there are two children I want you to meet.'

'I imagined they would be the two children I had seen through the window upstairs. As soon as the two children saw us they came towards me smiling.

'Hello, how are you?' said the boy. 'Are you Francesca, the new Francesca?' He continued by introducing himself. 'My name is Chen Chian; would you like to play with us?'

'I smiled but I did not know what to say. A few minutes later, Jon Chian came out of the house with his wife and called to his children. 'Let's go children,' said the Chinaman. 'Mr and Mrs Curro are very busy and tired from the travelling.' Turning to me he said, 'You can come and play with Chen and Meilin any time you want, but for now we must say goodbye.'

Nunziato and Battistina thanked Jon and Giovanna for all they had done and said they would see them very soon. It seemed to me that he and his wife had told his friends all about me.

Months passed and I met many more people and I was accepted as Francesca Curro. I started going to school, I remember being terrified on my first day, but I was never left alone. Every morning Chen and Meilin would come and fetch me and I felt safe, it was as though I had a new brother and sister. The children at school did not really bother me, but if anyone started to make fun of me, Chen would stop them straight away, threatening to tell the teacher.

Every day after school I was allowed to play with the Chen and Meilin at my home or at their house, and every Sunday morning we would go to church, then to the Chian household to play in the afternoon. It was there that Mr Chian began to teach us the art of self-defence. At first I did not take it seriously, but as time went by I really wanted to learn, not only for my personal defence, but because in the back of my mind I thought that one day I would go back to avenge my father's death and reclaim the hacienda, my hacienda, and this skill would help me achieve my goal.

As the years went by, Nunziato and Battistina were very happy to have me with them, I could see the expressions in their eyes, they were very proud of me. Some evenings we would all sit together at the table, they would enquire about everything I done at school and what I had learned and sometimes they even asked me light heartily if I had a boyfriend yet. Nunziato often helped me with my homework, especially with maths, as I did not find that subject particularly easy or should I say honestly, I didn't like it. Occasionally we would sit and play draughts, in the evening.

'Oh dear God! I'm sorry, Papa Joe, I didn't realise I had been talking for so long, you must all be so tired, I should go now. But we will have lots of time to talk in the near future if everything goes as I have planned.'

'Well Rosita, we're all pleased to see you again after all these years, for us it's a miracle and we are filled with joy that you had a good and happy upbringing. We wish you all the luck with your plans, goodbye and may God go with you.' said Joe Onanusi, opening his arms and hugging Rosita, he still couldn't believe she was alive and back here after all these years.

'Goodbye Papa Joe, I hope to see you all soon.' They all hugged Rosita, and then she mounted her white palomino and set out for the hacienda. On the way there, she thought that it only seemed like yesterday that she had left her home, all be it forcibly and returning now incognito was so exciting and daunting at the same time.

Not far from the hacienda, she caught up with a group of Negroes returning from work and stopped to ask if they were going in her direction. One young woman was carrying a baby on her back and was also laden with tools and food and looked as if she was struggling.

'Yes, Miss.' answered one of them.

'Good, then pass me your baby,' said Rosita, stretching out her arms to the young woman, who looked shocked and scared 'Let me relieve the weight from your back.' The group looked at her in surprise; they could not understand why a white woman should offer to help them. This just didn't happen here. Rosita guessed what the woman was thinking.

'Don't worry; I'll give you back your baby before we get to the gate of the main house.' Rosita smiled at the woman. Slowly and tentatively the woman handed her baby over, the baby did not stir and seemed to like Rosita. They all walked together in silence.

As promised, when they approached the gate, Rosita handed the child back. She said to them. 'My name is Francesca Curro and I have come to visit my Uncle Vincenzo.'

Again the Negroes looked at each other dumbfounded; they had not expected any politeness from this woman. Rosita then slapped her palomino and trotted to the gate, by now the sun was setting and there was a light-refreshing breeze. Many people were coming back from work now, as soon as she entered the gate she was face to face with the mansion which she knew so well. For a few brief seconds she felt scared, the shock of seeing the house where she was born, and where she'd seen her father murdered. This sight frightened and alarmed her almost to the point of panic. But she managed to keep it together as always, after all, she hadn't come here just to visit the place where she was born, she came here for an important reason, in fact the most important in her whole life.

In front of the Mansion she saw people coming and going, close to the front door she saw two men talking. One was Don Camillo Ferrero she recognised him immediately. The other was a young man, and very handsome too! Three other men were just dismounting from their horses and two maids were walking towards the house, each carrying a basket full of fresh vegetables. She saw a full cart of people returning from the fields. As she rode her horse into the main entrance, all eyes were upon her and she hesitated for a few seconds contemplating her next move. She decided to waste no more time.

'Good evening, gentlemen, can you tell me please, where I might find Don Vincenzo Curro?' She paused for a long few seconds and repeated, 'Don Vincenzo Curro?'

Don Camillo Ferrero approached her and took off his hat.

'Good evening, Miss. With whom do I have the pleasure of speaking to? I'm the master of this hacienda,' he said looking into her deep dark eyes, which were regarding him petulantly like a cross child.

'My name is Francesca Curro.' She answered, outwardly smiling but churning inside.

'I'm pleased to meet you,' replied Don Camillo. Delightful, he thought as he surveyed the beauty in front of him. Rosita extended her hand to shake his. Then the young man who had been talking with Don Camillo ventured forward and gazed up at Rosita. He knew he had a cousin but not such a beautiful one!

'Good evening,' he said. 'I'd be glad to accompany you to Mr Curro, I'm his son.'

'Ah, then you must be my cousin, Angelo,' she exclaimed. 'Father is always speaking of you and would be very pleased to see you again.'

They shook hands and then Rosita dismounted. After saying goodbye to Don Camillo they both left together. She took off her hat letting her long wavy brown hair fall onto her shoulders, then shaking her head she gracefully released her curly main to show its full glory.

'I hope you have had a good journey?' asked Angelo thinking again what a beauty she was. He looked into her beautiful dark eyes, which were looking at him in the same intense way he was looking at her. He couldn't help it; he had to touch her in some way. He stopped in front of her and he said, stretching his hand out with a devilish smile on his sensual lips. 'I'm very happy to see you again after all these years.'

Rosita returned his smile and her eyes sparkled like stars at night.

'Yes, the journey was good thanks be to God,' she said, blushing. 'The heat was stifling but I travelled well because I took my time, taking many breaks in the shade of trees on the way. And my journey was made better by the many good and friendly people I met along the way. Anyway how are your parents keeping?' she blurted, then realising what she had said, she could have bitten her tongue. How could she have forgotten about his mother's death? She was mesmerised by his voice and his hypnotic gaze. Angelo hesitated for a moment before replying.

'Father is well but we lost Mother nearly two years ago.' A sadness fell over his eyes.

'I'm so sorry,' said Rosita and they continued in silence for the rest of the way. They arrived at the front of the house and Angelo turned to her.

'Do you mind waiting here for a minute?' he said. 'I'd like to warn my father before you come in. You know, he is not getting any younger. When we lost Mother he took it very badly, he misses her very much.'

Rosita nodded, and Angelo went in.

'Hello, Father.' he said, putting his hands into his trouser pockets casually.

'Hello, Angelo, you're early tonight, but that's good because dinner's nearly ready.' he said, giving a quick glance at Angelo then turning back to what he was doing.

'Wait a moment, Father, do you mind stopping what you're doing for a second, I have something to tell you.' His father turned to him again. 'Outside there's someone who came from far away to visit you, so would you mind coming out to greet her?'

'Who is it? Who would come to see us?'

'It's my cousin, Francesca, Father, Uncle Nunziato's daughter.' For a quick moment Angelo saw something strange in his father's face, surprise, confusion, sadness, but why? He thought he would be thrilled to see her.

'No, that's impossible.' Was his father's answer. His brother Nunziato would never permit such nonsense.

'Father, I'm serious, wait a moment.' Angelo went out and called her, she came in and greeted Vincenzo and then embraced him. Vincenzo could not say a word, he just cried with joy at seeing her. But his old mind was asking, what's going to happen now? Vincenzo was getting too old and was not in the best of health, he knew that the girl was not who she said she was but in fact Rosita Miserendino. In fifteen years Vincenzo had seen her only twice. On the few visits to his brother Nunziato, but they had not had much contact. He had seen his brother a few more times, when Nunziato had come to the hacienda in the summer to work. But then stopped coming, as he could not stand the pain in his heart, the memories of his daughter and his best friends' violent death were too much for him to bear. For a short while the three were silent, Angelo decided to break the silence.

'Well I don't know about you two, but I'm starving,' he said, not knowing why his father's joy of seeing Francesca vanished so quickly. He set the table with his cousin's help, and Vincenzo served out the meal, which had been his job since his wife had died. They started to eat, the food was good and Rosita complimented him on it. Vincenzo had not said much to her, he was in deep thought.

But suddenly he took her hand in his and said. 'You're welcome in our house; you do not know how happy I am to see you again. How are your parents and why did they let you come here alone?'

'Well Uncle Vincenzo, as a matter of fact they were not so happy about me coming, but they let me follow my heart, as I had desired to for a long time. You know that I love Mother and Father very much, but each of us has our own destiny waiting for us, and I feel my destiny is here.'

'And what do you plan to do?' asked Vincenzo, trying to control himself, but from what? He didn't even know what he really felt, if the feeling in his gut was fear, anxiousness for Rosita or happiness to again see someone he once loved as a child. 'And how long do you intend to stay here?'

Angelo now detected that something was different in his father's voice.

'Father!' Angelo interrupted, thinking his father had offended his cousin Francesca. 'What are you saying? Francesca has only just arrived.'

Vincenzo ignored Angelo's comment. He just waited for Rosita's answer.

'I'm here to look for a job,' she replied, giving him a cheeky look. 'I cannot live off my parents' backs forever.'

'I see, but what sort of work can you do? Dear God, Francesca, this is no place for you; there are some heartless people here. You know what I mean?'

'Don't worry Uncle; you'll see, everything will be all right.' Was her reply.

Angelo was baffled at his father's reaction and expressions, but decided to give in for now, as he knew it was getting late.

'Angelo, go and prepare the room for your cousin,' he said, still wishing Rosita had never turned up. Not because he didn't love her, but for the simple reason that he was worried sick for her life.

'Uncle, I'll help you to clear the table.'

'No, leave it Francesca, this little job is mine, I'll do it tomorrow morning, let's go and get your things in from outside.'

'Thank you, Uncle, but all my possessions are in this bag.'

'What! A young beautiful woman like you, travelling with just a few things?'

'Calm down uncle, the rest of my things are on their way, all being well they should be here in a few days! I sent them by train; you know how the railways work here, they always take their time. And once they arrive at the station, they will be delivered.

'Uncle, if it is inconvenient for me to stay here, please tell me, I won't be offended and I will find a place somewhere in the village.'

'Don't even think it,' was his response. 'You are here and you will stay, there's a room for you and even if there wasn't. We would make room for you, Francesca.' Then her uncle embraced her and whispered to her not to let Angelo hear their conversation. 'Be careful, my dear, it will not be easy for you to do what you have in mind. But remember, many people will be eager to help you, me being the first of course.'

'Thank you Uncle Vincenzo, I know that already, I felt it in my heart. And please don't be concerned, I'll be very careful.'

The three of them spent the rest of the evening catching up on what had been happening in each other's lives. Before they all retired to bed, Angelo asked if she would like to go with him the following morning.

'I'll take you for a long ride and we'll go by the mountains if you are not too tired.'

'With pleasure, Angelo. I'll be down before you, good night Uncle, Angelo, I'll see you in the morning.'

Rosita entered the room her cousin had prepared for her, she didn't care what it looked like, and she was too tired to think about anything at all. She stretched herself out on the bed falling asleep almost immediately.

CHAPTER TWO

When Rosita woke she heard voices outside and the noise of passing horses and carts. She got up, and went to the window and was surprised to see people on their way to work. The night had gone, and she realised she had slept without even undressing. She went downstairs to find her uncle in the kitchen.

'Good morning Uncle,' she said, her face lighting up with a smile like a ray of sunshine, which bought a lump to her adoptive uncle's throat. He hadn't felt like this since his wife had died.

'Good morning, Francesca. Did you sleep well?'

'Yes, Uncle, I slept like a log. Is there somewhere I could have a wash please?'

'Come with me to the back room, there is water in a tin bath, It's cold of course, but there is a saucepan full of hot water on the stove, and there are some clean towels in the back room too.'

'Thank you Uncle. Is my cousin up yet?' asked Rosita.

'Yes my dear, he's getting the horses ready. Here's your hot water, now make haste as breakfast is almost ready.'

'That's lovely Uncle, I'll be ready in ten minutes.'

Rosita quickly washed and by the time she had finished, the horses were already saddled. They all sat down together for a hearty breakfast of eggs, bacon and fried potatoes.

'Uncle, this is delicious,' exclaimed Rosita appreciatively. 'My stomach is so full; I don't think I could eat another thing for a week.'

'Ha! You think so? After about three or four hours riding in the fresh air, you just wait and see how hungry you'll be. Anyway, hurry up, time's getting on and the sun will soon be up high and you will get burnt. Take this bag with you, there's food inside for your lunch,' said Vincenzo.

'And what did you put in it, Uncle?' asked Rosita, feeling the weight of the sack.

'Just a few things,' he answered, smiling at her. 'Cheese, tomatoes, some bread and fruit. The water canteen is already with the horses. Francesca, this evening on your return, we'll go to visit Don Camillo and Donna Teresa, after dinner of course.' Rosita raised an eyebrow, and looked at her uncle Vincenzo straight in the eye, as if to say, are you joking? Vincenzo understood her perfectly. 'If you wish to stay here, we must request his permission and at the same time you can ask if he can give you work,' he said, seriously. He wanted her to realise that he was not joking, and that he meant what he said.

'As you wish Uncle.' She replied as she stood up to leave.

'Good bye now, see you two tonight,' said Vincenzo.

Rosita and Angelo left together and no words passed between them for about ten minutes. Rosita was busy taking in her surrounding, and thinking about what her uncle Vincenzo had said. She did not realised that Angelo was looking at her all the time, and was wondering to himself what was wrong with his cousin, maybe she was still tired or perhaps he had offended her unintentionally. He decided to be the first to break the silence.

'Good morning, Francesca.'

She turned around and looked at him wondering why he'd said that. Then she realised why. He was being cheeky. She had been deep in her thoughts, and had forgotten she had company.

'Oh, I'm sorry, Angelo, I was just admiring the fields, they are so well cultivated, I do not remember them being so well maintained. You see, when I was a child and my parents used to come here to work. I was always sick and I hardly ever went out, you do remember that, don't you? So I never saw the fields look so beautiful.'

'Yes I do remember,' answered Angelo, thinking how strange all this was, and how his father had behaved toward Francesca yesterday when she arrived. He sensed that something was not right, and couldn't wait to find out what it was all about. He wasn't born yesterday; he knew his father had been secretive in the past. But his father had told him it had been for his own sake. 'You were always very pale, and the doctors…' He hesitated not wanting to say the wrong thing. 'But now you've grown into such a beautiful woman, who would have believed it? It just proves that doctors can make big mistakes too… Francesca, do you really think I believed you when you said you were thinking how well the fields were cultivated? I know you have something on your mind. You can't fool me, so why didn't you tell me, don't forget, I am your cousin, maybe you have left your sweetheart behind? Or you are worrying about your parents?'

'Neither!' she laughed. 'See, you're wrong too, not only the doctors!' At that, they both laughed together and continued on their way. 'I do love my parents, Angelo, and I do miss them, but like I told Uncle Vincenzo they have done enough already, I have to work and support myself. Tell me Angelo, which part of the plantation are we heading for and what work do you have to do today?' asked Rosita.

'Today, I must do a general sweep of all areas to check for any problems. For example, to see if any animals are loose from their pens or if there are any broken fences and I must make sure that everything is running smoothly,' finished Angelo, his eyes glistened as he spoke to her. Angelo being a tall, handsome man with wavy fair hair and a beautiful pair of brown, almond shaped eyes was pleasing to Rosita's eyes. He is the type of young virile man who any woman would love to be involved with. Kind and gentle towards everybody, especially with children and women, but God help any man who tried to cross his path, because he is strong and capable of defending himself.

His father, Vincenzo Curro, had also been a handsome man in his youth, but now, at sixty-seven year old, is a tall and distinguished looking man but starting to show his age due to the stresses of life. An Italo American, whose parents were one of the first families who left their country, to find a better life in Argentina. He was one of the lucky ones who had found good work, but of course many had found disappointment and poverty. He had worked at the Hacienda Antigua for over forty years. Unfortunately, not long ago Vincenzo lost his wife, and now devastated by the loss of his dear companion, keeps himself busy looking after his son Angelo, his only child. Who also misses his mother terribly, and now he is concerned about Vincenzo's health. Angelo would like his father to retire and move away to a village, preferably somewhere nearer his brother Nunziato. But, Vincenzo is a stubborn man, and for some reason, he had said to his son, that he could not leave the hacienda Antigua. Vincenzo's brother is a few years younger than him, and since the death of his daughter Francesca fifteen years ago, had visited Vincenzo only twice.

'Today you will sample the fresh mountain air in your lungs, and I'm very lucky to have somebody who looks so angelic to share it with me,' blurted out Angelo. He couldn't stop himself saying those words as he was smitten by this beautiful girl. To his eyes, she really did look like an angel.

'Thank you kind sir,' said Rosita. 'But what would your true love think of you going out alone all day with another woman? I shouldn't think she'll ever speak to you again if she found out.'

'Well, you are mistaken my dear cousin,' Angelo replied reminding himself that she was out of bounds as she was his cousin. 'It is not as you think.'

'Really? She must be a very trusting and tolerant woman not to say a word?' asked Rosita playfully. She really enjoyed being out with Angelo, if only he knew how she felt, and who she really was!

'She wouldn't say a word and do you want to know why?' He hesitated. 'Because I don't have a true love as you put it. Where would I find the right girl for me in a place such as this? There is only work and problems here.'

'Problems?' replied Rosita inquisitively, pretending to have no knowledge of the matter. 'What sort of problems are you talking about?'

'Not today, you've only just arrived. There's plenty of time to tell you, if you stay long enough, but I think you'll soon see for yourself. Anyway, you have to promise me something,' said Angelo, suddenly looking pensive.

'What's that?' asked Rosita, perceiving a wanting in his voice.

'Last night…' began Angelo, but was distracted by a rustling noise coming from a field close by. He quickly went for his rifle thinking a dangerous animal had maybe picked up their scent. Or possibly one of Don Camillo's men was playing God with some Negroes. 'Don't move,' he whispered to Rosita. He dismounted quickly and quietly to check. Swiftly Angelo moved into the green field of two-metre high corn in the direction the noise had come from. It didn't take long to find the cause of the noise. He found a wild dog devouring a rabbit about six or seven metres ahead of him. Angelo thought nothing of it and turned to leave, but the dog heard Angelo and went for him. Hearing the dog running for him Angelo turned on the spot, raised his rifle, took aim and shot the dog in a split second.

As he turned again to go back, he saw that Rosita had dismounted and moving towards him, she was holding her rifle up ready to shoot. Her heart was thumping in her chest, so much so, that for a long moment she couldn't say a word to him. Angelo saw the look of relief on her face as she walked quickly to him, and he understood instantly what she was thinking.

'It's okay, I'm all right, it was just a wild dog. Unfortunately it went for me so I had to put it down, he could have had rabies. Are you all right?'

'Yes Angelo, I thought you may have bumped into one of Don Camillo's men or a bandit. When I heard the shot I thought they…' She stopped, she was now too emotional; Angelo stretched out one hand and pulled her to him.

'I'm so sorry, Francesca, I hadn't planned for this to happen, I wanted your first day out with me to be a wonderful one. You don't need to worry about me I haven't got any enemies here. So now, give me a smile, then we will be on our way.'

She obliged him with a genuine smile, as a single crystalline tear escaped from her dark eyes. Looking down at her face Angelo thought to himself, what a beautiful picture this would make.

'I'm sorry Angelo, I don't know what came over me. I'm not usually a person who gets scared very easily.'

'You are forgiven, my beautiful cousin. And you don't look like someone who gets scared easily,' he said, helping her to mount her horse by holding her knee in his cupped hands and giving her a boost up. They rode on for another five minutes without saying anything. Then Angelo broke the silence again. 'I think there is something you and my father are hiding from me, I hope you two don't wait too long to confide in me, I'm a big boy now.'

She smiled at him, and for once she felt speechless.

'Ah! Now that I remember,' continued Angelo, 'what I was trying to tell you earlier. Last night when you arrived, did you see three men standing to the left of Don Camillo's house as you look at it?'

'Yes, I saw them, but I did not take too much notice of them,' she said, wrinkling her forehead in recollection.

'Good. Let it stay that way! Don't look at them and keep away from them, they cause nothing but trouble, they are bad news.'

'Hey! What happened to the happy face you had a moment ago?'

'Again, I must apologise dear, Francesca, like I said before I brought you out here with the intention of spending a lovely day out together, but instead I'm giving you lectures.' He said, looking ahead of him. 'We're here.' What was wrong with him? He asked himself. She had only been here twelve hours and he already felt responsible for her. He should get a hold of himself, if not, he would look ridiculous. Behaving more like her father instead of her cousin.

'Oh, look at that little house,' she exclaimed, 'Over there. Does anybody live in it?' Forgetting for a moment all the trouble she could get into asking too many questions. It's too early to be inquisitive; she should behave like a girl who's lost without her parents. But she found it difficult especially around her adopted cousin.

'No,' replied Angelo. 'It was built for the men who come to work in this area, sometimes they stop over for a couple of days, it's safer for them in there. At the bottom of the mountains there are many wild animals and at night they come looking for food.' The terrain around them looked sombre; the ground was very dry, as there hadn't been any rain for some time now. All the grass and bushes were shrivelled dry husks.

'How beautiful, a mountain stream,' remarked Rosita, happily.

They dismounted, and led the horses into a small yard beside the little house, where they unsaddled the horses. The two horses went straight to a large container, which was full of fresh water collected by means of pipe directly from the stream.

The stream opened up into a small pool behind the house, in which people often bathed, and then wound its way down the mountain. Rosita asked Angelo if he came to this place very often.

'No!' he replied, carrying the saddles into the shade, while Rosita took care of the food supply. 'Only three or four times per year. Others come here to repair broken fencing, replenish stocks or take away livestock,' he explained. 'Listen Francesca, if you are tired you can wait here while I go to check around the area.'

'No, I'll come with you, you can't leave me here alone, I'm not that tired, and anyway a walk will do us both good after the long ride.'

'Good, we'll take a canteen of water with us as it's so hot,' said Angelo, happy that she'd decided to go with him. He felt as if he wanted to hold her in his arms and protect her. They started to explore the immediate vicinity and check the area for necessary repairs, occasionally they would come across the hacienda's horses and cows eating what little they could find, which at that time of the year was mostly dry because of the drought. By the time they had finished their rounds it was eleven o'clock. Angelo suggested they climb the mountain they were at the foot of, enough to be able to see most of the hacienda. So, they picked up what was needed, and started to climb.

They stopped at the same stream but further up the mountain, to drink the crystal clear fresh water, which gushed out of the top of the mountain and flowed through the pool behind the small house. Angelo and Rosita kicked off their boots, and paddled their hot sweaty feet in the clear bubbling water.

'It has been ages since I've had such a wonderful day,' said Angelo wistfully. 'It seems I am always busy and I'm doing a good job of keeping myself unhappy. I miss two people very much,' he proceeded, with a sigh, looking into the clear water as if he was expecting something to appear at any moment. 'A little girl who I used to play with as a child, who disappeared a long time ago and the other is my mother who left us a few years ago. When she died I lost every will to be happy. I never plucked up enough courage to leave this place, and it's something I do not understand really.' Angelo stopped, looking up meeting her oh so beautiful brown eyes. 'I'm sorry, I must be boring you?' She looked different, pensive as if she was ready to say something.

'Not in the least, please carry on talking, it's good for the soul,' she said, smiling. He laughed at her good humour. If only he knew what he'd just said, and who she really was. Angelo splashed his feet in the cool water. And she decided not to ask any more questions… for now.

'Once, my father told me that if I wanted to leave, he wouldn't stop me. But how could I leave him alone. And then there is my recurring dream, which makes my life impossible,' he said, looking at her again.

'A dream?' Rosita asked, wrinkling her forehead. 'Is it a nightmare? What sort of dream?' She enquired, devouring him with her eyes.

'Well, not always, but my dream is about a little girl with long dark hair. I'm on the mountain. I hear her screaming for help and I find myself running towards her cries. When I find her, she is hanging from a rock over a cliff edge. I stretch out my arm to help her, but I'm too late and she slips from the rock and falls into the valley. I then feel so helpless and upset, but as I turn to leave I see her again sitting on a rock. She's laughing at me and says, 'Don't be stupid, it's just a game, look I'm alive' and then she laughs again. 'And I always wake up confused and scared.'

Dear God, he looked so… so handsome, she thought. And wondered what he would say if she told him who she really was, that she was the little girl in his dreams. Of course she would tell him, when the time was right.

She looked away into the horizon and she tried to remember what he looked like when he was young, when they used to play in the back garden of the hacienda, and in the fields near the house.

'Have you ever spoken to anybody about this?' she asked, feeling sorry for him.

'Yes, I had told my mother many times, God bless her soul.'

'Well, what did she think of it?' asked Rosita.

'Oh, I don't know, she told me that dreams have something to do with your past lives. Anyway, let's forget about my dreams for now, I'm hungry, what about you?'

'Starving!' answered Rosita; they slipped their shoes back on and started to climb down the mountain. After a couple of minutes Angelo challenged her.

'Let's have a race. The last one down will make some fresh coffee to go with our lunch.'

'You're on,' she answered. 'Hey Angelo! What's that noise?'

'What noise?' he asked, stopping and looking around them, thinking it was probably a snake or another animal nearby.

'Over there!' said Rosita pointing towards a bush about ten metres away.

'Just a moment,' he said taking the rifle off his shoulder. 'I'll go and check,' he said, and started to walk towards it. As soon as he had his back to her, Rosita immediately started to run down towards the small house. 'Hey, where are you going?' yelled Angelo realising she had tricked him. 'Cheat!' he said, chasing after her and watching her descend the mountain with such agility. They reached the bottom almost simultaneously, and then made their way slowly to the little house giggling and catching their breath.

'All right,' said Rosita, breathless. 'I'll make the sandwiches.'

'Agreed,' said Angelo, laughing. 'And I will make the coffee, where did you learn to cheat, and run so fast?'

'I grew up with two great parents and had two very special friends to grow up and play with. We learned over the years to respect one another like family.'

As they ate, Rosita complimented Angelo on the coffee, and he was pleased. He talked about life on the hacienda. Rosita listen very carefully to what he was saying, and her mind worked over time. By the end of their lunch break she had a clear picture of what exactly was going on here, and what she had to do to put it right. As she concentrated on her plans, the relaxed expression on her beautiful tanned face changed to a rather anxious look. That didn't escape Angelo's watchful eyes; he thought maybe she was tired.

'We ought to leave now Francesca, as we have another area to check before we swing by the hacienda, don't forget we must officially introduce you to Don Camillo' said Angelo.

'Yes, I have not forgotten, I do hope my belongings arrive on the train soon, I can't go and visit people with my clothes smelling like this,' she said quickly, Angelo didn't miss that either, as she deliberately changed the subject.

They saddled the horses, and now Angelo and Rosita had to take the long route round the mountain. They passed under many trees that provided welcome shade and the breeze was blowing soft and fresh, there was an air of peacefulness around. The wind caressed Rosita's face and she imagined it was her father who was welcoming her back. As they made their way home, Angelo and Rosita saw many people working for Don Camillo, and as they passed by them, they were acknowledging her with a smile and bows of their heads. She noticed that and so did Angelo. What was going on here? He thought to himself, but decided to let it go for now. Rosita, of course knew why, and her thoughts went straight to Papa Joe. He had obviously wasted no time in telling the working people of the hacienda, that Rosita was alive and had returned as Francesca Curro. And that soon she would be needing a lot of help from all of them, to restore peace and happiness to the hacienda, as it was before when they were like one big happy family, all united and without violence or prejudice.

Angelo, having noticed the behaviour of the workers more and more as they were riding, looked back a couple of times after they had gone past groups, to try to fathom what was going on! He turned to Rosita; looking at her quizzically wondering if it was just her pure beauty and charisma that was having this effect on these workers. She looked calm and happy. As if she had sensed Angelo looking at her, she turned and saw him staring at her. They smiled at each other as if they were two people in perfect harmony with each other. He could not keep his eyes off her.

'Francesca,' he said. 'Is there something you haven't told me?' He moistened his lips unconsciously, as his eyes were fixed on her mouth.

'I'm sorry? I do not know what you're getting at,' she answered.

'Are you sure?'

'Very sure. Why, what did I do?' She knew that he hadn't missed the behaviour of the people working in the fields.

'It's nothing you did, but the reaction of the people we have been passing for the last few kilometres is making me wonder. Normally when the other men and I come this way, it's as if we don't exist,' he proceeded, with his head leaning to one side and forward so he could see her face better. 'Today I am here with you and these people are greeting us. But it's all for you, not me.'

'Of course, they're greeting me, it's because I'm more beautiful than you. You're not jealous are you?' teased Rosita, playfully.

'No, no, I'm not jealous. On the contrary, I'm very happy for you because I too like you very much. You don't know how happy I am, to have my cousin staying at my home, the only cousin I have and a most beautiful one at that.'

'Hey now!' exclaimed Rosita. 'Don't embarrass me with all these compliments.'

'I'm just stating the truth' said Angelo sincerely.

'And I thank you from the bottom of my heart, dear cousin. I know that you and your father are happy to have me here.'

'Yes, but I still think that you and my father are hiding something from me,' he said, never taking his eyes away from hers. Rosita was returning his eye contact with the same amount of attraction. In that very moment they both felt a sudden mutual desire for each other, some strong magnetic power, which was pulling them closer and closer together. In fact, he had such a strong desire to wrap this woman in his arms and to protect her. He wanted to be able to feel her every curve, vibration and to inhale her scent deep into his lungs. Angelo wanted to tell her how he felt, but he couldn't put his feeling into words. After all, this was his cousin.

'Angelo', she whispered, breaking this intense moment and blushing from head to toe. 'Just for the time being I cannot give you the answers to your questions.'

'Then I was right to suspect that there's something going on. Well, I promise, for the time being, that I won't ask any more questions. But I want to stay near you at all times to offer protection, if you need me. I want to make sure nothing untoward happens to you,' he said, giving her one of his most sensuous smiles.

Rosita's breath caught in her throat and a tremor of pleasure went through her like a bolt of lightning. What was the matter with her, she'd never felt like this before. She had been looked at by many other men, but they'd never made her feel... like this man does, so desired, so beautiful and so alive.

'Thank you, Angelo. I know I can rely on you,' she said, in a hoarse whisper, their eyes still locked and the two of them having difficulty tearing away from this clinch of eyes.

The rest of the way home passed quickly. Even though the sun was still hot, she felt a chill down her spine. For a while there was silence between them, both were deep in thought.

'Well, Francesca,' he said, as they went into the house. 'Would you like to bathe first and I'll wash afterwards?'

'No, thank you, I am going to have a chat with your father so you can go first. In any case, if I go after you I can take my time.'

'I should have known!' he laughed.

Rosita walked into the kitchen and greeted her uncle who was about to make coffee.

'Any for me?' she asked, going to him and planting a kiss on his brown cheek.

'Only if you've got time to stop for a minute,' laughed Vincenzo, as she disappeared up the stairs.

'Yes, Uncle I'm coming straight back down, I must fetch a change of clothes.'

She reappeared within a few minutes, and went to join him for coffee, and now Vincenzo wanted to know how her day had been.

'It was wonderful,' she enthused. 'It was such a pleasure to spend some time with my cousin.' Vincenzo and Rosita carried on chatting congenially together and after a while Angelo reappeared, half-dressed in only his faded jeans, his fair wavy hair still dripping on his shoulders looking so damn handsome. Rosita's eyes went to his golden haired chest and down to his waist where a trail of golden hair disappeared beneath the waistline of his jeans. A hot flush reached her face when she realised that her cousin Angelo was watching her admiring him.

'Have you finished already?' she asked, trying to hide her embarrassment.

'Yes, were you two talking about me?' he wanted to know.

Rosita couldn't look him in the face; she stood up, picked up her things and with humour she said, 'No, we weren't talking about you, but a certain cousin of mine!'

'I'm your only cousin,' he laughed, and his eyes devoured her shamelessly. He couldn't help this attraction he had towards her, it was too strong even for him to resist. Rosita too was incredulous to what her eyes were showing her. She remembered how handsome a young man Angelo was fifteen years ago, but she never expected him to grow into such a lasciviously desirable man. She then remembered, she wasn't here only to avenge her father, but because of Angelo as well. Rosita had had a crush on Angelo at the age of eight, and she had never given any thought to any other man since. A childhood crush that had remained and developed. She licked her lips, and then got up and went to wash, allowing this astonishing male sexuality to cause her imagination to run wild. Before she came out of the washroom Rosita noticed her travelling clothes, which she had left in the morning had already been washed and ironed and placed on the dresser. She went straight to Vincenzo and hugged him.

'What's that for?' he asked, smiling up at her from his chair, where he was busy cleaning some vegetables.

'Just to say thank you for doing my washing,' she answered, tearfully.

'You don't have to thank me; they needed doing so I did them.'

'Well I'm old enough to do the washing. So from tomorrow onwards, I'll do all the washing,' she said.

'Oh, you will, will you? And then what will I have left to do? Anyway, if you go to work all day, you won't have enough time to do the housework.'

All this time Angelo was sat with his elbows leaning on the table, and his hands supporting his chin, watching Rosita intently. And wondering how it could be, that when Francesca was very young she was always ill, the doctors had told his Uncle Nunziato that she would never live past the age of ten. But she had grown into such a beautiful healthy specimen of a woman. 'I could eat her alive,' he thought to himself, with a grin on his sensuous and kissable lips. Rosita asked if there was any coffee left.

'Of course there is coffee, when I make coffee, I always make plenty,' answered Vincenzo, smiling at her and wondering at the same time why on the earth his brother Nunziato had permitted Rosita to return to the Hacienda Antigua alone. She would have been safer in Bella Vista. She wasn't afraid of anybody, or anything and that could mean trouble, could complicate her life and others' too. Rosita smiled and went to the stove. There was a tinkling sound as her trembling hand placed the small cup onto a saucer. Her uncle quickly got up and went to her.

'What is wrong, Francesca?' he asked, instinctively. 'If you don't feel well we can go to see the boss tomorrow.' He realised that she must be more than a little nervous because she had to go to the house which she once lived in and was truly hers. She also had to meet her mother again, face to face, with her second husband, who was playing the master of the house, which once belonged to her father. There was a strong chance that maybe her mother may recognise her. This was a big risk, and if she did, would she say something? Donna Teresa never cared much for Rosita when she was a little girl, so hopefully she will not recognise her, for everybody's sake.

'Oh no Uncle, I assure you I am fine,' she said, not looking Vincenzo in the face.

'Well I'm ready to go, I'll wait for you two outside,' said Angelo, sensing something was not right. He hadn't missed any of the conversation the other two had just had. He must keep his eyes open; and he wondered why his father hadn't ever told him anything about his cousin before. He must have a good reason of course, but the two of them did not fool him.

'I'll be ready in a few minutes,' replied Rosita, while father and son walked outside together.

'Father, why do you suppose Francesca was tense a few minutes ago.'

'I can't say for sure, son,' said Vincenzo, not looking his son in the face. 'Maybe she's afraid to meet Don Camillo, or perhaps she's tired, anyway we will talk about this another time,' said Vincenzo. He knew his son was no fool, and anyway sooner or later he would have to find out. But this was not the right moment.

'Father, Francesca doesn't strike me as the type of girl who is afraid for no reason, and she doesn't look tired to me. Do you know something that I don't?' asked Angelo, leaning forward to brush something off his trousers.

'Son, like I told you a minute ago, we'll talk about this another time,' and before Angelo could press his father further, Rosita appeared.

'Here I am. Aren't I the lucky one tonight, to be accompanied by two handsome young men?' she teased. Then the three of them set out together towards Don Camillo's mansion.

CHAPTER THREE

As they were approaching the main house, they came upon a group of Negroes walking towards them. It was Papa Joe and his family. They were all carrying gifts of some description, one had a bunch of flowers, one had a pigeon, and Bimpe, Joe's wife, had a fresh herbal loaf of bread. Papa Joe was the first to come forward.

'With your permission, Don Vincenzo,' he started, and then turning to Rosita he continued. 'We have brought a small gift to welcome your niece, Francesca, and we would like her to accept our friendship. Should she need help of any sort, we are at her disposal.'

'Thank you very much,' answered Rosita. 'I'm pleased to accept your gifts and I am grateful for your friendship.'

At that moment Don Camillo appeared from the door of the mansion, accompanied by the same three men Rosita had seen the day before and had been warned to steer clear of.

At this, Papa Joe made a move to leave, saying, 'I think it would be better for us to return home now, we know you have things to do.' Obviously he didn't like Don Camillo's men. And all the family had an apprehensive look on their faces.

'Just a moment, Papa Joe,' intervened Vincenzo. 'Why don't you and your family go to my house? The door is always open to you; we shall not be long here. There's coffee on the stove, just make yourselves at home and we will meet you there shortly.'

The three men who intimidated the Onanusi family left Don Camillo standing at the door waiting for them to approach. Vincenzo was the first to greet him.

'Good evening, Don Camillo,' he said, with a forced smile on his mouth.

'Good evening, Vincenzo,' he replied. His eyes moved to Rosita, looking at her from top to toe, arrogantly and without shame.

'My niece has come to thank you and Donna Teresa in person for allowing her to stay on your hacienda, at my home with me. And she would like to re-acquaint herself with your lady wife.' All the time this banter was going on, Rosita didn't move her eyes from the man she hated so much, with a printed smile across her face, while at the same time panic-stricken in case they recognised her. Her insides were churning with anger.

'I'm sure my wife would like very much to see Francesca again after so many years, please come in.'

Vincenzo went in first followed by Rosita with Angelo one step behind her. She gripped hold of Angelo's hand tightly. He was surprised, and he thought that this was the third time he had seen her in such a state. He was now certain she must be afraid of something and he was going to find out who or what was scaring her, as soon as he could. Don Camillo's voice interrupted his thoughts.

'You will find my wife in the kitchen with the cook, Vincenzo. Take your niece in to see her. Angelo, as you are here I have some things to discuss with you.'

As Rosita followed Vincenzo into the corridor to the left which led to the kitchen, she shot a distressed look at Angelo, without realising she had done it. They arrived at the kitchen door. They both paused before knocking. Vincenzo looked at Rosita with a questioning expression on his face. She took a deep breath, winked at him and nodded that she was ready.

'Come in, the door is open.' Donna Teresa's soft voice came from behind the kitchen door. They entered and saw her seated at the table, and Maria the cook busy at work by the stove. Thank God, the kitchen was not brightly lit, thought Rosita.

'Ah! Vincenzo,' she said rising from her chair, a surprised look on her face, she hadn't expected Francesca to visit so soon. 'I see you have brought your niece to see me,' she exclaimed. 'Come, come nearer. My God, Francesca, you've grown up into a beautiful young lady,' she said, as she moved nearer to embrace her. Donna Teresa's face suddenly changed colour, for a split second Rosita thought that she had recognised her. She had been afraid until that moment, thinking that her mother would come to embrace her and she didn't know how she would have reacted to that. 'How are your mother and father?' asked Donna Teresa.

Rosita hesitated to answer for a few seconds; she couldn't help thinking how beautiful her mother still was at the age of sixty.

'They are in good health, thank you, they send their regards.'

'Thank you, who would have imagined that you would grow into such a lovely thing?' repeated Donna Teresa, looking at Vincenzo.

She didn't look bad herself, thought Rosita again, looking at her with hatred in her heart. She had to look away to hide her distain, so she used the opportunity to greet Maria the cook, as she wouldn't have another chance to once Donna Teresa started talking. She went over to shake Maria's hand and as their eyes met a look of shock flashed across Maria's face, she looked as nervous as Rosita felt, for sure something must have crossed her mind.

'Do you remember how ill you always were?' continued Donna Teresa.

Her eyes showed a hint of sadness. Rosita wondered if she remembered her daughter at all, if she missed her, or if she even felt guilty.

'Yes, of course I remember, how could I ever forget? I also remember a little girl about my age, with dark hair, in fact, if I'm not mistaken it was the same colour as my hair. She used to come and visit me, how is she? Is she still here?'

Donna Teresa looked at Vincenzo, who shrugged his shoulders. She quickly changed the subject so as not to show them that she felt uncomfortable with the question, and asked if she could offer them something to drink. Just for a moment she thought she saw her little Rosita staring at her through Francesca's eyes. A shiver ran down her spine, she shook her head, as if to say to herself she was imagining it.

Vincenzo saw her expression, and for a second his heart seemed to stop beating. If she does recognise her, what would happen?

'Well that is very kind of you, as long as it's no trouble,' he answered, in a whisper.

'No trouble at all,' she replied.

'A glass of milk for me please,' said Rosita.

'A coffee for me,' said Vincenzo.

They sat at the table while the cook prepared the drinks. Donna Teresa wanted to know about Francesca, how she had passed her time all these years, and she wanted to know if she was engaged.

'Not yet,' replied Rosita.

'And how long are you staying with us?' was her next question.

'Well, I hope to stay a couple of months,' Rosita replied. 'But only if Don Camillo and yourself permit me to stay and work on your hacienda. I'm sure at this time of the year you will need lots of help harvesting the crops.'

Donna Teresa eyebrow rose quizzically, then she burst out laughing.

'But what kind of job can my husband find for a girl such as yourself? What could you do on a farm?' she said, still laughing.

'I assure you, Donna Teresa, that I can do anything on a farm. I'm able to look after animals, drive ploughs, handle a horse and cart and milk the cows and goats.'

Just then, Don Camillo entered the kitchen with Angelo. Rosita's eyes met with Angelo's dark eyes. He gave her a searching look, she smiled at him to reassure him she was fine, but he still didn't think so. Even though he hadn't known her for long, he could read her like a book.

'What a good smell of coffee, is there any spare for us? And I'm as hungry as a wolf,' said the master, placing his hands in his trouser pockets, staring at Rosita and smiling at her. He looked her over from head to toe again, making her flesh creep.

'Really, darling,' replied his wife, blushing as red as a tomato, seeing her husband looking at their beautiful guest in that manner. 'Don't you worry, supper is nearly ready.'

Vincenzo was the first one to get up. 'Well, we will be on our way now, thank you for the refreshment,' he said, looking at Donna Teresa and praying to God that she hadn't recognised Rosita.

'One moment!' said Donna Teresa. 'Don't leave yet.' She turned back to her husband. Rosita and Vincenzo held their breath, thinking that she was about to divulge Rosita's identity. 'Vincenzo's niece needs a job, and she's told me she can do anything on a farm.'

'Of course,' he replied, smiling at Rosita again and looking at her through his thick long black eyes lashes. 'There is plenty of work for you. In fact your cousin Angelo can find a suitable job for you, I'm sure, and if you wish, you could work together. He told me that you were riding with him all day today, and you don't look that tired, so you must be able and strong.'

'Thank you very much, Don Camillo,' said Rosita, trying to give Don Camillo a warm smile. But she didn't quite manage it, then proceeding quickly. 'You won't regret this, I promise you, and you'll be satisfied with my work. As you were with my father's work years ago.'

She said good-bye to Donna Teresa and her husband, as did Vincenzo and Angelo. As the three left the house, they remembered that Papa Joe Onanusi and his family were waiting at Vincenzo's home.

'Do you think they're still there?' asked Rosita.

'I think not,' answered Vincenzo. 'We spent a longer time at Don Camillo's than I had imagined.

Angelo took hold of Rosita's hand. 'Well, cousin, from tomorrow, we're working together so I can keep an eye on you, and make sure you do things right,' he said, raising an eyebrow. Rosita laughed.

'Well dear cousin, you'd better just behave yourself, or you'll be sorry,' she answered, looking into his eyes. Angelo laughed, and pulled Rosita to him and gave her an affectionate long hug.

'You must be really hungry and your brain's not functioning properly. Come on we'll be home soon and we can see what Father has cooked for us,' said Angelo, feeling in his heart that he would like to keep Francesca close to him always, to protect her. Like the little friend he had once, a long time ago. But she had disappeared, probably dead, and occasionally he wondered what had really happened to her.

'Do you ever do the cooking, Angelo?' asked Rosita.

'What? You must be joking; the kitchen is too small for the two of us. We would be at each other's throats within minutes.'

'Don't believe what he says,' interrupted Vincenzo, laughing. 'I don't let him near my cooker, and anyway, I have more time than Angelo. He works all day, I work only a couple of hours in the morning on our own produce.'

It didn't take them long to arrive home, and there, waiting patiently was Papa Joe Onanusi with his family

'Forgive us, we did not think we would be so long,' said Vincenzo, apologetically.

'It doesn't matter,' answered Papa Joe. 'But if you don't mind, we ought to go as it is late and we still have to cook. We will have to go to bed without dinner at this rate!'

'Oh no, that won't happen,' interrupted Rosita. 'If Uncle doesn't mind, you can all stay here to eat; I'll cook for everyone. In the mean time you can all chat together, it won't take long.'

'Of course, my pleasure, you're very welcome,' said Vincenzo, happy that Rosita had taken it upon herself to invite these loyal friends.

'Well Uncle, you'd better come and show me where everything is!' she said moving toward the kitchen.

'What do you want to cook?' asked Vincenzo.

'That depends on what you've got in your cabinet.'

'Well, there's rice, meat and vegetables. There is dried pasta, fruit and salad.'

'Thank you Uncle, you can go back with the others, and sit outside for a chat. I'll get on by myself and when dinner is ready I'll call everybody,'

Rosita started at once, and very soon the delicious aroma of her cooking began to waft outside. She moved round the kitchen like a woman who'd lived there all her life and she knew what she was doing. She was whistling away and feeling good for the first time since the day before when she had arrived.

'What a wonderful smell,' remarked Bimpe Onanusi from the kitchen door. 'What's cooking?' she asked.

'Just be patient,' replied Rosita. 'You'll see soon enough.'

Angelo appeared behind the two women and said just loud enough for her to hear, 'Father, I have a feeling she'll be burning everything!'

'You're talking too much! said Rosita, laughing. 'As you are here you'd better come and make yourself useful by laying the table.'

Angelo moved nearer to her, placed one hand on her shoulder, and gently eased her towards him. Then he said, 'If it tastes as good as it smells then we're in for a treat. How long will it be? I'm hungry.'

'In ten minutes everything will be ready,' she replied.

'I can smell something else too, have you got anything else cooking too, like cakes? Let me see,' he said going to the oven, and went to open the oven door.

'If you go near that oven I'll smack your hand,' scolded Rosita, jokingly. 'If the door's opened now, everything will be ruined.'

'Bossy boots,' said Angelo. He found some bread and cheese, which he cut and placed on a dish, then took it out to the table.

Once the meal was ready, Rosita served the main dish onto eight dinner plates. Finally she placed a jug of water in the middle of the table. Everything was now ready and so everyone was called in.

They started to eat and after a few mouthfuls, everyone was complimenting Rosita. She had cooked the meat and vegetables, in a hot chilli sauce, accompanied by simple boiled white rice. For dessert, she had prepared a fruit sponge. It was something simple made from fresh eggs, milk, sugar, flour, sultanas and dried prunes. Rosita was a little worried that they might not like it, but it all quickly disappeared. After they had their coffee, Bimpe Onanusi began to yawn.

'Excuse me, but my eyes won't stay open any longer,' she said, getting up. 'Thank you very much for your hospitality, the meal was excellent, but we really must be going.'

'I understand,' said Vincenzo, and everybody stood up. They all shook hands and said their goodbyes and Joe Onanusi and family were about to leave when Vincenzo stopped them.

'Wait a minute, I'll go and get my horse and cart for you to ride home, and tomorrow one of us will come and collect them. You are all too tired to walk at this hour.'

They consented to his generosity, thanking Vincenzo again, as he left to fetch the horse and cart. Then turning to Rosita, Joe Onanusi said, 'We are all so happy to see you again and we hope that everything goes well for you.'

Presently Vincenzo reappeared and they mounted the cart one by one, Papa Joe took the reins and they were on their way. Vincenzo, Angelo and Rosita went back inside, they were also tired.

'We'd better go to bed now; we can tidy this up tomorrow morning,' said Vincenzo, yawning.'

'I'll get up early tomorrow morning, and help you clear everything away,' offered Rosita.

'We'll see about that,' said Angelo, playfully, 'I suppose you'll expect early morning coffee in your room to wake you?'

'Hey, I know I'm tired but not so tired that I couldn't wake up earlier than you,' she retorted.

'All right then, I'll see you tomorrow morning,' he said smiling and then left the kitchen.

Rosita turned and quickly kissed Vincenzo good night, then swiftly followed Angelo up the stairs.

'Are you going to bed without saying good night to me?' she said, taunting him.

They both reached the upstairs landing and turned to one another.

'It's not that I ran away because I was afraid of you!' he said joining in with the joke. He then rested his hands gently on the ridge of her shoulders, with his thumbs sitting in the shallow behind the top of her collar bones, he pulled her to him. His hand on her shoulders felt like a feather, but she still sensed he was shaking.

'Good night, dear cousin.' He kissed her forehead. 'It's a pity we've lived so far apart for all these years. If we had grown up here, together, we could have had many happy times together,' he said. His thumbs were resting against her carotid pulse, which was beating faster under his touch. He was now looking straight into her eyes. Slowly his gaze lowered, stopping at her oh-so-inviting lips and stayed there for a long few seconds. Then he gave her one of his devastatingly sensual smiles that almost sent her pulse through the roof. Her legs weakened and her cheeks flushed, she prayed to God that he hadn't seen these tell-tale signs of how she felt.

'Good night, Angelo,' she replied, after what seemed like an eternity that they had been looking at each other.

'From tomorrow on, we will have plenty of time to talk together,' he said, releasing her from his hold. He watched her turn and waited until she was in her room, and then scolded himself by tapping his fists against his forehead for what he had very nearly done. He walked to his room and closed the door behind him. Undressing and getting into bed, hoping but not succeeding, that he would fall asleep quickly.

Five minutes after Rosita was in bed and the house had gone silent, she started to pray.

'Heavenly Father, I thank you that I am alive and back where I truly belong. I pray to you for guidance and that everything I do will turn out for the best. Amen.'

CHAPTER FOUR

Rosita woke suddenly and stretched her limbs. She turned her head on her pillow and wondered what the time was, as she could see from a crack in the curtains that it was already light. There was not a sound anywhere. She rose from her bed quietly and found a dressing gown hanging on the back of the door. She assumed it must have belonged to Vincenzo's late wife. She put it on, and swiftly went downstairs and started to prepare coffee. While the pot was coming to the boil, she began to clear the table of the previous evening's meal. She washed up, and then poured out a cup of coffee and took it to Angelo's room. Knocking gently on the door, she entered without waiting for an answer. She placed the coffee on the bedside table.

'Wake up, wake up! It is late,' she urged, shaking him roughly.

She then turned away and went back down to get herself some coffee. Five minutes later Angelo appeared in the kitchen, his eyes still half closed.

'In the morning I like milk in my coffee,' he said grinning.

Rosita returned his smile, and said. 'I think I should take some coffee to your father, how does he like it?'

'That won't be necessary, he's already on his way down,' replied Angelo.

At that very moment Vincenzo entered the kitchen and smiling he said, 'What's going on here? Doesn't anyone like to sleep in the morning any more?'

'I'm sorry,' said Rosita, 'it is my fault. The coffee is ready. Can I pour a cup for you Uncle?'

'Hey, you've done everything already!' remarked Vincenzo.

'Not quite, the breakfast still has to be prepared, but I thought you would like to do that, Uncle, and in the meantime I'll go to collect the cart from Papa Joe.'

'You mean, we will go and get the cart,' intervened Angelo. 'There are many people around at this time of the morning and not all of them are nice. I wouldn't like you to be out on your own where someone may take advantage of you,' said Angelo.

'Well, I'm not afraid, but I won't argue with you,' she said. Before they left, they told Vincenzo they would be about three-quarters of an hour. On their way to Papa Joe's house, Angelo and Rosita again had to pass Don Camillo's Mansion. The thought of him living in her father's Mansion like a king made Rosita's skin crawl. And the thought of him sleeping in her father's bed with her mother, that really made her blood boil.

'The day of judgement is near!' she thought to herself. The morning air was fresh. The sun rose in the sky, sending the first heat from its rays. The smell of jasmine surrounded her and with great pleasure she inhaled deeply with her eyes closed, remembering the aroma from when she was young. There must have been a field full of people picking flowers ready to be taken to the factory where perfume and soap products were manufactured. The breeze was blowing gently on their faces, the leaves on the trees rustled faintly above them and both of them were now deep in thought. Angelo not knowing Rosita very well yet felt disquieted at the thought of her being alone in some places, and encountering some of Don Camillo's more unsavoury men. Dear God, he thought to himself, if anything ever happened to her, he would go out of his mind. From now on he must make sure not to let her out of his sight, for his peace of mind, and for the sake of his uncle and auntie.

'It's absolutely heavenly, at this time of the morning,' said Rosita, looking at Angelo. He turned and surveyed her radiant face.

He smiled at her, and then he said, 'For me it's more than heavenly, because you're with me! In the last forty hours you have changed my life. It has happened so fast that I feel so confused, but very happy,' he finished, holding her hand. Suddenly, ahead of them in the distance they saw a stationary cart in the middle of the road. There were two men aboard. One Negro and one white and by the cart were two figures on horseback. As they approached the group, Angelo recognised them as Don Camillo's men, one was Pietro Tonto and the other one was Don Ciccio. These were two of Don Camillo's most trusted men who were extremely sadistic and violent, and it was very dangerous to be approached by them.

'What are they doing up at this time of the morning?' asked Rosita.

'Can't you guess? They have been out all night in the village and they are probably still drunk. God knows what havoc they have caused.'

As they drew closer, they realised that the two men on the cart were being intimidated by Pietro Tonto and Don Ciccio. They were demanding to know what they were carrying on the cart.

'And what is going on here?' asked Angelo, authoritatively, looking first to the two men on the cart, then at Don Camillo's men.

'We are delivering these containers on the cart to a Miss Francesca Curro,' answered the white man on the cart.

'I am Francesca Curro,' she said,' and you're on the right road. Thank you for taking the trouble to bring me my luggage.' Then she turned to address Don Camillo's men. 'Have one of you left something on this cart? If not then your work here is done.'

'No, we want to know what's on board,' answered Tonto aggressively.

'Really? Have they not already told you, that the containers on the cart belong to me?'

'Listen to this bitch,' sneered Ciccio, the ugliest and most disgusting man she had ever come across in her entire life. He was not very tall, had a big belly, was unshaven, his eyes red from being drunk. And while he was talking to them unashamedly broke wind.

'She doesn't know who we are! If you want to stay on this hacienda, you keep your mouth shut and do as we say!'

Rosita's inner rage pumped the blood within her straight to her head. Her fingers slowly reached for the rifle strapped to her horse but Angelo quickly intervened.

'It's better that this is stopped right now, we don't want to waste any more time and I'm sure Don Camillo has work waiting for you two.'

It was plain to see the two men were more malicious being drunk. Tonto moved nearer to Angelo, regarding him seriously for a few seconds. Then he said, 'You always seem to be the peacemaker amongst us, but I can see in your eyes that you have no fear. I wonder what goes on in that mind of yours. Come on let's go,' he said to Don Ciccio. Reluctantly they rode off, still looking back over their shoulders for a few seconds. Angelo told Rosita to accompany the two men on the cart home.

'I'll carry on to Papa Joe's,' he said, never taking his eyes off the two drunken henchmen, until they disappeared behind the bushes at the bend in the track one hundred metres away. 'I'll get back home as quickly as I can to help you unload.'

'All right,' she agreed. 'I'll be off then, see you in a little while.' She and the rail men soon arrived at Vincenzo's house. 'Uncle!' she called out. 'Come and see what we've got here. Look, all my things have arrived from the station.'

'Good morning, gentlemen,' said Vincenzo, moving toward the cart. 'Let me help you boys get these things off the cart,' he said, happy for Rosita.

'No Uncle, these two young men will give me a hand, and in any case Angelo should be back very soon.'

The two railway porters started to untie the containers. They were smiling because they could see how happy Rosita was to have her belongings arrive, as well as being so keen to help them. She was full of energy, and very friendly. They helped to carry the containers upstairs for her. They had left the largest of the chests until last as it was extremely heavy.

'Miss Curro, what do you have in this case? Stones?' joked Tunde, the Negro porter.

'More like a dead body!' spouted the other.

'You what? Oh no, sorry. They are mostly things of sentimental value. My father gave them to me before I left. Well, we've nearly finished anyway.'

As Rosita finished speaking, Angelo arrived.

'Why didn't you wait for me?' he said.

'Well, you know, times are hard I couldn't afford to pay more than two wages! Anyway, I think you should go and have your breakfast, it's getting late,' she said, showing vitality and eagerness, as she was walking towards the house.

'What about you?' he asked, admiring his cousin Francesca. He wondered to himself how on earth he was going to work beside her every day, without being able to take her into his arms and kissing her until she could take no more.

'I'll eat something on the way to work. That is if you are capable of making me a couple of sandwiches?' she joked. He consented and disappeared into the house, and she went back to the cart again, to help the others finish unloading. When the last chest had been put away, Vincenzo invited the two railway porters for coffee, and breakfast if they wanted. Rosita ran down the staircase, as happy as a child who had just received a wonderful present.

'I can't believe it, all my belongings have finally arrived. Don't you think this is wonderful?'

At that moment Vincenzo was putting the sandwiches he'd made for her and Angelo in a leather bag. Slowly he raised his eyes to meet hers, and with a grin on his face, he said, raising an eyebrow.

'That is wonderful for you. But clothes are clothes and you seem to have accumulated many of them.'

His gaze had become quizzical now. Vincenzo was no fool; all of those chests and boxes and some of them far too heavy to be clothes. He wondered what she really had in them. Rosita was holding his gaze in a knowing way. Angelo was stood in the doorway wondered what all this was about. Why were his father and Francesca looking at each other in that conspiratorial way? He waited for her to leave the kitchen, and when she was out of sight, he went over to his father, took the bag with the sandwiches and murmured into his ear.

'I, dear Father, can smell a silent conspiracy between you two, and before the sun sets tonight I promise you that I will find out all about your secret.'

Vincenzo laughed and then while he was taking dirty dishes to the sink he said, 'Go to work, son, it's getting late. And please take care of Francesca; she can be a handful sometimes.'

'I will do just that and with great pleasure. And you please look after yourself,' Angelo said, shaking his head.

At that moment Rosita returned to finish her milk. She said goodbye to her uncle and the two railway porters, thanking them for their help. Then she went back out and quickly mounted her horse.

'Hey, wait for me, and don't forget the water canteen,' shouted Angelo, as he ran after her. 'Are you trying to give me a hard time this morning? Don't be in such a rush, we're not going very far today.'

Angelo mounted his horse, but kept his eyes on his cousin. He swore to himself under his breath. Being near her was agony for him. She was so beautiful, and he was falling more and more in love with her every minute. He did not know how long he could resist it without touching her. Neither could he understand what was happening to him. He felt a mixture of elation for the emotion of love he was feeling, and shame because this was his cousin. But his overwhelming sensation of joy every time he was near her trumped any other feeling. Logically and physically, he understood his not having been with a woman for a while was part of this whirlwind he was trapped in, but this had never happened to him before, having such a strong attraction towards a woman. To say he wished only to touch Francesca was an understatement, she had him under her spell, he could think of nothing and nobody else. What he really wished was to take her to the same place where he'd taken her on their first day out together. Up into the mountains at the water spring, to make passionate love to her, naked under the sun until they both collapsed with exhaustion.

'I don't mind where we go,' she said, to break the silence. 'I enjoy the time I spend with you wherever we are.'

Hearing her say these words, made Angelo's heart beat even faster still. A warm excitement ran through his body as he looked into her deep dark eyes. With his hungry eyes feasting upon her loveliness, his lips curled up into a devilish smile. Then his mind went to the little sham between her and his father earlier. He wondered what a beautiful woman like her was doing in this horrible place, and why of all the jobs this beautiful creature could find in the world, she'd decided to do a man's manual work on a farm. She was obviously far better than this. Was he in a dream? If he was then please God let him carrying on sleeping he thought to himself.

Today's job for Angelo and Rosita was, along with many others employees, to plant and water thousands of young lettuces. They worked hard all day and Angelo made sure his cousin was never out of his line of sight. He spent most of the day thinking non-stop of how he should deal with this situation. After going around in circles in his mind, he concluded that perhaps he should discuss it with his father later. The time had seemed to pass quickly, thank God, and they began to prepare to return home.

***

Meanwhile back in the village of Bella Vista, Nunziato and Battistina were worried sick for Rosita. Even though they knew that with his brother Vincenzo and their nephew Angelo she was in good hands, they also knew Rosita's temperament so they couldn't help worrying. The trouble with Rosita was, if she believes she is in the right about something, she would fight for it tooth and nail. Rosita could ride a horse as well as any man and shoot a rifle with uncanny accuracy. Nunziato and his wife had tried for years at turning her into a perfect young lady. But they had completely failed. Her mother had numerous attempts at stopping her doing martial arts lessons and again she'd failed. Rosita had been sent to the best school in the area. Having to use all of their savings, in the hope that one day it would make a lady of her. They wished only the best for her, as they would have their own daughter; that one day Rosita would meet and marry a rich handsome man who would expect his wife to behave like a lady. But no such luck.

Battistina was stood at the sink with her head down as she did the washing up, trying not to let her husband see the tears accumulate in her eyes. Nunziato sat with his head behind the newspaper, looking at the pages, but not being able to concentrate enough to read even a few lines. He missed Rosita like hell. Since the day she'd arrived in their home it had never been as quiet as it was now, both he and his wife missing her happy laughter.

'Why don't you go to visit your neighbours, Nunziato?' suggested Battistina, feeling sorry for her husband. 'Jon Chian was inquiring about you; he wanted to know how you were, and why he hadn't seen you lately.'

She continued talking to him, determined to break the horrible silence that was dragging them both down. Nunziato at sixty-two years old, a few years younger than his brother Vincenzo, didn't show his age. His brown hair still thick and curly, he was fit as a fiddle and still an attractive man. He worked hard and he liked to continue with his exercise. He also, like Rosita, enjoyed martial arts. Over the last couple of years, he and his wife had done well with breeding chickens and selling eggs. Nunziato kept himself busy by doing a few handyman jobs here and there, as well as locally helping on a small ranch.

As the years passed by, Nunziato thought that the pain in his heart, for what had happened fifteen years ago at the Hacienda Antigua, would have gone away by now. But it hadn't. The image of Don Sebastian Miserendino's horrible last moments at the hands of Donna Teresa's lover still haunted him. Nunziato tried many times to convince his brother Vincenzo to move away from the hacienda, but he'd failed. His brother told him he was more useful where he was. He'd always dreamed that one day Rosita Miserendino would return, and he and his son Angelo with the help of a few close friends would be needed there.

There was a knock on his door, which broke Nunziato away from his disturbed thoughts.

'Come in whoever you are, the door is open,' said Nunziato. The happy Chinese faces that came through his door quickly put

Nunziato in a better mood. 'I'm afraid you have arrived too late, you can only help Battistina with the dishes now.'

Jon and his son Chen made themselves at home sitting at the table next to Nunziato. Whilst Jon Chain's wife, Giovanna and daughter, Meilin, went over to Battistina to give her a warm hug and offer help. The Chinese family had arrived in the village of Bella Vista, nearly at the same time as Nunziato and his family, over twenty years ago. Since then they have been the closest of friends and often relied on one another for help both physically and emotionally.

CHAPTER FIVE

'Oh my goodness, I think my work must have been unsatisfactory today,' remarked Rosita.

'Sorry, are you speaking to me?' asked Angelo, looking at her from under his hat. He'd avoided directly looking at her nearly all day, because each time he did his heart did a somersault. It was killing him, not being able to take her into his arms, and smother her with kisses.

'No, I was talking to myself,' she answered crisply. 'What is wrong with you? All day you've been preoccupied. If I've done something to upset you, please say so. Maybe you resent me for staying at your house because you have no privacy to bring someone special home any more? If so, it would only take a couple of days for me to find another place to stay in the village.'

Angelo was shocked at her outburst. Had he been that rude today? Dear God, if only she knew.

'What are you saying Francesca? Please forgive me for behaving like an idiot; it's not at all what you're thinking. You are the best thing that has happened to me in a long time, and I like having you around.'

He was trembling now. 'I only wish you were not my cousin!' he blurted out. 'You see…' There was a long pause while he thought carefully about what he was about to declare. 'I… I have been struggling with this since you arrived and I am rather confused because I think I'm falling in love with you,' he confessed.
Rosita didn't say a word, she just kept looking at him. Tears started to well up in her eyes; her bottom lip began to tremble.

Angelo could not resist it any longer. He reached for her and gently locked her in his strong arms.

'Please, sweet Francesca, don't cry. I'm sorry, I shouldn't have said that. This was neither the time nor the place for me to...' He couldn't carry on. His heart felt as if it was going to burst through his chest, he had to stop and take a breath. He groaned deeply, pulled her tightly to him and rocked her like a child. The heat from his body was tangible and pressed so close to her, she smelled the dusky scent of this man and the fresh sweat of hours of work. Rosita slowly raised her eyes to meet his. She saw anxiety in his eyes. This was not fair; she should tell him the truth about herself. But she had wanted Vincenzo to be the one to break the news to him. But now things had changed, and she couldn't wait any longer. She raised her hand to touch his face, he closed his eyes, inhaling deeply the smell of her hair mixed with the sweet fragrance of her perfume, making Angelo feel dizzy.

'Angelo, can we stop someplace before we get home, where nobody can eavesdrop. I have something important and private to tell you. That is if your father hasn't already told you?'

Angelo nodded his consent saying, 'I know the perfect place.'

They rode for about ten minutes into an opening of grass with a solitary acorn tree in the middle of it. They could see for about eighty metres around them that there was nobody else to listen to their conversation. They sat under the tree facing one another. He sat silently looking at her, not knowing what to expect but preparing himself for the worst. He thought he had overstepped the mark and she was about to put him in his place.

'Angelo,' she began slowly, 'I am sorry I did not tell you this before, but I hope you will understand when I have finished why I couldn't.' She took a deep breath and carried on. 'I am not the person you think I am.' She paused to let this information sink into his already over active thoughts. He didn't say a word, he just held his breath.

'The day the hacienda was attacked, your uncle Nunziato happened to be there in my father's study, thank God. He and I witnessed my father being killed and who had killed him. Your very brave and loyal uncle managed to sneak me away just in time or he and I would have been killed just like my father. Francesca Curro, your cousin, sadly died from the illness she had that very night the Hacienda was attacked fifteen years ago.' He looked as if he was in shock but she carried on. 'Anyway, your uncle and aunt buried their daughter the next day on the road to Bella Vista. They never told anybody outside of family and very close friends about Francesca's death. And to protect me, they bought me up as their daughter, Francesca. I grew up with them, and they have treated me as their own daughter. You don't know for how long I've been planning to return, but until now, I hadn't had the courage to leave Nunziato and Battistina.' His face was now starting to flush but he still said nothing. 'So, I am not your cousin, Francesca.' She continued, 'I am Rosita Miserendino.'

His heart was beating faster and faster by the second. He couldn't believe what he had just heard; his breath was getting heavier in his chest. Then he whispered, 'Rosita, my beautiful little Rosita, you're alive?' he said. He didn't want to believe his ears, it must be a dream, and he would soon wake up.

'Yes, Angelo,' she whispered.

'Please, be quiet,' he commanded as he embraced her again. 'Rosita, my Rosita,' he murmured into her hair. They kissed with passion, almost losing control of their senses. Suddenly they heard voices in the distance. Angelo now kissed her forehead and said, 'It's getting late; I think we should leave now. We can wait for the right place and for the right time for you to tell me everything. Now I know why my father hadn't told me before, it was for my own safety.'

After looking at each other for a few long seconds, they started their journey home.

On their way there, Angelo could not keep his eyes off Rosita; their horses were moving at the same pace, and almost touching.

'I'd like to ask you a question,' he said.

'Of course,' she replied.

'Does my father know the whole truth, that you are not truly Francesca?'

'Yes, he knows,' she said, smiling. Her face turned red, remembering how it felt in his arms, and how sweet his kisses were. He grinned, suspecting what she was thinking.

'This,' he began, shaking his head, 'explains a lot of things to me. And what do you intend to do, now?' he asked, taking her hand.

'For now, nothing. I'll remain as Francesca Curro, hopefully nobody will recognise me. Then when the time is right, I'll take back what is rightly mine.'

'Does Papa Joe know who you really are?'

'Yes, he knows, but I think it's better not to talk about this any more, in case we are overheard.'

When they arrived home, Vincenzo was sitting outside waiting for them. As soon as he saw them, he got up quickly. 'Where have you two been?' he said, 'Didn't you want to come home tonight?' He was not cross, but concerned. Rosita dismounted and apologised to her uncle.

'I'm sorry Uncle, it's entirely my fault, but don't worry about us, we are old enough, and intelligent enough to look after ourselves,' she said jokingly.

Vincenzo laughed.

'Intelligent? You two? Get away, and get washed quickly, dinner will be getting cold.'

Angelo and Rosita did as they were told. At the table they were very quiet, just occasionally exchanging knowing smiles. Vincenzo soon realised that something had gone on between them. He was not stupid; he could see it written on their faces.

'Well, may I ask what's going on? Have you two no energy left to talk? Come on, tell me everything, what has happened today?'

'Nothing Father, nothing has happened,' said Angelo, looking at his father with pleading eyes, telling him not to ask any question. Vincenzo was now looking at Rosita.

'I don't mind. As you said Francesca, you're both grown up now, of course you have your secrets and you don't need to consult me any more.'

'That's not true,' interrupted Rosita. 'We are grown up, yes, but we still do need your help and support. Angelo, you tell your father what went on today, I'm going to fetch coffee.'

'Ha!' exclaimed Vincenzo. 'I was right! I bet you had your first disagreement!'

'No Father, we didn't fight, but we cleared up a few things.'

'Carry on,' said Vincenzo. 'I'm all ears.'

'Father would you please stop interrupting me!' said Angelo, cheeks flushing as he looked at Rosita. She understood Angelo was feeling a bit embarrassed and she thought it appropriate to speak up.

'Well, Vincenzo!' she said before going into a whisper. 'The first thing to tell you is that I told Angelo today that I am not his cousin. He now knows my true identity.' She left a little pause for the news to sink in and then continued. 'And the second is, we are very much in love.' Vincenzo's face became serious for a moment, but then he broke into a wide glowing smile.

'I'm very happy for you two, but I hope that nobody heard you talking about this today. It is imperative that we continue calling you Francesca; you never know who is listening. And please be discreet when you are together. We would not want to have to explain why two cousins are romantically involved.'

'Well Father, we made sure of that, but anyway we weren't talking for long,' replied Angelo, 'and there are still things I would like to know.'

'Yes, son. I'd wanted to talk to you about this for a couple of days, but it never seemed to be the right moment. I am sorry I kept you in the dark all these years. But it was for your own good. What do you want to know?' asked Vincenzo, mortified that his son had to find out this way.

'For example, what does Rosita; I mean Francesca, intend to do now she is here? It could be very dangerous for her around here, especially if anybody found out the truth.'

'It's not going to be dangerous if we are very, very careful,' interrupted Rosita. 'The majority of the people here are on my side.' She was right, most of the people on the hacienda would do anything to help her. And it wouldn't be only for Rosita's sake, but also to regain their own peace and tranquillity.

'But Father, how can we spread the word and trust them with the information?' Angelo wanted to know.

'I already trust them,' said Rosita, answering his question. 'They know that I am here, the reason why I am here and to be careful to address me only as Francesca Curro for the time being.' She looked very relaxed and confident.

'What?' said Angelo. 'How do they know about you, you've only been here three days?'

'Why do you think that Papa Joe came here with his family? To welcome her and let her know they had spread the word of course,' answered Vincenzo.

Angelo was still puzzled. 'How could all these people here believe so easily that you had returned and really were Rosita, when everyone had believed you had perished in the assault fifteen years ago?'

'Because,' she said, smiling up at him, 'the day, I arrived, before I came to find you and Uncle Vincenzo, I went to see Papa Joe and his family, and explained everything to them. Providing evidence which was indisputable.'

'Ha,' exclaimed Angelo. 'Now I understand why all the people we passed yesterday were acknowledging you in the field. They already knew about you!' He shook his head, and somehow he knew he should get ready for a lot more surprises to come. Rosita noticed Vincenzo had already started the washing up, so she said to Angelo.

'Well, dear cousin! I think we've talked enough for tonight; I must help your father clear away the dishes. Your father cannot be expected to do everything now there are three of us and don't forget, Angelo, you must report to Don Camillo about the day's work.'

'OK bossy boots, I'll try to be quick. When I return if you are not too tired we'll go for a walk,' said Angelo, looking at her with desire in his eyes. Seeing his meaningful smile she imagining what he had in mind, Rosita's heart skipped a beat and her cheeks went from a pinkish shade to red all-over in a few seconds.

'Yes, of course,' she blurted out. 'Hurry up, I'm not too tired.' She got up from her chair, and moved toward the sink with the intent of helping her uncle.

'I told you I can manage here, you go and do your own things.' said Vincenzo playfully.

'I do wish you'd let me help you Uncle, I'm used to helping with the housework.'

One hour had passed and Rosita was impatiently waiting for Angelo to return. She went to sit outside with her uncle.

'Where are you two intending to go tonight?' he asked.

'I don't know, Uncle, I'll go wherever Angelo takes me. I expect we'll not go far, maybe to the place we used to go when we were young. Look here he is!' she said, jumping up like she had springs in her legs.

'Hey, Angelo, you were gone so long, I was about to go by myself!'

'I don't believe you,' he laughed. 'My father wouldn't let you go on your own. Are you ready?'

'Yes I am,' replied Rosita. 'Are we going on foot or horseback?'

'We'll just go for a short walk around the house, under the stars,' he replied, taking Rosita's hand. They left bidding Vincenzo a goodnight. He stood watching them walk away, and soon the two figures disappeared into the trees.

'Do you know where I'm taking you?' asked Angelo.

'Not exactly, but I have an idea,' she answered. She felt Angelo's hand tighten its grip, and then he stopped, turning her towards him. He gently gathered her into his arms. He kissed her forehead, then both cheeks and then found her lips. They kissed passionately, his mouth increasing its pressure on hers, until Rosita thought she'd faint. Angelo broke away and led her towards a large tree on top of a hill, from where they could see the Hacienda Antigua mansion, as well as Angelo's house. They moved slowly, holding each other closely, and when they arrived at their destination, they knelt down under the tree.

'Please God, I don't want this to be a dream or I'll die of unhappiness,' said Angelo, holding Rosita close to him as if someone was trying to take her away. He wondered how on the earth he and his father had stayed away from his uncle Nunziato for so long. Of course, there was a reason for everything.

'No,' said Rosita. 'It's not a dream. I'll pinch you; if you're dreaming you'll wake up!' Angelo went to kiss her again but stopped as he heard a scream. 'What was that?' she whispered.

'Shh! Listen!' replied Angelo quietly.

They heard a girl's voice crying out, pleading, 'Please let me go!' Followed by a man's voice saying menacingly.

'Shut up if you want to see tomorrow's sunrise. Let me do what I want and I'll let you live.'

Angelo told Rosita to stay put and he would go to check out what was happening. But Rosita had her own ideas and unknown to him she followed. When he got nearer the source of the disturbance, he could see nobody, so said in a raised voice.

'Whoever you are, leave that girl alone!' Angelo had already recognised the man's voice as one of Don Camillo's men, Pietro Tonto, but pretended he did not know him. There was no response. 'I said let the girl go!' repeated Angelo.

The man got up and was now in Angelo's sight. He rushed towards Angelo and produced a knife. Angelo stepped back a couple of paces, looking around desperately for a weapon of defence. At that moment Rosita sprang out from nowhere.

'You scum, you'll pay for all the suffering you've inflicted on these people!'

'You crazy bitch! I'll cut your face, that'll teach you to keep your nose out of other people's business.'

He had hardly finished what he was saying when Rosita, moving like lightning, lurched forward bringing up her right leg, striking him in the stomach with a sharp front kick. She spun round to her left and deftly kicked his arm, sending the knife flying from his right hand. He was taken aback and stumbled to the ground, winded.

'Damn you!' shouted Tonto struggling to get the words out, and looking like a dangerous wounded bear. 'When I get my hands on you ...'

Rosita pushed a surprised Angelo towards the bushes, ordering him to get the girl out of harm's way. He still couldn't believe what he had just witnessed.

'Go!' she repeated. 'I'll take care of this animal!'

For a few seconds Tonto had lost sight of his assailant, swearing away to himself, he was becoming very anxious.

'Where are you? Let me see you, you bitch,' he shouted, spinning around and looking into the undergrowth. Rosita was hiding behind a tree just behind him.

'Hey, are you looking for me?' He turned around but could not see her. 'I'm here!' she said. As he moved forwards she darted out and aimed a sharp snap kick to his groin. He dropped to his knees and groaning deeply, doubled up in pain. Again and relentlessly, Rosita's foot struck his face. The man rolled onto the floor, but rose again quickly. His anger at being struck by a woman overrode some of his pain, but before he regained his balance completely, Rosita's right leg swung round in a high arch in the air and struck a fatal blow to his neck. He slumped into a heap on the ground, just as Angelo reappeared, worried sick and mad at himself for leaving her at the mercy of that dangerous bandit. The relief on his face was evident when he saw her.

'Are you all right, Francesca?' he asked, still breathless from running back to her.

'Don't worry about me,' she replied, as he pulled her to him, and held her tight. It took her breath away, and for a moment she thought she would faint. After a long moment, he loosened his grip and she asked. 'Well, what are we going to do with this scum?'

'I saw his horse not very far from here,' Angelo answered.

'Good, bring it here, we have to get him as far away as we can, so nobody suspects us of anything.'

Together they hoisted the dead man's arms over their shoulders. He was a terribly heavy dead weight. They managed to place his body unceremoniously across the horse's back, strapping him onto the saddle with his belt, then led the animal out to the road. Rosita slapped the horse's rear sending it immediately galloping into the distance away from the hacienda. Then they returned to the tree to gather their thoughts. They decided what they were going to say as an alibi if anyone should ask them if they knew anything about the death of Pietro Tonto. Rosita was also worrying about the Negro girl. She'd seen Angelo and even though he'd rescued her from the bandit, she might talk if under duress someone questioned her and if she talked, of course that would mean the end of her plans.

'Don't worry,' said Angelo, 'I told her to go straight home and say nothing to anyone. But you tell me something before we leave, where did you learn to fight like that?'

'A friend of your Uncle Nunziato taught me martial arts,' she replied. He took her in his arms and kissed her once more before taking her by the hand and saying, 'Shall we go now? My father will be waiting for us to come home before he goes to bed. Please don't tell him anything that went on tonight.'

Vincenzo was reading a book when they arrived, not that he understood much of what he'd read. His thoughts were full of Angelo and Rosita, being out at that time of the night. Knowing what could happen if any of Don Camillo's drunken thugs were out there.

'Hello Uncle!' said Rosita, trying to look tranquil. 'You're still up. You didn't need to wait up for us, you could have gone to bed.'

Slowly he closed his book, 'Goodnight you two lovebirds,' he said, and with a grin like a Cheshire cat he turned and left. They wished him goodnight in return, looking at each other like conspirators. Angelo grabbed her hand and pulled her to him.

'I love you, wildcat,' he said, kissing her fervently. Almost bruising her lips, searching for her tongue with his, exploring the contours of her mouth. She pulled away licking her lips and looked down at Angelo's right hand which was resting on her left breast, the nipple erect from his gentle caress. He smiled and brushed his lips across hers once more, then looking down to his hand himself he said, 'I think I went a bit too far, there. I should say I'm sorry, but I'm not sorry. So I think its best now if we retire too?' he suggested.

'Yes you're right,' she replied, and they went up the stairs together hand in hand. They stopped in front of her bedroom.

'Goodnight Rosita, my love, I'll see you in the morning,' he said, kissing and hugging her lightly, not wanting to let her go.

'Your room is that way. This, if I recall correctly, is my room,' she said, opening the door, but still Angelo did not move, instead he stayed looking at her, until she closed the door.

For nearly half of the night, Rosita tossed and turned thinking of what had gone on in the nearby copse that evening. Her uncle's snores could be heard throughout the whole house but eventually she fell asleep.

CHAPTER SIX

There was a knock at Rosita's bedroom door, which woke her with a start. It was already morning.

'Come in, it's not locked,' she said, rubbing her eyes. In walked Angelo, followed by the aroma of freshly brewed coffee.

'What's the matter? Are you not feeling well?' he asked as he kissed her cheek.

'No, I'm fine, why?' she answered, smiling up at him, and looking at his freshly shaved face.

'It's late and I've already got the horses ready, breakfast is waiting for you,' he said, rubbing his finger sensuously up and down her neck, making her body shake with excitement. He was making her pay for leaving him behind her door the night before.

'I'll be down in a few minutes,' she replied, looking at his puffy eyes. She realised he hadn't slept much either.

Reluctantly Angelo left her. Quickly she put on her clothes and went downstairs. 'Sorry Uncle, I overslept,' she apologised. 'I'll go and quickly wash my face,' she said, pinching Angelo's bottom as she passed by him.

He gasped, and almost followed her out. The nerve of the woman he thought to himself, God knows how much anguish it would cost him to control himself from making love to her. All night he had been permanently aroused. This morning when he woke her up, and had seen her rosy cheeks and her sleepy eyes, he almost climbed in with her. Dear God, how long could he resist the temptation to make love to her? Angelo didn't realise how long he had been standing staring at the door through which Rosita had exited, from, until his father dryly interrupted his thoughts.

'If I were you I would close your mouth, before an insect flies in. Sit down, and have your breakfast, it's getting late.' Angelo looked at his father, and they both burst out laughing. After washing, Rosita joined the two men at the breakfast table. 'At what time did you go to bed last night, Francesca?' asked Vincenzo.

'Only ten minutes or so after you Uncle,' she replied, 'But I was unable to sleep straightway, I had a lot on my mind.'

Angelo looked at Rosita with a questioning expression on his face, and she knew what was going through his mind too. That he wanted to tell his father what had happened the previous evening. Discreetly she shook her head at him to tell him no. At that moment Vincenzo rose from the table and disappeared out the back of the house. Rosita took the chance to speak to Angelo.

'Tell your father not to mention to anyone that we were out walking last night,' she whispered.

'How can I do that? If I do, he'll suspect something,' he whispered back.

'Please Angelo,' she pleaded with him.

'All right, I'll try,' said Angelo. He knew that she didn't want to worry Vincenzo.

They were almost ready to leave for work when Vincenzo, having noticed the knowing looks between these two young people, asked Angelo what was going on between him and Rosita. He didn't give Angelo time to answer; he just looked at his son with a serious expression on his face, as if to say, I know something is afoot.

'I think it's better if you two go to work now, it's getting late and by the way, I wasn't born yesterday. See you two tonight, and God be with you,' said Vincenzo, shaking his head.

Angelo took his opportunity to instruct his father not to mention their walk the night before, when Rosita walked out to the horses. Vincenzo did not react or question Angelo's request, because he had had a very early visit from one of Papa Joe's friends, letting him know everything that had happened the night before.

Today's work for Angelo and Rosita was to help guide all the cattle through a large disinfecting tank, and then to brand them with the hacienda's stamp. Rosita was given the task of making a list of the number and type of animal as it passed through. And Angelo was helping to tie the animal's legs together ready for them to be branded. Half the day had already gone by and it was time to eat their lunch. As there were many workers in one place today, the vaquero's cook was on hand to prepare hot food. They would eat well this lunch time. There was roast beef, beans and plenty of fresh salad. Rosita washed her hands before joining the many men who were already queuing with plates in their hands for their food. Two other men were helping the cook to cut the bread and meat, and two were serving.

Rosita and Angelo were nearly at the end of the queue. Today she'd dressed in baggy suede trousers, a short sleeves cotton blouse and a suede fringed waistcoat that she had draped over her saddle. Even though she had worked half the day under the sun, she didn't look too flustered. Her long dark hair tied back with a piece of a blue ribbon. As she was chatting to her fellow workers, her eyes were exploring all around her, she looked fixedly at some people she didn't like very much. She noted how the Negroes sat apart from the white workers with their heads bowed. They appeared to be afraid to look at their fellow men for fear of retribution.

'When my father was alive all the workers would sit together, chatting and joking, there was a good atmosphere then,' thought Rosita to herself. She felt a great sorrow in her heart as she remembered this. Just then a man on horseback came galloping directly towards one of the foremen. Once dismounted, he gave the news that Pietro Tonto had been found dead.

'How did it happen?' demanded the foreman, grabbing hold of the rider's jacket lapels.

'I don't know, Don Ciccio,' answered the poor messenger. 'They think he was drunk and fell from his horse and broke his neck.'

Don Ciccio, seething with anger, called one of his men over.

'Jesús, I'm leaving you in charge, report to me tonight,' said Don Ciccio, then he jumped onto the messenger's horse and rode like the wind into the distance. Pietro Tonto had been Don Ciccio's best friend; he could not believe he was dead. They had been drunk together many times before, so it wasn't as if it was the first time. How had he managed to lose control of his horse this time? Something didn't add up in Don Ciccio's head. He knew they had both done a lot of horrible things to too many people on this hacienda, so it may have been revenge for something. He would have to find out. But for now he would have to be very careful and watch out for his own back with extra care.

Angelo and Rosita exchanged a quick knowing look to one another. For the next hour, after they had eaten, everything was calm, some people were dozing and others playing cards. They had lain on the ground under the shade of a tree for a while. Angelo was lying with his hands behind his head and his hat over his face. She thought Angelo was asleep, so Rosita got up and went to her horse and started to saddled it, suddenly she felt a hand on her shoulder and she spun round. It was Angelo.

'Are you thinking of leaving without me? Where you go, I go too. Understand.' he said. Rosita smiled and shook her head. She should have known she could not fool Angelo, especially now that he knew what she was capable of. He knows she's not afraid, and that could easily get her killed.

'I just wanted to check around for a few minutes,' she replied.

'Well my tigress, you just tell me where you want to go and I'll take you there.'

'Nowhere special, I just want to see where these roads over here end up.'

Angelo wanted to stop her, but he gave in. If she had made her mind up to go nosing around, then nobody could stop her.

'All right, but what's going on in that head of yours?' he demanded.

She laughed and then she said in a whisper, 'I don't know yet, I need to find a place.'

'A place?' he repeated.

'I mean, somewhere not many people would pass through. A place where there are a lot of trees and bushes for cover.'

'All right, as you wish, but I'm coming with you,' reiterated Angelo as they set off. 'I knew the instant I saw you go to your horse that you were looking for trouble.'

Five minutes into their ride, they spotted two negroes leaning against a nearby tree, watching Rosita and Angelo as they approached. Rosita slowed her mount to acknowledge the two men. They smiled at her and bowed slightly, and one of them said, 'Buenos dias, Miss Curro, if you need us we're at your disposal.'

Rosita didn't want to stop to talk with them at that moment, but she appreciated their offer. For sure the news had been spread round very quickly. She was delighted, but there was still a lot of planning to do.

'Come and see me tonight behind the stable, but make sure that nobody sees you,' she replied, before going on her way with Angelo. They cantered along together for about half an hour, and then Angelo stopped.

'Francesca, look over there,' said Angelo, as they approached some high bushes. 'Behind those trees there is a deserted house and a big barn. Nobody's been there for years, my father told me that...' He hesitated looking around to make sure nobody was about, then whispered. 'A long time ago your grandparents lived there.'

'Really!' she said, showing a keen interest.

'It's true,' he proceeded. 'When I was a young boy my parents worked in this area and I explored the house. I went inside and there were still many pictures hanging on the walls, and all the furniture was still there, although in bad condition. And from what my father told me, your grandparents were very happy in this house, and even after building the new mansion, they still used this place as a kind of retreat. He told me that as the hacienda's business grew and more and more people came to work for your grandfather, mostly Negroes and Italians. He built small houses for them, and they in return treated him like a king. Your father grew up and started to help about the hacienda, and workers came to respect him as they did your grandfather.'

Rosita was listening very carefully to what Angelo was telling her. Her eyes were glistening, filling with tears ready to cascade down her peachy soft cheeks. She blinked her eyes several times, and then she focused so she could see clearly all round under the tall trees next to the house that once belonged to her dear grandparents. The instant she saw the place, she knew it was the right place to use as her headquarters. Here she would recruit and train anybody who wanted to help her on her quest to one day take back what was rightly hers. She felt sad about her grandparents; she didn't remember them at all, it was as if she had never even met them.

'It's strange, I don't remember my parents ever speaking to me about my grandparents,' remarked Rosita, a bit confused; surely her father had spoken to her about his parents.

'I don't know.' Angelo replied, 'Maybe it had something to do with your mother. I'll tell you something else; your grandparents' graves lie just behind this house. Come, I'll show you. Then we will return to the others, otherwise people will ask questions about where we've been.'

They ventured through the high bushes that were overgrown, untouched for many years, they almost covered the house. The asparagus fern that climbed all-over the surrounds of the house, and the high trees would make the best hiding place one could hope for, thought Rosita. It looked so desolate, but once it had been a happy house with happy people living in it. The whole area looked deserted. Yes, she thought. This was the ideal place. This was the place where her plans, with the help of her grandparents' spirits, would become reality. Rosita raised her eyebrow and looked pained, it was an unpleasant feeling she had in her gut. She wondered if Don Camillo had anything to do with her grandparents' death, as well? Dear God, if that was the case, he has a lot to answer for!

They made their way to the graves; Angelo had the feeling that he would regret this one of these days. He shouldn't have brought Rosita to see this place, but it was too late now.

'Look, here they are,' said Angelo, pointing to two metre high statues half hidden with more overgrowth at the head of the graves. The horses looked uneasy. They sensed that maybe there was some wild animal around. Angelo feared it could be a poisonous snake. But he didn't mention anything to Rosita. She slid slowly off her horse and approached the stone figures. Looking at them intently she stroked the face of one, as if it was her grandmother. Tears misted over her eyes, and in no time they began to fall down her face.

"My dear grandparents, I promise to return to you soon. I will restore this place, so you will receive the respect you deserve," she murmured.

'Francesca, we must go now,' urged Angelo feeling very nervous.

'Yes, I'm coming now.' She realised the risk they were taking, as Don Camillo's men were everywhere looking for trouble. Angelo and Rosita returned to work. Her eyes were still a little bloodshot from the crying she'd done. She was thinking through how the new discovery was going to fit into her grand plan. She felt emotionally drained having discovered more about her family and she thought the afternoon's work would never end. Angelo noticed how she was suffering, but could not help her in this situation. The job Rosita was assigned to do was finished, all the animals had been processed so she asked Angelo if she could help him or the others with some other job.

'If you wish,' answered Angelo,' but we're almost through now.'

'Well in that case, I'll go and get the horses saddled,' she replied. As she approached the horses, she came upon a group of Negroes who were making their way to their cart to go home. Rosita pointed at the two she spoke to earlier.

'Hey, you two, come here,' she said with authority. At this all of them turned around. 'You, and you, come here,' she repeated, 'saddle these two horses,' straight away they nodded and did as they were asked. 'I'm sorry, I have forgotten your names,' she whispered to them as they approached.

'Tunde,' said one of them, continuing with his task without looking at her.

'Gideon,' answered the other.

'Good,' she said, moving around her horse as if she was looking for something. 'I've changed my mind about you two coming to our stable, it's too dangerous. Do you two know that there is a house not far from here where the old founder of this hacienda used to live?'

'Yes, we know about that,' answered Gideon, 'but, for many years people have been afraid to go there. Some say the spirits of the couple haunt the place.'

'And, do you believe that?' asked Rosita. 'Because we're going to meet there on Sunday afternoon. You and any other young people like yourself that you can trust. Of course you know how important it is that this is kept from Don Camilo's men. I must have the place cleaned so it is habitable. Also, near the house there is a big barn that needs repairing and converting into a school.'

'A school? What sort of school, Senorita?' asked Gideon, not sure if he understood.

'A school of martial arts. You have heard of this surely?'

'Yes Miss, I have.' replied Gideon. 'Who will be the teacher? If you don't mind me asking?'

'I will teach all you young people as much as I know. Because when the time comes, we'll need to defend ourselves as best we can.'

'Very well Miss, we'll do our best,' said Gideon, impressed with Rosita's frankness and courage.

'You'd better go now,' said Rosita to the two boys. Then leading the horses she returned to Angelo, and saw he had finished his work. She gazed at him for few long seconds, and as if he'd sensed her looking at him, he turned around. Their eyes met and when she saw his eyes arrogantly looking up and down the length of her body, she blushed and had to look away for an instant. His intense gaze lit a spark in Rosita's body, and in no time she was on fire. His broad smile, told her that he knew how she felt.

'Hello, dear cousin, would you care for a lift?' she joked, trying to forget how she felt.

'That depends where you're planning on taking me,' he answered cheerfully.

'Well, if you will allow me, I'll take you to a place where there is homemade spaghetti and tomato sauce with chilli!'

'Ah, the perfect place for us. In that case I'll accept willingly!' he murmured into her ear. He took a quick glance around to see if anybody was nearby to witness what he was about to do. When he was happy that the coast was clear, he pulled her behind one of the horses and gathered her into his arms, kissing her hungrily. She responded to his kisses passionately, then pushed him gently away to catch her breath.

'Oh! Mr Curro. What do you think you're doing? There are people about here who could see us!' she said breathlessly.

'What are you afraid of? That they'll think that I don't kiss you very well?'

'Buffoon,' she cried squeezing him tightly and kissing him back fervently, taking him by surprise. Then she pushed him away and jumped onto her horse leaving at a gallop and waving at him. 'See you at home,' she said laughing.

'Wait for me!' he yelled, speedily mounting his horse. What a woman, he thought, while he tried to catch up with her. She had slowed her horse to a gentle trot, and Angelo caught up with her and drew alongside. He reached over, and bodily pulled her from her mount so she was sitting sideways in front of him. He held her tightly in his arms and whispered into her ear, while she melted against his strong warm body. She loved the smell of his body; mixed with his after shave it made her feel a bit light headed. His kisses threatened to carry her away into a shameless response.

'I love you so much, Rosita.'

'And I love you so much too, Angelo,' she replied. She got back onto her horse and they continued on their way home in silence for a while, content just being in each other's company. Rosita looked around at the lush bounty of spring that surrounded them. Fertile beauty in the midst of bloody violence. This was truly a time when the will of the Almighty was needed.

'Do you truly wish to reunite these young people?' asked Angelo, his eyes never wavering from her face as he waited for her answer. He could see her fighting with her thoughts, whatever she was thinking.

'Yes, Angelo, you know we need them.' Angelo was happy with her answer, and then he turned his attention to the richness of the crops surrounding them and the various men and women who still at that time worked hard to harvest them. There was food enough for everybody. So why were some people still living in poverty without food? And was all the violence necessary? Of course not, but greed and racism had no bounds.

Temporarily, it seemed that all her problems from the past had been forgotten. Angelo felt so happy that he started to sing a Sicilian song. Rosita laughed and slapped her horse, setting off at a gallop again.

'Let's see who gets there first!' she cried.

'You are always cheating!' complained Angelo, taking up the challenge. They arrived in the yard as if they were being chased. Vincenzo heard the horse hooves and rushed outside, thinking the worst.

'What's going on here?' he shouted through the swirling dust, but he realised what was going on, when he saw the two lovers laughing together.

'Hello Father!' said Angelo with a twinkle in his eye, not looking at all tired.

'Hello Uncle! How has your day been?' asked Rosita, still laughing.

'Very well, how about you two? Have you heard the news?'

'What news,' she replied, looking at Angelo.

'About Pietro Tonto, they found him dead this morning,'

'Oh! That. Yes we heard, someone reported it where we were working, I believe he fell off his horse in a drunken state,' she answered swiftly. At this point Rosita went straight inside to the wash room, thinking that Vincenzo may start asking her awkward questions.

Later they all congregated around the kitchen table.

'Not that I'm complaining about what we have, but a promise is a promise!' proceeded Angelo. 'Not only what I've been through with you, just a minute before we left the field, but...'

'What's happened?' interrupted Vincenzo; he'd been deep in his own thoughts and didn't get the gist of the conversation, until he looked at his son and Rosita. She quickly had to say or do something to hide her embarrassment.

'Well grumpy, what you missed out on this evening you will eat tomorrow. I'll make tagliatelle. I'll prepare them tonight, then tomorrow Uncle Vincenzo just needs to prepare the sauce.' No more was said on the subject, but they all knew what had passed.

After they had had their coffee, Angelo went straight to see Don Camillo. Vincenzo started to clear away the dirty plates and Rosita went to wash out some of her clothes. On completing that task she began the preparation of the fresh tagliatelle, thinking how lucky she and Angelo were, that Vincenzo hadn't pursued the matter about Pietro Tonto. But she was wrong; she should have known Vincenzo better. He meandered over to her and stood to her side while she mixed the pasta dough.

'I want to ask you something,' he said looking straight at her. 'Did you or Angelo have anything to do with the death of Pietro Tonto?'

Rosita stopped what she was doing and looked at him, not really wanting to answer because she didn't want to worry him, but she didn't want to lie either.

'Well,' she said after a short hesitation. 'Yes, we were there when it happened. But where his body was found with his horse was a long way from here, so I don't think anyone will suspect us.'

'I expect you are right, I'm sorry. I had to ask you as I had a funny feeling you knew something about the situation.'

'Believe me Uncle, we didn't go out looking for trouble, but an innocent young girl was in grave danger and we couldn't just let it go on. But don't worry about it Uncle, we were very careful,' she said.

After about an hour Angelo returned from Don Camillo's. He explained to his father all about the event of the night before, and how Pietro Tonto had died. But Angelo had a lot more to tell his father. He had seen that there were many new ugly faced types of rogue at his master's house, and they were armed to the teeth. That made him wonder what they were doing there and what his master was up too. Maybe he was expecting trouble from somewhere. They certainly didn't look like business people to him. Since the arrival of Rosita, Angelo could see things more clearly. Don Camillo wouldn't hire these type of men to keep them idle or just riding their horses around the hacienda. He hoped that this didn't have anything to do with Rosita. Don Camillo had definitely changed his manner towards him, since Rosita arrived. It could be a coincidence, but from now on he was going to take extra care of her. Because with her quick temper, one of these days she would go too far and that would be the end of her big plan.

'A penny for your thoughts,' asked Rosita, when she saw him looking seriously at her.

'Yes, well, what about the tagliatelle, you haven't even started yet!' he joked.

'Of course I've started, I've already made the mixture, now you have to knead the dough.'

It took nearly two hours to finish the tagliatelle. By the time they had finished, there was more flour on their faces and the floor than on the table. Angelo had never done this before, but he found it turned out to be fun, or was it her company that was fun? In the background, Vincenzo enjoyed watching his son and Rosita making fools of themselves. He was happy for them, they had found each other. They started to clean themselves up, and the mess they had made.

Angelo looked at his wristwatch. It was too early to go to sleep, so he thought he would ask Rosita if she wanted to go for a walk, and hopefully this time they wouldn't encounter any troublemakers.

'If you want to forget all about this mess, come for a walk with me.' he suggested hopefully.

'Not tonight,' answered Rosita, directing her eyes from the sink where she was washing up towards Angelo. 'I don't really want to go out, my legs are so tired, but we can sit outside for a while. I'll play the guitar and you can sing for me.'

'But I don't know any songs.'

'That's not true,' put in Vincenzo. 'Do you not remember when you were in your teens I played the guitar, and you used to sing with your mother.'

'But Father, didn't you say you were very tired?' said Angelo, 'and anyway I don't remember the song very well.'

'Once you start to sing, it will come back to you, I'm going to fetch my guitar too,' insisted Vincenzo. 'It's about time there was music in this house again. Francesca has brought a new light into our lives.' On that note Vincenzo disappeared upstairs to fetch his guitar, then rejoined Rosita and Angelo who were already sitting outside.

The gentle evening breeze was refreshing as it blew across their faces, relaxing their bodies from the hard work they had endured all day, forgetting for a while all the problems that lie ahead of them.

'Come Francesca, let me hear you play,' said Vincenzo. They started to strum a few notes to tune their guitars and then played some chords together. It wasn't long before they were in unison with each other. Angelo recognised the tune of a song he had once sung and was soon singing as he had never sung before. Looking into Rosita's eyes he told her in the song and with his eyes how much he loved her. The three of them enjoyed a pleasurable evening relating stories, laughing and exchanging jokes. Under the millions of twinkling stars, they had the feeling that their relationship had been truly sealed.

By now they were tired and it was time to retire to their beds. Vincenzo said his goodnights, and was the first one to go in. Rosita and Angelo took each other's hands and headed in too. They kissed goodnight at the bottom of the stairs, and then followed Vincenzo up for the night.

CHAPTER SEVEN

Rosita had slept like a log. After she had stretched like a cat does after sleeping, she sat up in the bed wondering what time it was. There was a knock at the door.

'Come in,' she said cheerily. It was Angelo who had brought coffee up for her.

'Good morning, Miss, are you ready to get up,' he asked, kissing her slowly and softly on her lips.

'Good morning, Angelo. Yes I slept very well thank you,' she replied sarcastically.

'I know,' he replied dryly, 'you've been snoring all night!'

'What! I don't snore,' she said, pretending to be hurt by his remark.

'Well, all I know is somebody kept me awake all night. Actually, I thought I should have come to your room to keep you company, but I changed my mind.'

'What made you change your mind?' asked Rosita, thinking to herself that she had had that same exact thought.

'I was afraid you'd throw me out. Instead I had a cold shower.'

'Idle chatter,' she retorted. 'Now I think you'd better leave and give me a chance to get dressed. Thanks for the coffee,' she said. He left after he'd given her another slow soft kiss. She quickly dressed and was soon down for breakfast.

'Do you know that today we only have to work until lunch time?' exclaimed Angelo.

'Really?' she replied joyously. She was pleased. 'Great, then I can ride to the old hacienda.'

'Looking for trouble again? Really Francesca! You never cease to amaze me. For goodness, sake, do you know what danger you put yourself in, not to mention the people around you who are involved.' said Angelo, angrily. He felt like locking her in her room, until he could find out more about Don Camillo's plans. 'I'm sorry Francesca, I shouldn't have spoken to you like that, but I'm so worried about you.' he said, calming down a bit. 'We could go to the old hacienda together,' he suggested, still looking at Rosita, and shaking his head to stop her talking. He didn't want his father to find out, not yet anyway. But it was too late, Vincenzo had heard some of their conversation.

'What hacienda are you two talking about?' asked Vincenzo. 'There aren't any near here.'

'I know that Father, we're fooling around. Anyway we'll be off now, bye, see you later.'

'Wait, I don't think I'll be here when you two return, I'm going to the village shortly. Francesca, do you need anything?' he asked, looking from one to the other.

'Well Uncle I need many small things, but I have to prepare a list and then we'll go together one of these days. Thank you all the same, and do not worry if we are late returning tonight.'

Angelo and Rosita's work today was to pack all the fresh vegetables such as tomatoes, green beans, aubergines and peppers into boxes, and help to load them onto the lorries which came from the big cities of Tucuman and Mendoza, and some from the villages nearby. By the time they arrived at the barn where they were to work, they found many workers who had already been there a few hours picking the vegetables before sunrise. Angelo's main job was to document and grade the vegetables. Both Anglo and Rosita's attitude towards the other workers was one of authority, but with politeness.

Angelo did not carry a crop like some of the others in charge in the hacienda.

At this time of the year there were many temporary workers who slept under the stars at night. They brought their few possessions with them on their wagons. It was a sorry sight to see all the workers, from mixed ethnic origins, slaving away to make a pittance for themselves and their children, who could be seen in and around the area.

'A place as this should have an area where these people can wash and sleep like decent human beings,' remarked Rosita. She worked as hard as the others, and very often she glanced at them admiringly.

It was nearly mid-day. They had almost finished loading the lorries, when a Negro woman carrying a box of tomatoes on her head suddenly tripped forward onto her face. The box toppled over spilling the contents all over the ground badly bruising them. Rosita saw the whole thing happen, and she ran over to help. But before she could get to her, the foremen, who had put his foot out in front of the poor woman, making her trip, was there with a crop. He raised it above his head to thrash her with. But Rosita arrived just in time to stop him by grabbing his wrist and forcing him backwards.

'What are you doing?' she cried. 'This woman is not a wild animal! Someone tripped her on purpose, and I know who.'

'This damn woman just ruined a box of tomatoes,' he shouted angrily, ignoring what Rosita had said.

'I know it was not intentional, why don't you ask her if she's all right instead of beating her?' demanded Rosita, furiously, helping the woman up.

'You're new here aren't you? I think you should mind your own business, if you know what is good for you!' shouted the foreman angrily.

Rosita doesn't know when to stop, thought Angelo to himself. She wouldn't back out of any trouble, no matter who was causing it.

'And if I don't mind my own business, what are you going to do about it?' she answered, defiantly. The ugly son of a bitch really was trying her patience. He regarded her with detestation for a few seconds and then raised his crop as if to strike her. But his crop came nowhere near her, as she reacted quickly in defence. In a split second a well placed kick struck his groin and brought him to his knees, doubled up with pain. Two other men approached to see what was going on.

'This man insulted me, and tonight I'm going to report him to Don Camillo,' announced Rosita. Gesticulating to the woman who had dropped the fruit to move away from the area. Then Angelo arrived and took hold of Rosita's arm.

'Let's go now, Francesca,' he said. 'There is no reasoning with these people.' Then he led her away from the scene, and as their morning's work was complete, they mounted their horses and started out on the road for home. As soon as they were out of earshot of everyone, Angelo started to speak.

'My God, Francesca! I can't leave you alone for five minutes without you starting some trouble. As soon as we get home, you'll get a good hiding from me! Then I'll lock you in your room.'

'Ha! And what do you mean by that?'

'Well, I can't show you what I mean now, or what I would like to do to you, I'm too tired, hungry and hot, but when I've had some lunch and a wash you'll see!'

'If you so much as to touch me I'll tell your father!'

'You won't have time to tell my father, or the strength.'

Rosita already knew in her heart that Angelo was right. She shouldn't have lost her temper so quickly; she swore to herself that in the future she would try hard to control her emotions. If not for her, at least for Angelo and Vincenzo, she owed that much to them. But deep down inside her, she couldn't help feeling good having hurt the son of a bitch! She looked at Angelo from under the brim of her hat, he was looking ahead of him deep in thought. She wondered what he was thinking. A few minutes ago he was mad at her. She hated that silence, she wasn't used to this, Angelo was always so carefree, joking and laughing with her. She loved the way his eyes shone when he looked at her. Suddenly she had had enough of this horrible silence.

'Angelo.' she called.

'Yes,' he answered curtly, with a hoarse voice. He was very sorry for speaking to her in that way, but she had to learn to control herself for everybody's sake, he dreaded the thought of seeing her hurt. 'Are you all right?'

'Yes… no, I'm not all right, unless… unless you forgive me for my behaviour. I behaved in an immature way,' she said, fighting back her tears. Angelo sensed the emotion in her voice, and that she was about to burst into tears at any time now.

'Francesca, my dear, I'm not cross with you. What you did was right and justified, I'm just worried about you, I dread to think what might happen. You don't have any idea how much I love you!' He whispered, bringing his horse closer to hers.

'I know, and I love you too!' she said, with tears beginning to slide down her flushed face. He couldn't stand it any longer, he wanted to hold her in his arms. He quickly dismounted his horse and reached for her. For a few seconds she stopped breathing, she thought he wanted to beat her. She was wrong, he only helped her to dismount. He gathered her up in his arms and began to kiss her fiercely, she responded to his kisses with equal passion. They were so engrossed in each other that they didn't realise that people were passing by, until someone said. 'Buenos tardes, Señor Curro.'

It was one of the men who had worked with them all morning, and his wife, Margarita, on their cart.

'Buenos tardes, Julio, Señora,' replied Angelo, grinning shyly, a bit embarrassed for being caught like a teenager, on his first date.

'Oh God, Angelo what will they think of us now?' said Rosita, hiding her face against his chest.

'They may think that we're human, and sometimes we can't control our desire. And now Señorita Francesca Curro, let's go home, or there is a chance that someone else will find us here and maybe in a worse position.' The rest of the journey home passed quickly, as they laughed and joked with each other.

'Do you know what I was thinking?' said Rosita, while preparing something to eat for their lunch.

'Not until you tell me,' he answered.

'I thought I'd go to my grandparents' old house after lunch,' she said nonchalantly, to test his reaction.

'Oh no you won't, not without me!'

Rosita laughed, because she knew he would say that. After eating lunch, they packed a few things to take with them. Angelo wondered what she really had in mind, but he chose to wait until she decided to tell him.

'Angelo, could I ask you a favour?' she said, interrupting his thoughts. 'Would you stay with me tonight in my grandparents' old house?'

'Francesca, you're not serious!' he said, in disbelief.

'Yes, I am. We'll leave a note for your father telling him that we'll be out all night. We can take a couple of blankets and enough food for dinner and breakfast. Your father, or anyone else, will not suspect the real reason why we'll be going there, they'll just think we want to be alone, won't they?'

It didn't take too much persuasion on Rosita's part, for him to consent. He thought he was in for a wonderful evening alone with the woman he loves, in fact, his body started to stir immediately, thinking he would make passionate love to her all night.

'Well, aren't we going to be two lovebirds tonight?' teased Angelo.

'Of course we are!' she laughed, flinging her arms around his neck. Angelo scribbled a note to his father and Rosita got a few things together that they would need, not forgetting a canteen of water and her guitar, as usual. Angelo was very excited at the prospect of spending a whole night alone with Francesca, but he was in for a big surprise. Because when they got to their destination he would find a lot of other people waiting there. Their journey didn't take very long. As they neared the supposedly deserted area, the road changed into a rough track.

'Stop!' said Angelo, in a loud whisper. 'Don't make a sound, I think I heard voices.'

'Of course you heard voices, that would be Gideon, Tunde and Bayo.'

Angelo looked at Rosita with a confused expression on his face.

'Sorry, I forgot to tell you, but we will not be alone here tonight. You see, if we are to renovate this place, we need a lot of helping hands.'

At this, Angelo smiled to himself; his night of passion with Rosita had gone up in flames. He slapped Rosita's horse and they continued on. Soon the two new arrivals dismounted. Gideon and Tunde approached and took the horses, and bowed their heads slightly.

'You heard us coming?' asked Rosita.

'No, Señorita, you were seen. We have four men on guard duty on the perimeter,' replied Gideon.

'Good. Have you been here long?' she asked, excitedly. Angelo was getting more and more curious.

'No, we've just arrived, but there are others who have been here since this morning.'

'There are others too?' asked Angelo astonished. 'How many of you are here altogether?'

'We number about ten, and already the barn has been cleared. But it's not safe; it's in great need of repair. There's lots of wood available, but as yet, we don't have any nails or tools,' said Gideon, with an apologetic note in his voice.

'Very good,' answered Rosita, 'but now let's go and meet up with the rest of the men.'

When they got to the barn, she found the men waiting expectantly for her, standing in a row. She was shocked at the state of some them. The scars on their faces, the clothes on them were like rags and the expression on their faces were like those of people who had been chased by wild dogs. However, a couple were in good shape. After Rosita had observed them all carefully, Gideon began to introduce them to her one by one.

'I am pleased to have you all here,' she began, 'but you must not forget that we are trespassing, we have no right to be here, and we have to tread very carefully.'

Gideon interrupted her at that moment. 'Señorita, I have something to confess. Five of these men do not belong here. They escaped several days ago from another hacienda, where they treat Negroes very badly, far worse than we are treated here, and they have come to seek refuge with us.'

'Gideon, as far as I am concerned, they can stay, but it is dangerous for them in this area. They cannot light a fire because the smoke will be seen, and they will need food but I can't come here every day. For a while I could only come once or twice a week.'

'Do not worry, Señorita,' replied Gideon. 'Tunde and I will look after them,' he proceeded, looking at Rosita questioningly. He didn't know what to expect from his decision, and the responsibilities he was taking without thinking of the consequences.

'Buenos, Gideon, let's not waste any more time. I've brought some nails and a couple of hammers, and I'll see if there are any more tools left around anywhere that we can use. Next week I'll go to the village and start to buy a few more things that we'll need. Not all at once though, because there is only one store and maybe people will wonder what's going on.'

'I have a suggestion, Señorita,' put in Gideon. 'If you can provide food and blankets, we'll provide the tools. We can take these from the hacienda little by little, no one will notice.'

'Right,' she agreed, 'that's a good idea, but you'll be taking a huge risk doing it.'

'I know, but it's a risk we are happy to and have to take,' he replied. 'There is one more thing I have to tell you, Señorita. You said you would teach us some martial arts.'

'Yes I did,' she replied.

'Well,' he said pointing to a small group of young men. 'One of those boy's is very good, he can teach us when you're not here.'

'How good is he?' she asked.

'Very.' was Gideon's response.

'That's fine with me, it gives me more time to plan other things,' she said. Rosita continued making plans with Gideon and the others, while Angelo moved around the buildings carefully, checking all was well and that nobody uninvited was nearby snooping. And wondering how the hell they could help all of these people at the same time. They needed food and blankets straight away, but with Don Camillo's cut-throats all around the Hacienda Antigua, it would take a miracle to do anything undetected. He and Rosita must think of something clever at once.

Meanwhile, inside the Mansion, Donna Teresa and Don Camillo Ferrero were getting ready to receive some dinner guests. At forty-seven, Donna Teresa still looked young and beautiful, and as vain as ever. Donna Teresa had been born in 1907, in the city of Buenos Aires. She was the daughter of a German mother, and a Spanish father. They had been established in Argentina since the 1850s She married Don Sebastiano Miserendino in 1929. At the time he was betrothed to one of Donna Teresa's sisters. But, Donna Teresa being selfish, and mischievous, tricked Don Sebastiano, by seducing him, and telling him nasty things about her own sister. He was trapped, her beauty blinded him. Ten years later it cost him his life, being assassinated by Donna Teresa's lover. She spent a lot time looking after herself, visiting her beautician, and hairdressers trying to keep her hair the same colour as she always had. She amused herself by entertaining herself and her husband's friends.

'Darling, what do you think about that new girl? I mean, Francesca Curro,' she asked, looking at herself in the mirror, just in case anything had appeared during the night, like a spot, or a wrinkle.

'What about her?' he replied, trying to fasten the cufflinks on his spotless white shirt.

'You know?' she said.

'No, I don't! You're not starting to get jealous again are you? If you do, you're wasting your time, darling. I only have eyes for you.'

'Oh you big ugly liar, I don't mean that anyway. It's just… well. I don't know. It's something about her. I can't put my finger on it.' She proceeded, looking serious for a few long seconds. 'You know, when she came to visit the other day, I looked into her eyes and for a split second I… I… I don't know what I saw but she seemed very familiar.'

'Really my love, I do not know what you're worrying about. She's a hardworking girl, and she's being watched twenty-four hours a day by Angelo. My vaqueros are telling me that she and Angelo are working very well together. So, now please stop looking at yourself in the mirror, come here and help me on with my cufflinks darling,' he said playfully, a wary grin curling up his moustached lips. Don Camillo Ferrero did love his wife, but he was no saint. Of course he'd noticed Francesca as a beautiful woman, and it had even crossed his mind to try to seduce her. But then, he would have to try to prize Angelo away from her for a while because he stuck to his cousin's side like glue. He considered him a good worker and a friend, and he trusted him with his life.

But what he didn't know of course was what lay ahead of him. He never suspected that one day he may have to cross swords with Angelo. Even Angelo didn't know it until a few days ago, but now he began to understand more about his master's malignant sense of humour. Maybe Angelo had heard things that his boss had possibly done in the past, but refused to believe it.

'What are you up to?' asked Rosita, walking towards Angelo, after she'd finished planning things with Gideon and the others.

'I'm starting a fire to make coffee,' he replied.

'Don't be daft, Angelo, someone will see the smoke!' she cried out, concerned. She was surprised at Angelo, didn't he know what a dangerous situation they were in?

'Francesca, we may have been spotted coming this way. Anyway, the wood is dry, so there won't be much smoke. It's late afternoon now, so I would think people will be having their siesta or preparing to go to the village. Any case don't you think it would be a good test to see if anyone notices it?' Changing the subject to stop her worrying he said, 'Do you know, inside the house, hardly anything has been touched, so there should be things the young men can use there, like pots and crockery. But I never ventured upstairs. I thought the floor was likely to be rotten.'

Rosita realised that she may have overreacted to the situation. She shouldn't have spoken to Angelo in that manner; he had been so supportive towards her, and very patient. She shouldn't have doubted him. He was a man, and what a man, strong, clever, and very sensually attractive. She would fight away any woman who got between them.

'Don't think about that now,' she said. 'Time is getting on; we'll look around the house properly tomorrow. When you've made the coffee you can call the others and ask them if they want to eat. There is enough food for everyone, and Angelo?'

'Yes, my love, would you like sugar in your coffee?' he answered sarcastically smiling at her. With that she understood he had forgiven her.

'I'm sorry, Angelo, I do not know what got into me! Please forgive me.'

Her sorrowful expression tugged at his heart strings. He didn't care if anybody was watching them or not, he took her into his arms, and ravished her lips with his kisses. She was breathless when he'd finished.

'I hope that was a nice way to punish you,' he said. She turned away from him. 'And where are you off to?'

'I'm going to tidy up my grandparents' graves before it gets too dark.' And with that she ,again, turned away from him and left him standing watching her walk away. His eyes rested on her hips, he really loved the way she moved her behind when she walked. He admired her for her beauty, but also for her courage, and for what she stood for, and the fact that she now belonged to him.

Rosita started to pull up all the weeds that were sprouting out from the edges of the gravestones and spied in the half-light some purple and yellow flowers growing wild at the base of a tall oak tree. She plucked a few up by the roots and replanted them at the foot of the headstones. After this she knelt down and her eyes filled with tears.

'Dear grandparents,' she whispered, 'give me the courage to carry out my quest and to always remain happy with Angelo, the same way that you two were. I promise that one day very soon your house will be happy again.' Rosita hadn't realised she had company until Angelo touched her shoulder.

'I have brought you some coffee before it all disappeared.'

'Thank you,' she replied, and stood up. He put his free arm around her, and when she had wiped away her tears, she took the coffee. Then she said. 'Angelo I've been thinking, it's probably better that we return home tonight.'

'You have changed your mind? You're trying to send me crazy aren't you?'

She turned to him, laughing now, momentarily forgetting about the coffee in her hand, which spilt onto his white shirt.

'Oh no, look what I've done.'

'Oh Francesca, it's nothing, it'll wash out. Now please tell me, why don't you want to stay any more?'

'Because my darling, if we go tonight we can leave our food and blankets for these people, and tomorrow morning we can go to the village and buy extra provisions and some clothing for them. Also, we need to buy more nails and paint. If only we knew of someone in the village that we could trust,' she said with a concerned voice.

'You know, I believe there are a few,' said Angelo, thinking out aloud.

'Who are they? Do I know them?' asked Rosita.

'I think you do know them, but we will wait and see,' he said touching her chin with his fingertip.

'Why can't you tell me their names now?'

'Oh well, if you insist. One is the doctor; he was one of your father's good friends. They grew up together. Maybe you remember him? He used to come and visit the real Francesca quite often, and he was your doctor as well.'

'Yes, I think I do. You think we can trust him for sure?'

'I feel we can. Also, he is a good friend of my father's. Actually I believe father had to visit him this morning,' Rosita was in silence for a few seconds, thinking and hoping that Vincenzo would not tell these people the truth about her, at least until she met them. Seeing her deep in thought, Angelo asked, 'Is everything all right, Francesca, are you ill?' He placed both hands on her shoulders.

'Angelo, do you think your father will tell him everything about me?' she asked in a concerned tone.

'All I can say is, if he has, then tomorrow we'll know for sure when we go to the village. But don't worry, my father is a great judge of character, he will only say what is necessary,' he replied.

'And what excuse can we make to see him?'

'That is very easy, my lioness. You can tell him you're staying here for a while and so want to reacquaint yourself as a patient with him and that you need a check-up soon. I am sure he will remember Francesca, as he used to see her on a regular basis. But let's wait until we speak to my father tonight.' They started to walk back towards the house together; Tunde and Gideon were walking towards them looking for Angelo and Rosita.

'What should we do now, Señor?' asked Gideon, addressing Angelo.

'Well, it's getting late now so you can get ready for your dinner. Please put out the fire when you have finished with it. We'll go back home now, and we'll come again sometime between tomorrow and Monday morning with some provisions for you all.' Angelo told them, looking at Rosita for her approval. She nodded her head and then he proceeded. 'Please could you tell your friends, not to move from this place during daylight hours. We're leaving all the food we brought with us; it should last through the day tomorrow. And if they want something to do, they could start to clean up the house downstairs, especially the cooking utensils, then the wood needs to be prepared for the barn repairs. If they are not superstitious, they could sleep in the house, but not upstairs, as it's probably unsafe. Are you two returning home tonight?'

'No patrón (boss), we're staying here tonight. We'll go back tomorrow,' answered Tunde.

'I'm not your patrón, my name is Angelo, and I want you all to call me by my name. I would like you to think of me as your friend.'

'Well, thank you, Angelo. I would prefer to call you by your name, but only when we're on our own if you don't mind, in front of the other people I would still like to call you patrón if you don't mind,' pleaded Tunde with his tone and his eyes.

'Yes of course, you are right,' replied Angelo, then he moved towards Rosita. 'Let's get ready to go back,' he said, placing one arm over her shoulders.

'I'll get your horses ready,' offered Stefano, and soon they were on their way, waving goodbye to the others.

'Please, all of you remember to be very careful,' instructed Rosita as they rode off and out of view. In the old days her father had always been concerned about his workers as she was now. Nothing like her mother, so people said, she thought only of herself. On the way home they were chatting about how fate had brought them together. Things could have been so different, in fact Angelo could already have been married to some local girl in the village, and

Rosita could easily have fallen in love with another young man in the village where she grew up for the last fifteen years. But this had not happened. Instead they were together again as they had been when they were very young.

They had almost arrived home and there was an awkward silence, as Rosita started to think about her grandparents again. Angelo saw the change of mood in the woman on the horse next to him, the woman he loved so much. Right now he was worrying so much about her. He knew how dangerous what they were planning to do was, so, he started to tell a fairy tale to make her laugh.

'There was once a little girl called Red Riding Hood,' he began, smiling at her. 'Who went to visit her grandmother deep in the forest, but on her way she met a wolf who was very… very hungry. So he opened his big mouth…'

Rosita knew why he had suddenly come out with this children's story. She couldn't contain herself and burst out laughing. Angelo stopped his horse and dismounted.

'Now, what are you doing?' she asked.

But instead of answering her question, he walked round to Rosita's side and looked up at her sat on her horse.

'I want to walk hand in hand with you, and I think I deserve a kiss for telling you a story,' he said. Then he helped her off the horse. Her laughter slowly stopped and she looked down at him with love in her eyes. She slipped her feet out of the stirrups, swung her left leg over her horses head and slowly slid into his strong waiting arms. With his hands around her waist, he slowly let her down until her feet gently touched the ground. He held her close to him. They were eye to eye; gently he placed a kiss on her forehead. He shook with pleasure and with fear at the same time. If anything ever happened to her, he would be lost, he could never get used to living without her now that he had found her again. Angelo loved her more than anything in his life, more than the air he breathed every day out in the fields. She was his Angel, with eyes that melted his heart every time he looked into them.

Rosita also felt the need to be in his warm strong arms. She hadn't realised until she was there, very, very close to him, that she loved Angelo deeper and more intensely than she had imagined; she had loved him from their childhood. And she too was worried about him, with what was going on, anyone could get hurt. Dear God, please don't let him get hurt, she thought. Then she raised her big brown eyes to meet his, and sliding her arms slowly round his neck said to him,

'Come here, handsome, you can have your kiss but only if you promise to act like a real gentleman… '

CHAPTER EIGHT

At home Vincenzo was already in bed, he had retired early as he was not expecting them home tonight. As he lay in silence gently drifting off to sleep, he heard voices coming from the kitchen and got up instantly to investigate. He wondered who it could be, maybe one of the Negroes wanted to discuss a problem with him, as sometimes they did come to him for advice. But to his surprise he saw Angelo and Rosita preparing something to eat.

'Good evening Uncle, I hope we didn't wake you up,' she said.

'What happened?' he answered, 'Are you two afraid of sleeping outside under the stars?'

'No, my dear uncle, the truth is, we cannot sleep unless we're here with you.' They all laughed together. Now Vincenzo was up he wanted to know what they were preparing to eat and what had happened this evening.

'I'm having tomato and onion salad, and Angelo is having fried eggs,' answered Rosita.

'Now I feel hungry,' said Vincenzo.

'So, come and have some salad with me, Uncle,' she said.

The two men and their favourite woman started to eat. There was silence for the majority of the time while they were eating; Rosita and Angelo were busy thinking about what had happened today, what was being planned for the next few days and what reason to give Vincenzo as to why they had returned home tonight. At the same time Vincenzo was wracking his brain as to why the two lovebirds preferred his company, instead of being on their own like two normal people in love would do. In the end Vincenzo was the one who broke the silence.

'Well?' he began. 'Who's going to be the first to tell me why you came back tonight? Not that I'm complaining, but it doesn't look like you had a fight.'

'Very well, Father, I'll explain,' volunteered Angelo looking at Rosita for her approval. She smiled at him and discreetly nodded her consent. 'The reason we came back, is because tomorrow morning we need to go to the village to buy a few things.'

Vincenzo nodded but of course didn't buy their story for one second; he knew that there was a lot more to it.

'And what, may I ask, do you two have to buy that is so important? Today I bought enough food to last a month,' said Vincenzo, looking at Angelo then Rosita and then back to Angelo again.

'Well Father, you see, Francesca wanted to visit the village and also to reintroduce herself to the doctor.'

'Oh yes, I already thought about this,' answered Vincenzo. 'In fact, I saw the doctor today and I spoke to him about it.'

'Father, did you tell him everything about Francesca?' asked Angelo.

'Yes, I told him everything.' He hesitated for a second because he'd seen Rosita's expression change. 'Don't worry, he is an intelligent man; he knew that for the illness Francesca had, there was no cure and no hope. He would have worked it out for himself anyway, and would have been offended if I had lied to him. Don't you forget, Rosita, that your father and he were very good friends. And another thing; you have your father's looks. In fact it surprised me, that your mother did not see it when she met you again. But then I think she'd forgotten what he looked like long before he was killed.'

Angelo interrupted Vincenzo's momentary lapse in sensitivity.

'Father, do you suppose we can really trust the doctor?'

'I'm very sure, son, no doubts whatsoever' said Vincenzo, gently placing one hand on Rosita's elbow, to reassure her.

'And are there any more people we can trust like that?'

'Yes, son, there are many good people, more than you can imagine.'

Both Angelo and Rosita were very relieved to hear this news, it gave them more courage and confidence in what they were planning. After a short silence, letting this information sink in, Angelo piped up again.

'Father, if you're not too tired, could we talk some more?'

Vincenzo said nothing, he just nodded in agreement.

'Well,' began Angelo, 'first of all we thought we'd like to renovate the house at the old hacienda. You know, the one where Grandpa and Grandma Miserendino used to live, what do you think about that?' asked Angelo, waiting a few long seconds in suspense, thinking his father would tell him that he had lost his mind.

'Could I enquire why? asked Vincenzo, looking at Rosita.

'Uncle, this was my idea, I swore on my grandparents' graves that I would restore the house to its original state. I have such a strong desire to reunite myself to the family I was born into.'

Still Vincenzo was not convinced, so he said, 'Is there any more you two want to tell me, because restoring and living in a building that does not belong to you is a risky thing to do?'

'Well, Uncle, yes there is more to it. There are some people taking refuge in the old hacienda, who also need our help, and we want to make it into our base, where we can prepare everyone for the big day when we take back what is mine.'

'Don't you two think you're rushing things a bit?' asked Vincenzo calmly.

Angelo and Rosita just looked at one another. After a short silence he continued. 'In that case, you're a very lucky girl.'

'How's that, Uncle?' asked Rosita, showing her impatience, like a little immature girl.

'I recall, not long ago, that Don Camillo, or Donna Teresa, said they would like to get rid of that property.'

'Uncle, that's fantastic,' she cried. 'How could we find out if it's true?'

'Well, let's not run before we can walk. What I think is best, is that tomorrow when you two go to the village to see the good doctor, ask him what he thinks. He knows everything that goes on in the village, including the toing and froing in your mother's house. And when I see Don Camillo, I'll tell him that you two intend getting engaged and so would like to buy a property and peace of land somewhere near here. And, if Don Camillo mentions the old hacienda, I'll ask him if he would consider selling it to you two. But of course we have to check our finances. We may have to borrow some money from somebody or the bank, but I don't think it will be difficult,' said Vincenzo, all in one go.

'Oh, Uncle, thank you so much,' cried Rosita, ecstatically. 'I only hope that some day I can repay you for all your kindness, and understanding. But I think our finances will not be so bad, because when I left the hacienda at the time of the assault, my father gave your brother, Nunziato, a box containing some valuable gold coins. I believe my father intended that Nunziato should sell them, in case anything happened to him, and spend the proceeds on bringing me up. But he never used them, instead he saved them and gave them to me just before I came here.'

Vincenzo looked at Rosita, he scratched his head, then he looked at the old clock ticking away on the wall in front of him, and he realised they had been there for hours. It was nearly one clock in the morning.

'I think we have talked enough for tonight,' he said getting up and walking towards the door, 'and it's time we all went to bed. Good night, my children, I must sleep if I'm going to have a clear head tomorrow.'

'Good night, Uncle,' called Rosita, watching Vincenzo walk towards the staircase.

'Well, dear cousin, are we going to sleep too?' asked Angelo, lifting her chin up with his finger to look into her beautiful brown eyes.

'I do feel very tired, but I don't think I'm going to be able to sleep after today's wonderful revelations,' she replied.

'In that case, why don't you come to my room and we can talk further until you want to sleep, or you can read a good book?' said Angelo, winking at her with a cheeky smile splashed across his face.

'Angelo!' she tutted. 'What would that poor man upstairs think about that?'

'Come,' he said, holding out his hand for her to go to him, 'I'll be a proper gentleman, even if the desire to take you kills me.'

She moved closer to him, and he kissed her gently on her lips. And even though his body was burning with the pain of wanting her, and the agony of having to sleep in the next room to her was unbearable, he too wanted to wait for the right time. The both of them were sensible, with traditional old fashioned values and all jokes apart they were both going to be strong against this ever hungry temptation. For how long though, they didn't know.

'You know what, I think I believe you as well,' she said smiling at him, but not feeling so sure of her own self-control. She wanted him as much as he wanted her. Just a look from him, or a brush of his hand anywhere on her body would immediately make her feel like a quivering, fluttering flower waiting to be picked.

'Good, I'm going to get changed,' he said, running upstairs.

In no time at all they were sitting together on Angelo's bed, pillows behind their backs.

'There are a few books here, or would you like to look at some photos first?' he whispered. Then Angelo slid his arms around Rosita, as they began to look through the photos, Angelo explaining to her who was in and where each photos was taken. Occasionally they exchanged pecks on the lips, just happy to be close to one another. There were only about twenty photos but Rosita did not get to see the last few as she fell asleep in his arms. Angelo kissed her on her forehead, and wondered whether to leave her where she was, or to take her to her room. He chose the latter, because he wanted to sleep in his own bed, so he gathered Rosita into his arms like a little girl and carried her into her room.

The two of them slept deeply in their own beds, but not for long. It was early morning, a continuous knocking on Vincenzo's door was demanding it be opened. It woke the three of them, but Angelo was the first down to face who ever was outside. To Angelo's surprise, as he opened the door he came face to face with one of Don Camillo's bodyguards, Don Ciccio.

'Is it necessary to make all this noise so early in the morning and wake everybody up? said Angelo, grumpily. 'What can I do for you?' He sensed trouble. Had the Negro girl talked? Were he and Rosita in trouble? He tried not to panic. The man in front of him reeked of alcohol. He had probably spent half the night in a bar, drinking like a fish.

'The boss had sent me to wake you up. You're expected to be there, pronto. I will tack up your horse while you dress,' said Don Ciccio. His eyes were red. He really looked evil.

'Thank you, but no thank you. I can tack my own horse. Ride on and tell Don Camillo that I'll be there as soon as I can,' Angelo slammed the door closed in Don Ciccio's face without waiting for him to leave, he was furious. Vincenzo and Rosita had positioned themselves behind the door ready for trouble, so as he turned they almost bashed into one another.

'What's up?' asked Vincenzo, worried sick.

'What was all that about?' asked Rosita simultaneously.

'Nothing, calm down you two,' he said, looking at Rosita. They heard Don Ciccio ride off into the distance. 'Don Camillo wants to see me immediately. Something must have happened, I advise you two to go back to bed. It's not necessary to worry without knowing what has happened and...'

'Angelo, I'm coming with you,' interrupted Rosita. 'You may need me.'

'No you won't. I have to go and dress, Father; don't let her out of your sight. I have a bad feeling about this, but I don't think it has anything to do with us. Promise me you won't go out,' said Angelo looking into Rosita's eyes, pleading with her. She reluctantly agreed, with a slow nod of her head, but Angelo wasn't sure if she really meant it.

Angelo took less than a couple of minutes to splash some cold water on his face and to dress. He went flying down the stairs, taking the steps two at a time. 'I'll see you two later, Father. Rosita,' he said, staring at her for a few long seconds reinforcing his request for her to stay put. He then turned and walked out of the house. As soon as he stepped out into the dark of the early morning, the pure fresh air caressed his face and made him breathe in deeply. His thoughts were in turmoil; it had been a very rare occurrence that his master had called upon him in the middle of the night. Only when they needed help to gather cattle or horses when they had escaped or they suspected rustler activity. But this time he had the feeling it was something completely deferent. When Angelo arrived out front of the large white building, Don Camillo, and about ten of his men were already poised next to their horses waiting for him.

'Let's go,' said Don Camillo, as soon as he saw Angelo. And without any explanation they left at a gallop. Angelo was riding side by side with Don Camillo, and the rest of the men right behind them. 'You're wondering why I sent for you?' shouted Don Camillo, over the noise of the horses' hooves. Angelo nodded. 'The death of Pietro Tonto. I don't think it was an accident. So, Ciccio suggested we go and shake up the Negroes a bit, they may know something.'

Don Camillo had always treated Angelo with respect. And Vincenzo had never told Angelo of the bad things Don Camillo had done over the years. This is why after hearing this Angelo was shocked; this was his master speaking. The man he had learned to admire over the years. Angelo had never seen this side of Don Camillo before, because he usually got his henchmen to do all the dirty work. He never knew that this man would enjoy inflicting pain on his people, black or white. But tonight he saw his master in a different light, for the man he really was. Angelo suspected his master had been drinking, even though he didn't look drunk. But he could see the others had all been drinking before they decided to go out and molest these innocent people in the middle of the night.

Angelo was wracking his brain to think of something to prevent any of this happening. Dear God, help these people, he was praying. But it was so difficulty to think clearly, they were screaming like a bunch of red Indians ready to go to war, and he heard one of them, saying.

'Let's burn their shacks, with them inside.'

Angelo now thought of the young girl Pietro Tonto tried to rape, and how scared she had been. Surely as soon as she sees them, the girl would talk. And even if she didn't talk, these drunken vaqueros will still burn their homes, and maybe kill some of these people. As they were galloping through the night with the aid of the moonlight, a few clouds above them threatened rain. The beautiful oleander trees, whose flowers during the day released a sweet scent filling people senses. Now, thought Angelo, the beautiful plants looked grey and eerie, almost like ghosts, and just like Angelo felt right now.

Suddenly Angelo realised that Don Camillo was heading towards the South barracks, where mixed race people lived, and not north where the young Negro girl lived. He felt a little relieved, but still there was the second question. Why had they called him? Did Don Camillo think that bringing Angelo with them to witness their butchery would make him happy? Or maybe his master would feel safer with him by his side? The answer to that one he would have to wait for.

It took them less than ten minutes to reach the barracks. All was quiet and deserted, except for the burning fire in the centre of the camp, and a few old men seated around the fire chatting and keeping warm. Don Camillo's men didn't stop their shouting and surrounded them. Even in the dark, Angelo could see how afraid the poor men were. Two of Don Camillo men jumped off their horses and began to manhandle the two Hispanic men who were now on their feet.

The others were galloping around the barracks; non-stop yelping and screaming. Then they began shooting into the air, as if the shouting and screaming was not enough to wake everybody up. Don Camillo sat on his horse laughing at what was going on. It was then that Angelo understood his master was not drunk, but doped up on drugs.

Soon most of the people began to come out from their shacks and caravans. Angelo looked round and realised that none of Don Camillo's men were looking towards him. He went over to some of the people who were still confused as to what was happening to them. And told them to take the women and children away, if possible over to the old hacienda and to pass the word quickly to defend themselves, but not with guns. For a while the place looked as if it was hell, women and children were screaming. Angelo, still on his horse, kept moving from one side of the barracks to the other, making sure that Don Camillo's men didn't go after the women and children while they were escaping.

A couple of buildings in no time were on fire; Angelo saw two children and a woman getting out from a rear window. He was now seething, his blood was boiling. He wanted so much to kill all of these bastards. At that moment he wished a few of his friends were there with him. Suddenly from the corner of his left eye, he saw Don Ciccio dismounting his horse, and moving toward one of the shacks. Oh no you don't, he thought to himself. So he got off his horse and followed him over to where he was going.

'Come out, come out, wherever you are,' said Don Ciccio barging his way in. Angelo didn't wait to see if anybody was left inside, he went in behind Don Ciccio, and with the butt of his riffle he struck Don Ciccio in the back of his neck, knocking the bastard unconscious onto the floor. Angelo liked what he had done, in fact he felt much better. Now nobody could stop him. He turned around and walked outside again. As he stepped outside, another one of these bastards was there face to face with Angelo, he had a burning torch in his hand, ready to throw it inside the hut.

'What are you doing in there?' he asked Angelo.

'I was just checking if anybody else was in there.'

'I don't care who is inside,' answered the drunken animal.

'Well then, be my guest,' said Angelo, and stepped aside. As the man stepped past him to throw the torch into the hut, Angelo again using the butt of his rifle knocked the thug to the floor. Angelo hadn't seen a second man approaching behind him, who had witnessed his actions. The man swung his fist violently at Angelo's head. The punch narrowly missed him as he had seen it coming just in time.

'Why did you do that?' shouted the ugly man in front of him; his rifle was now pointed at Angelo's chest.

'Because he wants to burn this shack down and Don Ciccio is in there. I saw him entering a few minutes ago.' Blurted out Angelo.

'You're lying!' said the drunken vaquero.

'Why don't you go and check for yourself?' suggested Angelo.

Just then Don Camillo came over to them.

'Where have you been?' he demanded. 'I have been looking for you everywhere.'

'And I was looking for you, Don Camillo. Why don't I accompany you home? Donna Teresa is sure to be worried about you.'

Don Camillo's eyes, were now focussing on his man's rifle pointed at Angelo's chest.

'What are you doing? He's one of us, you fool.' barked Don Camillo.

'He knocked Giacinto down, to prevent him burning down this barrack. He said Don Ciccio is in there, but I don't believe him.' As he finished his sentence, Don Ciccio appeared in front of them holding his head in a daze.

'There, you see, he was right, you drunken fool. Now we ride home, I'm tired,' said Don Camillo.

The bastard, thought Angelo, maybe in the morning he wouldn't remember anything.

At home, Rosita and Vincenzo were waiting in the kitchen. She had been pacing the kitchen floor since he had left; she was worried sick not knowing what was happening out there. Was Angelo in need of help? Should she go, or send someone to check? Vincenzo was thinking the same thing, but he kept calm. If Don Camillo had wanted to harm Angelo he would have done it here, in his own home.

It was about four thirty in the morning, when they heard a horse approaching the house. Both, Vincenzo and Rosita ran outside, Angelo arrived as they got outside. They were both relieved to see Angelo back in one piece, and as Angelo dismounted, she jumped into his arms.

'Is everything all right, son?' asked Vincenzo. Angelo nodded. His father turned and left, he felt too emotional, and he wanted to leave his son and fiancée alone. Angelo's horse found its own way back to the stable, and after a long emotional hug, Angelo led Rosita back inside. Vincenzo sat at the kitchen table holding his shaking hands in his lap, a mixture of nerves and tiredness. Angelo briefly explained to them what had happened and then the three exhausted people went back to bed. Except Vincenzo couldn't sleep, his mind working overtime, the other two were also analysing the night's events but eventually fell into a deep sleep.

The following morning at nine o'clock, the house was very quiet, as it was Sunday. Angelo and Rosita awoke to the delicious aroma of cooking biscuits, and met each other outside their rooms on the landing.

'Good morning, my love, did you manage to get any sleep?' enquired Angelo.

'Yes, eventually' replied Rosita, 'But tell me, how did I come to be sleeping in my bed before you were so rudely called away?'

'Maybe you're a sleep walker, or maybe I decided to have a good night's sleep, instead of staying awake all night, looking at you,' he said, pulling her to him, folded her into his arms and kissed her good morning, then he said. 'I can smell something good, let's investigate,'

'What a good idea, darling, let's.'

When they got down to the kitchen, they found a very large tray of freshly baked biscuits just asking to be eaten. 'Hey don't touch,' Vincenzo scolded them, as they both attempted to steal one. 'They are for your engagement party,'

'Our what?' exclaimed Angelo.

'Well if you two want to convince Don Camillo that one of these day you two really want to get married, you must get officially engaged first. You have to do it in the proper way.'

'Father, you're a genius,' exclaimed Angelo. 'But Francesca and I have been discussing this and we are both concerned. Won't people wonder why two cousins are getting engaged, they may think the situation weird and start asking questions?'

'Genius! Yes that sounds good, I accept the compliment. As for you two; I know many people who have married their cousins, and you have the advantage of saying you didn't grow up together, so you are relative strangers, pardon the pun. And anyway, love is love and nothing can stop it.' He decided to change the subject. 'Are you still going to the village this morning?'

'Yes Father, after breakfast and a few of these delicious biscuits,' said Angelo, snatching up a couple of biscuits, and moving away from the kitchen table.

'Well, whilst you are there, you can buy sugared almonds for the favours in the general store, and if you can pick up a couple of bottles of liqueur too. This way at the same time you can let all the people know that you're getting engaged soon. And don't forget to visit the doctor as well,' continued Vincenzo. He didn't want to forget anything he had planned in his mind. 'And should anybody ask you the reason for being there, you can say you're taking Francesca for a check up. Take the baggage wagon with you to carry your wares home in.'

'Thank you, Father. Oh, and by the way, don't let that genius thing go to your head, it's big enough as it is.'

'Don't worry about my head, you just make sure yours is securely screwed onto your shoulders. Keep your eyes and ears open all the time, you never know who is listening in the shadows.'

Rosita came out of the wash room, and snatched up a few biscuits too. Vincenzo just smiled. She and Angelo went upstairs and dressed very smartly and when they returned to the kitchen, Vincenzo saw them. He whistled.

'If you two dress like this now, what will you wear when you get married?'

At Vincenzo's compliment, Rosita's face flushed from a natural pink to a beautiful rosy colour.

'Thank you, Uncle, you're very kind. You don't look that bad yourself,' Rosita took in a breath and hesitated. Vincenzo looked at her expectantly for a few long seconds, he sensed she wanted to continue talking, but she turned round and moved towards the door. But before she reached the door she stopped, turned round, she found him still looking at her questioningly. She smiled, and her face lit up like sunshine.

'Uncle, you've always been able to read my mind. OK, I have something else to tell you,' she said.

'I thought so! Go on,'

'I hope to go to Tucuman City very soon, with Angelo, of course. I would like to buy some finer clothes for special occasions,' she said.

'Well of course and rightly so. I would be happy to go with you if you need me to.

CHAPTER NINE

Soon Angelo and Rosita were on their way, and she started to explain to him about the wooden box that her father had left her.

'You know Angelo, as well as the coins, there were a few documents inside,' she proceeded.

'What sort of documents?' asked Angelo.

'Well, one of these documents is a will of some sort and in it is written that if anything should happen to my father, all his possessions would pass to me,' she said, looking into Angelo's eyes. She knew he would be happy for her, in fact his eyes started to cloud over with tears of joy.'

'That's marvellous, Francesca. But it is not going to be easy to go to your mother, and say, 'Mother, here I am alive and well, so hand over all my father's properties, and disappear from here, you and your nasty husband.'

'Oh my darling, Angelo, I know that, but this is not one of my priorities right now.'

'I know, my love. I was only joking, I wanted to see you laugh, it was a poor joke,' he said, putting his arm round her waist.

'I know, my darling. Don't worry, we will have plenty of time to laugh, to be happy, and not only the two of us,' she said, squeezing him tightly and placing her head on his shoulder.

'By the way, Angelo, could you please stop for a few minutes when we reach Papa Joe's house, I want to see how he is. Also I have noticed there is a cart catching up with us, so at the same time we could let them pass.'

'Of course, my love, we have got all day so we can do whatever your heart desires.' he said raising his eyebrows repetitively and suggestively.

'Stop it you cheeky man, can't you think of anything else?' She retorted.

'Not when I'm looking at you my sweet.' They laughed.

When they reached Papa Joe's place, they saw two of Don Camillo's men, one was striking Vittorio, Papa Joe's son, with a crop.

'Hey, you two, what do you think you doing?' shouted Rosita. 'He's not a wild animal.' She quickly jumped off the cart, ran over and stood between Vittorio and the two thugs.

'Why is he beating you?' she asked Vittorio.

'We were getting ready to go to church,' Vittorio started to explain. 'Then we heard them call us to come out, or they would burn everything.'

'What?' interrupted Rosita, with a murderous look on her face looking at the two trouble makers. 'You were beating him for going to Mass?' She had addressed the man with the crop, looking at him as if she wanted to kill him with her eyes. 'And what right do you have to stop him?'

'They are blacks, they shouldn't be seen in a white man's church,' answered the other man, looking Rosita up and down in a lecherous way to let her know he liked her.

'If you were God, then you could stop them attending if that was your wish. But you are not God. So, my advice would be to leave them alone, and if you don't like them being there, then stay away yourselves.'

Right at that moment the cart which had been behind them on the road was approaching. It was Don Camillo and her mother, and although they must have witnessed what was going on, he chose to ignore it and carry on his way. He said nothing, how could he? After all he had done the same thing himself the night before with his men. The bastard! Rosita thought to herself, your time will come. She continued with her onslaught regardless.

'In church, there are all kind of Christian people, people who believe in God, and not evil people like you. If I ever catch you doing this again, you'll live to regret it,' she finished.

Angelo all the time stayed silent, but he never took his eyes off Don Camillo's men. One of them came closer and glared at her.

'And I advise you to go back to where you came from and mind your own business,' he hissed at her menacingly.

Rosita did not back down but returned his glare second for second about twenty centimetres from his ugly face She could smell the stale alcohol and tobacco on the man's breath. The staring match seemed to go on for ages, until the man jerked his head forward to scare her, but in a split second she brought up her knee sharply and thrust it into his groin. He was taken totally by surprise and dropped to the floor holding his groin. His companion had started to laugh when his friend had faked a head butt, but his laughter instantly turned to horror as his friend hit the ground.

'I will only leave if the boss of this hacienda tells me to,' she shouted, so Don Camillo who had only just past them could hear. The master's cart came to a halt and Don Camillo turned in his seat. All this time Angelo had been monitoring the situation. He knew by now that Rosita was more than capable of looking after herself, but he thought they should continue on their way before Don Camillo started to ask questions. Rosita straightened her tunic and turned to face Don Camillo, and a shocked, Donna Teresa.

'I do apologise for losing my head,' she said, looking as if she was really sorry. 'I know I shouldn't behave like this on your property, but I don't like to see violence without a good reason,' she said, afraid that he might actually send her away. She really should learn to control her temper, she thought, she really could have kicked herself.

'You're excused,' he assented, 'this time!' Then addressed his two thugs. 'Get up you fool, and both of you get out of here.' He looked at Rosita again; she had for sure made him wonder if she really was who she said she was.

'Come on Francesca, let's leave,' interrupted Angelo, 'It's getting late,' he finished. But Rosita had something else to say to the temporary boss of her hacienda.

'Don Camillo, do you mind if I accompany these people to church?'

'Not at all, I may see you all there,' replied Don Camillo, as he turned himself back round in his seat, and then left at speed.

Rosita then called Papa Joe and said. 'We are all going to church together,' she announced, but Papa Joe was cross with her.

'What is going on in your mind, for you to jump to our defence like that? Don't you realise how much of a risk you are taking? And what will people think if you and Angelo arrive at church together with us? We're going alone, on foot,' put in Papa Joe, very cross with her. Hadn't she seen the look on Don Camillo's face? He may have recognised her, and what happens now if he had?

'If Francesca is happy to ride with you, then so am I,' suggested Angelo. 'After all, we do not care what people think or say. So, please let's leave, otherwise we'll be late for Mass.'

With that, they all climbed onto the wagon, and left at a fast trot. On arriving at the church they saw many people on their way in. Angelo engaged the wagon's handbrake, and went to find the nosebag for the horse. Rosita stepped down giving a helping hand to Mama Bimpe, and Vittorio helped his father and the rest of the family down.

'Let's go inside now,' said Mama Bimpe, after thanking Angelo and Rosita for the ride.

'I know it wasn't our original intention to come to church today,' suggested Rosita to Angelo, 'but I will have to meet the priest sooner or later. And today I suppose is as good a day as any. Do you know Angelo, when my father was alive he used to come to this church every single Sunday, and read a verse from the Bible. I would like to see who performs that duty this morning,' she finished, feeling a little emotional.

As they entered the church, they dipped their finger in the font's holy water, and made the sign of the cross. Then found seats near the front in the third row. The service was made lively by the priest and was about good versus evil. On nearing the end of the service, the priest raised his hands to the heavens and addressed his congregation.

'Today,' he said, 'is a jubilant day for God. We have a new member joining our flock today, who has come to listen to the Lords' word. What do you think, my brothers and sisters, if this person were invited to come up to read a verse from the Bible for us?'

There was a collective, 'Praise be to God!' from the congregation.

He then descended the few steps from the pulpit, and forwards along the aisle. Rosita thought he would ask Angelo, as he was directing himself towards him, but to her surprise he turned at the last minute and stopped looking straight at her.

She didn't know why, but he made the sign of the cross in front of her and then put his hands together as if praying and said.

'Bless you, my sister, would you do us the honour of climbing the pulpit and reading a verse of your choice from the Bible to end our service?'

Rosita was taken aback but rose immediately, nodding her consent. She had not expected this, and as she approached the altar, and came to the steps of the pulpit, her legs started to feel weak. She knew that everybody was watching, her long auburn hair and her dark hazel eyes complemented her elegant clothing, she was indeed a beautiful sight to behold. She climbed the few steps up to the top, opened the Bible at a random place and then slowly raised her eyes to meet the congregation. The first person her eyes focused on was her mother, who seemed to be regarding her with jealously in her eyes, maybe since her father's death it was normally her honour to read from the Bible wondered Rosita? Worse still, thought Rosita, maybe she had begun to suspect who she really was? She looked back down to the Bible and slowly flicked through the pages to find the verse she was looking for. Exodus 23:27-30. The one her father used to read to her a long time ago. She found it, paused, and looked to the priest for his signal to begin. There was complete silence, she couldn't hear a solitary sound, just her heart thumping in her ears. The priest nodded, she took a deep breath and began.

"And I shall send the fright of me ahead of you, and I shall certainly throw into confusion all the people among whom you shall come, and I shall indeed give the back of the neck of all your enemies to you. And I will send the feeling of dejection ahead of you, and it will simply drive the Hivites, the Canaanites and the Hittites out from before you. I shall not drive them out from before you in a single year, that the land may not become a desolate waste and the wild beasts of the field really multiply against you. Little by little I shall drive them out from before you, until you become fruitful and really take possession of the land."

As she finished, the tears were veiling her eyes, the priest approached her helping her down from the pulpit and thanking her by placing his hands into hers to comfort her. She gave a small smile. But the priest sensed something was not right.

'Sister, would you like to tell us your name?' But before she could reply, Angelo came forward showing concern for Rosita, after seeing how emotionally drained by the experience she had become.

'If I may, Father?' he interrupted. 'Dear people of the congregation,' he began, 'For those of you, who are not aware, I would like to introduce you all to my long lost cousin Francesca Curro. I would also like to take this opportunity, if it's all right with you, Francesca.,as we are in the house of God and I can't think of a better place, for me to announce our imminent engagement.'

The sound of applause rang out around the church, people rose and spilled into the aisle to congratulate the couple. Don Camillo was one of them, but Donna Teresa left without a word. The doctor was the last one to come to them and he embraced Rosita, saying warmly.

'I'm so glad to see you in such good health, even us doctors can make mistakes sometimes. Welcome back Francesca.'

Dr Francesco Pedrazza, whom Vincenzo had seen the previous day, had delivered Rosita at her birth and had watched her grow up until she had disappeared from the hacienda at such a tender age.

'And I would be very pleased if you two would come and see me before you go back to the hacienda,' added Dr Pedrazza.

'We had already planned to,' replied Angelo. 'We will come to see you after we've finished our errands around the village if that is acceptable, Doctor Pedrazza.'

'Excellent, in that case you two are welcome to stay for lunch if you have time,' offered Dr Pedrazza.

'If I'm not mistaken we've just received our first invitation as a couple,' laughed Rosita, already feeling better.

'That's very kind of you Doctor,' said Angelo just before they left.

Dr. Pedrazza turned to Rosita and said, 'Don Saverio Scalabrini, our priest is also a good and trusted friend to all of us.' He glanced at the priest stood beside him. But his eyes told the priest a lot more. Both Angelo and Rosita thought that Dr Pedrazza was trying to tell them something other than what the words meant. A hidden agenda.

'Is Father Scalabrini coming to lunch with us?' Rosita asked the doctor.

'Yes, of course, and we can all have a good long discussion over some wine,' he replied.

'Thank you for the invitation then, I look forward to it,' answered the priest.

Angelo and Rosita made their way out of the church, and across the road to the local bar. They found themselves a table inside and Angelo went straight up to the bar to greet his good friend who worked behind the counter.

'Hello, Juan, how are you?' said Angelo, embracing Juan over the counter. They'd know each other for nearly twenty years, almost the same amount of time as Nunziato, Angelo's uncle.

'I'm fine, and very happy to see you Angelo, but please tell me, who is the beautiful lady you came in with? asked Juan. He had taken the liberty of asking only because of their close friendship.

'Well, don't be too impatient; can't you wait until I introduce you to her?' laughed Angelo, beckoning Rosita to come over to the bar.

'Juan,' Angelo began as Rosita approached, 'I have the honour to introduce you to my fiancée, Francesca Curro,' he said, looking at his friend with a concealed laugh. 'Francesca, I would like you to meet my good friend, Juan,' he proceeded. 'Maybe he can help us in some way?'

'My God, Francesca Curro, Nunziato's daughter, I'm very sorry I did not recognise you. You have grown into such a beautiful young lady,' said Juan, blushing a bit for his mistake. He quickly walked around the counter and came to her with his arms open to embrace her. 'Francesca, you had always been like a sister to me, I cannot tell you how happy I am to see you again after so long. Also, I am so happy for your engagement to Angelo. Congratulations, you have captured the heart of the best man in town, my best friend. Now please tell me, what can I do to help you two? Are you in any sort of trouble?' asked Juan.

'No, I meant maybe you can help us with our engagement party. For a start, can you get us a kilo of sugared almonds?' said Angelo, smiling at his surprised friend.

'Yes, of course, my friend, my boss is in fact going to Tucuman City tomorrow to collect supplies for the bar, so they can be here in a couple of days. He'll be back soon!

'Thank you Juan. 'Can you do me one more favour, can you bring them to us when they arrive?'

'I will bring them on my day off, and is there anything else I can do for you two lovely people?' replied Juan.

'Yes, maybe there is, but we will talk in private when you come to see us.'

'I'll be there, you can count on it,' said Juan.

They chatted a little more until they'd finished their drinks and then left the bar to continue with their shopping. Angelo and Rosita were like two happy children as they walked arm in arm together to the nearby general store. But the smiles disappeared from their face as soon as they stepped inside the door, for they saw a small Negro boy at the counter with blood streaming from his nose. He approached them, limping slightly, to ask if he could assist them in any way.

'What happened to you?' asked Rosita.

A frightened look shot across the boy's face, he knew he should not talk to customers for any other reason than to fetch goods for them.

'Is your c… c… cart outside?' asked the boy. 'I'll carry anything you need to yo… your cart.'

'Where is Don Antonio, your boss?' asked Angelo.

Hesitantly the boy slowly turned his head towards a door behind the counter. Angelo went to the door and listened for a few seconds. After establishing that Don Antonio Marquis was enjoying himself with a lady friend he returned to the boy. What possible pleasure could Don Antonio gain from beating a poor Negro boy? Angelo thought to himself.

'I don't think your boss will be out for a while,' said Angelo softly. So, sit down and tell this lady what's been going on, while I fetch the cart to the door, and then we will find the things I need. I'll take them out myself.'

This was a good move on Angelo's part, as he could choose what he needed without fear of anyone seeing. The boy was stunned by the way these two white people were treating him so nicely. His gut feeling told him he could trust them: which helped him gain enough courage to explain to Rosita how he had been bought by Don Antonio and how he would punish him for any small mistake he had made. Dear God, she thought, to herself, he actually enjoys inflicting pain on this poor boy.

'What did you mean, your boss bought you? Where from and from who?'

'Please, Miss,' he pleaded, whispering, 'I cannot tell you that. If they find out I told you my family would be made to pay dearly.'

'OK. What is your name?' she asked the boy.

'Carlo, Miss,'

'Listen Carlo, this is against the law, you are supposed to be free to work where you want, do you understand what I'm saying?'

'Yes, Miss.'

'Then listen to me, do you know where the doctor lives?' Carlo nodded. 'Good, go to him straightaway, tell him I sent you and wait there for us, we'll take care of everything here.'

The boy, although afraid, did as he was told and moved towards the front door. As he walked out Angelo came back in. Rosita started to help Angelo with the things they needed and when they were through they left a note with some money on the counter. They both got onto the cart and started to make their way to the doctor's house. On the way there they came upon Papa Joe and his family, so Angelo pulled the horses up and Rosita jumped down.

'Have you anything else to do today?' she asked.

'No,' answered Vittorio, 'we've done everything we needed to do. Why? Do you need me to do anything for you?'

'Yes we do,' said Angelo. 'Can you drive our cart home with you, you'll get home quicker.'

'Yes we can,' replied Vittorio. 'But would you like one of us to come back and pick you up later?'

'No, thank you, I'm sure someone will give us a ride back. On the way back could you stop and tell my father we're staying at the doctor's house for lunch and not to worry?'

So with that, Papa Joe's family mounted the cart and left. Angelo and Rosita walked the short distance to the doctor's house. Angelo knocked at the front door. It was answered by a young Negro girl.

'Good morning Miss, Mister,' she said curtseying, 'the doctor is expecting you.'

They both smiled, and thanked the girl. 'This way, please,' she pointed. They followed her inside. She took them to the sitting room where they found the doctor and the priest, with a glass each in their hand, waiting for the two of them.

'Come in, come in,' the doctor welcomed them. 'Did you get everything you need?'

'Yes, thank you, Doctor Pedrazza. I hope you forgive us for sending you an extra guest. How is he?' enquired Angelo.

'He has been beaten quite badly,' replied the doctor.

'We know that, has he said anything to you?' asked Angelo.

'No, he just said you instructed him to come here to be checked over,' was the reply.

'Doctor, this poor boy has been purchased,' said Rosita, angrily. 'I thought this practice had been outlawed a long time since. Does it really still go on around here?'

'Listen, my children,' put in the priest. 'Right or wrong, the rich live by their own rules.'

That statement and the way it was delivered was enough for Angelo and Rosita to understand that, for the moment, they should let it go. So Rosita changed the subject.

'Anyway, Doctor Pedrazza, Don Saverio, I would like to let you know, that next Saturday Angelo and I are having our engagement party, and we would be honoured if you would both be able to be present?' she said all in one go.

'The honour would be mine,' said Don Saverio and the doctor in unison. 'And now please excuse me, I'm going to the kitchen to see if lunch is ready yet, I'm ravenous,' said Don Saverio leaving the sitting room, whistling. He knew that Angelo and Rosita had something to discuss in private with the doctor, even though he and the Doctor already knew much more than Angelo and Rosita imagined.

'I'd be really delighted to attend your party,' repeated the doctor.

'Thank you, Doctor Pedrazza, but now I have to ask you another favour,' said Rosita. Angelo interrupted her.

'Yes, we do need your help,' he said.

'What's wrong?' asked the doctor. 'You look concerned, Angelo. Of course you know I'll help you both in any way I can.'

At that moment the Negro girl came to inform them that lunch was ready. So they all moved to the dining room. It smelt so good, and they sat down with hearty appetites. They all agreed that compliments should be relayed to the cook as there was an excellent variety of foods, and it was delicious. After lunch they all went to sit outside under the shade of a tree to drink iced coffee. The doctor was watching Rosita very closely.

'Has anyone ever told you that you have a strong resemblance to your father?' he said, making Rosita's face go red all over. Not because she was embarrassed, but because she was mad. Mad at her mother, mad for what had happened fifteen years ago. For losing her dear father and the nice people she knew at the hacienda. But most of all, because she wasn't a man. But with God's will, she was determined, even though she was a woman, that she would successfully finish the job she had come here to do.

'Doctor,' she spoke after a few long seconds, she could feel Angelo's eyes watching her. 'If I look so much like my father, why didn't my mother recognised me?'

'Because, my child, I'm sorry to say that your mother had forgotten your father's face long ago. It was obvious for all to see that she married him for his money, and the social whirl that came with it. She didn't have any feelings for him. All her affections were saved for her longstanding lover, Don Camillo. Now she's started to age though, she thinks only about herself. There is no room in her life for anything else, a very selfish woman I'm afraid to say. But then, you knew that in your heart.'

Rosita took in what the good doctor was saying, and she secretly wished she could perform some magic, so she could go back in time and put everything right. But she and no one else had that power, so, now history was about to be repeated. There would inevitably be more killing, but this time for the right cause, to right a wrong, for justice. Her eyes were filling with hot tears, ready to escape, and for a long moment she couldn't hear anybody speak, she was in her own dimension. Then suddenly she heard Angelo speaking to Doctor Pedrazza.

'Doctor, Rosita and I would like to buy, if it's possible, her grandparents' old hacienda including the house.'

'My dears,' the doctor said, stunned 'there is plenty of better land in the area with good potential for productivity.'

'We know that, but there are many reasons why we want this place,' put in Rosita. 'First of all, there are people taking shelter there who need our help. Secondly it is strategically a good place to make our base. We need to form an army by gathering together any people who are willing to fight for their freedom and prepare them for the day when we take back our lives. A place to store medical supplies, weapons and provisions. But most importantly, I made a promise to my grandparents' at their graves, that I would restore the place to its former glory.'

'Wait a moment,' said the doctor. 'You sound as if you have it well planned in your heads, but don't you think we should check if it's even for sale first?'

The priest had remained quiet until now, but he decided to intervene here saying, 'May I suggest something?' They all turned to him and waited for his suggestion. 'What we could do, is invite Don Camillo and his wife to your engagement party and talk to them there. In fact, Donna Teresa is the one we really should speak to. If she declines your invitation to come to your party, then the doctor and I could pay her a visit ourselves, we know her very well. What do you think about this?'

'I think it's a good idea, my dear friend,' replied the doctor.

'That's settled then. Now, what are we going to do with the Negro boy?' asked the priest. 'He can surely never return to Don Antonio, or he will certainly suffer some more beatings.'

'I would like to take him with us and hide him with the others, at the old hacienda. With the help of the good doctor, and you, of course,' she said, pleading with her eyes.

'And what do you want us to do?' enquired the priest.

'For a start, we need to get back home, so could either of you lend us a cart or horses, and we'll return them tomorrow or later tonight?'

'We'll do better,' said the priest gladly. 'I can take you two home. I was planning on paying Papa Joe and his family a visit anyway.'

'Perfect. Thank you, Don Saverio,' cried Rosita with joy. 'I think we are all done here for today, so should we collect the cart and leave at once? I can sit at the front with you Father, Angelo can sit in the back and we can hide the boy under a blanket behind us. With you on the cart with us, Father Scalabrini, no one is going to stop us and ask questions.' Rosita spoke decisively, like a real leader. 'Do you suppose Don Antonio has discovered Carlo's disappearance yet?' she asked.

'Who knows? But I'm sure we'll find out when he does,' replied the priest.

'How?' asked Rosita.

'I suspect Don Antonio will send people out to search for him. I'm going to fetch the cart for you now. I'll swing it round the back here so nobody can see when we put the boy in the back.'

After a short while, Father Scalabrini returned. Rosita and Angelo managed to hide the boy as comfortable as possible in the back of the cart tucked underneath the front seat and covered by a few blankets. They piled some old clothes that the priest had collected behind him. Just as they were about to leave, the doctor handed Rosita a carpetbag.

'I would like to give this bag to you. It was given to me by my mother when I left home for this practice. It has been in the family for many years, but I'm sure you'll take good care of it.' Knowing what was ahead of them in the not too distant future, the doctor had filled the bag with medical supplies. Everything an army would need for a field hospital; bandages, bottles of antiseptic, basic surgical tools, antibiotics and more.

'I don't know what to say, Doctor Pedrazza,' exclaimed Rosita.

'There is nothing to say, just be careful, you're treading a dangerous path,' replied the doctor.

'I'm afraid it's something we have to do, Doctor Pedrazza, but of course we won't be taking any unnecessary risks unless we have to. Good bye for now and thank you for lunch,' Angelo was already on the cart with the boy, and was getting impatient. He was silently praying to God that nobody would stop them, as neither of them were carrying any weapons. Rosita jumped up onto the cart next to Don Saverio and they were on their way. Once they were at a safe distance and out of sight of the village, they uncovered the Negro boy so he could take in some fresh air. Not that anybody was sweating, as the air was getting fresh, all morning they'd expected some rain. God knows they could do with some, but the scent in the air hinted of snow. Hopefully it would keep dry for a while though. If not the people in hiding at the old hacienda would be in a difficult situation.

In a short time they were approaching Papa Joe's house. Thank God, they hadn't bumped into any of Don Camillo's drunken bandits.

'Would you like to come in with me?' asked the priest. 'I am not planning on staying long.'

'Very well, Don Saverio, we don't mind,' said Angelo, as Rosita nodded her approval. As they stopped directly outside, the front door opened. Rosita looked around to see if anybody was about and then indicated for the boy to slip inside the house unnoticed. Papa Joe and his family were happy to receive them. They chatted for a while, Mama Bimpe was going out of her way to make them feel welcome, and produced glasses of delicious fresh lemonade. Vittorio had not yet returned from Vincenzo's house, maybe he had stopped there for a while to help with a chore. As soon as they had finished their drinks, Don Saverio got to his feet.

'Thank you for the most welcome refreshment,' he said.

'Would you like some more?' offered Mama Bimpe, to the priest. And what about you?' she said directing her question to Carlo. He shook his head and a smile appeared on his battered face.

'We really must go now,' said the priest, Angelo went outside to check if the road was clear and then beckoned the boy to the cart, followed by Rosita and the priest.

'Please wait, Angelo,' called Papa Joe, 'before you go there is something I want you to see.'

'What is it?' asked Angelo. He felt an anxious tightening in his chest. With all the things going on these days, he didn't know what to expect.

'Come and see, it will take only a few minutes,' insisted Papa Joe. Angelo jumped down from the cart and followed the old Negro to the rear of his house, to some bundles of wood tied together. Papa

Joe, had always been like a father to Angelo, he would trust him with his life.

'Help me to move these, please,' commanded the old Negro.

The two of them started to hoist up the bundles of wood and presently a shallow pit was revealed which contained several boxes of rifles and ammunition. Angelo was taken aback.

'My God, how did you get hold of all of these?' he asked, examining the arms more closely. 'They look dated, where did you get them?' he repeated.

'Fifteen years ago, after the assault, I discovered them hidden under some bushes about a couple of kilometres from here, but it is only recently that I transferred them here. Do you think we can use them?' Asked Papa Joe.

'Oh yes, yes, we could use them, but it's too dangerous for you to keep these things here. I will come back with my father's cart on Saturday night and take them to the old hacienda.'

Papa Joe agreed and was relieved, because he knew that this risk he was taking would mean dire consequences if these weapons were found on his property. They quickly replaced the bundles of wood once more. Angelo rejoined the others and they departed. Don Saverio calling back to Papa Joe, said. 'Don't worry, I'll bring Vittorio back with me when I return.'

On their way back, for a few minutes they chatted about Angelo and Rosita's engagement, and then they embarked on plans for Carlo's future.

'Where are you going to hide this boy? You can't keep him at your home for long,' pointed out the priest, to Angelo.

'We don't intend to keep him at the house for long,' replied Angelo. 'I should think between tonight or tomorrow morning, we'll transfer him to the old hacienda with the others who are hiding there. At least he will be safe and have company there.'

'You're taking a big risk, I'll pray for you, my children.' said Don Saverio, touching the crucifix hanging round his neck. They pulled up outside Angelo's house, to see Vincenzo and Vittorio sitting outside playing cards. Vincenzo got up straight away to greet the priest.

'Don Saverio, what an honour,' he said.

'How are you Vincenzo? As you can see, I gave the two lovebirds a lift home,' he said laughing. Vittorio approached the priest and kissed his hand. 'Bless you my son,' the priest said as he made the sign of the cross. 'Today is a happy day for me. I saw you and your family at church. Rosita and Angelo's presence was the answer to all my prayers,' he continued, and moved towards the cart. 'Now, please help me to bring in some old clothes I have brought for those in need at the old hacienda.'

Vincenzo came forward to help, but Angelo stopped him.

'Father,' he said, 'don't worry. Vittorio and I will take care of those and you go inside with Don Saverio, please.'

Angelo returned to the cart, he hesitated for a few seconds, he looked around to make sure nobody was in the vicinity to surprise him. When he felt sure that there was no danger, he uncovered Carlo. Vittorio and Angelo exchanged glances but said nothing out loud, as some of Don Camillo's men could pass by at any time and they had to keep the boy's presence a secret.

Then Angelo asked, 'Can you help me take these up to my room?'

'With pleasure,' answered Vittorio. 'I'll be happy to do so.'

As quickly as they could, they put the clothes which concealed the boy into a large wicker chest then carried the pile into the house and upstairs. Rosita followed them bringing a glass of milk and a wet flannel to freshen his face, and soon after Angelo went back down.

'What happened to this boy, why is he in this state?' asked Vittorio. 'I know him, he works at the general store.'

'Yes, that's him,' answered Rosita. 'His master has reduced him to this. But don't worry, Vittorio, the day will come when he receives his just punishment.'

'Well, we're ready to support you, we just await your word,' said Vittorio.

'Thank you, but it's not yet time, things still have to be properly prepared. We need many more men,' said Rosita, moving to the window. 'We need people whom we can trust, Vittorio, otherwise many people will be hurt,' she finished, sighing.

'Please don't worry yourself so Miss Rosita,' replied Vittorio moving over to the window to stand next to Rosita. 'You can't expect that nobody will be hurt. That can only happen in dreams. Anyway, there are already more men behind you than you could ever have imagined. You see, this hacienda is very big and as well as the people who live here permanently, there are lots of others who come once a year for three or four months at a time, who are very discontent with the low pay and the bad treatment they receive. They deserve at least a roof over their heads and a bed to sleep in at the end of a hard day's work.'

'Vittorio, I do not know these people, and they do not know me. How can I ask them to risk their lives for me and how could I trust them?' said Rosita, turning to face Vittorio.

'I'm sure you can depend upon every one of these people to support you in your quest, once I've spoken to them.'

'Buenos, Vittorio,' she exclaimed. 'And in return, I'll be very pleased to help these people with their working conditions, once I've regained all of my father's property. But be very careful, if someone finds out what you're doing, your life and many others will be in jeopardy.'

'I promise you I'll take care,' he said.

'Very well, Vittorio, but we're all in God's hands. Let's go down now, and leave this poor boy to sleep. Later we can decide when to move him.' So, Vittorio and Rosita went downstairs to the kitchen to find Angelo with Vincenzo and Don Saverio, drinking liqueur together.

'I thought I could smell aniseed, why are you drinking without us?' laughed Rosita. She moved over to Angelo and she put her arms around his neck and kissed him affectionately, while Vittorio came and sat next to Vincenzo, saying, 'You know Vincenzo, even us Negroes drink liqueur sometimes.' They all laughed together. Two extra glasses were fetched for the two new arrivals to this trio, the glasses were filled with the same aniseed drink and the trio of glasses refilled again. "Salute" they all said, clinking their glasses together. A few more minutes passed as they relaxed and drank cheerily, savouring the company and the alcohol. Then suddenly, Don Saverio broke into the jollity.

'Can you tell me, before I go back home, when you intend moving the boy from here?' he said addressing Vincenzo.

'We don't know yet, maybe we should wait a couple of days, so as not to raise suspicion,' answered Angelo.

'And what do you have in mind?' asked his father.

'Well Father, as you know, every workday very early in the morning, a cart passes by here carrying Negro workers to the plantation, and Stefano and Mariano travel with it. I can forewarn them that on Wednesday they should stop by to pick up another passenger. We can prepare the boy to go with them and at the same time we could quickly load on board some provisions for the old hacienda.'

'Bravo!' the others chorused.

'Also,' continued Angelo, 'I'll ask Stefano to tell a couple of the people at the old hacienda to come to meet the boy and collect the food.'

'Your idea is very good,' said Don Saverio, 'I hope that Don Camillo's men don't see anything. I must go now. Are you ready Vittorio? I'll give you a lift, I don't want to be late for my card game with Dr Pedrazza.' At this Rosita broke into a laugh. It sounded funny to her, hearing that a priest was going to a card game, but on the other hand, should she expect anything less from Don Saverio. After all, he had openly and whole-heartedly joined in on her quest too, he was part of her plot even though he knew it would mean people would get hurt and even killed.

'I don't know!' she exclaimed. 'Priests, gambling?'

'My dear Rosita,' he began, while he was getting up from his chair. 'I am playing at the doctor's house, not in the church, a casino or in the whorehouse. Sometimes we play for the whole evening and into the night, just for a glass of liqueur. It's a pastime, you should join us some time. Anyway my children, goodbye and God bless you all, I'll see you on Saturday if not earlier.' The priest walked towards the door waving his hand in the air at Vincenzo and his family, with Vittorio following behind him. Vittorio climbed onto the cart helping Don Saverio up next to him.

As they were about to pull away, two of Don Camillo's men mounted on their horses rode by, heavily armed with rifles, ammunition belts and hand pistols on their belts. Vincenzo and Angelo raised a hand each to acknowledge the two men, and when the men had passed by looked at each other questioningly. They both wondered why their boss was keeping his men armed as if they were ready for a battle. Was Don Camillo expecting trouble from one of his enemies or had he discovered something about Rosita and her plot? If he had then they were all doomed.

As soon as Don Saverio and Vittorio had disappeared around the corner, Vincenzo, Angelo and Rosita went back in and sat at the kitchen table.

Rosita and Angelo had their concerns about Don Camillo's men, but it was Vincenzo who said in a whisper, 'We must be much more carful from now on. You saw how Don Camillo's thugs were armed to the teeth. Something is going on. From now on we must call you Francesca, even in the house. You never know. If Don Camillo suspects something he may send men to spy on us.'

'Well!' Vincenzo continued, changing the subject and no longer whispering. 'What happened today? Did you order the sugared almonds and the liqueur for your engagement?'

But before Angelo could answer his father, Rosita got up and said, 'You two handsome men, carry on chatting.' Then whispered, 'I will go upstairs to check on the boy,' Angelo and his father both nodded. Once she disappeared, Angelo answered Vincenzo's question.

'Yes Father, we ordered everything, and on Wednesday Juan Pellegrini will deliver them.'

'Ah, Juan,' mused Vincenzo. 'Yes, he's a very good and intelligent young man.'

'Yes Father, and he has many friends too, I plan to ask him if he is willing to help us in our quest.' Over the next few minutes, Angelo filled his father in with all the adventures of the morning. How two of Don Camillo's men were beating Vittorio, forbidding him to go to church, what had happened in the church, how they had rescued the boy, and the delicious lunch they had had at the doctor's house. But Angelo did not mention what Papa Joe had hidden in the ground at the back of his house.

'And did Francesca enjoy herself?' enquired Vincenzo.

'I think so, she looked happy enough.'

'Good, could you go and ask Francesca and the boy if they're hungry? As for tonight I have prepared a lamb stew with fresh vegetables.'

Angelo went upstairs to find Rosita standing beside the sleeping boy. Hugging her first, he asked if she was hungry.

'Well I'm not very hungry yet, but… ' she inhaled through her nose sniffing the air. 'Mmm, your father's cooking certainly does smell good.'

Angelo led Rosita out of the room where Carlo was sleeping and into the corridor. He stopped her and pulled her to him gently. He looked into her eyes and very slowly moved his lips to line up with hers. After brushing his lips backwards and forwards sensually along hers, he kissed her passionately for what seemed an eternity. He and Rosita were transported into their own worlds of blissful pleasure. After they had satisfied their hunger for each other, and with lips that were pink with the stimulus of kissing, Angelo confessed to her how much he needed, and wanted her. They walked slowly back downstairs to discover a mouth-watering feast set out on the table. And the smell of the freshly baked bread and stew instantly wet their appetites, so they sat down to eat.

'Where is the boy?' asked Vincenzo. 'Isn't he coming to eat?'

'No,' replied Rosita, 'he's sleeping, he's not very well and he is tired.'

'How will he sleep tonight if he sleeps now?' asked Vincenzo.

'I could look for some sleeping tablets for him in the medical bag Dr Pedrazza gave me, should he need them, then he won't feel the pain of his wounds,' answered Rosita as she rifled through the medical bag. 'And guess what else I've found in the bag!' she exclaimed. Father and son looked at her expectantly.

'What?' asked Angelo.

'Money, believed it or not,' she said,

'How much?' asked Angelo again surprised.

'Quite a lot,' she replied, then going silent for a few long seconds. 'And some photos of my father,' she continued, with a sad expression on her face.

'What? May I see them?' asked Angelo.

'Yes, of course,' she replied. 'Here they are,' she said, handing the photos to him.

'Should we count the money too?' He asked, trying to change the subject and lighten the blow on Rosita's emotions. She looked at him sideways raising her eyebrow, telling him she had seen right through his attempt at protecting her feelings. They stared at one another for a few seconds and then both laughed out loud together.

'Wasn't your father young here, and handsome,' remarked Angelo.

'Well, where do you think I got my magnificent looks from?' joked Rosita. 'I hope that if I have male children in the future, the boys will be as handsome as he was.'

'And what about me?' asked Angelo, putting on a hurt voice. 'Am I not handsome too?'

'Of course you are, my darling,' she said, pulling at his cheek with her thumb and forefinger. At that point Vincenzo got up, as he had finished eating. He looked at Rosita and his heart warmed to see her and his son so happy.

'Take care of that money, Francesca, it is a godsend. You have enough money there for your quest and more,' he said. His face became dark as he dreaded the thought that she may get hurt. 'I think I'll go out for few minutes, I need some fresh air.' Vincenzo turned and walked out of the kitchen.

As soon as he was out of earshot Angelo whispered to Rosita, 'Can I come and sleep in your room tonight?'

'Really, Angelo!' she exclaimed.

'Well, sweetheart, Carlo is sleeping in my bed, so where do you suggest I should go? Your bed is large enough for two people to sleep comfortably together!'

Rosita studied his face and laughed.

'Angelo, I think you got too much sun today!' she said, then Angelo took hold of her hands and went down on one knee in front of her, his brown almond eyes were devouring her. He wondered to himself how he'd found the strength all this time to stay away from her bed.

'Go on! How can I sleep with a strange boy in my bed?'

At this Rosita roared so loudly with laughter that Vincenzo reappeared from outside, to see Angelo kneeling at Rosita's feet.

'And what is so funny?' he asked, finding it hard not to join in the laughter.

'Nothing father, I am just proposing to Francesca that she comes for a walk with me tonight.'

Vincenzo dismissed them with a grin, then he said, 'Well, I am very tired, so, I'm retiring for the night. If you two want to go for a walk, that's your business. And by the way, Angelo, there is a spare bed in my room.' Angelo ignored this last remark, and as his father disappeared up the stairs, he pulled Rosita to him.

'What I am going to do with you?' he sighed.

'Simple, my dear, just let me be, I want to go to sleep now too.'

'Surely not yet, It's too early, only old people go to bed at this time,' complained Angelo.

'Very well,' she consented. 'Let's walk, but first we should change into some dark clothing so we won't be seen,' she added, as an idea popped into her mind.

'What for?' asked Angelo. 'What's going on in that little head of yours? There are not many people out and about at this time of night, apart from some of Don Camillo's drunken cut-throats.'

'Please don't think that I'm crazy, but I want to go to the main house to check something out,' she said.

'Francesca, what are you talking about?'

'Don Camillo's mansion, darling. Do you remember outside at the back of the mansion there is a set of iron rungs, which went up onto the roof?'

'Yes I know them,' he said.

'There was a small wall at the top, behind which we used to hide when we were children.'

'So, what does this have to do with us now?'

'Please Angelo, let me finish,' replied Rosita. 'Do you remember that behind the wall was a small door which was always locked and you wondered why? Well, once I was playing in my parents' room…'

'What does your parents' room have to do with this?' interrupted Angelo again, now getting a bit worried about Rosita's idea. This beautiful woman was surely looking for trouble tonight, so whatever she suggested, he was going to have to agree and go along with or she'd only try this mad adventure by herself and get into some nasty trouble.

'Angelo, will you please be quiet for a minute and let me finish! That day I hid myself in the wardrobe, pretending the Indians were coming. I could have only been about six or seven years old, suddenly my mother entered the room with someone. It was a man, they were giggling together, and my mother told him that they wouldn't get caught, as my father was away from the mansion. I was there in the darkness of the wardrobe really afraid that she would discover me. I blocked my ears, I was shaking with fear. As I moved myself away from the wardrobe doors and closer to the wall I touched something with my elbow and a shallow opening was revealed. My heart was beating so loud in my chest, I thought they would surely hear it. It was a low passageway, but wide enough to accommodate the width of two people crawling side by side. There was a very small source of light at the other end of the passageway which was about three to four metres in length. I held my breath and slowly inched my way into the passageway and I ventured towards the light at the other end. It seemed like an eternity, but I was moving very slowly so as not to accidentally knock against anything in the dark. When I finally reached the light source and my eyes were used to the low level of light, I found a door and very slowly slid across the bolt that was holding the door secure. The door opened silently bringing me out onto the roof. That's when I discovered the wall we used to hide behind. I think it had been built to conceal the passageway's exit. On the other side, of course, were the iron rungs leading from the roof to ground level.'

'Oh Francesca, why didn't you tell me about this passageway when we were young?' asked Angelo.

'I'm sorry, Angelo, it was my little secret,' she replied, 'and today I can finally make use of it.'

'For what?' asked Angelo, now a bit more worried.

'You will see later,' she replied, begging him with her eyes. He loved her too much, and didn't like the idea of her being in harm's way, but he consented because he knew how important this was for her, and that however much he begged her not to go she would do what she wanted anyway. They went upstairs to change. Angelo was ready first, and Rosita followed not long after. Angelo looked her up and down, his breath caught in his throat. She looked so sexy and physically agile in her tight black leggings and long sleeved roll neck top. Her hair was tied back in a bun and covered with a black bandana.

'The boy is sleeping peacefully,' he said, tearing himself away from his thoughts about what he would like to do to her right now.

'Good, come on, let's get going,' she replied. 'And by the way, Angelo, thank you. I know what I ask is too much sometimes, but I do need you beside me to support me.'

CHAPTER TEN

Creeping out the back of the house they took the long route to the rear of Don Camillo's mansion. It took them an hour and a half to get there because they would stop frequently to check for Don Camillo's men but luckily they didn't encountered anybody. They approached the back of the main house slowly and quietly. Waiting patiently for a good few minutes about fifty metres from the boundary. Angelo looked around the immediate area for any signs of movement, while Rosita concentrated on the house itself. Once they were satisfied that the coast was clear, they moved quickly and efficiently to the back fence. They stopped again to check for any presence of guards within the compound before advancing.

As they were about to go over the fence, they heard a guard approaching them. They crept back about three metres behind a low shrub. The guard stopped right in front of them looking out into the darkness. He was smoking a cigar and was carrying a rifle and hand pistols. He flicked his cigar stub out into the darkness. It landed at Rosita's feet but she didn't flinch, her eyes were glued to the guard.

As soon as the guard was out of range and they had checked the vicinity again they made their way over the fence. Staying in the shadows, they crept over to the iron rungs, which they climbed steadily, and soon they were standing at the top of the roof, behind the wall which was in front of the small door leading into the bedroom.

'How are we going to open this blessed door without making any noise?' asked Angelo, raising his voice.

'Shh,' whispered Rosita, 'it's easy, I'll show you how to do it. I've fixed it so the door can be opened from both inside or outside.'

Angelo was impressed by Rosita's ingenuity, as she had invented this simple but clever method to get in and out, when she was only eight years old. She had made a hook with a piece of string on the inside, so she could open it with a stick from the outside. He squeezed her round the waist and kissed the side of her neck, but Rosita ignored Angelo - not because she didn't enjoy it, but because she had other things on her mind.

'Listen, Angelo, I thought I heard a noise in the trees in that direction,' whispered Rosita, gesturing towards them.

'I think your ears are playing tricks on you. If someone was in this vicinity, they would have captured us by now,' said Angelo.

'Well, I think we're just lucky. Whoever is out there is probably busy doing something else, or we'd be in big trouble.' Hopefully they're on our side, she thought. Angelo of course believed her, so he moved to the edge of the wall and listened again. For the first few seconds he could hear only his heart throbbing in his chest.

'Yes,' he whispered, when he returned to stand next to Rosita, 'you were right, I heard it. Someone certainly is out there, and you know who it could be.'

The noise they'd heard was the sound of a twig snapping under someone's foot. They both went to look over the edge of the roof in the direction it was coming from.

'Look over there. Can you see the shadows of those two men with rifles on their backs?' asked Rosita. At this, Angelo pulled Rosita back behind the wall. 'They must be guarding the mansion. I wonder how long they've been here.' she asked, almost to herself.

'I didn't know there were this many guards here,' replied Angelo. 'What can we do now? We can't stay here on the roof all night!'

'No. We'll have to go inside, and with some luck we'll be able to leave by the front door,' answered Rosita.

'Rosita, this is not a joking matter,' he said, in desperation.

'But Angelo, I'm serious. If my mother is sleeping we can cross her bedroom and she won't see us. I know that she sleeps with an eye mask. Let's hope that Don Camillo is out, because from her room we can go out into the corridor, then down the stairs and out the front,' said Rosita, trying to convince herself that everything would go as she planned.

'That is if we're lucky enough to find your mother asleep. What if we meet someone on the way down?' he said, worrying more for her life than his own. At this point Rosita felt guilty, she shouldn't have asked Angelo to accompany her, putting both their lives in danger was not necessary. She should have come on her own, but it was too late now so they must both keep calm.

At that moment they heard a woman giggle. Both of them looked at each other and smirked in unison, as if to say: that's why the guards didn't see us, they had a woman with them. This was fortunate for Angelo and Rosita.

'Listen my love, I know you're right, but we don't have time to think about this, we must act quickly,' she whispered in his ear.

'If we get through this unscathed, I swear I'll never come back to this place any other way than the front door,' murmured Angelo, leading Rosita to the passage door.

She opened the trap door and they stepped gingerly into the passage closing the outer door behind them. They moved very slowly towards the inside of the house allowing their eyes to become accustomed to the diminishing light. Approaching the inner door, which led into the wardrobe they heard Donna Teresa's muffled voice, she was not yet in bed. Instead she was speaking in a very agitated way to her husband.

'Why don't you come to bed early any more? Am I too old for you? There's always an excuse. Where are you going tonight? To see another woman?' she was saying.

'No, you know how much I love you. What's going on in that head of yours?' was his reply.

'You want to know what's in my head? Well I'll tell you. I saw the way you were looking at that girl in church.'

'Which girl?'

'The new girl, Francesca, Vincenzo's niece.'

'Ha! That's why you left in a huff, I thought there was a reason why you stormed out.' This time he had raised his voice.

'You see, now you're shouting at me, and you do that rarely. What other reason could I have to be mad at you, could you please explain that to me?'

'Nothing my dear, I think you'd better go to sleep, it's getting late for you,' he said with less hostility in his voice this time. He didn't like to raise his voice to her, but right now he had lots on his mind. And so he should, after all, he had made many enemies in the past.

'No, I can't sleep until I know what you were thinking.'

'If I tell you, you won't sleep anyway.'

'Is it something bad?'

'I do not know, Teresa, perhaps I'm mistaken but if it's what I think, there will be a big problem. I was looking at Francesca Curro, but not because I wanted her as you think. Did you look closely at her? How do we know that she is who she claims to be?'

'Yes I did look at her, why? Are you trying to confuse me with some fancy story? Because you had better think twice before you do.'

'Today in church, while she was reading the Bible, I saw your late husband for a moment. She had his eyes and his facial expressions,' he explained. His face darkened, he had a distant look in his eyes, fifteen years distant, in this very house, in the corridor when he'd stabbed Don Sebastian Miserendino in cold blood. But his wife hadn't seen that, she couldn't even imagine the scene that was running through his mind.

'Camillo! What are you saying? That the girl could be Rosita?' she asked. Then as if to herself she said, 'Wouldn't that be wonderful. Maybe we want to believe she is, but you know very well that she's gone. Anyway, even if it was her, why has she waited all these years to come back?'

'It's a possibility,' he said looking out of the window, into the courtyard. It was deserted, apart from his men with their rifles slung over their shoulders and a pistol on their belt. A family of bats were flying round above the mansion, and grasshoppers were singing their night song safely contented on the trees enjoying the fresh breeze.

But Don Camillo at this moment had nothing to enjoy, he was searching his brain for a way out of this mess. He had decided to hire some more mercenaries, just in case his hunch about Rosita was right. He knew his actions of the past were a good reason for a revenge attack, but his wife had no idea. She had been kept in the dark about the truth of what had happened all those years ago.

'No, Camillo!' Teresa finally ranted loudly. 'Rosita died, nobody could have survived in those flames that burnt down the barn with all those people in it. Those poor people were burnt so badly nobody could be identified. I don't want to think about it anymore.'

'I'll tell you what I'm thinking though, just to be sure, I would like to send someone to the cemetery in the village of Bella Vista, the place where Nunziato Curro lives. I would like to check if there is a grave for Francesca Curro. I do remember you telling me that the girl was ill and hadn't long to live,' he said, turning to look at his wife.

'Yes, Camillo, I did but doctors aren't always right in their diagnosis. So, maybe she grew out of all her illness,' she said calming down a bit.

'Well, my love, you could be right, but I'd like to be sure for our piece of mind. So, tonight I'm going to the village to see someone who travels there often.'

'Do I know him?'

'Yes, it's Antonio Marquis, the general store owner.'

'Oh yes, of course, I know him,' she said moving behind him and circling her arms round his inflated waist. She placed her head against his back. She was trying to calm him down using her body; she had always been good with her body language, pawing over him like a cat.

'I'm sorry, my love, I didn't mean to shout at you. But you see, I'm so lonely some days, I just miss you when you're not here.'

As if he hadn't heard what she had said, he carried on talking about what he had going on in his mind.

'I'd heard he's going to Bella Vista tomorrow, and I'll ask him to do me this favour, so when I have peace of mind over this matter I can relax.'

'All right, my darling, but why don't you go tomorrow morning?' she pleaded. Then turning him to face her she fluttered her eyelashes and said, 'Please stay with me tonight and keep me company.'

'Yes, my dear, you are right, I'll stay. I have been very busy lately, and I've neglected you, forgive me,' he said, praying to himself that she never finds out the whole truth about what happened here fifteen years ago. He had a lot on his plate right now to deal with, so relaxing would probably help him to work things out more clearly.

'There is nothing to forgive; you should forgive me for being a silly girl. Why don't we go and have something to eat with a glass of wine, then we can come back to bed?'

'As you wish, my dear,' he said.

With relief Rosita and Angelo heard the sound of the couple leaving the bedroom.

'They have gone,' whispered Angelo.

'We're in luck then,' she replied.

'Quickly then, let's get out of here,' he said.

'Angelo,' she whispered, 'supposing one of them returned?'

'There's no time to talk. Act now! Isn't that what you said?'

'Follow me, I know the way,' she said, closing the passage entrance door in the back of the wardrobe. Then they stepped into the wardrobe itself, parting the clothes inside. She very carefully pressed her ear to the door of the wardrobe that opened into the bedroom.

'I can hear them going downstairs, come on,' she whispered. They crept through the bedroom and towards the landing, there was no one around. 'Shh,' Rosita mouthed again, her finger to her lips. She listened at the bedroom door and then gently eased it open. Together they tiptoed towards the stairs that lead to the ground level.

'Thank God, there's nobody about,' whispered Angelo. They held hands, to give each other encouragement. Rosita went down the stairs as silently as a cat, followed swiftly by Angelo. At the bottom of the stairs, on their right was a corridor leading to the kitchen. They listened for a few seconds for any movement. Hearing nothing, Rosita signalled for Angelo to check outside the front door. He swiftly walked over to the door and opened it gently, first listening then looking to see if anyone was passing. At the same time, while his heart was pounding in his chest, wondering what on earth he was doing there. Then he signalled for Rosita to join him and she ran nimbly to the front door. Luckily for them the coast was clear. They closed the door gently behind them and made their way round to the back of the house again, making sure to stay in the shadows at all times. Within a few minutes they were again over the back fence, and on their way home.

After running all the way back they entered the kitchen, breathless, their legs were burning and shaking with the effort the long run had taken. Their hearts were beating rapidly and the adrenalin was giving them a head rush. They embraced one another and then for no reason burst into uncontrollable laughter. Rosita placed her hands onto Angelo's cheeks.

'One of these days you'll despair and curse the day I came back,' she said. 'In future I'll do this kind of night work on my own. Please forgive me, I just wanted to see if the passage was still there.'

Angelo put his forefinger across Rosita's lips.

'Be quiet, and listen. I never want to hear you speak this way again. What do you take me for, a little boy? Of course I was afraid tonight, but not for myself, my fear was for you. You have no regard of danger to yourself, so I have to protect you. Fifteen years ago when you disappeared, I missed you so much, I cried a lot on my own thinking of you, thinking I'll never see my best friend, my only friend ever again. My mother and father's comfort helped me come to terms with my loss, but now that I've found you again I think I would die if I were to lose you once more. I love you so much, my Rosita,' he whispered into her ear.

Rosita of course, knew that he was right. But she couldn't help it, she had to make sure for future reference.

'What we did tonight was very risky but rewarding,' replied Rosita. 'If we hadn't gone, we would not have discovered that Don Camillo suspects my true identity.'

'This, my dear, means that from now on, we'll have to prepare everything and everybody even more quickly and carefully,' said Angelo.

'I agree, but it's late now, let's go to sleep, we can think about what we need to do next, tomorrow,' she answered, and the two of them made their way upstairs.

'Goodnight, my love, sleep well,' said Angelo, kissing Rosita as if he would never see her again. He loved everything about her, what she smelt like, the taste of her, and he wanted her so much that his loins were often in pain. But at this moment he was tingling all-over.

'Only if you come to sleep in my room, especially after what we've been through tonight,' she said.

Without saying anything, Angelo picked her up in his arms and carried Rosita into her room. He laid her on the bed and returned to close the door and then lit the paraffin lamp on the dressing table. Rosita got up to shut the window and drew the curtains.

They began to slowly undress, kissing each other teasingly at the same time. Angelo was ready first, and sat on the edge of the bed while his eyes were having a feast dancing over Rosita's beautiful body.

'I'm sorry, but I haven't got my pyjamas here,' he said sitting there in his boxer shorts. He teased her with one of his wicked smiles, then she turned her back to him to place the last piece of clothing neatly on a chair. He turned down the paraffin lamp, then reached across to her and gently pulled her toward him, he took her into his arms and began to stroke her with his fingertips. His lips glided over her shoulder, nipping lightly at her soft flesh. Moving his lips over he found her earlobe and began nibbling at it, making her tremble with the pleasure it gave her. Rosita ran her hands over his smooth back, her desire accelerated, her head whirled. She could feel his lips against hers, they were moist and hot.

Gently he caressed her breasts then her stomach, murmuring words of love. Then he moved downwards with tantalising slowness, Rosita was lost in her own little paradise, all her worries melted away, masked by the ecstasy she was experiencing. She thought of nothing but the sensations fluttering in her belly and the tingling heat spreading all over her body. His hands were exploring her womanly curves, his finger finding all her secret sensitive places she had longed to be discovered, experiencing what seemed like outer body pleasure. Suddenly there was a tremendous feeling of urgency, and a soft moan emanated from deep in her throat, followed by his controlled moan of pleasurable sensation, that fired through his body. It shook him to the core.

CHAPTER ELEVEN

The next morning, Rosita was awake first. She stretched her arms and touched Angelo's sleeping form. She jumped.

'What are you doing…' she started to say, but then sighing with satisfaction, remembered the previous night and how they'd made love so passionately many times until early morning. Angelo was still in a deep sleep, so she carefully rose from the bed so as not to disturb him. Quickly slipping into her dressing gown, she noticed the bedside clock showed the time was five a.m.. She went down to the kitchen to prepare some coffee and there she found Vincenzo sitting at the kitchen table.

'Good morning, Uncle,' she said cheerily.

'Good morning, dear. Did you sleep well?'

'Yes, very well,' she answered, blushing. 'I thought you would still be sleeping.'

'No, I've been up a little while,' said Vincenzo.

'Why, are you feeling ill? asked Rosita.

'Not at all, I went to check on the boy, to see how he was. He was awake, and I made him a drink and something to eat. I think he has gone back to sleep now. I woke early because I have a feeling of foreboding.'

'About what uncle?'

'I don't know, it's something in the air or a feeling in my heart.'

'Well, I think you may be right about this feeling. I should tell you what happened last night,' ventured Rosita.

'I heard you go out, last night,' said Vincenzo. 'I thought you went for a walk, but that wasn't the case. What did you get up to? I wanted to see if you'll tell me the truth.

'Well, what we did last night was in one way extremely stupid, but in another way very useful,' she whispered, a little mortified. 'You see Uncle, last night we sneaked into Don Camillo's mansion.'

'Have you two lost your heads? Suppose someone had seen you!' he hissed.

'Uncle, if someone had seen us, we wouldn't be here now in one piece. Anyway we heard a very interesting conversation between Don Camillo and my mother.'

'What? Do you think your mother suspects something?'

'That's what I would have expected but it's not my mother who is suspicious Uncle, but Don Camillo,' she said. Sadness again fell over Rosita's face. Vincenzo felt for her. 'In fact he is sending somebody to Bella Vista to check if there is a grave for Francesca.

'What have you done to make him suspicious?'

'I think it was yesterday at the church. When the priest saw a new face he called me to read a verse from the bible, and I read the same verse my father used to read occasionally. Do you remember it, Uncle? You used to come with us, the reading was Exodus 23. verses 27-30.'

'Yes, Francesca, I do remember very well.' At this point, Rosita suddenly felt emotional. Her eyes clouded with tears, Vincenzo placed one hand on her shoulder. In order to fight through her emotions she changed the subject and told Vincenzo the rest of the details of Don Camillo's conversation with her mother. Then going back to her previous thoughts continued by saying, 'I need to tell you Uncle, I used to be so proud of my father when he used to get up to read in the church. He was my idol,' she said, smiling at Vincenzo.

'We all were, my dear, I'm happy to say,' replied Vincenzo still talking in a whisper. 'You were very important to him too. And today you are very important to all of us; there are many people who are relying on you and ready to do anything for you.'

'I know Uncle,' she said, embracing him. 'And we must get everything organised as soon as possible.'

At that moment, Angelo appeared at the bottom of the stairs dressed only in his trousers, still half asleep, his fair hair untidy and wild. He saw his father and Rosita embracing.

'Hey, you two, what are you doing? She's my fiancée! Come here, I want to do that,' said Angelo, and pulled Rosita to him. 'Did you sleep well? he asked her tenderly.

'Yes, very well, Angelo. And I told your father about last night.' Angelo looked at her questioningly. 'I thought it best to tell him everything we did last night,' she said softly.

'Everything?' he exclaimed, whispering.

'No, you buffoon, not that,' she laughed.

'Hey, you two lovebirds! Come and sit down for breakfast so we can talk things through,' called Vincenzo. Then he whispered, 'First of all, about the boy, Carlo. He must leave today. Vittorio and Stefano will soon pass by here. Today they'll be working with you two. You must take the boy with you, on the way you have to decide where and with whom you're going to leave him. Tell Stefano to send word to your uncle in Bella Vista, about what you heard Don Camillo say last night. Nunziato should be told about this as soon as possible,' said Vincenzo, calmly. He was the strongest among all of them, thought Rosita, Vincenzo always kept cool.

Suddenly Angelo had an idea.

'Father.' Angelo interrupted, 'Stefano has a cousin who works on the Bella Vista train. Maybe he could get the message to Uncle Nunziato very quickly.'

'Very well, whoever, as long as the message gets through,' replied Vincenzo. 'And in future, think twice before you go running off on your next escapade! Those people are not playing around you know. Even though Francesca knows the inside of the mansion very well, next time, and I hope there isn't a next time, if you cannot get to the front door without being noticed, that would be the end of everything.'

At this Angelo and Rosita looked at each other with surprise. How could Vincenzo have known that they had come out via the front door? They had only told him where they'd been, and about the conversation they'd overheard. They had not made any mention of climbing the steps and entering the wardrobe via the passageway or leaving through the front door.

'Father,' enquired Angelo, still whispering. 'Did you by any chance follow us last night?'

'No, I'm not as crazy as you two, or as young. I didn't go out, but out there are people watching Francesca's back day and night,' he replied smugly.

'Just one moment Father, can I ask you something?'

Francesca already knew Angelo's next question.

'We're thinking the same thing now?' she said, laughing.

'Wait, Francesca let me ask. Father, last night we risked our lives to enter Don Camillo's lair. You know why we did it? And you know what we did! We saw two armed men behind the mansion, so we couldn't go back the same way. Are you telling me that those two men were there to protect Francesca?'

'Not those two at the back, Angelo,' replied Vincenzo seriously, not giving anything else away. 'But if what you told me is true, things are more serious than I imagined. I'm afraid we cannot wait too much longer to carry out our final mission. Well, my children get yourselves ready for work,. As soon as Vittorio and Stefano arrive, you must all leave. I'll go to wake the boy.'

As quickly as they could, Rosita and Angelo went to the back of the house to saddle their horses while Vincenzo went to get the boy ready. A few minutes later, he brought Carlo down. The poor boy looked lost.

'And what is your name?' asked Vincenzo, to make some sort of conversation, but the boy did not reply. 'Don't be afraid, if you don't want to tell me I don't mind, but don't forget we're your friends. We only want to help you.' After a minute or so, the boy plucked up the courage to speak.

'My name is Carlo,' he said hesitantly.

'What did you say, son?' asked Vincenzo.

'I said, that my name is Carlo but I'm not used to anybody asking me my name. Usually people say, "hey you" or" boy!"'

'I'm sorry, I hope that this dreadful behaviour will soon cease.'

At that moment Vittorio entered the house.

'Hurry, Vincenzo,' he said. 'We must get the boy onto the cart quickly. I saw many strange faces on the way here and I wonder which filthy holes they crawled out from?'

'From the very hole Don Camillo keeps them in, until he needs them,' retorted Vincenzo. He knew something like this would happen one day, but hadn't expected it so soon. They hid Carlo on the cart under some blankets, and soon they were on their way. Angelo and Rosita following the cart on their horses. When they were out of sight of the house and in open countryside, Stefano asked Angelo to join him on the cart, as he wanted to speak to him.

'I'll take the cart Stefano,' suggested Rosita. 'You take my horse and ride with Angelo.'

They exchanged places, so Stefano and Angelo could talk whilst following the cart.

'Angelo,' Stefano began. 'We are very concerned with all these strange faces around, do you think they know about Francesca?' asked Stefano, 'Papa Joe thinks that Don Camillo has even more men coming, to keep her under surveillance.'

'What do you suppose gave Don Camillo the idea that Francesca is not who she says she is?' asked Angelo, while his eyes were scanning the surrounding area in case of any trouble.

'Well, Papa Joe thinks it's because of the way she stood up for Vittorio against his men yesterday at the church. And also, the way he was looking at her when she read from the Bible at church,' said Stefano, suddenly looking over his shoulder. He felt as if someone was watching them. Angelo looked questioningly, at him, but Stefano shook his head as if to say it was nothing.

'Yes, that is true,' replied Angelo, 'We found out he suspects something last night. We know that he's going to see Don Antonio Marquis today.'

'About what?' asked Stefano.

'To ask him to visit the cemetery in Bella Vista, to find out if there is a grave with Francesca Curro's name on it.'

'Dear God, Angelo. Don Antonio will do this for him for sure, and more. He's an evil man.'

'I know, my friend, that's why my father wants us to contact our friend, Juan's brother, who works on the railway, and ask him to warn my Uncle Nunziato.'

'I would do this with pleasure, if it was possible, but what reason can I give to go to the station?' replied Stefano. There was a short pause then, 'Wait I have an idea, why don't we ask Juan to take the message to his brother Manuel. He is white, he is free to go where he pleases. As Manuel's fiancée is from Bella Vista, he could easily get the message to your uncle Nunziato, while he is on a stop over there. What do you think?' Angelo looked at Stefano, pretending he was thinking and then he said. 'You know, for a Negro, you're not that stupid.'

They both laughed heartily and then bumped fists with each other in a brotherly manner.

'Hey, did I miss something?' called Rosita turning to look at the two of them laughing.

Suddenly, Vittorio who was sat on the cart behind Rosita, by Carlo's side, cleared his throat a few times to attract their attention.

'What is it?' asked Rosita, turning back around to look where she was going.

'Look who's coming this way.' Vittorio looked at Angelo and pointed with a movement of his eyes. Two heavily armed men were approaching on horseback from their left flank, Rosita turned to catch Angelo's eyes. He smiled and winked at her, he of course had seen them too.

'What are we going to do if they want to search the cart?' asked Vittorio.

'Quickly, uncover Carlo,' ordered Rosita.

'But why?' asked Vittorio, panicking a bit.

'Listen, uncover his body but keep his face concealed as if he's asleep, they'll just think he's one of the workers,' she urged.

'He's not the only concern,' said Vittorio, 'There are other things on the cart as well,' Rosita looked questioningly at Vittorio. He spoke with one hand partly covering his mouth to conceal his words. 'We're carrying the boxes of rifles and ammunition too, Father thought they should be moved at the earliest opportunity. Hey look, there are three of them.'

Another ruffian had joined the two men approaching.

The three men, armed to their teeth, stopped in front of the cart. One of them had rough ugly features and he stared at Rosita intently.

'Who are you and where are you going?' he demanded. Angelo moved his horse to the side where Rosita was sitting; meanwhile Stefano went to the other side of the cart and reached in for a stick.

'We are the ones who'd like to know your identity and ask what you are doing trespassing on Don Camillo's land! No, don't bother answering, just go back to where you came from,' commanded Angelo, forcefully.

At that point, the two men who were fiddling with their guns in an agitated manner moved closer to Angelo.

'Ha, we are working for Don Camillo too,' one of them smirked.

'Well, now that we've finished with the formalities, do you mind removing yourselves from our way? We have a little further to go before we reach our place of work,' ordered Angelo.

Things were getting hotter and hotter, thought Rosita, looking back at Vittorio. They understood each other.

'You're not going anywhere till we let you,' was the reply by the thugs. Rosita decided that they had been delayed long enough, and now was the time for some action. She mouthed something to Angelo, trying to make her lip movement as little as possible.

'Tu capisci Sicilianu? (You understand Sicilian?)' Angelo nodded. 'Allura e meghiu chi di sbarrazzamu di iddi, prima chi finisci malu! (Well I think it's best if we get rid of them before this ends badly!)'

'Puru io penzu cosi- (I think so too,)' he replied. Rosita slowly slid her hands down her thighs and past her knees to her boots. She gave Angelo the nod, then as quick as lightning she pulled out two knives and threw them at the two men in front of her. The knives met their target with deadly accuracy, dead in the centre of their chests. Angelo had pulled out his rifle and crashed it down onto the head of the third man. The three men slumped onto the ground at virtually the same time. Stefano jumped off his mount and finished the third man off with the stick he'd retrieved from the cart.

'Quick! We'll have to get rid of them before someone comes,' said Stefano, breathlessly.

'Come on quickly everybody, we must put them on their horses,' ordered Angelo.

'Where are we going to hide them?' asked Vittorio, breathlessly.

'Not very far from here is a quarry that the hacienda uses as a refuse dump,' Angelo responded.

'I know it,' said Stefano. 'It's not far from here, just behind those trees, and there is a very deep stretch of water too.'

They hoisted the dead bodies onto the horses and two workers from the cart led the horses to the dump. Angelo and Vittorio accompanied them, while Rosita waited with the rest of the men. They managed to hide the bodies very well under wood and weeds in the dump. Then they slapped the horse's rump, and they sped off. They returned to the cart, a little out of breath.

'Angelo, what's our next move?' asked Rosita.

'Well, we go to work and carry on as normal, as if nothing had happened,' he replied.

Within ten minutes they had arrived at their destination. Mariano and the other workers had arrived long before, and had already dug a pit ready to hide the boxes of rifles and ammunition in. Very quickly with the help of all the workers, the guns were concealed in the pit and covered with brambles and other foliage. Two of the men were from the old hacienda and had been waiting to take Carlo with them; they left together after the guns had been hidden, taking food and provisions as well. Everyone was carrying on with their work as if nothing had happened. Today their duty was to prune the fruit trees as the fruit had already been picked, and then all the branches they had cut off had to be burnt. Adjacent to the fruit trees was an open piece of ground and this was to be prepared for vegetables to be sewn. Stefano was working next to Angelo, digging lines of troughs. Stefano nudged Angelo discreetly with his elbow.

'What is it?' he asked.

'Don't make it obvious, but look to your right,' said Stefano.

There were a few men watching them from behind the trees about fifty metres away.

'I know,' said Angelo, whispering. 'And you look to your left.' Stefano straightened up and made pretend to wipe his brow with his cuff. There were another two men to the left. They carried on working normally, trying to ignore the strangers. Rosita approached Angelo and Stefano offering them water from her canteen.

'I didn't know we had guests for lunch today,' she joked quietly.

'Come here my observant little minx, you left me all alone over here,' answered Angelo, pulling her to him.

'Not true, you had Stefano to keep you company,' she said, as Angelo kissed her forehead then took a drink from the canteen.

'Do you think I should do this to Stefano?' Angelo was holding the open canteen over Stefano's head as if he was about to pour water over him. Stefano overheard his remark.

'Why don't you just try it and see what will happen to you?' he suggested. The three of them laughed together. They were putting on an act as if nothing was bothering them and all was normal.

'It's nearly time to eat, what is there for lunch today?' Rosita asked Angelo. Then not waiting for an answer she proceeded. 'What do you think if we eat those two on my right for starters and the ones on the left for the main course?' she said mischievously.

'Francesca!' Angelo hissed. 'Do not go looking for trouble, we have enough of that to deal with right now.'

'No, I'm not joking, I think they intend to stay here all day just staring at us. I have the feeling they want to interfere with workers. They look exactly like wolves waiting to pounce on their prey.'

'Calm down, Francesca. If they are waiting there for this reason, there's nothing to fear because we are many, and they wouldn't dare take us all on.'

The day passed slowly, and at the end of the working day the people packed up their tools and belongings and started to get ready to go home. Rosita, Vittorio, Angelo and Stefano stayed until last to see the workers off. They knew that Don Camillo's men were still around somewhere watching them, and so they pretended to talk about the next day's work.

'Angelo, look, the men are leaving,' said Vittorio.

'What shall we do now?' asked Rosita.

I think we should go home,' put in Stefano. 'Perhaps they're moving out of view to make us think they're leaving, when really they're going to watch us for our next move?'

'You're right, let's go straight home,' said Angelo.

Vittorio and Stefano mounted the cart and Rosita fetched hers and Angelo's horses. Once ready, they all left together. On the way home they only spotted two of Don Camillo's men, who were watched them from a distance. They arrived outside Angelo's house without encountering any trouble.

'Would you boys like to come in for a drink?' Angelo invited.

'No, its better that we go home, otherwise our parents may worry about us,' said Vittorio.

'Very well. Goodbye boys,' replied Angelo. Rosita nodded her goodbye.

It was late at night, supper was finished and Rosita, Vincenzo and Angelo were drinking coffee.

'Excuse me boys, but I'm tired, in fact I feel rather dizzy. I'm going straight up to bed,' said Rosita. She kissed Angelo on his cheek and her uncle on his forehead, then wished them a good night. 'I'm sorry I can't help you to clear up tonight,' she finished.

'It doesn't matter, you've worked hard today,' replied Vincenzo, Angelo just looked at her but said nothing, he wondered if she was pretending to be ill, and would later find an excuse to go out for another of her nocturnal scouting trips. But before she even reached the stairs she slumped to the floor with a thud. Angelo ran to her side, he called her name a few times, frightened of what could have happened to his precious Rosita. He picked her up in his arms and Vincenzo rushed to fetch some water.

'My God, Angelo, what's wrong with her?' exclaimed Vincenzo, when he returned with the water. 'If she didn't feel well, why did she stay at work all day?'

'I don't know, Father, she was fine earlier today,' replied a distressed Angelo, as tears welled up in his eyes. Vincenzo dabbed her face and neck with a damp cloth to try to revive her. After what seemed an eternity but was actually only thirty seconds, Rosita opened her eyes and saw them looking at her with concern, the tears rolling down Angelo's face.

'Whatever happened to me?' she asked.

'You passed out and crashed to the floor,' explained Vincenzo.

How do you feel my darling?' asked Angelo relieved that she was now conscious. 'Oh Francesca, why didn't you tell me you didn't feel well today?'

'But I'm all right Angelo!' she insisted, 'I felt fine all day, I swear. Just a little while ago after I finished supper I started to feel strange.'

'Now then, I'm taking you to bed and I'm calling the doctor,' decided Angelo.

'That's not necessary. After a good night's sleep I'm sure that tomorrow I'll be fine,' she replied, but Angelo was adamant and took her up to bed, helped her to undress and put her nightgown on. When she was settled in, he touched her forehead.

'My God, Francesca you're scorching hot, your temperature must be well over a hundred,' he exclaimed. 'I'll tell Father to bring you some fresh water.'

'Angelo, please calm down. If you listen I'll tell you why I feel this way.'

'I'm listening,' he said and knelt on the floor taking hold of her hands.

'You see, the entire problem is that it's my monthly time and sometimes it affects me like this. Perhaps today I worked a little too hard in the heat,' she said, her face flushed, her eyes were glistening. She did look as if she had a very high temperature. Angelo took her hand to his lips and kissed it. 'I'll be all right by morning, you'll see,' she finished.

'All right, I believe you,' he said, 'but I'm still sending for the doctor. Maybe he can give you something to bring down your temperature, now try to get some rest.' At that point Angelo left her and went downstairs.

'How is she?' asked Vincenzo.

'The same, I'm going to call for the doctor, now,' said Angelo.

'It's not necessary, someone's already left with your horse,' replied Vincenzo.

'Who?'

'Mariano. He had come over to play cards with me, but as soon as he heard what had happened he offered to go. I hope that none of Don Camillo's scum stops him on his way.'

The two of them started to clear up the kitchen, both with their minds on Rosita. Within fifteen minutes the kitchen had been cleared, everything washed, dried and put away, food packed away, floor swept and mopped. They had just sat down to drink a camomile tea when suddenly they heard voices outside; it was Donna Teresa with Maria, one of her servants. Vincenzo let her in.

'Good evening, Donna Teresa,' said Vincenzo; he was somewhat surprised and taken aback to see her here so late.

'What's the matter with you tonight, aren't you going to ask me to sit down?' she said.

'I do apologise, Donna Teresa. I wasn't expecting such an important visitor so late, what can I do for you?'

'Nothing for me,' she said, looking around the kitchen as if she was looking for something, or maybe inspecting if the house was clean. 'I came to see what had happened to Francesca.'

'How did you find out so quickly about her being ill?' asked Angelo, pretending naivety.

'One of our men saw Mariano galloping by like the wind and they stopped him, I'm very sorry to say.'

'Yes, she is ill, she fainted this evening after supper and has a very high temperature,' started Angelo, putting a handkerchief to his eyes. Making the matter a bit more dramatic, so Donna Teresa could report it to Don Camillo how worried they were for Francesca.

'May I see her?'

'I think we should wait until the doctor has seen her,' replied Angelo.

'Mm… perhaps that's for the best,' she said, shaking her head, thinking to herself how wrong Don Camillo was thinking that this girl was Rosita. She had presumed that this illness was a remnant of the sickness Francesca had had as a child.

'May I offer you and your maid a drink?' Vincenzo asked.

'A glass of fresh lemonade would be welcomed,' responded Donna Teresa. Her maid nodded as if to say, me too.

Vincenzo began to prepare camomile tea to take up for Rosita and two glasses of lemonade for the two visitors. After a few minutes, Angelo took Rosita's drink up. She was half-asleep; he sat next to her on the edge of the bed. His heart was breaking to see her in this state; he had forgotten momentarily that Rosita had said she'd be okay the following morning.

Presently Dr Pedrazza arrived along with Mariano.

'Good evening Vincenzo, Donna Teresa? Where is Francesca?' he asked, going straight to the sink to wash his hands. 'What exactly happened? I came as quickly as possible.'

'She's upstairs, she just passed out,' replied Vincenzo. The concerned doctor hurried upstairs, into Francesca's bedroom, he checked her pulse then felt her forehead. Angelo was right behind the doctor and he whispered that Francesca had said she was on her menstrual cycle.

'She's burning up,' interrupted the doctor. 'Quick Angelo, fill a bathtub with cold water.'

Like lightning, Angelo did as he was bid, asking his father to bring the bathtub up from the washroom together with a couple of large clean towels. They filled the bath with buckets of water brought up from down stairs by Angelo and Mariano. Rosita was very weak and had very little strength, so Angelo lifted her up as she was, and laid her gently in the bath supporting her neck and shoulders. Her beautiful auburn hair cascaded onto the floor behind the tub.

Meanwhile, Donna Teresa was impatiently pacing the floor downstairs. She wanted to know if Francesca was really sick, so she made a decision to go and see for herself. She marched up to Francesca's bedroom. Gingerly now she peered around the door, and saw to her surprise the girl's flushed face in the bath. She ventured forward.

'May I help?' she asked.

'No, thank you,' replied the doctor. 'For now we have to bring her temperature right down and keep her cool. If you want, you can fetch a cool sweet drink for her, as she could do with some fluids packed with energy.'

'I'll do that straightaway,' she replied, disappearing out of the room.

'I wonder what she's doing here?' asked Angelo. 'She surely isn't concerned for Francesca's wellbeing.'

'She must have an ulterior motive,' replied the doctor in a whisper.

Donna Teresa soon returned and handed a cool orange juice to the doctor. Meanwhile Rosita opened her eyes, and looked at the three faces around her. She closed her eyes again and reopened them to return her focus onto Donna Teresa, her mother. Angelo was secretly worried that Rosita may utter the word 'mother' in her delirium. Rosita was weak but not delirious, she was wondering to herself what on the earth this woman was doing here, and tried to raise herself from the tin bath, but Angelo stopped her.

'Yes, it's Donna Teresa,' he whispered in her ear.

'Well, I think she'll be all right now,' announced the doctor, 'Donna Teresa and I will go down together now. Angelo, help Francesca out of the bath, get her dried and dressed. Put her into bed, covering her lightly.' The doctor took Donna Teresa by the arm and led her out and downstairs.

'What was she doing here in my room?' she uttered softly. Angelo kissed her forehead.

'You should know why she's here,' he replied speaking softly into her ear as he stripped her of the wet clothes and dried her naked body with a soft towel. After dressing her in a dry nightie he helped her into her bed placing a sheet over her. He held Rosita for a couple of minutes, telling her how worried he was and how much he loved her. Then he left her to rest, going down to join Vincenzo, Donna Teresa, and the others.

'She's all tucked up,' he said, and joined them at the table.

'Well, I'm going to make a final check on her as I must go now,' said the doctor. So he went up and approached her bed. 'Do you know you gave us a scare, Francesca?' he said. She smiled at him. 'I've had a thought that Donna Teresa seeing you in this condition could be to our advantage,' continued Dr Pedrazza. 'She may now reconsider the doubts that she and her husband have that you're not really who you say you are. But to convince her even more that you're not Rosita, I think you should stay in your bed for a week.'

'Are you joking? Tomorrow I'll be well enough to go back to work, I know I will.'

'No you won't! I'm going down now and I will say that I need to do some blood tests on you and then I'll accompany Donna Teresa home. I'll return here tomorrow, hopefully with some good news for you. Francesca, I'll leave you two tablets for the period pain, but I'll tell the others that I've left sleeping tablets. Goodbye for now and stay in bed,' he insisted.

The doctor made his way back down and spoke to Angelo with concern in his voice.

'Angelo, I've left a couple of sleeping pills on the bedside table, can you take her a glass of water so she can take them. She'll sleep all night. I'll be back tomorrow to check on her, and do some tests. Please make sure she doesn't try to get up, she's very weak.'

'Do you think she'll be all right, for Saturday?' asked Angelo.

'I hope so, son,' he answered, and winked at him.

Donna Teresa had listened to every word they'd said. After all, that's why she was there.

'Why Saturday? Do you have to go somewhere?' enquired Donna Teresa.

'Well, no! But we've planned our engagement party for this Saturday. I think we should postpone everything now,' answered Angelo.

'I'm very sorry, I hope she gets better soon,' Donna Teresa replied.

'Thank you! For your kind words Donna Teresa, we had actually planned to come to you in person this evening and officially inform you of our engagement.'

'I'm very happy for you, and I'm sure she'll get better soon. Anyway I must go now, tomorrow I'll send you one of my servants to look after Francesca.'

'Thank you very much but that won't be necessary, Donna Teresa,' put in Vincenzo, 'We already have someone coming tomorrow morning who'll stay with Francesca until she gets better. Good night Donna Teresa, and thank you again for coming to visit. Good night Maria.'

'Good night Angelo, Vincenzo. Doctor Pedrazza, are you coming with us?' she asked the doctor. Leaving the room not waiting for him to answer.

'Yes, I must be on my way too,' he replied, 'Francesca is in your hands now,' he said, addressing Vincenzo. Then he took him to one side and whispered, 'You found a good answer very quickly, but now we have to find someone before tomorrow morning.'

'You could do that for us,' suggested Angelo. 'When you pass by Papa Joe's house, would you stop to ask if Anna or Felicia could come over?'

'I can do that, but I must really go now, she's waiting,' nodding in the direction Donna Teresa had gone. He joined the ladies outside and taking Donna Teresa's arm they walked off together with Maria trailing behind them.

'Oh Father, I thought that woman would never leave,' exclaimed Angelo. Vincenzo chuckled, at his son's words.

'She had to make sure if Francesca was really sick,' answered Vincenzo. 'It's a pity that Mariano left as well, I wanted to ask him if he'd had a chance to see Juan while he was in the village.'

'Father, you should know by now, Mariano is a very quick-thinking young man. I think it's quite possible that he took the opportunity while he was there to tell him.' Just then, as Angelo finished talking, there was a knock at the door. Father and son looked at each other. With what was going on, they suspected the worse.

'Who's there?' called Vincenzo, as Angelo moved over to the washroom, where behind the door he kept his rifle. If the worse came to the worse, he would die fighting.

'Luigi!' came the reply. Angelo quickly went to open the door.

'Luigi, what are you doing here at this time of the night?' he asked. 'Are you looking for trouble? There are many of Don Camillo's men around, come in quickly.'

'Yes, come and sit down, son,' said Vincenzo.

'Thank you, Don Vincenzo,' panted the young Negro. He was out of breath. He said, 'My cousin, Mariano, sent me here to tell you that Don Camillo has just got home accompanied by two dangerous looking strangers, armed to the teeth they were. He told me that it's going to be very dangerous to go out tonight, that is the message I have to give you.'

'Thank you very much, Luigi,' said Vincenzo Then he proceeded, 'Tell me, where is Mariano at this moment?'

'Not very far from here,' the boy replied. 'He's watching Don Camillo's house.' Luigi looked a bit scared.

'Well, I think you should stay here tonight,' offered Angelo. 'It would be dangerous for you as well to be out tonight.'

'Thank you, but I'd better not,' said Luigi, standing up, and making for the door 'Mariano is waiting for me.'

'As you please,' replied Vincenzo, 'but if you need to come back we'll leave the back door open. Goodnight son and be careful!'

'Goodnight,' replied Luigi, as he departed.

'Father, I think it's time for us to get some sleep,' suggested Angelo.

'Yes son, but we'll go and check on Francesca first to see how she is,' he replied.

They crept into Rosita's room as quietly as possible. She was sleeping peacefully; Angelo kissed her on her forehead. 'Sleep well my love,' he whispered.

Vincenzo and Angelo retired for the night, and in less than ten minutes, they were asleep. The house was now quiet, and the only sound to be heard came from Vincenzo's snores. In her room, Rosita was moving around on tip toes, light as a feather. She quickly and silently dressed in black leggings and a black long sleeved top. She slipped on a black balaclava, tucking in her hair and put on some black gloves. Her mysterious looking figure stealthily moved around the house, first checking in on Vincenzo and then into Angelo's room and the doors were gently opened, then closed behind her. Going down the stairs making sure none of the steps creaked, she slipped out of the back door into the darkness of the night.

CHAPTER TWELVE

Angelo woke on Tuesday morning, he stretched and yawned. He had slept well. Getting up, he went out onto the landing and walked past Rosita's room intending to go down to make coffee. He suddenly remembered what had happened to Rosita the previous night and he turned back towards her room.

'My God, I slept right through without checking in on her once,' he thought to himself feeling very guilty. He entered her room quietly. She was asleep face down on the pillow, he went to her and kissed her cheek. She looked so beautiful and serene lying there, which stirred something inside him, he felt like taking her into his arms and hugging her, but he didn't want to disturb her. He could see she was sleeping peacefully, so he went down. He walked into the kitchen and to his dismay found, Anna, her brother Vittorio, Mariano, Stefano and Vincenzo huddled together whispering around the table.

'Hey, what's going on here?' asked Angelo, 'A reunion? Can I join in?'

'Good morning, Angelo,' they all said together, rather seriously. Anna got up.

'How is Francesca, may I see her?' she asked.

'She's sleeping, it's best not to disturb her,' replied Angelo. Anna sat down again, and Angelo found a cup, poured some coffee out for himself, and then joined them around the table.

'What's wrong with all of you this morning?' he asked. 'Why the long faces?'

Vincenzo explained what they had been talking about in Sicilian. 'Well son, last night while we were sleeping there's been a lot going on outside. Two of Don Camillo's guards were found dead outside his mansion. Someone broke in and killed one of the new men who arrived only yesterday. They, Mariano and his cousin saw the shadow of the killer who was dressed completely in black, head to toe and moved as swiftly and fluidly as a cat.'

'Please Father, stop speaking Sicilian, I just got up and I'm still half asleep,' said Angelo, but Vincenzo carried on in his native tongue.

'Will you be quiet, son, and let me finish. The walls don't have ears, but they can hear and bushes don't have eyes but they can see. Stefano told me that after the attack on Don Camillo's men, the person dressed in black came in the direction of our house.' At hearing this, Angelo was instantly brought to full consciousness, and he stood up.

'What!' he exclaimed. 'Please Stefano, tell me, after you saw this person dressed in black heading this way, where did he end up? Did you see anything else?'

'No, Angelo, sorry, I came straight here,' replied Stefano hesitantly looking down at the ground.

Angelo could tell he was not telling the whole truth. 'Here? You mean the killer came here to this house don't you?' Angelo demanded again. Stefano first looked at Vincenzo and then back to Angelo.

'Yes, Angelo. That person came in here and five minutes afterwards I came in, and I went to sleep on the chair. It was convenient for me to stay, and if anybody had seen me coming here my explanation would be that I was going to stay in case Francesca needed the doctor again.'

Vincenzo decided to intervene.

'Come and get ready for work, Angelo. Then have something to eat, it's getting late.'

'Father, I would like to stay here today,' was his reply.

'No son, you can't. I will make sure that young woman upstairs doesn't go anywhere alone from now on. Anna and I will look after Francesca,' said Vincenzo with authority.

'As you wish, Father, but don't let her leave her room.'

'Not to worry son, I think that she's fully aware that we could get another visit from a certain person, like yesterday,' finished Vincenzo as he was busy preparing a packed lunch for Angelo.

Very well, Father, but I'm not hungry now. I'll go and check on Francesca once more before we leave.'

Angelo washed and dressed, and before he went downstairs again, he entered Rosita's room. He leant on the bed placing one hand on either side of her, she was still lying on her stomach.

'God, I love you so much,' he whispered, as he rested one hand on the centre of her back. She woke, and smiled up at him.

'What are you doing here? Don't you ever sleep at night?' she teased. He smiled and placed his head next to hers, and began rubbing his nose with hers. Then he began nibbling her rosy lips.

'Mmm…' she moaned, 'you taste better than bacon and egg. I think I'm going to eat you all up.'

'You do, do you? Lady, don't encourage me, I don't need that. I'm already in pain for wanting you, so, you stay as you are, while I force myself to move from here. And anyway, it's not night, it's morning and I'm ready to go to work,' he laughed.

'Wait for me, I'll be ready in ten minutes, you're not going to leave me here, are you?'

'You know what? You've got a screw loose,' he joked, and then he kissed her once more and stood up to leave. 'And don't you dare move from this room, if you know what's good for you,' he said.

'Anna is downstairs, I'll send her up and she'll get you anything you need. And in any case, get ready, because tonight we have to have a serious talk. No more of your crazy nightly escapades, bye darling,' and with that, Angelo left for his day's work, hoping he could concentrate on what he was supposed to do with all this going on in his head. Rosita, from the window of her bedroom watched him and the others leaving for work. At that moment there was a knock at the door and in walked Anna with some coffee.

'Mm…' thought Rosita to herself, 'what a boring few days it's going to be.'

'Good morning, Francesca, and how are you this morning? Did you sleep well last night? Or maybe you tossed and turned and bumped into some furniture last night. If so, may I see your bruises?'

'Good morning to you too, Anna. Don't you people ever sleep? And how are you?'

'I'm very fine. Francesca, out there many people are very worried for you,' replied Anna.

'Well, tell them that I'll be out and about in less than a week, God willing.'

'Yes Madam. If God's willing, and if you obey the doctor and stay put,' said Anna, with an authoritarian sound in her voice.

'Come on Anna, spill it out, what have I done now? I have been in this room since yesterday.'

'Drink your coffee, it's getting cold. I'm going to get you some breakfast,' finished Anna, giving Rosita a stern look, for having put herself in danger. Rosita was wondering how they could have found out about last night's adventure so soon.

CHAPTER THIRTEEN

Juan had been at the train station since early morning. He was sitting on a bench, rolling a cigarette, waiting for his brother's train to arrive. While there he noticed two men who were heavily armed, pass by. 'I can smell trouble here,' he thought to himself. At that moment a whistle sounded the approaching of a train, and as the train pulled into the station Juan spied his brother looking out of the window shouting.

'Hey, Juan, over here!' Manuel's life revolved around the railway. He worked five days a week, spending his free time with his fiancée in Bella Vista Village. He enjoyed his job, although sometimes it was hard work when he came across awkward passengers. The train came gradually to a halt. It was several weeks since they had seen each other, and Juan felt very happy to see Manuel again. They hurried to each other and hugged. '

How are you?' asked Juan, 'And what have you got to tell me?'

'Todo bien, (all good)' he replied, for a split second Juan saw a hint of worry on his brother Manuel's face. 'I'm very pleased to see the best brother in the world, and tonight I'm going to see my fiancée, for two beautiful days, so I can forget about the trouble I face on the train some days. Today for instance there were two drunken men in the second carriage, I made myself busy somewhere else. You just don't have any idea how dangerous they can be.'

Juan being two years older than Manuel, had always been responsible for him. Juan thanked God his brother had grown up as a sensible, hardworking young man and had the brains to keep out of trouble.

'Good, I'm very happy for you, Manuel, when are you two going to get married?' asked Juan.

'When I make lots of money my dear brother!'

'Of course, when you became rich, my brother?' Juan laughed, but he knew his brother was a perfectionist, so in his mind Juan wished him well. Then continued by stating. 'If you wait until you have a lot of money Manuel, you'll never get married.' Juan laughed again and then spoke with a more serious tone. 'Anyway, enough of this, I would like to ask you a favour.'

'Hey, my brother, anything for you, but let me start unloading some cases while you're talking.'

'Better than that, I'll give you a hand,' Juan offered. The two brothers started to pull out heavy boxes from the carriage. On one box was written [Hacienda Antigua-Don Camillo]

'Hey, Manuel, what's in these cases, they are very heavy?'

Hey, armano,' replied Manuel, 'you never change, you're always putting your nose into other people's business. You said you wanted to ask me a favour? Don't forget I keep this job because I don't hear and I don't see anything! I keep my nose out of other people's business' said Manuel, scolding his elder brother.

'Very well, I get the message. Listen, do you ever go to visit Uncle Nunziato Curro, when you're in Bella Vista?'

'Yes, sometimes. In fact, I should go more often to see him and his family. We shouldn't forget what he and his brother Vincenzo did for us when we were young. Do you remember when no one wanted to know about us, it was him and his brother Vincenzo who fed us and taught us how to stand on our own two feet?'

'Yes, mi armano, they taught us the way to steer clear of problems. Well, Manuel, today is the day we can do something for them.'

'Of course, Juan, anything,' replied Manuel.

'Well for a start,' began Juan, 'as soon as you arrive at Bella Vista, go and see Nunziato, and warn him that at the end of this week Antonio Marquis is coming to check if there is a grave with the name Francesca Curro on it. He will also ask questions generally of the local people to see if they know if she is who they says she is.'

'One moment Juan, why would he ask that? Is there any doubt that Francesca is not Francesca?'

'Yes, mi armano, there is!' stated Juan, watching the expression on his brother's face change. 'And this is the information that Don Antonio would like to be able to confirm to Don Camillo. If they find out that Francesca is really…' He looked around then whispered, 'And this must not be repeated to anybody we do not trust. She is really, Rosita Miserendino.'

'What!'

'Shh! A lot of people will be in trouble if they find out. Anyway, you have many friends in Bella Vista, can you make sure that Don Antonio doesn't get too close to finding out the truth?'

'Wow! Don't worry, accidents happen every day, you know what I mean?' said Manuel, already getting excited, he was looking forward to an enjoyable couple of days at Bella Vista with friends.

'Manuel, do not use violence, unless it is absolutely necessary,' warned Juan.

'Very well, Juan, I'll do my best. I'll go to see Nunziato tomorrow night with Maria, and at the same time I can see Francesca again, I mean Rosita,' replied Manuel.

'How long has it been since you last saw her?' asked Juan.

'Well I'm ashamed to admit it, but not for a year or so,' he said, mortified.

'You should be ashamed, but if you want to see her, she's here at the Hacienda Antigua. She's going to be engaged to Angelo Curro, and at the moment she is working at the hacienda with him, and living at her Uncle Vincenzo's house. Anyway, what's in these cases?

'I thought you had already forgotten, I don't know for sure, but I think they are arms, and we shouldn't get involved. Look some people are coming this way with a cart, they must be coming to collect them.'

'Very well, mi armano,' said Juan, 'but tell me something first. Have you met any people who have heard what exactly is happening here? Why is there all this extra movement of hired thugs going on?'

'Juan, mi armano, Don Camillo has many enemies. Today, those two drunken men I was talking about a minute ago. I overheard them talking loudly about Don Camillo. Something about the fact that he hadn't kept his word on something, and the people he had let down were very upset and shouldn't be fooled around with.'

'Ha, now I understand why all these strange faces are around the village and at the hacienda,' said Juan. 'Don Camillo must be expecting trouble. Tell me, who were those two drunks on the train?' asked Juan.

'I really don't know, I never saw them before,' replied Manuel.

'Are they still on the train now?' Juan wanted to know.

'You're joking, they've gone. Someone must have thrown them off the train, they were talking too much, and I can't have been the only one to hear them. Somebody obviously didn't agree with what they were saying!' At that moment the train whistle blew loudly.

'Well I must go,' said Manuel, 'Juan, try to keep your nose out of other people's affairs! Because one of these days you'll find yourself in deep trouble.' The two brothers embraced each other and said goodbye, and Manuel hopped back on board just as it started to pull away. The train gathered speed, and Juan waved, yelling.

'Give my love to Maria!'

While this was going on Angelo was having a rough day working without his beloved Rosita, the work seemed harder without her presence. He also couldn't get out of his mind Stefano's story of the goings on the previous night. His suspicions were that Rosita had been responsible. His mind was so preoccupied with these thoughts that he failed to hear Stefano calling him.

'Oh, excuse me, Stefano. I was miles away, what is it?'

'Are you worrying about Francesca? Well don't, tonight you'll be sure to find her in good health.'

'No, Stefano, I'm not worried about her health so much, but about what happened last night,' he said, shaking his head. 'I think she found out something but we had no time to talk to each other this morning.'

'I'm very sure about it,' said Stefano, touching Angelo compassionately on his shoulder. Stefano loved Angelo like an older brother; he had always been there for him when he needed help of any sort. And Vincenzo too, they had both helped so many Negro families in the past. Now the time has come for all those people to return the favour. 'When you get home she'll tell you everything. In fact, why don't you go to see her now, we can get by here without you.'

'I know, Stefano, but if I go, some of Don Camillo's men may start to harass you.'

'Angelo, my friend, have you forgotten what we've got hidden here. We have no intention of letting them do what they want any more, especially now that we have a good reason in the shape of a good leader, Francesca. She's putting her own life in danger for our good, and this has given us courage.'

'I know,' agreed Angelo.

'And one other thing,' continued Stefano, 'Do you know that more people have arrived at the old hacienda?'

'What? Where from?' asked the shocked Angelo. 'How will they survive if we are unable to bring them provisions? We are being watched every hour of every day.'

Of course Angelo was damn right to be afraid, thought Stefano. But now there was no turning back, this battle was inevitable, and was not for greed but for justice.

'Angelo, please, calm down. One way or another with God's help, we'll find a way to help them. You know, these people have come from a place where conditions are very, very bad. They are treated much worse than we are here. They have to work fifteen hours a day for only twenty pesos. More than a third of that is held back to pay for the rent and what is left is hardly enough to buy food with,' said Stefano, angrily.

'I know you Negroes have a hard life, but I didn't realise that people were still treated this way,' said Angelo, really feeling sorry for all these people.

'Not only that,' continued Stefano, 'the majority of them are living four or five to one room, in very cramped conditions.'

'I do understand how desperate these people are, Stefano,' said Angelo, looking around to check if anybody was within earshot. Don Camillo's men were beginning to get to him too. 'How in the name of God can people work in peace, knowing they are being watched continuously by these ugly, ruthless and vicious men? But still, they come here risking everything, risking losing their very own lives. Do they know what danger they are putting themselves in?'

'Oh trust me, Angelo, they know. We've told them of the dangers, but they still prefer to come here to fight, because they believe that sticking together under Rosita's wing, they can defend themselves and rid themselves of this hell once and for all. They have no life anyway. Recently some people have been arrested for no reason whatsoever and they are never seen again. Angelo listen, here in Argentina there are many immigrants, but for us Negroes, life is getting more and more difficult. Anyway, I advise you to go home; you will be more useful there.'

'Very well, you've convinced me, I'll leave you in charge. Why don't you pop by later tonight and we'll have a catch up then. I'll make you a special Italian coffee,' offered Angelo.

'Bye for now,' said Stefano, 'and thank you for the invitation, but I was coming anyway.'

'What a cheek!' laughed Angelo as he went to saddle his horse.

Angelo was happy that he had decided to go home and couldn't wait to hold his beautiful Rosita in his arms. Meanwhile at home Rosita was getting mind bogglingly bored sitting in her room doing nothing. Anna was downstairs helping Vincenzo. Rosita remembered Jon Chian telling her that martial arts should be practised daily for one to remain alert and supple. So to break her boredom she decided to do some exercises. As usual when practicing martial arts, her mind became absorbed in what she was doing, focusing on every movement and channelling all her energy into the exercises she was doing. She imagined herself being in one of Jon Chian's classes.

She was so concentrated on what she was doing that she did not sense Angelo slowly opening her bedroom door. He stood watching her for a few seconds in the doorway and as she turned sharply throwing a high kick in his direction, she saw him. Dropping her leg she screamed for joy and ran at him. He stood his ground waiting for her to jump into his arms, flinging her arms around his neck and her legs around his hips.

'Hey, hey just a moment! I was supposed to do this. After all, I was the one who left my work to come and see you,' he said. They kissed passionately for a few second before being rudely interrupted by Vincenzo's voice coming from the kitchen, asking Angelo if he would like to eat something.

'One moment Father, I'll be down soon,'

'I'm hungry, how about you?' asked Angelo, devouring Rosita with his eyes.

'No, I'm not,' she said sadly. 'I've been so bored stuck in here by myself that I have been picking at food since morning.'

'Then I'll leave you to finish your kicking and punching while I go down to eat. I'll be back as soon as I've finished. Be ready to answer a few questions I have for you.'

Angelo went down and Rosita carried on with her exercises. After a few minutes, Anna appeared. She'd brought up some fresh lemonade, so Rosita had to stop again.

'Francesca, you're sweating a lot,' scolded Anna. 'Dry yourself quickly, before you get ill again from the draught. You don't want to be really ill just before your engagement do you?'

'All right, nanny,' retorted Rosita mockingly. 'I'll do as you say, but I need some water to wash myself first.'

Shaking her head, like a mother does with a spoilt child, Anna went down to fetch a bowl of warm water for Rosita.

As soon as she entered the kitchen she saw Donna Teresa coming in. Discreetly Anna signalled Angelo to go upstairs. As he stood up, for Donna Teresa's benefit she said, 'Quickly Angelo, go upstairs, Francesca isn't feeling too good, I'll follow as soon as I can with a bowl of cold water.'

Angelo entered Rosita's room, quickly explaining in a whisper. He ordered her to lie in the bed as if she was asleep. Not one minute after, Anna and Donna Teresa walked in. Anna started to dab Rosita's sweaty forehead with a wet cloth, Angelo sighed heavily, pretended to be worried about her condition. Donna Teresa asked Angelo what the doctor had said the previous night.

'Well,' began Angelo, placing one hand on his forehead as a sign of despair, 'he doesn't exactly know what's wrong with her. So he said he would come this morning to take some blood for tests, and would return tonight with the results.'

Rosita, still with her eyes closed stirred a little, pretending to wake up and let out a few groans of animated discomfort. She partially opened her eyes and in a pained whisper addressed Angelo.

'What is happening to me? Angelo, help me please. I feel my head is about to burst at any moment, call the doctor, call the doctor for me please.' Angelo took her hand into his as if to comfort her.

'Try to stay calm, Francesca, the doctor will be here tonight, try to sleep now,' he said. Donna Teresa had taken in all that was going on. Francesca all red faced and covered in sweat, Anna's caring attentions, Francesca's moaning and groaning and the way Angelo woefully tended to her, Donna Teresa really believed that Francesca was very sick.

'Well, I can do nothing here to help,' she said. 'It is best if I get out of your way. When the doctor comes, Angelo, would you let him know that I need to speak with him please. He is expecting an answer from me, and perhaps I can give it to him tonight.'

'We will tell him, Donna Teresa, and thank you very much for your kind visit,' replied Angelo. Anna accompanied Donna Teresa down the stairs holding a handkerchief to her nose as if she was weeping, but actually stifling the giggle she was fighting to control. Once Donna Teresa had stepped into the kitchen, Anna closed the door behind her and went to the washroom. She took in a few deep breaths in an effort to control her laughter. The parts the three had played had worked to perfection.

'Dear God,' she said to herself, 'please make that woman leave very soon.'

Donna Teresa had stopped in the kitchen to talk to Vincenzo. But after less than a minute there was a knock at the washroom door.

'Who is it? It's open,' Anna responded. Vincenzo entered.

'Are you all right, Anna?' He asked.

'Yes thank you, Don Vincenzo. Did Donna Teresa leave?'

'Yes, she's gone but she told me something very interesting before leaving.'

Anna hadn't heard Vincenzo's last few words, because she'd burst out into a loud raucous laughter, she laughed so much that the tears were rolling down her face.

'What's happened to you?' Asked Vincenzo, smiling at her obvious amusement. Angelo came to see what was going on, and seeing Anna still laughing uncontrollably, set him off too. He'd guessed why she was laughing, and they held onto each other's arms and laughed some more.

'Is there something I should know?' asked Vincenzo.

'Sorry, Father,' said Angelo, 'but when Donna Teresa had arrived, Francesca had just finished her exercises and she was dripping with sweat. So when Donna Teresa came up to see Francesca, she was lying in bed with me and Anna trying to cool Francesca down. We gave a very convincing performance! Oh Father, you should have seen Donna Teresa's face.'

'But son, I did see Donna Teresa's face, she was looking very concerned, and would you like to know what she told me?' he asked, looking serious.

'What Father, what did she say?' asked Angelo.

'Well son, what the lady told me, I'm going to tell Francesca first,' he said even more seriously. Anna and Angelo were a little more concerned now at the tone of Vincenzo's voice.

Meanwhile upstairs, Rosita had got out of bed, and had watched through her window as her mother was leaving. Each time she saw her mother, she wondered what was going on in her head. If she still thought about her at all? Is she as selfish as she was fifteen years ago? And what would she say if Rosita confronted her, what would she say? Would she really report her to Don Camillo, the man whom once used to sneak into her mother's bedroom, while her father was away? It made her angry to remember that soon after her father was killed, her mother married Don Camillo, the head of a bunch of bandit's. But very soon now, he would die by her hand. Everything she had imagined the previous night had deserted her, and she sighed in despair. There was no sense fighting with her mother, at least not yet.

Vincenzo led Anna and Angelo up the stairs, as soon as he reached the landing, the old man knocked at Rosita's bedroom door, and he entered at her request.

'Come in, it's open,' she said jovially.

'Well, we're all ears,' said Angelo and Anna in unison to Vincenzo whilst sitting on Rosita's bed. Angelo was now a little worried about what his father was going to say. Vincenzo settled himself carefully into a chair, and clasped his hands over his stomach.

'Well, my dears,' he began, 'Donna Teresa told me that the old hacienda…' he hesitated, then he said, looking direct at Rosita's face, 'The hacienda, will be an engagement gift for Angelo and Francesca, and they may start to renovate it as soon as they wished.'

Rosita screamed, and began jumping up and down on the bed. She embraced Angelo, then Vincenzo and Anna. That, of course was indeed good news. The men who were hiding in the old hacienda could start cleaning the place up immediately, and work on the land.

'Uncle,' she said after they all calmed themselves down, 'If Papa Joe and his family didn't want to work for the Hacienda Antigua any more, would they be in trouble?'

'Why are you asking me that? I didn't know that Papa Joe wanted to leave the hacienda!'

'No, Uncle, it's not that Papa Joe wants to leave, it's I who want him and his family to come and work for me at my grandparents' old hacienda,' she said, looking at Anna, as if she could provide her with the answer. Even though in the back of her mind she knew that at her request they would jump for joy.

'Well, my dear, in that case if they would like to work for you, I don't see how Don Camillo could stop them. Anyway, my young people, don't expect too much all at once.'

'Well,' began Rosita, rubbing her hands together. 'I don't think we have much to fear right now,' she replied, and looking at all three of her bedroom guests, as if it could help her to recapture all the adventure of the previous night.

'What makes you think that?' asked Angelo.

'A little bird told me that Don Camillo is in a real mess. He has made lots of enemies with his greed.'

'And who is this little bird?' asked Angelo, rubbing his stubbly cheek and thinking he really needed a shave.

He was sitting on the bed with his legs crossed. Rosita glanced at him, he looked so handsome, she thought, with his strong long legs in his black leather trousers, his white shirt and black waistcoat. Those eyes, those brown almond shaped eyes, were devouring her, she had to look away or she would forget what she was about to say. She looked for a few long seconds at Vincenzo. He was leaning back in his chair with his back against the wall. Then she looked at Anna who sat on a chair next to Vincenzo.

'Sorry, I cannot tell you right now, perhaps one day soon.'

'Listen, Francesca, my dear,' said Vincenzo, 'Do you think we don't know about your little escapade last night? It was a crazy thing to do, but thank God nothing happened to you. Now, we are waiting for you to tell us what you discovered, tell us something!' commanded Vincenzo.

Rosita thought she could get away with it, but as they had found out what she had been up too, she thought she'd better spill the beans. After all, they were her family, and her best friends.

'Very well Uncle, if you insist, I'll explain it all. Please forgive me firstly for not telling you what I had planned to do last night; I didn't want to worry any of you.' She took a deep breath and then continued. 'It was easy getting past Don Camillo's guards; two were distracted chatting with some women. They were relaxed because they knew there were guards and dogs all around. But you see, Uncle, I went prepared. Did you notice a rabbit had disappeared from the back of the wash room?'

'No dear, I hadn't noticed, but we'll discuss that later,' he said. They all laughed. 'Carry on,' said Vincenzo, and looked at her with amusement.

'Well, I took the rabbit, and cut it up into pieces and sprinkled some sleeping potion onto them, which my good friend Jon Chian had given me before I left Bella Vista. He said I maybe would have need of it someday, so, when the two dogs sensed my approach...'

Rosita hesitated for a long moment; she was recalling a mental picture of what had happened the night before. Then she proceeded, licking her lips and inadvertently making Angelo's body tingle with the desire of tasting those now moist lips.

'When they ran towards me, it was lucky that they hadn't barked. So, I threw the pieces of meat to them, which they devoured in an instant, chewing and crunching through the bones. Having eaten the meat they were calmer towards me, sniffing all around me for more food and pretty soon were sprawled on the ground asleep. I entered the mansion from the passage that I showed to Angelo a couple of days ago.' Rosita, breathed in deeply again, and from the bed she moved to the window as if she needed some fresh air, then slowly she turned to face Angelo.

'As you know, Angelo, the passageway led straight to my mother's bedroom. Luckily nobody was around, the corridor was deserted too. Then suddenly I remembered that in my mother's room behind the picture of the Madonna holding the baby Jesus Christ, there was a safe without a lock. My father used to keep his money there, and my mother kept her and my grandmother's jewellery in there too.'

Vincenzo was looking at her with an expression of concern etched into his face. His mind was working overtime, imagining Don Camillo and his men turning everything in the house upside down, and then killing them all.

'You didn't take anything, did you?' he asked her, praying to God she hadn't brought any of the jewellery home. 'Because if they come looking and find them here, we're as good as dead.'

'Come on, Dad! You don't really think Francesca would do such a thing?' asked Angelo passionately, coming to Rosita's defence.

'Thank you, Angelo,' she said gratefully. Then looking again at Vincenzo she continued. 'Please don't worry Uncle. I know you don't think I'm that stupid? I took everything, yes, but hid them elsewhere in the hacienda, in a secure place. One of these days we'll need them, anyway. After I'd hidden the jewellery, I ventured downstairs and was surprised not to see any guards hovering about. But I was of course mistaken, as they were all in the kitchen eating. I did not want to push my luck but before leaving I managed to overhear the conversation going on in the kitchen. This conversation explained to me why all these new men have been brought in. It's good news for us; we can be more relaxed in our movements as the men are not here on our account.' Rosita stopped. But Angelo suspected that there was a lot more to it than that.

'One moment, my dearest,' he said, smiling at her. 'Why don't you tell us how it really happened, when you were eavesdropping on Don Camillo and his friends? We have been told that there was a fight, and someone was badly wounded.'

'Oh that, yes,' admitted Rosita. She thought she could again get away with it. 'I got into a bit of a fright. I was listening at the keyhole when I heard the door to the corridor open. The first man who came out had a scar on his cheek and was very fast with his gun, he told me to put my hands up and that if I moved he would fill my stomach with bullets. The second man who had a round baby face said, "Hey look at what we've got here, a shy one! He's covered his face."' Thank God, they did not realise that I was a woman.

'Anyway, I had my hands behind my head. Quickly, because there wasn't any time to think, I pulled out two concealed knives which I'd strapped across the back of my shoulders. I waited for my chance, and as soon as the man with the scarred face turned and spoke to Babyface, telling him to call Don Camillo, that is when I threw the knives at them.

'Scar-face went down silently because the knife hit him in the throat, but Babyface had a chance to scream because the knife lodged in his chest. That was bad luck for me, because five seconds after Babyface's scream two more men emerged from the kitchen...'

She stopped for an instant and looked at their shocked faces.

'I knew there was no way to escape out of the front door, so I ran back towards my father's old study, luckily managing to dodge their bullets. I managed to lock the door behind me to buy me some time.

Luckily for me nothing had changed in the room. I managed to hide in the secret passageway I'd escaped through fifteen years ago just in time. I heard the study door being broken down and two men came into the room to search for me, I heard their heavy boots racing around the floor. Then one man said he couldn't find anybody in here and that he, meaning me, had disappeared into thin air. I waited sitting absolutely still for five minutes to make sure no one was around. At first I thought I'd get out via the passageway, but I decided to go out the same way I came in, through my mother's bedroom, even though I knew it was very risky.

I'd heard the two men running down the corridor back towards the kitchen. I opened the secret door very slightly, enough for me to check that all was clear. I crept out into my father's study and back out into the corridor. There was uproar in the house, but it was now concentrated outside. They were looking for me thinking I must have got out of a window, so I left the study very quietly.

On tip toes I crept in a semi-squat hugging the wall and I snuck into my mother's bedroom. It was dark in there but I knew where the wardrobe was, so I got down on all fours and cat walked over to the wardrobe, getting into it just in time as they both began to stir. From inside the wardrobe I could hear Don Camillo and my mother's raised voices demanding to know what was going on and what was all the shouting about.

I entered the passageway and made my way out onto the roof. I was worried about the few men I had left down there searching for me, so, very carefully, I looked over the ledge and saw them running around looking for me. I had to wait about twenty minutes for the search to calm down. Two of them stopped just below where I was hiding. One of them was holding his lantern up to the trees and a revolver in his other hand, obviously thinking that I could be hiding there. The other one was about five metres behind him holding a rifle and just below where I was hiding.

'What I did next was my only chance to get out of there, so I jumped onto the second man, landing directly on his neck breaking it instantly. I think he died the second we slumped to the ground, not even having the chance to utter a single sound or cry,'

Rosita hesitated. Her audience of three people were still looking and listening to her dumb struck. She stopped for a few long seconds as she poured some water from a jug into glass and gulped it down all in one go.

'Where was I? Oh yes. The man with the lantern obviously thought that I was his companion because as he backed away from the trees he said, 'Well there doesn't seem to be anyone around here.' 'I pulled his head back by grabbing a handful of his hair, and I slit his throat with the small dagger I carry in my belt. Soon after that, I saw another two men a bit further away, I slipped into the shadows and crept away from the hacienda. When I finally reached home, I approached from behind the house and I entered the stable. I stopped in there for twenty minutes in case anyone was around, to regain my composure and to get changed out of my black outfit. I then slowly crept to the front of the house, but nobody appeared, so I slipped inside the front door. That's all that happened. The rest you all know.'

Vincenzo sat there with his legs stretched out, looking at Rosita and rubbing his cheeks with his hands, again thinking how lucky she'd been not to get caught or hurt. He prayed silently thanking God for her safe return. Angelo still didn't think she had told them everything, so he probed.

'You haven't told us what you discovered inside, am I right?'

Rosita smiled. 'Ah... yes, very well.' So, she began to tell them what she had heard. 'A couple of years ago Don Camillo had made a contract with two powerful Italian and two Spanish families from Tucuman City. Their association owned a large warehouse, where they stored and packed their goods such as meat, fruit and vegetables for retail markets. He took a lot of money in advance from these people, but then went back on his agreement to give them his crops, instead preferring to sell them to foreign contractors who paid him a better rate. This happened two years in a row, and he'd given the excuse that the crop yield had been poor, and he'd make it up the following year. Now these people are becoming agitated and impatient because now there are many warehouse workers out of work and less food on the markets. I get the impression that if we do not do something very quickly, we will all be in the middle of it with a ton of trouble.'

'Mmm…' muttered Vincenzo thinking to himself this girl is a real leader, she has real balls and more courage than any man. 'And what can we do about this?' he asked her. 'We don't even know who these people are.'

'Don't worry, Uncle, I know their names and I know where I can find them.'

'Really, Francesca, and how can we approach these people?' asked Angelo, he was thinking exactly the same thing as his father about his fiancée. 'They'll think we're spying for Don Camillo,' continued Angelo. He was right of course, these people could take them for spies, but he was sure that Rosita had already thought of this and had something hidden up her sleeve.

'I'll make sure that they don't think this. With my strategy I promise that everything will go well,' assured Rosita.

'Francesca, you're not really thinking of meeting these people face to face?' Angelo asked.

'But I must my darling, not alone, but with you. You see, today when the doctor comes back, with his help we can arrange it.'

'Darling, what you're trying to do is madness!' exclaimed Angelo.

'I beg you Angelo, trust me and you'll see, everything will be all right.'

'May I interrupt?' asked Vincenzo. 'I want to ask you a question. You said that you know the names of these people, can you tell us?'

'Of course, Uncle, I can tell you but not right now,' she said flicking her eyes sideways at Anna.

'Yes, I understand,' said Vincenzo.

Rosita didn't like to say too much in front of Anna, because if anyone stopped her to interrogate her, she may divulge something out of fear of being hurt. Vincenzo got up.

'I think we've talked enough now, I'm going for an afternoon nap outside, in the fresh air.'

'Me too,' said Anna, following Vincenzo.

'Well, I'm staying inside to keep Francesca company,' said Angelo.

'Hey Francesca, if he behaves badly just tell me and I'll kick him out,' said Anna, jokingly. They all laughed as Anna and Vincenzo went downstairs. Angelo grinned at Rosita and he went to shut the door.

'And what do you think you're doing?' asked Rosita, with a twinkle in her eye.

'What I should have done hours ago, I'll just shut the door so we won't be disturbed. They went to sleep outside, we'll sleep here.' What Angelo had said he meant, they settled themselves on the bed and soon dozed off, embracing one another, as if it was a winter's night. A couple of hours later they woke to the sound of cartwheels, and horses' hooves approaching.

'Oh dear God, Angelo, if I'm not mistaken, the doctor's here!' said Rosita.

'No, it's too early for the doctor,' he replied.

She went to the window to check.

'Quick, it is him, we must get dressed,' she said. They hurriedly dressed and Angelo went down and into the wash room to splash his face with cold water. He then went outside to welcome the doctor who was talking with the others.

'Hello, Doctor,' said Angelo. 'Francesca's getting up now. Would you like something to drink?'

'Yes, thank you, something cold.'

'Is freshly squeezed orange all right?'

'Yes son, it's good for me,' replied the doctor. Angelo asked his father and Anna if they wanted something to drink too. They accepted, and at that moment Rosita's head appeared out of the bedroom window.

'Hey! Don't forget me!' she cried.

'How could I forget you?' Angelo answered, going back inside. The doctor and the others laughed.

'Listen to those two love birds,' said the doctor, 'I have good news for them.' At this Anna got up, thinking the doctor would want to speak to Vincenzo alone.

'I think I should give Angelo a hand,' she said, 'and Doctor, I think they know the good news already.'

'They do, do they?' laughed the doctor.

'Shall we go in?' invited Vincenzo, to his guest.

'Good idea,' replied the doctor. So, they followed Anna in, and sat themselves at the table. It was more pleasant outside, as a fresh breeze had begun to blow gently, but inside was more convenient, as they could speak without worrying if anybody could over hear them. They waited for their drinks, and not long after, Rosita appeared in the kitchen.

'You are all cruel people to leave me alone upstairs,' she said jokingly. 'May I join you?'

'Of course, my dear,' said Doctor Pedrazza, getting up at Rosita's arrival, 'but only for five minutes. Come and sit next to me.' He put both his hands out palm up to invite her to go to him. 'I have something to tell everyone.'

Rosita placed her hands in the doctor's. 'Doctor, it's a pleasure to have you with us here. But speak now, you have our undivided attention.' At that moment, Angelo arrived with the drinks.

'Ha, about time!' said Dr Pedrazza, taking a glass and drinking it down quickly.

'That's better, now I can speak. Well, last night when I accompanied Donna Teresa home, we were walking along talking. So I told her that you two were interested in buying a piece of land on which to build a house, ready for when you get married, if you can get together enough money. I then, said to her, that I recalled she had said once that she wished to sell the old hacienda.'

Dr Pedrazza, proceeded, with a wide grin across his face. 'So, she asked me how much money you'd got, and I replied that I wasn't sure, and that maybe you'd have to borrow money from the bank. Then Donna Teresa stopped walking and turned to face me, she said that maybe you two won't need to borrow the money. She'd wanted to get rid of that piece of land for a long time now, because it belonged to her ex-mother and father-in-law and she never really got on with them. Actually, she said she loathed them, but she wanted to speak with Don Camillo about it first and if I was coming this way again today she would give me a definite answer. Which she has, so she and Don Camillo have agreed to giving you two the old hacienda as an engagement and wedding present as long as you agree to stay working for them at the hacienda! And what do you think about that, my lucky children?' finished Dr Pedrazza, all excited.

Angelo told Dr Pedrazza that Donna Teresa had come back again at lunch time to see how Francesca was doing. He also told him in great detail about all the play acting they had done in her presence to fool her, and how good their performances were. He then went on to tell the Doctor that Donna Teresa had already told Vincenzo about the old Hacienda, and that she wanted to see Dr Pedrazza again later, after he visited Francesca again.

'Maybe she wants to confirm her intention to me?' Said the doctor.

'I hope so,' said Rosita 'Now I want to ask you a favour, doctor.'

'What is it, dear?'

Suddenly there was a great clanging sound, in the kitchen. They all turned around towards where the noise had come from, all startled, and confused. Four pairs of eyes were trained on one mortified Anna, who had just dropped a pot full of vegetables onto the stone floor. Anna was so embarrassed that she didn't say a word and didn't want to hear what they had to say to her, so she made herself busy clearing up the mess. They all looked at each other and then burst out laughing.

'Well,' began Rosita, 'what I would like to ask is, when you go to see Donna Teresa, would you tell her that you wish to send me to a specialist in Tucuman City for a second opinion and further tests.'

'Why there, in that city? And so far away too!' interrupted the doctor.

'Please, let me finish, because there's a big hospital there with better facilities for blood testing, and all the latest equipment.'

'My goodness,' exclaimed the doctor. 'What fancy plans have you got whirling around that pretty head of yours now?'

'Well doctor, what do you say?' pleaded Rosita totally ignoring his question, her beautiful brown eyes looking straight into his, searching for a clue as to what he was thinking. 'Can you do this for me? Can you tell her tonight? Because I need to make this trip in order to fulfil my plans.'

'Well, if you look at me with those beautiful puppy dog eyes, how can I refuse?' he replied. 'I'll do my best, Francesca. Now I must go if I am to see Donna Teresa, if I have any important news I'll come back again tonight,' said Dr. Pedrazza. He got to his feet, thanked them for the refreshment and left. He went directly to see Donna Teresa and Don Camillo.

CHAPTER FOURTEEN

Meanwhile things were afoot outside of Las Cejias. Things that would play their part in the final plan.

In the City of Tucuman, the families of Salvatore Ruvolo, Francesco Maiorana, Rosario Mendoza and Miguel Mendoza were beginning to organise a very big party for the upcoming wedding of Giuseppina Maiorana, Francesco's daughter to Miguel Mendoza of the Mendoza brothers.

At the same time while the women were organising the details of the party, the men were preparing a meeting to discuss their future plan to pay Don Camillo back for his treachery by attacking the hacienda. These families stood to lose a lot of money thanks to Don Camillo's underhand tactics and were worried about the future of their businesses and their worker's livelihoods. Very soon Don Camillo and his other business associates, who had all colluded to dishonour their contract, would be in for the shock of their lives. The three Tucuman families were no longer prepared to let things go on as they had been. Rosita had found out details about these families and their plans. So as a matter of urgency, she had to meet with these families before they carried out their assault on Don Camillo's hacienda. She was worried that too many innocent workers had suffered enough already and that they may accidentally get mixed up in this fight and maybe lose their lives. They weren't to know of Don Camillo's corrupt deals outside of their work.

In the village of Bella Vista, on the Wednesday evening, Nunziato Curro had just opened the front door to a surprise visit from

Manuel Pellegrini, and his fiancée, Maria Rossos. It had been a long time since they'd seen each other and Nunziato had been expecting to see his friend Jon Chian at the door. Nunziato stood silent at the door, so Manuel spoke first.

'Hey, Uncle, are you going to make me stand here, on the doorstep? Aren't you going to invite my fiancée and I in?' He joked, as his uncle looked at him with joy in his eyes.

'Of course, Manuel, come in, come in.' Nunziato embraced Manuel as a father would a son. Nunziato's wife, Battistina came down at that moment, wanting to know who was there. Then she saw Manuel.

'Dear God, what a surprise,' she said as tears welled up in her eyes. Manuel embraced her and a lump formed in his throat.

'Forgive me for not coming before,' he croaked, 'it doesn't mean I have forgotten about you though.'

Maria, Manuel's fiancée felt a little left out, so she interrupted. 'Can I be one of the family too?' she asked, smiling.

'I'm sorry,' blurted out Manuel, 'Uncle, Auntie, this is my fiancée, Maria. Maria, these two lovely people are my adopted parents.' Maria felt a little confused but she shook their hands and kissed them on both cheeks.

'Well,' said Battistina, 'you two arrived just in time, supper is ready so you can eat with us.'

'You're very kind,' answered Manuel, 'but you did not expect us, and have only prepared for two. Please excuse us and carry on eating.'

'Nonsense, we'll share what we have as we did when you were young,' insisted Nunziato.

In the end, it was Battistina who convinced Manuel and Maria to stay and share their meal. They all sat together at the kitchen table to eat. They chatted for a while about the past and the future, filling in some details for Maria. Manuel and Maria complimented Battistina on the food.

'I know,' laughed Battistina, 'that the pasta with Pinto beans I make is the best! Can you smell anything else?'

'No,' Manuel answered, 'I can only smell the pasta.'

'Then I'll tell you what we have next on today's menu. Cannoli ripieni!'

'Ah!' responded Manuel, his taste buds activated at the sound of this. 'A Sicilian sweet! You usually make them for the feast of Saint Joseph.'

'Yes,' Battistina replied, 'in fact, in three days' time it is Saint Joseph's Day.'

'What, already? How could I forget?' Manuel exclaimed. 'That means Easter is almost upon us.'

'Yes,' said Nunziato, his voice subdued and sad, 'and this year we'll be on our own.'

'That's not necessarily true, Maria and I can keep you company,' replied Manuel. 'Maria and I will invite ourselves over for Easter day, how is that?'

'You are joking, aren't you? Maria's family will be expecting you to spend this special day with them.'

'No, Auntie, I'm very serious,' said Manuel. 'In fact we can spend a couple of days with you, and we can even sleep here if there's room.'

'Of course there is,' answered Nunziato.

As the evening passed, after the bean pasta was devoured, the tray of a dozen cannoli was transformed into a tray of crumbs.

'I'm so full, my stomach feels like it will burst,' said Manuel. 'We have finished everything.'

'You're wrong,' said Battistina, laughing, 'we have still got lots left for Saint Joseph's Day.'

'Bueno,' said Manuel, 'but I must go for a walk now, to aid my digestion.' Manuel really needed to speak with Nunziato. He didn't know how to start, as he hadn't seen Nunziato for a long time. He felt awkward, as he had to tell him that the real reason he had come to see them was to bring a message from his brother Vincenzo.

'What do you think, Uncle, shall we go together?' he suggested.

'With pleasure,' replied Nunziato getting up, 'we can visit a friend of mine at the same time. Jon Chian, he lives not far from here, do you remember him?'

'How could I forget him?' replied Manuel, feeling a bit ashamed again for staying away for so long from his best friends. But when you are young and go out in the world, to fend for yourself, it's easy to lose yourself in your own life and forget important people or things for a while. They excused themselves from the two women and went out. Once outside, they took a few steps and Nunziato stopped Manuel by taking hold of his elbow and looked him directly in the eye.

'Have you got a problem you need to speak to me about?' he asked.

Manuel gave a small knowing smile.

'It's a long time since we saw each other. I'd almost forgotten that you could read my face like a book. I'm ashamed for staying away for so long, Uncle, but don't worry I'm not in trouble. Uncle, yesterday I saw my brother, and he asked me to bring you news about Francesca, and I'm here to pass it on to you.'

'My God! Has anything happen to her?'

'Calm down, calm down Uncle. Francesca is in good health and she's happy. Do you know that on Saturday they are having a party?'

'I know, it's Saint Joseph's Day, everyone celebrates this day,' said Nunziato smiling.

'No, Uncle, not only that. Angelo and Francesca are going to be celebrating their engagement too.' Nunziato was overcome with this news and the tears started to well up in his eyes.

'Are you all right?' asked Manuel, 'aren't you pleased?'

'Of course, I'm very pleased, you can't imagine how much. May God bless them; I pray that one day Francesca will find peace in her heart. You know how much joy she gave us.'

'I do know that,' said Manuel. 'Listen, Uncle, is there some place where we can sit and talk without being overheard?'

Nunziato nodded his head yes. 'Come Manuel, I know a place not very far from here,' said Nunziato. He suspected that there was more news, but very different from what Manuel had given so far. Rosita had probably organised an attack. It was too early, and it was very dangerous. He hoped that in the process of the battle she wouldn't be hurt. They walked for almost ten minutes, and presently arrived at a place which from outside its tall fencing looked just like woodland. But then they came to a high wooden gate which they entered.

'I have been here before!' exclaimed Manuel, as he remembered this was Jon Chian's residence. Such beautiful flowers and plants surrounded them. A soft breeze was blowing, there was an air of tranquillity about the place. Suddenly a voice interrupted his thoughts.

'Welcome, my friends.'

Manuel, turned to face a smiling, white-haired old man who was not very tall, it was Jon Chian.

'I was admiring your beautiful garden,' said Manuel. By now the old man had recognised him and the two bowed to each other the Chinese way, before embracing.

'I'm very happy to see you again, son,' said Jon Chian. 'Hello Nunziato, I was thinking about you, come I will get my wife to bring you something to drink.'

'No thank you my friend, perhaps later,' said Nunziato, 'Manuel here came with a message from Francesca, and he doesn't want any strangers to overhear it, so that's why I brought him here to speak freely.'

'Very well, I'll leave you, and you two can speak together,' said Jon Chian.

'No Jon, that isn't necessary, you can stay. We have nothing to hide from you.'

'Very well Nunziato, if you wish we'll go and sit under that tree over there.'

They sat together, and Manuel started to speak. He began with the visit he had had from his brother Juan at Las-Cejias, and the message he gave to him to bring to Nunziato. Then went on to tell them that Don Camillo was trying to find out details about Francesca.

'Why would he want to do such a thing?' asked Nunziato, 'How can he suspect anything? What has Francesca done to make him suspicious?'

'It's not only what she did but Francesca has a few of her late father's physical features. As well as his character,' said Manuel.

'This is true,' agreed Nunziato.

'Anyway, as I was saying. Don Camillo has asked one of his friends if he would ask around about you and your family and, if he would go to the cemetery to check if there is a gravestone showing Francesca's name. Anyway, Don Camillo wants all these particulars and you know, Don Antonio Marquis has all the right contacts so that he can find this out quickly.'

'Don't worry yourself, Manuel. You see, they don't have anything to find out about us,' said Nunziato, and he began to form a plan in his mind. He had heard about this Don Antonio Marquis, he had a reputation of being a nasty piece of work.

'Uncle, don't forget, people like that make up information if they can't find what they want,' proceeded Manuel. 'But anyway, I already told a few of my friends who work on the railway, that when Don Antonio Marquis arrives in Bella Vista, he should be followed. And if he makes a wrong step he will accidentally get his neck broken for sure.'

'When do you think this man will arrive here?' asked Jon Chian, addressing Manuel.

'Well, if it's like my brother told me, it will be tomorrow afternoon,' answered Manuel.

'Very well,' said Jon Chian, 'I too have a few tricks up my sleeve for him. You'll see that Nunziato and his family will be left in peace very soon.'

'Thank you, my friend, it's times like this that you find out who your real friends are,' said Nunziato, patting his hand on Jon Chain's shoulder. These two had been like brothers for years.

'Very well, we'll keep an eye on this nasty piece of work. If there's any news, I'll let you know straightaway and if I cannot come personally, I'll send one of my friends,' said Manuel.

'How are things going for Francesca at the hacienda?' Nunziato wanted to know. Not only was he missing her like hell, but knowing her character so well, he was also worried about her. What's more, he had to listen to his wife talk about Rosita incessantly and he had to put up with her crying night after night. They both prayed to God to protect her and not let her come to any harm in any way. The only way he could help his wife was to hold her in his arms, and reassure her that nothing would happen to their adopted daughter, because she has many friends around her to protect her. Sometimes though, he wished he could totally believe this for himself.

'It depends on what you're asking specifically, Uncle,' replied Manuel. 'If you want to know about friends, she has many, if you want to know about risks, yes there are those. You see, things are getting a bit complicated.'

'How is that?' asked Nunziato.

'Don Camillo has got many new men posted around the hacienda, and some also in the village itself. But this is not so much about him suspecting something about Francesca, but he is afraid of other enemies he has made. With the extra manpower, not only is Rosita in danger, but all the workers at the hacienda are too,' said Manuel, unable to hide the emotion in his voice. He was getting more and more emotionally involved in this matter, more than he thought he would. After all, apart from Maria, these people are the only family he has.

'Do you know who these enemies of Don Camillo's are?' asked Jon Chian.

'No,' answered Manuel, 'I do not know them personally, but I know they are not the kind of people who take kindly to being messed around.'

'Would you like to explain to us what exactly he did to them?' persisted Jon Chian. So, Manuel began to explain how Don Camillo had gone back on his word to give his hacienda's produce straight to them, even though they had paid in advance. They found out that he had sold his produced to a foreign trader. On hearing all this, Nunziato had become very serious and it hadn't gone unnoticed by Jon Chian; they had been friends for so many years. And he knew exactly what he was thinking.

'Nunziato, don't be afraid,' he said. 'Francesca is a very intelligent girl, and I know she will find a way to stop any unnecessary violence towards the workers at the Hacienda Antigua. If she does as I think she will, and we do our job right with Don

Antonio Marquis, Francesca will have only one problem to solve. Anyway, my friends,' continued Jon Chian, 'it's getting dark and it's not so nice to stay outside any longer, the mosquitoes are coming out to feast on our blood.'

'Yes you're right Jon,' agreed Nunziato, 'I think its better that we get back home before Battistina and Maria start worrying.'

'Oh no you don't!' retorted Jon Chian. 'You have to come in for ten minutes, at least to say hello to my wife, Giovanna, and we can drink a glass of something together.'

Nunziato and Manuel accepted Jon's invitation, so the three all rose together and walked towards Jon's house. Before they went inside, Jon spoke to Nunziato, and told him that he had a very good idea.

'What about?' asked Nunziato.

'Let's go and have a drink first, then I'll tell you.'

Nunziato smiled at his friend, and placed one arm around his shoulder. Jon was much shorter than Nunziato, but deadly, if someone crossed his path. He was a master of martial arts and had taught his son, his daughter and Francesca these skills as well.

'You, Jon, are always mysterious in your way, but I'm very happy to be your friend!'

'I'm very happy too, to have you and your wife as neighbours,' said Jon, as they reached the house. Jon opened the door for them and they all went in. Giovanna Chian was in the corridor waiting for him, she looked a little concerned but smiled and bowed her head to her guests, Nunziato and Manuel.

'What's the matter?' Jon asked his wife.

'Nothing bad, Chen has arrived with his future wife.'

'Ah! Very good, come in my friends,' he gestured with a wave of his hand, and they all filed into the kitchen. Chen was there and as soon as he saw them, he got up and moved away from the chair.

He then approached his father and embraced him. This gesture was not a Chinese tradition, but as they had grown up closely with Nunziato's family they had adopted the Italian way of showing their affection with family and friends. He then greeted Nunziato and Manuel in the same manner. Jon bowed to his son's fiancée, Sandra, and asked his wife to bring drinks for his friends. Giovanna went and did as her husband asked and soon returned with a tray of glasses and bottles of liqueur.

The two women then left the kitchen. Jon poured out some liqueur for the four of them and they raised their glasses and toasted each other. 'Salute', they all chorused, then downed the shots in one go. Jon refilled them again and rose his glass once again.

'We drink this to Francesca's Victory,' he said. They all rose and repeated 'To Francesca's Victory', downing their drinks again and sitting back down. This time Chen refilled the glasses and stood again with his glass raised.

'Drink with me now, to our conquest,' he requested, looking his father straight in the eyes. It was a challenge. Jon smiled, he knew very well what Chen had meant and in his mind he agreed with his son. The others followed suit, they looked like the four musketeers but with glasses instead of swords.

'I know what you're all wondering,' he said. 'What am I doing here? Well, we're in the company of friends and I now I can speak freely. Up until a couple of years ago, I enjoyed my job and the people I worked with, but recently things have changed and I can no longer work in that place. It's not only for myself that I have decided to leave, but for my future wife too,' continued Chen looking at his father again. 'There is no future for anybody now, you know this, Father. I felt like one of a flock of sheep surrounded by wolves, when one got hungry they would open their mouth and swallow us. Father, I swear to you that I get the impression that all those rich people and people with authority are not human. I only hope that you can understand me, Father?' said Chen emotionally. There was a sadness in his eyes. Jon got up and put one hand on his son's shoulder.

'Of course I understand you, my son,' he said. 'Who else if not me? Now I know why your mother looked concerned when we came in.'

'Father,' interrupted Chen, 'this is not the only reason why I left my job…'

'What is it, my son?' asked Jon, although he knew already what his son's next answer was.

'It's about Francesca; you know she is like a sister to me.'

'Yes I know that too,' Jon answered, 'Francesca is in our hearts and lives too.'

'Father, I thought I was the only one who felt this way, about wanting to support her.'

'No, dear son, at this moment in this room all four of us support her fully.'

Chen's mood brightened, he got up once more and refilled the glasses for a final toast. Up until now Manuel had remained silent. He plucked up some courage to speak but his head was starting to spin, as the liqueur was strong.

'Now you have to drink with me,' he cried dizzily. 'To my new job, as I resigned my railway job tonight!'

Instantly, Nunziato, Jon, and Chen all looked at each other and then started to laugh. They were pleased that they had all made this decision together.

'I think,' continued Manuel, now unsteady on his feet, 'we should be on our way, the women will soon be sending a search party out for us!'

'Yes,' answered Nunziato, 'we'll go straightaway. Good night Jon, Chen,'

'Goodnight,' replied Jon and Chen in unison. 'It has been a pleasure, we'll see each other tomorrow one way or another.'

'I hope our business tomorrow is finished quickly,' slurred Manuel, holding on to Nunziato's jacket to stop himself from overbalancing.

CHAPTER FIFTEEN

While Manuel and the others had been getting drunk in Bella Vista, back at the Hacienda Antigua, Rosita and the others were celebrating, because Dr Pedrazza had come back from Donna Teresa's with the confirmation that she had definitely decided to give the old hacienda to Francesca and Angelo as a wedding gift. The very respected doctor described how Donna Teresa had said to him, with tears in her eyes, that she had strangely developed a fondness for Francesca like a mother would for a daughter. Apparently she had already had the legal documents prepared for the transfer of ownership, and all she had to do now was sign them in the presence of her lawyer with the doctor himself and Don Saverio Scalabrini the priest present as witness.

Rosita was overflowing with excitement, so much so that she went around the kitchen kissing everyone, and thanking the doctor especially with a big long hug. She was so emotionally punch drunk that she was unable to hold back tears from welling up and stinging her eyes. She had to excuse herself and rushed to her room to compose herself. Of course she felt happy for the way things were going but at the same time she had to suppress the feelings of anger against her mother for how she had betrayed her father all those years ago and abandoned her as a child.

Angelo waited a minute or so then headed up to check on her. He found her sitting on the floor with her back against the bed. He didn't say a word, he just sat next to her silently, placing his right arm around her and just held her. He knew why she was crying, of course, she had been denied her mother's love when she was very young. When she'd needed it most, a mother's love, a cuddle when she felt afraid, or words of comfort when she'd fallen and hurt herself. Only the people around her used to do that, as her mother was too busy thinking about herself and having an affair behind her father's back. Angelo too remembered all these things about Rosita when she was young, as he used to spend lot of time with her, playing adventure games, board games, hide and seek and many more.

It was then that the seed of love was sown for this pair and so cruelly torn apart at such a tender age. But this love lay dormant for many years, not diminishing in any way, and now, at this very moment with all the love he had for her, he couldn't find the words that would comfort her. He just held her for the ten minutes it took her to stop crying. She was so strong physically and mentally but occasionally, emotionally, she had these lapses. Angelo finally felt it was the right time to say something.

'How do you feel now, my angel? Do you want to talk about it?'

He turned and tilted his head down to see her face properly and discovered she was asleep against him. He kissed her on her forehead very gently and then slowly repositioning himself, he took her up into his arms like a baby and laid her on the bed. Then he tiptoed downstairs and informed the others that she was asleep. Angelo apologised to the doctor for Rosita leaving them like that.

'It is totally understandable.' said the doctor. 'I can tell you why she is so upset. She is emotionally drained. Until today every ounce of her hated her mother or at least she thought she hated her. But deep inside, really, really deep inside, she loves her and still needs her love in return. One of these days, the time will come when the hate she holds in the forefront of her thoughts for her mother will slowly disappear.'

He hesitated for a few seconds for the others to take in what he had said, then proceeded changing the subject. 'By the way, Donna Teresa, also said that if you two wanted, you could start immediately on the renovation of the property and the land adjacent.'

Almost before the doctor had finished his sentence, Anna was on her feet.

'What's wrong with you?' asked Angelo.

'Well, I know that Francesca would want to do this as soon as she heard this piece of news.'

'Would you like to explain?' Angelo enquired.

'Yes, I'm going to my family to tell them, if they want, they can move to the old hacienda, as soon as they wish,' finished Anna, even more excited than Rosita and the rest of them had been.

'Hold on a moment,' said Vincenzo. 'If they move there now, where are they going to live? The house is old and is still dangerous in its present condition.'

'Don Vincenzo, I don't think my family will mind that much, sleeping outside until there is a place ready for us to stay. After all we're in the middle of the summer,' she said, confidently. 'Also, if we are there, we can be at hand to help with the renovation.'

'Excellent idea, Anna,' said the doctor. 'It won't take long to prepare the house to a safe standard, because we'll have the wood and the other materials we need delivered immediately, I'll see to that.'

'That's very kind of you to arrange that for us Dr Pedrazza. But we need a lot of money for that, and at the moment we must concentrate on financing more important matters,' said Angelo giving the doctor a knowing look. The doctor smiled slyly at this remark because he knew things that nobody else did.

'Angelo, I know you may not have that much money at the moment, but Francesca on the other hand, even if she doesn't know it yet, has got plenty of money. And if she needs it now, she can have it. But of course, first I must speak with her.'

'Speak with whom?' Rosita's voice surprised them all as she stepped into the kitchen.

'I hope we didn't wake you?' asked Dr Pedrazza.

'Oh nobody woke me,' she replied. 'I have to apologise for the way I left you all,' she said. Then looking at Angelo, she wanted to apologise to him personally later, for falling asleep in his arms. But she'd felt so safe by him, a comfort that she had not felt for years.

'Don't even think about it,' answered Dr Pedrazza. 'We all need to cry and let things out sometimes.'

'How do you feel now?' asked Angelo, and held one hand towards her for her to come to him.

'I feel revitalised,' she said, walking toward Angelo feeling like a little girl who had been offered a sweet by somebody, and she couldn't say no. 'Did I hear my name mentioned earlier?'

'Yes, you did, in fact the doctor has some good news for you,' said Angelo, pulling her onto his lap, shamelessly, and kissing her cheek.

'Well,' began Dr Pedrazza, 'if you need any money it's there waiting for you.'

'Hold on, doctor, it is very kind of you to want to lend us money and it would be easy for me and Angelo to say yes to your generous offer, but how would we pay this money back to you?'

'Give me a chance, young lady, and I'll explain something to you,' proceeded Dr Pedrazza, 'I don't want to lend you any money. I only want to give you what is yours.' At this, Rosita looked at Angelo, then Vincenzo with a puzzled look on her face, and returned her attention to the doctor. 'You see, when you were young, your father and I bought some shares. His shares he bought in your name and made me the trustee. He did not tell your mother anything of this

231

transaction because he suspected she was being unfaithful to him with Don Camillo and should she leave him and want half of his estate, he wanted your shares protected.' Dr Pedrazza, enjoying seeing the surprised looks on the faces of Rosita and Angelo. He hesitated for a few seconds before continuing with the details.

'You see, the dividends from the shares have been coming to me over the years as I am the trustee and I have been saving it all for you. I can get hold of this money and give it to you without anyone suspecting anything What do you say about that, Francesca?' finished Dr Pedrazza, looking at Rosita's expression of incredulity.

'Well, I do not know what to say. In fact, I'm speechless, I'm astonished. Well at the moment I don't know what to say, the best thing is for you to do what you think is best, Doctor,' she replied.

'Very well, in that case I will go and buy everything you'll need for the old hacienda. And thank you for putting your trust in me, I must go now, I have been reminded of your father and what a good man he was, and I feel a bit upset, I will call in on Papa Joe and his family on the way and will speak with him about moving into the old hacienda.'

'Thank you, Doctor, I will be happy when they move there,' said Rosita. 'It's safer for them because the situation with the hired thugs is starting to get worse.' She looked at him with pleading eyes and asked. 'Doctor Pedrazza, I know you have helped me a great deal already and you have a busy schedule yourself, but would you be able to help me to arrange for provisions to be taken to the old hacienda? There are many hungry mouths to feed there and they need blankets and clothes as well. As I cannot openly do anything right now due to doctor's orders, and I have the feeling that there are going to be more people there now, than when I left the last time I was there.'

She sounds more and more like her late father, thought Dr Pedrazza, always putting others first. She either doesn't even have an idea of what danger she is putting herself in by helping these people, or maybe she knows and doesn't care and is very good at concealing her feeling and emotions, by not showing any fear.

'Do not worry, Francesca,' said the doctor, 'I will see to everything as soon as possible.'

CHAPTER SIXTEEN

It was very early Thursday morning; the crowing of a cockerel awoke Manuel. He was home in his own bed. He had passed the night fitfully, after consuming too much liqueur and thinking how he had to break the news to Maria, the love of his life, the woman he promised he would soon marry. He could not imagine how she would react to the news that he'd decided to give up his job on the railway for Rosita's cause. In his heart he was sure that he had made the right decision though, because he wanted to repay Nunziato and Vincenzo for how they had brought him and his brother Juan up from such a young age, without parents or any other relatives to look after them.

Manuel rubbed his eyes, wondering what time it could be. He tried to get up slowly by swinging his legs off the edge of the bed and onto the cool floor. He managed to do that much even though his head was thumping, but when he tried to take a few steps, the room started to spin, and he slumped back onto the bed, taking his head onto his hands. He tried to call Maria, but his throat was so dry a croak came out instead. Maria's eighteen year old brother, Julio heard him as he came out of the bathroom and at once hurried into Manuel's room.

'Que passa, amigo?' he asked, seeing Manuel holding his head.

'Help me, Julio, I can't get up!' whined Manuel, hoarsely, 'the room is spinning!'

'My God, it smells like a distillery in here!' exclaimed Julio. 'Manuel, how much did you drink last night, an entire barrel? Dios Mio! Manuel, let's open the window first!'

'How can I, I can't even stand up,' groaned Manuel. Julio covered his nose with his hand, and stifled a laugh and went himself to open the window.

'How did you manage to bring my sister home last night?' Asked Julio.

'Don't ask me Julio, I don't even know how I got home myself, I only know my head is feeling like it's going to split in two at any minute,' he mumbled.

Julio took his arm and led him into the washroom, where there was a tin bath full of cold water. At first Julio had thought to just freshen up Manuel's face with cold water, but standing by the tin bath, he changed his mind and being tall and built like an athlete it was easy for him to pick Manuel up like a baby.

'What are you doing?' complained Manuel indignantly.

Without answering, but with a wide grin on his face, Julio briskly lowered Manuel, pyjamas and all into the cold water. Manuel instantly found his voice and strength, yelling at the top of his voice, while trying to get out of the tub. But Julio held him down saying, 'With this your headache should soon disappear!'

The rest of the Rossos household were awakened by the screams and went to see what was going on. They came in alarmed but half-asleep, and couldn't believe their eyes at the sight of Manuel, who by now was sat up in the tub unrestrained but soaked from top to toe like an unwillingly bathed dog. Julio turned to see his mother first, then his father and sister standing there. He expected his parents to be angry with him, but they were all laughing and when they'd calmed down a bit, Mr Rossos managed to ask Manuel why he was taking a bath in his nightwear. Poor Manuel didn't answer, but was looking at Julio crossly, wondering to himself how he was going to get him back for this prank.

'Come on Julio, let's get out of here and have some coffee,' said Julio's father, and they all went out still laughing, leaving Manuel sobering up in the cold water to sort himself out. Slowly he raised himself, took off his wet pyjamas and clambered out of the tub. He grabbed a large towel and went to his room to dry himself off and change. As he hadn't intend getting up yet, he found another pair of pyjamas and put on his dressing gown, then proceeded downstairs.

'Good morning, everybody,' he said, in a subdued voice as he joined his fiancée's family at the kitchen table. Maria got up to pour some coffee for him.

'Drink this my dear,' she said, feeling a little sorry for him for being so poorly after the amount of liqueur he must have imbibed the night before. 'And then go back to bed, you don't feel very well, do you?' She then scolded her brother Julio for giving her fiancé a cold bath.

'I must speak to you first, Maria, it's important,' Manuel closed his eyes, and brought one hand to his forehead. He didn't know where to begin or how to explain what he was about to tell her. Knowing Maria, her reaction would be to slap his face.

'One moment, my darling, I need to say this right. Then if when you have heard what I have to say you decide to beat me around the head, then I won't feel any more pain than I do right now.'

Maria looked at him startled and the other members of the family exchanged glances.

'Would you like us to leave the room?' Asked Mr Rossos.

'It's not necessary Papa, because what I have to say will effect everybody. And I may need you as a line of defence from Maria.' answered Manuel, still holding his forehead.

Maria's heart ached for him, she felt so sorry not being able to take his nasty headache away. She was now doubly concerned as to what he was about to say, but at the same time, she had to cover her mouth with her hand to conceal a smile. She adored him with all her heart and was thinking how handsome he was. This morning, even with a hangover from hell he looked as sexy as ever. He belonged to her, and very soon this five foot six, curly dark haired man, with the longest eyelashes she had ever seen would be her husband. He was a hard worker too, and Maria's family worshiped him.

'You all have to know this,' began Manuel. 'Anyway, last night as you know, Maria and I went to see Nunziato Curro. I had delivered a message to him from my brother. I found out through the course of the evening that Francesca needs our help, you do remember her, Nunziato's daughter?'

'Well,' said Maria, impatiently, 'what are you trying to tell us? Why are you afraid I'll hit you?'

'Please Maria, let me finish, I am already finding it hard enough to find the right words to say this.' He hesitated for a deep intake of breath. 'After all I heard last night, I felt I must help these people in whatever way I can, so I have decided to leave my job with the railway.'

Maria stood up abruptly and started to shout at him.

'Are you crazy, Manuel,' she cried. 'If you don't work and make money, how can we get married?'

'I understand what you're saying Maria and you are right to be cross, but give me a chance to finish and I'll tell you why I feel I need to do this. You see, when my parents died, my brother and I were abandoned, we had nobody to care for us, we were hungry and not old enough to work. Those two Curro brothers, Vincenzo and Nunziato, and their wives gave us food and roof over our heads. They brought us up until we were old enough to work and then we left to make our own way in life. I'm ashamed to admit this, but by leading my working life away from the Curro families, I had as good as forgotten them. Now it is obvious to me that they need me, and it gives me an opportunity to repay some of the kindness they showed to Juan and me when we needed them. I want to do this for them, to repay their kindness.'

Manuel finished speaking. He felt proud of his decision, and he knew with time Maria would understand. Mr Rossos stood up and approached Manuel, and laying a hand on his shoulder, he said, 'Manuel my boy, I'm proud to have you in my family, we're all behind you one hundred percent. I wish you good luck and if you need a helping hand in any way we will be only too happy to help.'

'Thank you, father,' answered Manuel, 'and to all of you for having the patience to listened to me. Now I'm going back to sleep, as this afternoon I start my new job.' Manuel rose from the chair, leaving Maria and her family watching him. He proceeded to climb the stairs to his room and got into bed.

Maria was not yet convinced; she was more confused than before. Was this an excuse? Was Manuel leaving her? And what sort of job was he talking about? She looked at her family asking.

'What job is he going to do?' she asked, addressing her father.

'Oh, it will be to work in the field,' replied Mr Rossos. Manuel is a bright young man and he knows what he's doing, you should know this already, Maria. Later when he get's up, you'll apologise to him for being childish.'

'Yes, father, you're right,' she replied.

***

It was now midday. Not many people were in the village streets, most of them had returned to their homes to eat lunch or take their siesta. A carriage was passing through the centre of the village; the driver was a grey haired old Chinese man with a long moustache. He looked new to these parts, and he stopped near the station. On a bench, there sat a young Chinese man. He was waiting for the train to arrive to try and make some money by offering to carry passenger's luggage.

At the house, Maria woke Manuel up. He tried to lift his head but he was unable to, it felt very heavy still as if someone had strapped lead weights to his head.

'Manuel, my love,' she was saying, 'you should get up and try to eat something. Also, there's a friend of yours waiting for you down stairs.'

'Who is it? And what time is it?' He asked drowsily.

'It's midday, Manuel.'

'My God, help me to get up,' he winced, as a sharp pain shot through his head 'Is it my friend who works at the station?'

'Yes, but don't worry, he's not in a hurry, in fact he's staying to have lunch with us. Come along my love, I'll help you get up and into the washroom.'

'Oh no, not another cold bath,' exclaimed Manuel.

'No, mi amor, I promise I won't do such a thing.' Maria accompanied him to the washroom and left him to wash, then returned downstairs. As soon as her brother saw her, he joked.

'Maria, do you think Manuel needs my help again upstairs?'

'Be quiet, you big bully, and leave him alone.' Maria was not at all amused with her brother's joke. 'He is still feeling very delicate.' she snapped sharply. At this the rest of the family who were all sat around the table eating started to laugh again, joined by their guest Romero, who had heard all about the state of Manuel earlier and the dunking Julio had given him. After finishing their meal, they were drinking coffee when Manuel entered the dining room quietly and approached the table slowly. He raised his hand feebly to greet everyone and Julio could contain himself no longer and laughed out loud.

'Father, please tell my brother to be quiet?' demanded Maria, furious at her brother's bad manner. Mr Rossos turned to Julio but as soon he saw his son's face, he too could not stop himself from succumbing to loud laughter. Maria realised she had lost the battle to stop her family laughing at Manuel. So, she left the room in a huff. Manuel drank a few sips of coffee and turned to his friend Romero.

'Que passa, amigo? Have you got any news for me?' he asked.

'Yes, my friend,' answered Romero. 'The train arrives at four o'clock and everybody is in position, exactly as you told me to do yesterday.' Manuel nodded his approval then Romero continued, 'Before coming here I did a quick visual sweep around the village and I saw two suspicious people.'

'What do you mean, suspicious, who were they?' asked Manuel again holding his forehead.

'I don't know them,' answered Romero. 'Two Chinamen. One was driving a carriage, waiting outside the station. The other one, a younger man sitting on the bench within the station itself.'

'Ah, those two,' answered Manuel. 'Don't worry Romero, they are part of the family.'

'What's going on, my brother-in-law?' Asked Julio, Mr Rossos interrupted his son.

'It's not your concern, Julio,' he said, 'wait until somebody tells you.'

'But, Father,' complained Julio, hurt, 'I want only to help Manuel, in some way.'

'It is very good of you to offer Julio.' said Manuel. 'I don't think we'll need your help yet, but when I do I'll let you know.'

Maria returned into the dining room, having realised that she should have seen the funny side of the situation earlier, and she pandered to Manuel.

'How do you feel, my sweetheart? Has your head ache eased?'

'Yes, Maria, a little,' answered Manuel.

'Manuelito, mi amor, where are you taking me tonight?' Maria cooed to him.

'You stupid girl, how can you women be so heartless?' exclaimed Julio, trying to give the impression that he was the man of the house. 'Father you should slap her face and send her to her room,' said Julio, proud of himself.

'Ha, you should never have been born!' retorted Maria.

'Why don't you learn to hold your tongue,' shouted Julio.

'By now her father had had enough, he stood up, shocked and embarrassed at the both of them. Manuel too had had enough, so he quickly intervened before the situation escalated any further.

'Excuse me please!' he said. 'I could do without this right now. I still have a nasty hangover and lots to think about. If I make a little mistake many people could be hurt, including myself. All this bickering is unnecessary. Julio, thank you for trying stand up for me. And Maria my darling, I'll take you out a little later. Please, both of you don't fight amongst yourselves any more, especially in front of your parents, would you promise me this?'

'Yes, Manuel, you are right, I promise,' she said, looking towards her mother and father, expecting at least a smile as a sign of forgiveness. She knew this time she had gone too far, she had regretted the way she had spoken to her brother, as soon as the words had left her mouth. She went over to her father and mother and embraced them both saying, 'I am sorry!' She loved her family dearly, especially her eighteen year old brother, Julio. She didn't know what had come over her.

'You're forgiven,' her father replied, 'but next time you'll get your face slapped,' finished Mr Rossos, very sternly. He had never seen her daughter speak to anyone in that way before.

'Well my sweetheart, you can go to get ready now,' Manuel said to Maria. She'd hardly given Manuel a chance to finish, as she shot away to get herself ready to go out. Julio and his father prepared to go back to work. Julio was working in a general store in Bella Vista. His boss, an Englishman called Keith Smith, was a friend of Don Antonio's. They were in the same trade of exploitation of other people, and Don Antonio was sure to make his first stop there. So, just before Manuel left with Maria, he called Julio over.

'Julio, a little while ago you told me you wanted to help,' he said.

'Yes, Manuel, and I meant it.'

'Well thinking about it, you can do something for me, but you have to be very discreet.'

Julio nodded in agreement eagerly.

'When you go back to work, you must keep your eyes and ears open, especially if your boss receives a visit from any strangers. What I need you to do, and be very careful not to get caught, is to try to listen in to what they are saying, but don't make it obvious, if they ask you any questions about Nunziato Curro's family, just say you don't know them very well, can you do that?'

'Of course I can,' said Julio, happy that he could do something for his brother-in-law. It made him feel special.

'Very good,' said Manuel nodding. 'If you find something out, don't get over excited, just wait until you see me next to tell me, you don't need to rush back immediately. I don't want it to look obvious. It would put you in danger and I wouldn't want that little brother.'

'All right, Manuel, I'll see you later tonight,' said Julio, trying to control his excitement.

Manuel and Maria left for Nunziato's house. The Curros had been preparing a small party for the celebration of the engagement of their daughter Francesca, which would take place on Saturday.

Battistina had to remain at home getting everything ready today as they wanted to mark the occasion with a few close friends beforehand. This had been Nunziato and Jon Chian's joint idea. They thought that if Don Antonio turned up unexpectedly for any reason, he would be more convinced that Francesca was who she said she was. Manuel and Maria arrived, and saw Giovanna, Meilin and Sandra already there and were helping Battistina to make the finishing touches.

'Mmm…! What a mouth-watering aroma,' exclaimed Maria,. 'What have you lovely people prepared here?'

'Well what you can smell,' began Battistina, 'among other food, is the cakes we have just made for later on.'

'My goodness!' exclaimed Manuel surprised. 'There is enough food here to open a shop! Have you been working all night?'

'Almost! We worked half the night and half of today, with the help of these marvellous girls,' answered Battistina.

'Well, I think we've talked enough now,' said Manuel jokingly, 'my mouth is watering. I'll have to taste some of the cakes, just in case they are not fully cooked.' joked Manuel, moving toward the small banquet, licking his lips.

'Don't eat them all,' laughed Battistina, 'I have to take some to Francesca.'

'I'm sure she'll be very pleased to receive some of these,' said Manuel. Then he asked. 'Auntie, when you say you have to take them to Francesca, do you mean you are coming to see Francesca too?'

'What are you saying Manuel? Of course I'm going to go and see my daughter.'

'Well Aunt, I was thinking that it wouldn't be a good idea for you to go, as things are very unsettled in Las Cejias,' said Manuel with a pained smile on his face. He didn't want to upset her, but right now Las Cejias was no place for an elderly lady like Battistina to be.

She would be an added worry for everybody around her. He was half expecting her to start an argument with him, but to his surprise she just calmly addressed him.

'Bravo, Manuel! You're right. Even though I desperately want to be with her, I do not want to be in the way when the real trouble starts. I know that everybody has their own part to play and mine is to stay here and wait until I am needed.' Battistina, touched Manuel's arm as if to say it's all right, before turning toward Maria and the other girls.

Manuel stopped her and said, 'Aunt Battistina, you're the dearest lady that anybody could meet,' and he embraced her. At that moment his Uncle Nunziato approached them, having heard and seen everything.

'Hey, Manuel, do you know that is my wife you're holding?' Nunziato said, smiling.

'Sorry Uncle! I was hugging my mother!' He kissed her forehead, and wished that she were really his mother, then he turned to face his uncle. 'And where did you come from? Looks like you just got up!' joked Manuel.

'Actually, I did just get up. This morning I rose very early, I couldn't sleep for worrying about how I was going to break the news to Battistina that I wanted to go to support Francesca. But I needn't have worried, she woke as restless as I did and I told her then, and she understood as she always does. After that, neither of us could sleep any more, so we occupied our time by preparing food for the engagement party! At daybreak, Jon Chian turned up, he was also unable to sleep and when he saw what we were doing he called his wife and daughter to help us. So I went back to sleep for a while. Anyway, why don't we change the subject and talk about what's going on in the village?'

'Everything is going well Uncle, and I hope there will be no need for any violence,' answered Manuel.

'Me too,' said Nunziato, 'but that depends on Don Antonio.'

'I wouldn't worry if I were you, Jon and Chen are already at the station, they will be sure to follow him everywhere. I've got a couple of friends around in case he brings bad company with him, we'll be ready to teach them a lesson if they try anything.'

At Nunziato's house the party was going well, people enjoyed chatting and eating the delicious Italian cakes, and drinking home-made liqueur, and wine. In the village some people were busy keeping their eyes alert in case any trouble occurred. It was almost four o'clock on Thursday afternoon. Chen, was disguised in a Chinese style wig with a long plait and a false moustache, he had been waiting at the station for the train which was now pulling in. He moved closer to get a better view of the passengers. The sun was beating down on them, but they had to do what they had to do. It was for a good cause. There were about ten other people waiting on the platform. For a few minutes there was a flurry of activity as passengers were getting off and on to the train, Chen was wondering how he would be able to recognise Don Antonio. He had no idea what he looked like, his eyes were darting backwards and forwards along the platform and he scratched his head, hoping he wouldn't miss him. Suddenly there was a loud voice above the general din.

'Hey! Porter!' Chen walked toward the man who'd addressed him. He was tall, plump and had hard facial features.

'Are you calling me, sir?' asked Chen.

'Yes, who else?' The man said impatiently, Chen instantly thought that this must be Don Antonio Marquis for sure.

'Yes sir,' said Chen, bowing slightly.

'Hurry and find me a carriage!' he ordered. Chen picked up the man's two large brown leather cases and made his way towards the station exit, to where a carriage was waiting. Don Antonio climbed inside and settled his large frame into the seat while Chen struggled to load the cases onto the back. After doing this, Don Antonio pressed a few coins into his hand.

'Tell the driver to take me to the tavern, and tell him to make haste, I don't want him wasting my time going the scenic route.'

Chen uttered a few words in Chinese to his father, and the carriage left speedily. As the carriage disappeared into the distance Chen looked at the money in his hand. He shook his head and with a smirk of disgust, threw the coins onto the dusty road. Some people are just pigs he thought to himself, he then smiled to himself, very content at the way things were going and the thought of all the little surprises Don Antonio would encounter shortly.

'You cursed man,' he said to himself and started to walk home. On the way he stopped by Nunziato's house. He joined Manuel and Nunziato, who were sitting outside the house drinking coffee together, because after the previous evening, Manuel had no stomach for alcohol. Smiling as he approached Chen told them, 'The big bad wolf is here, he's alone and he looks agitated.'

'Ha! People like him are always annoyed with the world, all we can do now is wait for the plan to unfold. We'll see what move he makes, and guide him like a puppet,' answered Nunziato.

'Well, I feel like breaking someone's neck,' hissed Chen.

'Please,' said Manuel, 'don't talk about hitting anyone, I've still got noise in my head that doesn't want to go!'

'I know what you need to remedy that,' said Chen, then hesitated for a few seconds. 'A couple of glasses of my father's liqueur.' The three men suddenly burst out into uncontrollable laughter.

***

At the cemetery, two of Manuel's friends, Orlando and Romero had started to look around and pretended to be busy, as if they were working. After about one hour of them being there, two other men came by carriage into the cemetery. One was Don Antonio and the other was an English friend of his, Keith Smith, who was the storeowner from Bella Vista. He had a similar superior way of behaving towards people as Don Antonio has, but was not a violent man. The Englishman, Keith Smith, addressed the two men who appeared to be cemetery workers, from the carriage.

'Hey, you two, can you come here please?' he asked, smiling at them.

'Are you speaking to us, Señor?' answered Orlando.

'Yes, both of you, can you come here please?' repeated Keith Smith. So, the two young men put down the tools they were holding and walked to the front of the carriage, looking at each other as if to say what have we done? They both took off their hats and held them tightly to their chests, creating the impression of two simple, frightened workers. In fact both Orlando and Romero were very impressed with their own performances.

'What can we do for you, Señors?' asked Romero, 'we're very busy today?'

'I would like to ask a favour of you two,' proceeded, Keith Smith, displaying a wad of money in his hand. He peeled two ten peso notes from the wad, enough for a day's wages each. Orlando and Romero looked at each other with blank expressions and then back to the two fools on the carriage without saying anything. Keith Smith thought that maybe he hadn't offered enough money, so he took out two more notes, saying.

'The job I want you to do for me is not very heavy work.' He pulled out a piece of paper from the in breast pocket of his fine long grey jacket, 'Here,' he said handing it to Romero. 'We need to know if the grave of this person is in this cemetery, it is very important to us and nobody must know we are looking. Understand?'

Romero took both, the paper and the money. The name written there was as they had expected, Francesca Curro.

'Hey, do you trust me amigo?' laughed the Englishman.

'No, I don't trust anybody and I'm not your amigo,' replied Romero.

They both turned and took a few steps away. They suddenly heard Don Antonio's irritated voice.

'Hey, you two, I want this done today, so don't waste time, I'm a very busy man!'

Orlando went back and stood by the side the carriage.

'We'll do this favour for the Englishman, but not for you, Señor.' He then bowed to them and turned away again.

'If you were working for me, you wouldn't address me that way!' Don Antonio barked at him angrily.

'Well, we are not working for you, so you can do nothing to us,' retorted Orlando taunting him even more.

'And what makes you think that?' demanded Don Antonio, his face was getting rosier by the seconds and not because of the heat.

'We're not Negroes, señor, we kick back,' was the reply.

Don Antonio's face flushed bright red with anger. If his eyes were guns, the two young men would be dead by now.

'Let's get out of here,' he ordered his friend. They turned the carriage round and set off, but Orlando was not finished yet, he shouted out after them.

'Hey, Señor Inglés, why is your friend so angry?'

The Englishman ignored this comment, but instead instructed Orlando and Romero to bring any information directly to him at the general store as quickly as possible.

'Buenos Señor. We'll see you later,' said Orlando. As soon as the carriage was out of sight, the two men sat down to enjoy a cigarette. They allowed a couple of hours to pass, smoking and telling jokes and then started back toward the town. When they arrived at the general store, they found Keith Smith in his office and reported that they hadn't been able to find the name they had been given on any of the gravestones.

'Are you sure, very sure that you looked thoroughly, everywhere? This news is very important to my friend.' emphasised the Englishman.

'Si, Señor. My friend and me looked at every grave, we're sure, honest Señor,' Orlando promptly answered.

'OK, but if we find you two have lied, my friend won't take it lightly. I promise you.'

'We know that, Señor Smith. We know what people like your friend are capable of doing,' answered Orlando, looking at Romero, with innocent eyes. Romero nodded in agreement. 'Um… where is your friend at this moment Señor Smith? Is he asleep to cool himself down?' enquired Orlando. The Englishman looked at the two young men with amusement. He liked these two spirited boys.

'He went for a walk, he needed to get some fresh air, he's very good at doing that.' replied the English man.

'You have to worn your friend, Señor Smith, sometimes too much fresh air can damage one's health,' said Romero. Of course the two young men knew that he was sure to be at Nunziato's house by now. They said goodbye to the Englishman and left content at having played their part.

***

Meanwhile, Don Antonio had in fact arrived at Nunziato's house. Chen, now out of his disguise, had seen him approaching from the kitchen window, but carried on drinking and chatting with Nunziato and Manuel, as if they had not noticed him.

'Good evening, Señors.' He addressed the three of them from the kitchen doorway. Nunziato looked over his shoulder at him, then rose and took a few steps toward him.

'Good evening, Señor. What brings you to these parts?' asked Nunziato, smiling. He didn't show the newcomer the anger that was eating him up inside. Nunziato really wanted to physically attack this man and break all the bones in his body, for the evil man that he was.

'Nothing in particular, Señor, I'm a stranger here, I'm just stretching my legs. Are you Italian, Señor?' asked Don Antonio, a white handkerchief in his hand, nervously dabbing the sweat from his forehead and face. The long walk had made him perspire more than usual. He was obviously worried that they may suspect why he was there.

'Yes, we're Italian,' answered Nunziato. 'Can we offer you some refreshment?'

'Yes, please, I have worked up quite a thirst,' said Don Antonio, looking around at all the festive food that was displayed on the surrounding tables. 'Are you celebrating someone's birthday?' he asked.

'Oh no,' replied Nunziato. 'It's no one's birthday, but we're celebrating my daughter's forthcoming engagement.' Nunziato, then called his wife who was inside. As she appeared on the doorstep. 'Battistina, please could you bring something fresh for this gentleman to drink?'

'Is wine all right for you, Señor?' she asked the stranger.

'Yes, thank you kindly, Señora,' he answered, then directed himself back to Nunziato. 'May I congratulate you and your wife on your daughter's engagement? Is your lucky daughter here for me to congratulate in person?' He asked, hoping Nunziato would ask him if he would like to take a seat on the patio. His eyes at that moment resting over the beautiful healthy trees in the garden and the cool shade they produced. A large orange tree took centre stage, with olive trees and other smaller citrus trees surrounding it. There were lots of varieties of flowers dotted around too, among them some red and white roses climbing up the wall with their sweet scent.

'No, I'm sorry you cannot,' replied Nunziato, enjoying seeing Don Antonio perspire so profusely. 'She's not here right now.'

'Isn't she? Where have you hidden her?' Don Antonio tried to joke. Even a child could see the obvious route Don Antonio's mind was taking, his nerves and the heat only served to add to his discomfort. Battistina served Don Antonio his wine and Manuel approached Nunziato and the sweaty guest.

'Where do you come from, Señor?' asked Manuel.

'Oh, I'm from Las-Cejias,' he said vaguely, trying to think of a different subject.

'Really!' intervened Nunziato immediately. 'My daughter lives there, on the Hacienda Antigua with her uncle and fiancée.'

Don Antonio feigned surprise. 'What a coincidence, then maybe I know your daughter?'

'Maybe! It's a possibility,' answered Nunziato.

'What is her name? I would be more than happy to deliver any message to her for you,' offered Don Antonio.

'Thank you, but that won't be necessary,' replied Nunziato. 'Francesca's engagement party is on Saturday and as she is my only daughter, I plan on being there. Perhaps we could travel together? Sorry I forgot your name, what did you say your name was?'

'Ha, I didn't say, how rude of me. My name is Antonio Marquis.'

'I'm pleased to make your acquaintance,' replied Nunziato. 'I'm Nunziato Curro, and this is my friend, Manuel Pellegrini. You know it's strange, I used to go to work for six months a year in Las-Cejias, I do not remember you, how long have you lived there?' asked Nunziato, looking straight into his guest's eyes and seeing his fear.

'You must have been away from Las-Cejias a long time. I moved there nearly fourteen years ago,' answered Don Antonio. 'Anyway,' he proceeded, 'as you were saying before, unfortunately it will not be possible for us to travel together; tomorrow morning I'm catching a train to move on.' He didn't want to say where he was going to. During the last few minutes Don Antonio's attention had continually been drawn back to Chen, who was still sitting quietly not very far from them.

'Excuse me, young man,' he called over, addressing Chen. 'Haven't I seen you somewhere before?'

'I don't think so!' answered Chen, 'I've no recollection of ever meeting you before, I hardly ever leave this village.'

'Perhaps he's right,' whispered Don Antonio to Nunziato. 'These Chinese people all look the same to me. Well gentlemen, I must go now, Mr Curro, Mr Pellegrini, thank you for your hospitality and please thank your kind wife for the wine. Whenever you come to Las-Cejias you're welcome to visit me and we'll have a drink together.'

'Thank you, I won't forget that,' replied Nunziato.

Before leaving Don Antonio looked at Chen again, and shook his head. As soon as Don Antonio was out of earshot, the three men laughed heartily together.

'Well my friends, it looks as if everything went as smoothly as we'd planned,' said Nunziato,. 'Tomorrow we can leave for Las-Cejias with no worries.'

CHAPTER SEVENTEEN

Morning burst out upon the fields of Bella Vista, with bright sunshine and clear blue skies. The birds were singing in the trees, the flowers in the garden were ablaze with colour and the bees were waking to busy themselves about the flowers and vines. The Curro household was filled with a solemn atmosphere; you could cut it with a knife. After skulking around all morning, hardly saying a word to his wife, Nunziato embraced his wife and said his goodbyes. Twenty minutes after that, at Bella Vista station four well-dressed men were ready and waiting for the train. One Sicilian, one Spaniard and two Chinese, father, and son.

Nunziato, Manuel, Chen and Jon were on their way to join Rosita in Las-Cejias. There was an air of contentment about them all. They knew that their arrival in Las-Cejias would be welcomed with joy, and they knew they would be needed there; Rosita's quest to regain her father's property was in the throes of completion. The men regretted having to leave the women behind and indeed the women let their men go with heavy hearts, it was like they were going to war. Rosita though was an important part of all their lives, the risks involved made it necessary for the women folk to stay behind this time. Their partners understood this, and hoped that one day soon they too would be able to make the trip without fear and celebrate their freedom together.

The train drew up slowly and only a few passengers got off. The four men smiled knowingly at each other but said nothing; they led their horses onto the train's livestock carriage and then went to find their seats, placing their personal belongings onto the racks above their heads. They all sat in a line in the same row, Nunziato at the left window with Jon next to him and Chen in the aisle seat with Manuel by the right window. Manuel was being uncharacteristically subdued; he leant his elbow on the window frame and rested his cheek on his hand, staring out onto the platform. He could only think of one thing, his beautiful Maria. He didn't know when he would next see her, and he wished he could hold her in his arms once more before the train left. But she had insisted it would be too upsetting for her to say goodbye at the station, but he was still hoping and checking to see if she had changed her mind. The other three had noticed his sullen mood and understood his pain, the pure love of a young man was always harder to deal with.

Suddenly he saw her running along the platform. He yelled, 'Maria, my Maria!' He turned to ask Chen if he could get out of his seat, but Chen was already up and out in the aisle with a smile on his face. Manuel with a grin the size of a canyon spread across his face, scooted over looking up at Chen who bowed his head slightly.

Manuel ran along the aisle towards the back of the carriage almost knocking over a lady in his rush, apologising to her as he disappeared around the corner. He jumped down off the train and ran towards Maria. She really looked breathtaking with her auburn hair cascading over her shoulders, a pair of large gold gypsy's ear rings, her beautiful green eyes and her slender body in a smart black two piece suit. She jumped up at him and he caught her around the waist with both arms and held her tightly rocking her side to side and kissing her passionately.

'Maria! Oh, Maria, how I love you,' he whispered into her ear.

'I love you too, my Manuelito,' she answered, tears rolling down her slightly freckled face.

'I promise you, when things calm down and there is a safe place for us, I'll come for you and then we will start our lives together.'

'I'm sorry, Manuel, I didn't want to cry, I thought I was going to be strong. I had to see you again… ' Before she could finish the train whistle blew.

'I must go now, my love,' said Manuel, looking into her green eyes, for a long instant, then he kissed her again, as the train started to move. He left her and ran to the carriage door and jumped onto the train. The train picked up speed but they kept waving until the train was too far for them to see each other. She stood silently in her thoughts for a minute still looking at the spot where the train had disappeared, as if she was expecting the train to come back. Maria felt a hand lightly rest on her shoulder.

'Come, let's go home, you'll see, he'll be back before you know it,' said her father reassuringly. They made their way home in silence. Her mother was waiting at the front door for them to return and took Maria into her arms.

'Don't cry, you know I don't like to see you crying. Anyway, it's not worth crying over men, they only make you suffer even more.'

Maria's brother, Julio, was ready to leave for work and overheard his mother. He went to the front door and said, cheekily.

'Mother, I'm going to tell my Father what you just said. And Maria, I'm happy that Manuel has gone, maybe you can do more for me now.'

Their mother laughed, she knew her son well and how he liked to joke, but as usual Maria failed to get the joke, so she took off one of her shoes and threw it at him.

'You selfish animal,' she shouted.

He dodged the flying shoe, slammed the door behind him and run as fast as he could down the road giggling to himself.

'Calm down, Maria, in the name of God! Your brother was joking,' said her mother trying to placate her. But she ran up to her room, at least there she could cry without being disturbed.

***

At Nunziato's house everything was very quiet. Battistina was feeding the chickens in her own thoughts when suddenly she heard a familiar voice behind her.

'Aunt Battistina!' She turned to discovered Meilin, Chen's sister.

'Meilin, what are you doing here? What happened?' asked the poor woman.

Meilin answered with a lovely sweet smile.

'Why, must there be a reason for me to be here?' she asked.

'Oh no, I didn't mean it like that. I meant why aren't you at home helping your mother, now that you father and brother are away?'

'That's right, that's the reason I'm here, Aunt Battistina,'

'What do you mean?' asked Battistina, still not understanding.

'I mean, Mother has sent me here, because she didn't want you to be on your own. I'll help you with your work, and then I'll help my mother, and please don't refuse, my mother won't accept no for an answer.'

'Back on the train, the four men, Nunziato, Manuel, Jon and Chen were more relaxed now and were laughing uncontrollably about the events of the previous night while they were sleeping. Nunziato had been informed of the goings on by one of Manuel's friends before they had left this morning. Apparently, Don Antonio had not been satisfied with the outcome of the enquiry at the cemetery; he did not trust the two gravediggers he had paid to look for Francesca's gravestone. So he had instructed two of Keith Smith's cronies to double check the cemetery at night. He was determined not to go back to Don Camillo with nothing to report.

From the moment Keith Smith's two men had arrived at the cemetery in the middle of the night, they'd felt uneasy. They felt they shouldn't be there, that the dead should be left alone to sleep in peace. Even with their reservations the two men knew they must go through with the job or be in trouble with their boss. Within a few minutes of them starting their search they'd begun to hear funny noises. An hour into their search for the name on the gravestones, they found themselves at the far end of the cemetery with tall trees now surrounded them, which were blocking out the little light there was from the moon.

Suddenly, the two men stopped, frozen to the spot with fear. They had heard many noises over the last hour, some of which could be explained away like creaking branches, twigs breaking, groaning, hissing and slurping. But this was not normal, in the distance they could hear chains being dragged along the ground.

In normal circumstances one would laugh, but in the dark, in the middle of the night, in a cemetery, the mind played games with the two men. They were staring at two dark shadows coming from the direction they'd heard the sound of the chains. After what seemed an age staring at the apparitions, which were now slowly moving towards them, one of them felt something touch the back of his neck. He let out a spine chilling scream and they simultaneously dropped their torches.

'Screw the money and Don Antonio, I'm getting out of here!' said the other one and began to run for his life, with his companion close behind him. Leaving behind their torches and two young men, friends of Manuel, rolling about with stifled laughter.

CHAPTER EIGHTEEN

It was Saturday morning, and it was St Joseph's Day. At Vincenzo's house everyone had been very busy, not just in preparation for the feast of St Joseph, but for another important celebration as well. Today was Rosita and Angelo's engagement party. So many good things had been baked. The table was laden with a multitude of savoury nibbles as well as home-made biscuits, cakes and sugared almonds. There was also an abundance of alcohol on show, from bottles of wine, red, white and rosé, as well as many flavours of liqueur. Now everything was ready and the room had been left neat and tidy. The families were off to church before the party began, Angelo went out to get the horses and carriage ready. As he left the room he shouted.

'Father, Francesca, come quickly?'

'What's wrong?' asked Vincenzo, a little concerned as he hurried out, closely followed by Rosita. What they saw made them cry out with joy, for there stood four very smartly dressed men on horseback. They were Nunziato, Manuel, Jon Chian, and his son Chen. With big smiles on their faces, they dismounted and Rosita was the first to rush forward and fling her arms around Nunziato's neck. Then she hugged Jon and Chen at the same time, and finally Manuel. Angelo and his father also took their turns at embracing the four men affectionately. The moment was especially emotional for Nunziato, because it was only the second time he had returned to the Hacienda Antigua since the assault had taken place all those years ago.

'You caught us just in time,' said Vincenzo, as he started to help to unload the few things they had brought with them. 'We were just on our way to church.'

'Would you men like to come with us?' asked Rosita.

'We'd love to come,' answered Nunziato and Manuel.

'We'll come too,' said Jon Chian. 'We're not Catholic, but we'll be going to a house of God, and that is good enough for us.'

Rosita, with tears of joy still in her eyes, asked Nunziato how her mother was.

'She's in very good health and she misses you like mad,' he replied. Francesca threw her arms around Nunziato again.

'Oh! I've missed you both very much too,' she whispered into his ear. 'Thank you for coming to be with me today. Thank you all.'

'Today, my dear Francesca, and every day until the job is done and you don't need us here anymore. You have many good friends and family behind you, Francesca, and we all love you,' replied Nunziato. She knew exactly what he meant, because she could see the determined look in the four men's eyes; she understood that they were here ready to fight by her side.

A few minutes later, they were all on their way to the church with Rosita, Angelo and Vincenzo, in the carriage, followed by Nunziato, Jon, Chen and Manuel on their horses. Angelo couldn't tear his eyes away from Francesca. He could feel her excitement; she felt more relaxed having Nunziato and the others here by her side. He took her hand and kissed it gently, his desire for her radiating from his eyes. After her bath this morning, Rosita had decided to wear a figure enhancing cream lacy blouse, with a smart small collar and three quarter sleeves, over a rose pink coloured skirt which clung smoothly to her hips before draping gracefully to her ankles. A pair of cream, ankle-length stiletto boots covered her feet. She had left her wavy brown hair unbound, so the trestles, still damp from being washed, cascaded over her shoulders and halfway down her back.

Angelo not being able to help himself leant his head against hers and whispered into her ear, 'Rosita, you're more beautiful than words can describe.'

'Don't embarrass me in front of everybody,' she said enjoying every moment of his lovemaking. He could not take his eyes off her. He had to consciously drag his eyes away from her, as he knew behind them there were four pairs of eyes looking in their direction. Oh, how he wished he could smother her with kisses.

As they passed the front of Donna Teresa's mansion, everything looked deserted. The people must either all be at the church or preparing for the festival. Vincenzo and Angelo looked at each other, and thought the same thing. Don Camillo's hired thugs had either taken a day off, or they were hiding.

'Well', thought Vincenzo to himself, 'they would not worry about that problem today. It was the feast of St Joseph and the engagement of two people very dear to him. But try as he might to push away that feeling from the back of his mind, he felt in his bones that something horrible would happen very soon.

As they arrived near Papa Joe's house, they slowed down, but there was no one around here either.

'They must all be at the Church,' said Rosita. 'Let's carry on.'

When they finally approached the church, there were many people standing outside, consisting of those who had come out from the first mass and others waiting to go in for the second mass. They were all chatting and exchanging good wishes for St Joseph' Day.

As they drew up, everybody turned to look at them. They were dressed so elegantly and with the four figures on horseback following the carriage, two to the back and one on either side, it seemed as if Angelo and Francesca were being escorted like a young prince with his princess. When they stopped, Vincenzo got off the cart and went to tie up the horses, as did Nunziato and the others.

Angelo helped Rosita to step down from the carriage, and they went inside the church. The others followed. Jon and Chen bowed their heads to the priest, who was surprised to see two Chinamen walking into his church. The others went to the font to dip their finger in the holy water before making the sign of the cross, as Catholics do when entering a church. They all found seats near the back of the church.

All through his sermon the priest kept looking to the back, he tried to resist it, but his eyes kept returning to the new arrivals. Donna Teresa was sitting at the front and she was very curious to see who the priest was looking at, she was eager to know who it was who had come into the church and was distracting the priest. After resisting the temptation for a while she finally succumbed and turned around to see who it was that was drawing the priest's eye to the back. She made no bones about it, she turned her body halfway around then her head the rest of the way and lifted herself up slightly to see better. Once she had seen the group, she turned back to face the front satisfied in herself that there was no problem.

After half an hour, the mass was over and the people started to file out. The priest said goodbye to Donna Teresa and Don Camillo and the other people near the altar. Vincenzo and the others stayed behind in their seats until everybody else had gone as Vincenzo wanted to introduce Manuel, Jon and Chen Chian to the priest. As Donna Teresa was leaving the Church, she saw Nunziato and stopped. He rose and approached her, and he shook her hand.

'My deepest respect to you, Donna Teresa,' he said.

'Nunziato, how lovely to see you again after so long! How are you?' she exclaimed.

'I'm very well,' he replied, 'and how are you, Donna Teresa?'

'I'm very well too thank you, and how is your wife, Battistina?'

'She is in good health too, thank you for remembering her,' said Nunziato, his stomach tightened into knots.

'Why is she not with you?' asked Donna Teresa.

'Well, we couldn't leave the few animals we have, someone had to stay to look after them,' he replied.

'I see, you must be very proud to have such a lovely daughter.'

Nunziato turned and looked at Rosita, then back at Donna Teresa.

'Yes, I am extremely proud of her,' he replied. They were so busy talking that they had almost forgotten Don Camillo's presence.

'Ha, Nunziato! Meet my husband, Camillo, he used to come to the hacienda very often. Do you remember him?'

Nunziato looked at Don Camillo coolly and shook his hand. For a few long seconds his mind flashed back fifteen years to when he last saw this evil man with a dagger in his hand, the dagger with which he had killed his dearly loved employer and friend, Don Sebastian Miserendino. Nunziato tried very hard to put a smile on his face.

'How could I forget him, Donna Teresa?' answered Nunziato and instantly his body began to shake.

'Anyway,' proceeded Donna Teresa, 'you're staying for a little while I presume, so we'll have plenty of time to catch up. Goodbye for now, we'll see you later at you daughter's engagement party.'

And with that she acknowledged the others with a nod of her head and left with her husband. Then Nunziato walked towards the priest. He stopped face to face with him. They stood looking at one another blankly for a few seconds and then they embraced one another as two brothers would after a long separation. Vincenzo had already introduced Jon and Chen to the priest. He was very happy to see Nunziato again and he offered to put up the new arrivals.

'There's not enough room at Vincenzo's house,' said Don Saverio.

'That's very kind of you,' said Vincenzo. 'We'll see you later at the party and we'll talk about it further.'

Don Saverio Scalabrini accompanied them to the door of the church. Before they all departed, Don Saverio Scalabrini called back Nunziato and told him how proud he was at the way he had handled his meeting Don Camillo again, knowing how hard it must have been to resist shooting him on the spot.

On their way back to Vincenzo's, Manuel asked Nunziato if he minded if he stopped by to say hello to his brother, Juan, at the bar.

'But of course, you can,' answered Nunziato. 'He'll be happy and surprised to see you. In fact, I think I'll come with you.' So they peeled off towards where the bar was.

Not hearing the horses behind him, Angelo stopped the carriage and turned around to see what they were doing.

'Is anything wrong, Uncle?' he asked.

'Everything's fine, don't worry, it's just that Manuel and I are going to see Juan at the bar.'

'Very well, Uncle. And Manuel, remind your brother Juan that I'm expecting him to be there tonight, it won't be a party without him!'

'Don't worry, I shan't forget,' replied Manuel.

Nunziato turned to Jon and Chen, and asked, 'What do you think; do you want to come to the bar with us? So when we go back to the hacienda we can bring Juan with us.'

'Well I don't know,' began Jon, looking at Rosita. He was thinking it wasn't very polite for all of them to go off. But Rosita sensed this and intervened.

'Stay with them,' she said, smiling. 'It's only for a little while, and you can sample the local beer. We'll go on, because there are a few things for us to finalise and cook at home.'

'Right, let's sample some beer then,' said Jon content that he hadn't offended anybody. 'We'll see you later.'

***

The four friends entered the pub and instantly they saw Juan. He was busy behind the counter. He was serving one of the locals and continued with his job. Presently he looked up to see who had come in and it took just a few seconds to realise who the people standing in the pubs doorway were.

'My God! What the he…' he exclaimed 'I'll be back in a few minutes,' he said to the other man behind the counter, as he rushed to Manuel. 'Hey, armano! Che passa!' He hugged his brother and they slapped each others' backs whilst embracing, then he turned to Nunziato to speak, but there was a lump in his throat so he just hugged him emotionally for a few long seconds. 'I'm so pleased to see you,' he said eventually, 'how is Aunt Battistina?'

'She's very well, son, and she'd be happy to see you if it were possible,' replied Nunziato.

Juan bowed in a Chinese manner to Jon and Chen, and then embraced them too.

'Come and sit down at a table,' suggested Manuel, 'and I'll bring you all some beer.

They made themselves comfortable and waited for Juan to bring their beers. They all held up their glasses and chinked them together.

'Salute,' they all cried. Juan was so happy to be surrounded by those he thought of as his family, he could hardly believe they were really with him after being apart for so long.

'Well, what's the news from Bella Vista, in the past few days?' asked Juan. The four men at the table with Juan knew what he wanted to know. What exactly had happened with Don Antonio?

'Oh yes,' answered Nunziato, 'two days ago there was a lot of activity going on.'

'That's all? Don't I get the finer details?' probed Juan.

They all laughed and then Manuel answered.

'Well armano, we had a very important visitor. Don Antonio Marquis in person, he came to see Uncle Nunziato but he left looking very sorry for himself.'

'Why, you didn't hurt him, did you? Not even a little bit?' asked Juan.

'No... Mio armano, nothing like that happened,' continued Manuel, 'he just wasn't able to gain any useful information and there was no one to beat! We were all ready for him,' Manuel explained to Juan how Jon and Chen had waited at the station while he had remained with Nunziato at his house, and had arranged for Orlando and Romero to pose as cemetery workers. And that everything had gone as planned, no violence had been used. Then he told how they had then all decided to come to Las Cejias to offer their help to Rosita.

'And you left your job and your lovely fianceé Maria?' exclaimed Juan to his brother, 'How could you?' laughed Juan. He was proud of his brother.

'We all left our jobs,' said Nunziato.

'And our families,' put in Jon, 'but we're very happy to be here by Francesca's side, so we can be of use to her,' he proceeded.

'Very good,' answered Juan. 'And you Chen, what do you have to tell me? Are you married?'

'Not yet,' he answered, 'but I have a nice girl.'

'That's a good start,' said Juan.

'Juan,' interrupted Manuel, 'Angelo sent a message to you; he said not to forget you're invited to the party tonight and to bring your guitar.'

'Not to worry, my little brother, I'm not going to forget,' he replied, 'and I'm bringing four beautiful dancers, with me. My shift here finishes in an a few hours.'

'Oh, we thought you may come with us now,' said Chen.

'Chen, my friend, we have all tonight and tomorrow to talk,' answered Juan. 'But now I must return to work, I'll see you all later. Don't go looking for trouble, at least not until I get there!'

The four of them laughed, as they watched Juan returning to his position behind the bar. Then they all got up and made for the door. Chen was the first one to reach it, but before he had the chance to open it, four of Don Camillo's men, totally drunk, burst in knocking Chen back into Manuel, and they both fell to the ground. Nunziato and Jon were taken aback. They both aimed a glare at the four drunks and prepared themselves for a serious fight.

One of them with unsightly facial features looked at Chen and said, 'I thought dogs were forbidden to enter this place.'

Juan who had seen everything and was already on his way from behind the bar, rushed to intervene. The locals fearing a brawl made their way out, while the other three drunks were laughing wildly at what their friend had said. By now Chen and Manuel were up on their feet and ready to plant their boots firmly into these thugs, but Nunziato stopped them.

'Manuel, don't do anything stupid, it's not right to start breaking bones on the first day we're here.' Nunziato had successfully stopped Manuel and Chen, but was battling to refrain from getting involved himself. At that moment the pub owner came out.

'What's going on here?' he demanded. Juan's boss was not a violent man, he never gave anyone any trouble and did not like it when anyone came into his bar to cause trouble and scare away his customers. Juan explained quickly the situation, and as soon as he had understood what was going on, he reached behind the counter and took out a rifle, then made his way to the four drunkards. He pointed the rifle at the one who had started the trouble and said. 'Whoever comes here into my bar, comes for a drink and to socialise and it matters not to me their skin colour, as long as they cause no trouble. What do you people want, anyway?' asked the pub owner.

'We want some beer,' slurred one of the drunken men, making fun of Don Filippo by trying to imitate his voice. Don Filippo ignored this and gestured to one of the staff to serve them. It seemed the situation had been diffused.

'It's better to leave now,' said Nunziato. 'I am sure Vincenzo and the others are waiting for us, for lunch.'

They waved goodbye to Juan and made their way outside, mounted their horses and the four of them left, with straight faces, deep in thought, thinking that the situation here was worse than they had imagined. In their mind they saw Don Camillo's men as bandits, or cut throats, but for today, as it happened to be St Joseph's Day, and the engagement of Angelo and Rosita, they had to control their urges to retaliate and everything must go smoothly.

With Nunziato and Jon out in front and Chen and Manuel diagonally behind them, they only needed swords to look like the four musketeers! Rosita was the one who heard the four men arrive and rushed out to Nunziato as he was coming out of the stable. She kissed him saying, 'You know Father, we've prepared a tomato sauce with chilli; your favourite!'

'And yours,' the others said all at the same time. Rosita turned to Jon and slipped her free arm through his and accompanied both men inside.

'Well, lunch is waiting for you when you're ready,' she informed them.

'Mmm, what a good smell,' remarked Manuel, from behind them. 'I can smell something else too, and it's not tomato sauce. What is it?'

'Beef escallops and meatballs,' answered Angelo. 'And today the taste is much better because I helped to make them,' joked Angelo, making everybody laughed.

'In that case, let's go out to eat,' retorted Chen.

'Hey, I take that as an insult,' laughed Angelo, 'Francesca has already tried them, what do you think, my love?'

'Well, they are just about edible,' she said laughing. 'Now stop looking for complements, my love, and help me bring the spaghetti to the table.'

They all sat down around an extended table together, in a convivial atmosphere to enjoy the meal Rosita and Angelo had prepared. It turned out to be delicious, as always. After coffee everyone helped to clean up and put everything away and they went to sit outside under the shade of a tree.

***

Later on in the early evening, the guests, friends of Vincenzo and Angelo, started to arrive. The people were of mixed origins. There were Italians, Spanish and Negro families and they brought with them drinks and food for the celebration, as well as a small present for Angelo and Rosita.

Rosita being a great hostess was happily chatting with all her guests, but every so often her eyes returned to the road. Somebody dear to her was missing, who hadn't show up yet. Angelo had noticed this, but for a while he was also busy with their guests and couldn't go to her immediately. But he managed eventually to make an excuse and worked his way through the crowd sidling up behind her, placing his arms around her waist and gently kissing her cheek.

'I'm sorry, my love, for having left you alone for so long, I haven't forgotten about you though,' he whispered. Rosita turned to face him and draped her arms around his neck.

'I know, my darling, I cannot expect you to be with me always,' she said looking into his hungry eyes.

'Don't worry, Papa Joe and his family will be here soon,' said Angelo.

'I'm a bit concerned, Angelo, I hope nothing's happened to any of them. I didn't see them at the church this morning or at their home when we went past.'

Vincenzo who was passing behind Rosita, overheard her comment, and stopped to talk to her.

'Papa Joe will be here much later,' he said. 'I'm sorry I didn't tell you earlier, but this morning we were very busy and I forgot to mention that they were moving house very early this morning. That's why our other cart is not outside.'

'But why didn't they tell me?' she asked sounding hurt. 'I could have helped. Angelo, did you forget to tell me too?'

'No, my dear, I was in the dark about this as much as you,' he replied.

'Francesca,' said Vincenzo, 'Angelo did not know. It was under the specific request of the doctor. He thought that if you knew about it you would have acted in the same way as you had before. Anyway, they were not alone; Doctor Pedrazza was there, with Stefano and

Mariano too. Doctor Pedrazza used the excuse of helping Papa Joe with his belongings to go to the old hacienda to take provisions, and check the health of the people already hiding there.'

'Very well, Uncle, I understand. You were right not to tell me,' admitted Rosita, feeling silly. She should have known that today was a big day for her, so she had many things to do without having to worry about anything else. And if she'd gone to help Papa Joe, they couldn't fool Donna Teresa and Don Camillo. Vincenzo didn't want her to feel silly in front of other people, so he said.

'You'll have to forgive me, dear,'

'No, Uncle, there's no need to ask for forgiveness, there's nothing to forgive, I only have to thank you for all you do for me.'

Angelo thought they'd done enough talking for now, so he interrupted saying.

'I'm going for a walk, which of you would like to come with me?' But before either could answer, he offered his arm to Rosita and said, 'Excuse me, Father. I'm leaving you in charge of the castle for a few minutes!'

'Have a nice walk then!' Vincenzo said with a smirk on his lips.

Angelo and Rosita left arm in arm, hearing the sound of music starting up behind them, coming from the gramophone, which was playing for the guests to enjoy until the musicians arrived. Angelo wouldn't have left the guests if he hadn't been worried about Rosita. As soon as they were both out of eyesight, he pulled her to him. He squeezed her in a full embrace, and then kissed her as if it was the first time, with passion and intensity. Her response was willing and equally as passionate.

'I have such a powerful longing for you, my love. I aim to have you very soon,' said Angelo, taking her head in his hands, his thumbs caressing the prominence of the satin sun-kissed skin covering her high cheekbones, moving in slow hypnotic circles, feeling the texture of her every cell. His fingers then wandered and trembled in the silken mass of her auburn hair. His kisses were now not gentle, but a bold assault on her mouth that was no surprise to Rosita. She knew he wanted her as much as she wanted him. His tongue plundered her, and she answered with the same intensity that drove him wild.

Then he stopped abruptly. He raised his face in the air; he inhaled deeply the night air, smelling the strong scent of freshly ploughed soil and oleander flowers that surrounded them. They were all along the fence, with their many beautiful colours, red, white and pink. And for a long moment as he was lost in the intoxication of his love making to Rosita, he couldn't even hear the night song of the crickets and frogs.

'I'm sorry Francesca; I was almost tempted to made love to you right here where we stand with our guests waiting. But this is not the time or the place. I only took you away from everybody because I want to talk to you, to ask you if anything was the matter?' he said, still trembling. They both continued to walk a bit further from the house. After a few minutes they came to a stop and Angelo turned to face Rosita, cupping her chin in his hand.

'What's happened, Francesca? Don't tell me it's just Papa Joe not being here, that's upsetting you?'

'No, Angelo, it's not that. It's that woman! I hope she doesn't come tonight with her husband!'

'That woman?' he said nodding, and smiling at her at the same time, 'You mean Donna Teresa? My dear, you must have patience for a little while longer, if we lose our heads now, we will lose everything we've prepared for so far.'

'I know, Angelo, but I cannot get out of my head what she said to Dr Pedrazza. That she loved me as if I was her own daughter. How can she say such a thing? She never loved her daughter when she was younger so how could she love Francesca now all these years later?'

He had to admit she was right to feel bitter towards Donna Teresa and for so many reasons too; Donna Teresa had betrayed her husband when he was alive. Then she married the man who had been her lover after her husband's murder. She had never been a good mother when Rosita was very young. In fact she didn't even recognise her own daughter when face to face with her, not that Rosita wanted to be recognised, not right now anyway or she would be easy prey for Don Camillo.

'My dearest Rosita,' he whispered, 'you're not dead, you're alive, and as beautiful as ever, the most beautiful woman I've ever known in my whole life. I'm sorry, I shouldn't use your real name, my dear Francesca. When Donna Teresa was young, she was very egotistic. But I am convinced that she's regretted not being closer to her daughter many times over the years, she maybe even thinks she'd be with her now if she had looked after her better.'

The noise of approaching horse and cart interrupted them. They turned round to see two carts. The first one carried Dr Pedrazza, Stefano and Mariano, and the second, Papa Joe and his family. They drew to a halt beside the couple.

'What are you two doing here?' asked Doctor Pedrazza.

'Welcome,' Rosita greeted them, clearly happy to see them. 'How are you all and what took you so long?'

'Very well!' they all answered in unison. So Angelo and Rosita climbed onto the back of the cart being driven by Doctor Pedrazza and they headed back to the house. Dr Pedrazza asked Rosita how many of the guests had arrived so far. Even though it was nearly dark, Dr Pedrazza could see the anxiety in Rosita's face.

'Enough,' was her reply. 'The front yard is full and I think we'll have an enjoyable evening!'

'I do hope so,' said Dr Pedrazza. 'All I want tonight is to sit and drink a couple of glasses of wine, and to converse with my friends.'

'Doctor,' interrupted Angelo, 'you asked what we were doing here. Well, Francesca was worried about not seeing any of Papa Joe's family today.'

'Oh I see, it was for this reason you two were here alone!' replied the doctor with a knowing look. 'Well my son, she's right to worry with Don Camillo's men always around sticking their noses in and causing trouble.'

'How is everything going at the old hacienda?' asked Rosita. 'Is everything running smoothly?'

'Oh yes,' answered the doctor. He stopped the cart about twenty metres away from the house. He did not want anyone else to hear what he was about to say.

'Angelo, Francesca,' he whispered, 'the only problem we have now is how to feed the ever growing army that is forming!' At this Angelo and Francesca exchanged a quick puzzled glance with each other and then looked back at the doctor, questioningly. 'The word, my handsome couple, has spread far and wide, and quickly, that you two need help here. The old hacienda is not such a good hiding place anymore; it's more like a refugee camp! There are Negroes, Italians, Chinese and Spanish, and some native Indians all living together and sharing the little food there is and the workload. They don't have many home comforts, but they're getting on very well, and they have already repaired the barn.'

'I can't believe it, Doctor!' Rosita exclaimed all excited. She wished she were there, so she could see for herself and help.

'All of the young people have been getting battle ready by practising martial arts daily. While the others have been helping with anything that needs doing, from working the land to guarding the perimeter. Or preparing makeshift weapons, to cooking and sharing out the little food that they do have. After only one week you wouldn't recognise the place.'

'I want to go and see for myself,' cried Rosita excitedly, and squeezing Angelo's hand with both of hers.

'I'm not saying another word on the subject until I have had something to eat and, more importantly, to drink.' replied the doctor. 'Now your guests are waiting and we're going to join the others if you don't mind.'

'Of course, let's go,' she responded.

Everybody got down from the carts and were soon mixing in with all the other guests. Rosita felt very happy and secure to be surrounded by all of her family and friends. She took Papa Joe's family straight to Nunziato, who embraced Papa Joe for a long few seconds, then Mama Bimpe, and the rest of the family like long lost friends do. Then Rosita introduced Jon and Chen to Papa Joe and his family.

Once the initial confusion of introductions had calmed down, Doctor Pedrazza walked over to Nunziato. Without any words being exchanged they fell into each other's arms like two brothers who hadn't seen each other for so many years. Then moved away from the crowd arm in arm to have a good long talk, they had a lot to catch up on.

Until now everything had been running smoothly, none of Don Camillo's men had showed their faces. The negative outcome to Don Antonio Marquis's investigation had worked in Rosita's favour, to get Don Camillo's men off their backs. Or possibly, only for today, as it was a special occasion, they had been ordered to stay away. Nevertheless, the Curro families were ready with all their faithful friends to defend themselves until the last drop of blood. The party was in full swing when Juan Pellegrini arrived, accompanied by four lovely women dancers. Angelo ran to welcome them, dragging his beautiful fiancée along behind him.

'I thought you were never going to get here?' he laughed, slapping his back.

'Hey, I said I would be here, amigo,' Juan replied, pretending he was hurt. 'Look I have brought my guitar, go and get yours now,' said Juan, raising his eyebrow, and smiling like a Cheshire cat.

'Oh no, please,' answered Angelo, 'today is my party, you go and play with the other musicians. I have to stay close to Francesca, just in case she gets bored?'

'Oh, I like that!' laughed Rosita, as she pinched him for glancing over at the dancing girls. 'You said it Angelo, stay close to me and look only at me, or else!'

At this Juan moved away in the direction of his brother Manuel, still laughing at Rosita's comment.

Angelo and Rosita started to mingle with the guests. Everyone was enjoying themselves, especially now as the alcohol was beginning to take effect. Juan got together with the other musicians, a trumpeter, two more guitarists and one man on a tambourine. They started playing traditional Spanish songs and the young man with the tambourine started to sing. The four beautiful girls Juan had brought with him were dancing on the makeshift wooden dance floor. Angelo had prepared this earlier with the help of his friends, so that not too much dust would be kicked up while they were dancing. All the guests were rocking and dancing to the music too.

It was almost ten o'clock, when Donna Teresa and Don Camillo arrived, accompanied by two armed men. The music stopped, and everyone turned to see the reason why. Vincenzo went to welcome them, followed by Nunziato and Angelo. Rosita watched them from the back of the crowd with disdain. One of Don Camillo's henchmen was middle-aged, smartly dressed with a distinctive over curly moustache. She thought she had seen his face somewhere before and continued staring at him through eyes that could have killed. Manuel noticed this and approached her slipping his arm through hers.

'What are you thinking, Francesca?' he asked her quietly. 'This is not the right moment for any trouble, come on,' he proceeded, with a smile on his face. 'Let's go and say hello to your newest guests.' Manuel guided her forward to stand directly in front of Donna Teresa.

'Good evening, Donna Teresa,' said Rosita, 'it is an honour to have your presence here, and I thank you very much for the lovely present you and your husband have made to Angelo and I.'

'It's a great pleasure for me,' replied Donna Teresa. 'If my daughter were alive today, I would have given it to her, but you have taken her place in my heart, and I wish you and Angelo many years of happiness together.'

'Thank you very much,' replied Rosita bowing her head to Donna Teresa for a few seconds. Her facial muscles seemed to be straining with pain through forcing herself to smile. She took a deep breath and proceeded. 'I hope that one day we can repay the kindness that you and your husband have shown to us.'

At that moment Don Camillo came forward to shake Rosita by the hand, keeping his two men behind him still. Angelo came and stood behind Rosita, and Manuel breathed a sigh of relief because Rosita had kept her cool.

'Don't you think, dear, that we are very honoured to have important guest like this?' said Angelo.

'Yes darling,' she replied, but her attention kept diverting to the man with the moustache. She knew this man, she was sure she'd seen him before, she told herself again.

Angelo invited Donna Teresa and Don Camillo to a place where they could sit down like the guests of honour. He placed them opposite the musicians. A woman quickly brought over a tray holding four empty glasses and two bottles, one of whisky and one of wine.

'Is wine all right for the lady, or would you prefer a soft drink?' asked the woman, placing the tray on the table. Angelo took their orders and started to pour out the drinks for his guests. Rosita was sitting opposite her mother, and noticed she was wearing a three strand necklace of pearls that she remembered her father had given to her mother on their tenth wedding anniversary.

'Strange,' thought Rosita to herself. They had not been in the safe when she, had raided it. Obviously Donna Teresa kept them separately. She did not hear Angelo calling her at first, but his voice broke into her thoughts.

'Francesca, I asked you if you would like to dance with me?'

'Oh yes, darling, with immense pleasure,' she replied, and stood up.

Angelo took her by her hand, excused himself and Rosita from Donna Teresa and the others and led Rosita onto the dancing area. The band was playing a tango and Angelo led Rosita expertly around the dance floor.

'Francesca, I didn't realise you could dance so well!' he whispered into her ear.

'Well you never asked me,' she answered, enjoying every second in Angelo's arms. 'Anyway, we've hardly had much time to talk about dancing,' she proceeded. 'Angelo, did you get a good look at the two men who arrived with Don Camillo?'

'Yes. Why?'

'Don't you think it rude of him to bring these two undesirable thugs with him to our party?'

'Yes, my dear, especially as they were not invited, but they haven't done anything wrong and maybe he feels more secure with them around!'

'What! Even here amongst all these celebrating people he's scared?'

'I don't know, my dear. Would you please calm down, nothing will happen tonight, there are too many people here. If anyone makes a wrong move, there are enough of us to deal with it swiftly and sharply.'

'You're right, darling, please forgive me. I just get anxious when he is around.'

The musicians stopped for a break but Angelo and Rosita continued to mix with and entertain their guests. There was an abundance of colour at this party; the young Spanish guests were dressed in their traditional costumes of red and black frilly dresses and the men in smart tight fitting trousers and fancy shirts. The people native to this land were dressed in their very colourful and ornate attire with brown wide rimmed bowler hats, also including bones and feathers similar to the native Indians who were in their full regalia. Then there were the Chinese families who wore their traditional bright silk outfits. Angelo looked across the crowd and spotted Manuel talking to his brother Juan, who both at the same time glanced over to him. He wondered what those two were up to! He was sure they were talking about him. In fact a couple of minutes passed and the two brothers approached him.

'Come on, amigo, come and play something with us!' said Juan, 'We're going to sing a song together.'

'One moment, my friends, please?' pleaded Angelo. 'I cannot permit myself. I promised Francesca that I wouldn't leave her alone for one minute.'

'That's not so,' intervened Rosita, 'Of course you should go and play your guitar with your friends and sing to me. I promise I'll not go and disappear anywhere!'

'You know what, I believe you,' said Angelo, as he looked at her, his eyes full of love. 'Come,' he said, finding her a place to sit opposite the band. He kissed her forehead and then went to discuss what song they were going to sing.

All the guests started to gather around and soon a Spanish melody began to fill the air. Rosita was very proud and her eyes remained glued to Angelo for a while. Her man's striking good looks shook her more than the dangerous bandits she had not very far from her. She couldn't see them from where she sat, but she knew they were nearby, protecting Don Camillo. Then as she moved her gaze around, she found Donna Teresa staring fixedly at her. Rosita forced a smile and looked back at the musicians. The song came to an end and everyone cheered and applauded. Rosita again looked over at her mother who was now chatting with Vincenzo and Nunziato. She scanned the crowd again to spot Don Camillo's men again, their presence really disturbed her so she wanted to keep a track of where they were at all times.

As she stared at them it suddenly came back to her where she had seen the man with the moustache before. It was at the hacienda when she was younger; he used to arrive with Don Camillo when he visited her mother.

'I bet you are one of the killers involved in the assault fifteen years ago, who disappeared with the others, pretending to be bandits,' she thought to herself. 'I would like nothing more than to strangle you right here and now.' But her thoughts were interrupted by Chen, who came to stand directly in her line of sight.

'Your face, Francesca, tells me you have grave intentions? You're surely not thinking of unleashing deadly force upon anyone without me, are you? Now that I'm here, don't you dare.' He moved round to face the same direction as Rosita and took her arm in his. He spotted the trio who Rosita was looking at, then said. 'Which one would you like for the first course? You cannot take them all at once!'

'Right now, I would like very much to get the one with the moustache. Don Camillo will be the last one. I want him to know who is going to be responsible for his death and the reason why?'

'I understand your anger, sister, but remember your training, you must pick the right time for every outcome. Tonight though belongs to you and Angelo. Let's keep it peaceful and enjoy ourselves.' Chen glanced over at Angelo, he was getting ready to play again but caught Chen's eye. A mere gesture of Chen's eyes towards Rosita and Angelo understood straightaway that he should not leave her by herself. Angelo excused himself from his friends, asking them to play the tarantella. The music started.

'Miss, may I have the honour of this dance?' Angelo asked, bowing slightly in front of her. She got up trying not to laugh, and said.

'Angelo, I cannot dance the Sicilian tarantella very well.'

'Neither can I!' he answered. 'We'll just watch everyone else and copy,' he said, as he pulled her onto the dance area. They soon picked up the steps to the traditional Sicilian dance and for the next few songs Rosita lost herself in the joy of being and dancing with her man.

After she had finished dancing with Angelo, she went to fetch herself a drink but couldn't take her eyes off the ugly man with the moustache, who sat behind Don Camillo. The more she looked at him, the more she was convinced that she was right about him being one of Don Camillo's long standing thugs, who used to accompany him when he visited the hacienda before the assault. She was wondering how long the tyrannical Don Camillo had planned to kill her father before he'd actually carried it out. Rosita was in such deep thought that she didn't notice Don Camillo approaching her. He stopped right in front of her cutting into her line of sight. He had a smile on his face, a cold smile, which didn't reach his eyes.

'May I have the honour of this dance? Please, Miss Curro,' he insisted. Other people were chatting next to them so his voice was not the only one speaking at that moment. Even so, his voice sounded strange in some way, and she didn't like it one bit. 'If your fiancé is not too jealous of course. I know I would be if I had a beautiful fiancée as you are,' he finished. His words were cold like a wind on a very cold morning. This made her feel very ill at ease, so she replied in haste so as not to let her emotions run away with her.

'I'm sure he wouldn't mind me having one dance with his favourite Master.' she said, getting up very slowly. 'Were you jealous of your wife when she was younger? I bet you were. In fact, I would bet you could even kill for her.'

Realising what she had just said, Rosita felt cold all over. She turned and moved slowly towards the dance floor with Don Camillo following behind her. She spotted Angelo, he was almost in front of her talking to his Uncle Nunziato, and he winked at her to reassure her. But it didn't help. Knowing she had to let the man behind her hold her in his arms, she felt numb, then a cold shiver ran through her body. She knew of course that he couldn't harm her; she was surrounded by many of her friends. But again with the thought of him touching her, made her feel sick. They reached the dance floor; Don Camillo took her hand and pulled her tightly to him with little ceremony. Rosita thought that he was punishing her, and she forced herself to smile to show him that she was not afraid.

'You know, Miss Curro,' he began, 'the more I look at you the more you look like someone I used to know.'

'Well, Don Camillo, being a very well-travelled and experienced man, maybe you have heard the old saying,' she said, hesitating for a couple seconds to find the right words to pacify him. 'That in this world there are seven faces that are alike. Maybe I am one of these faces you have come across before.'

Don Camillo laughed out loud, a guffaw that even with the loud music many people heard and turned around to see what was going on. Then he said, 'I doubt that very much. But I will get to the bottom of it, I always do, Miss Curro. May I ask you a personal question?' He proceeded, slowing his pace down, they were dancing a tango, and even at his age, he was a good dancer, thought Rosita. 'Are you really going to marry Angelo? I thought it was improbable, two cousins marrying, and this makes me think something is very wrong here. I can't understand why your parents do not do anything to stop you? Or your uncle, come to think of it?'

Her gaze, bright in the moonlight, rested on his eyes. 'What are you trying to imply Don Camillo?' she said as several things rushed through her mind. One of them was to swiftly knee him in the groin, so she would wipe the smirk off his face. 'Angelo and I are very much in love,' she said.

'Oh, everyone can see that.' said Don Camillo, hesitating whilst staring into Rosita's eyes. He was looking for some small sign that she had been compromised. But seeing nothing there and realising he had probably gone too far, he now began to back track and mellowed his tone. 'It is probably because you two have grown up in separate places and are relative strangers to one another.'

He was now wondering what had made him lose his grip. Because his gut feelings and hunches have hardly ever been wrong. Even his wife had been feeling restless about this girl lately, even though she hadn't said anything.

Don Camillo's words had got to her and his back tracking had come too late. She spouted out. 'Don Camillo, first of all. Could you please stop holding me like I am something that belongs to you. Secondly, to answer your question, in the past and present, many people marry first cousins. And this will continue happening even after you and I are long dead. Thirdly, it's none of your damn business and even though I'm on your property, this does not give you the right to offend me on the day of my engagement. Does you wife know how rude you are?'

The music had stopped during Rosita's outburst. Neither of them had realised this and that all the people were staring at them. Angelo rushed over to Rosita's side in no time. All her faithful friends were not very far from her, people began to move away slowly. Donna Teresa by now was getting impatient and upset with her husband's behaviour. Don Camillo's bodyguards placed their hand on their guns and started to step forward. But both of them changed their minds as soon as they felt something cold and sharp pressed under their chins. Juan and Stefano had a knife each in their hand ready to cut their throats. At that moment, the air was so thick with tension that it could be cut with those very knives. Don Camillo looked around him and saw that everybody was looking at him accusingly. Telling him he had managed to ruin the engagement party.

Angelo placed one arm around Rosita's shoulder. Then he said, addressing Don Camillo.

'Is there something wrong, Don Camillo? Did my fiancée offend you in any way. If she did so, please forgive her as she has not been very well recently.'

Angelo, of course knew it wasn't Rosita's fault for what had happen. He had imagined that Don Camillo hadn't come to the party to enjoy himself, but only to make a scene. Don Camillo of course knew there was no excuse for his behaviour and had no intention of apologising. So, he moved away in anger, pushing his way through the crowd and knocking over a Negro woman with a child in her arms, making her fall on the floor. Like a blind furious bear, he shoved everybody out of his way to make a space for him to get the hell out of there. He called his two men leaving Donna Teresa behind; he knew very well that he had managed to make a fool of himself in front of everybody.

Now Angelo understood why his father had left him ignorant about Don Camillo's nature and of what this man was capable of doing to other people and of what he had done in the past.

It was almost three in morning and the only guests left at the party were Dr Pedrazza, the priest Don Saverio Scalabrini and Juan. The priest had been the last one to arrive, very late, and he again offered accommodation to Nunziato and the others. They thanked him for his kindness, but had decided they would like to stay with Vincenzo, as they had a lot of catching up to do. So in the end they all shook hands and the three friends departed, leaving Vincenzo and the others to prepare themselves for bed, tired and worried, about Don Camillo's questions and Rosita's outburst.

CHAPTER NINETEEN

It was Sunday morning, about ten o'clock. Vincenzo, Angelo, Rosita and the others were cantering along on horseback to visit the old hacienda. Rosita was very excited, she was impatient to see all the people there, and how everything had been restored. The seven people on the horses were chatting as their horses were trotting along, but still keeping a wary eye out for any of Don Camillo's men. In fact they saw quite a few but none of them approached them to ask their business. When they had almost arrived at the old hacienda, it seemed as if the place was deserted. To their surprise they saw a high wooden gate, which had not been there before and when they came nearer, many young men suddenly sprung out, brandishing an assortment of weapons, such as knives and clubs. Vittorio with Stefano and Mariano appeared at the front, and Vittorio swung open the gate, apologising for the disrespectful welcome.

'There is no need to apologise,' laughed Angelo, followed by Rosita, as they saw a large sign written on the gate. *Private property, trespassers will be shot on sight.* They all rode through the gate. And immediately Angelo and Rosita caught each other's eyes, the place was unrecognisable. These people really had been busy, everywhere they looked there were tidy hedges and trimmed trees, new fencing and painted woodwork. They came to a stop near the big barn and dismounted. Nearby stood three young boys, two Spanish and one Negro aged about thirteen, who ran to them, smiling, and took their horses into the re-built stable. Nunziato looked at Rosita and said, 'We were all worried that there wouldn't be enough help, how did you find so many people so quickly in just two weeks?'

'Father, I didn't find them, they found me,' she replied, astonished by all the strangers who had never set eyes on her before, not knowing what was to be expected of them, and yet they all knew that very soon there would be a lot of trouble. Yet these people still came to help Rosita with her quest, and to begin a new happier life.

They started to make their inspection and the first place they checked out was the barn, which was being used as a martial arts school this morning. For a moment none of them uttered a word, they were amazed and impressed with the restored structure. The floor totally covered with tongue and groove wood, that had been found stacked in one of the sheds. Rosita noticed the determined looks on the face of the many young people who were practising martial arts, it seemed as though they were ready to fight. Jon and Chen had never expected to see so many youngsters interested in this place. The three young men who were teaching turned to see who had entered their makeshift kwoon. They were momentarily shocked to see someone entering, but only until they recognised Rosita and Angelo.

The three young men bowed their heads in acknowledgement, and the newcomers returned the gesture. Then the three young men approached Rosita and she introduced them to her father and the rest of the gang. They had a brief chat and went on with their inspection, accompanied by Antonio and Stefano.

When they arrived at the old house, Vincenzo said, 'Look they are preparing the house for when you and Angelo get married.'

At his remark everyone had a laugh. There were at least ten men working on the house, five on the roof, and others were putting up doors and repairing the windows. The house was big, and was an adaptation of a Spanish villa. It was run down, but soon these people would give the house a brand new facelift and make it as it was when it was first built ages ago. Adjacent to the house was a makeshift shack, which was a temporary residence for Papa Joe and his family.

As she hadn't spotted them yet, Rosita asked, 'Where are your family, Vittorio, I haven't seen them around anywhere?'

'They are in the field working, as there is nothing for them to do here,' replied Vittorio. 'They are with other families, preparing the land for the planting of vegetables.'

'But Vittorio,' exclaimed Rosita, 'today is Sunday, and I didn't bring them here to work every day, but only to do as much as they please.'

'Thank you for your kind words, mistress, but they know this. They are eternally thankful to you for freeing them, and they want to show their gratitude.'

Everywhere they went, people stopped working for a second to see who the new people were who dressed so smartly. One of the workers asked Vittorio who the visitors were with a gesture of his hands. Vittorio went over to the workers to explain, and they immediately started to applaud and cheer for Rosita. She felt a rush of emotion come over her, not only for the greeting they gave her, but also for the happiness she saw in their face.

Angelo saw the emotion on her face and swiftly slipped his arm under hers and led her towards the graves where Rosita's grandparents were resting. He bid farewell to the workers as they left and when they arrived at the graveside, she noticed that it had been cleared of the overgrown bushes and long grass, and the area was very tidy and clean with fresh flowers placed at the foot of the graves in a vase. She turned to Vittorio, as he and Stefano had accompanied them and said, 'Somebody has done a splendid job here.'

'Thank you,' he replied. 'My mother and father did it this morning.'

'Good, I would personally like to thank them. Where are they now?' enquired Rosita.

It was Stefano who answered.

'There is a road behind the barn, if you follow it for five hundred metres, you will find them on the left.'

Rosita thanked Stefano, and turned to the others.

'Please carry on the rounds without me, I would like to go and thank Mama Bimpe and Papa Joe.'

Angelo nudged Stefano with his elbow and signalled with his head for Stefano to follow her. As soon as Rosita was out of earshot, Stefano said to Angelo, 'By now, the word is around as to who the new visitors are, she will be safe here.'

But by now Angelo knew how Rosita's mind worked, if there wasn't any trouble, she would be looking for it or it would find her.

'Thank you for your reassurance Stefano, but I would like you to still keep an eye on her for me, please?' asked Angelo, pleading Stefano with his eyes.

'Of course,' Stefano said, as he turned and left to follow Rosita.

She had already mounted her horse and started out towards the field where Papa Joe and the rest of the family were. Stefano followed her on Angelo's horse, but kept his distance so as not to let her know he was following her. She trotted along casually. About two hundred metres along the road, she saw some men chopping down dead trees, and their women and children were stacking the branches into piles ready to burn.

Rosita admired the way the children were working so hard alongside their parents. There was one little girl who was about eight years old, she had long black hair, and as she turned round she saw Rosita approaching. The girl stopped what she was doing, smiled and waved her hand. Rosita smiled back at the little girl and winked at her. The little girl's mother saw this so she too smiled at Rosita and nodded her head in respect. There were also a number of men around who lifted their caps to Rosita as she passed by them. She acknowledged them with a nod of her head.

Presently she arrived at the field where she was told Papa Joe and his family were to be found. She stopped for a few long seconds while she watched the people working hard, with pride in their hearts. It almost brought tears to Rosita's eyes, seeing her grandparents' land reduced to this state, being forgotten for so many years. But now these wonderful people were working the land, not for money, but for the necessity to have a place to stay. They were a mixed race of people, and they were all happy to be working, as there was no pressure. Someone in the group was singing a working song.

Rosita noticed a girl nearly bent over double, who turned and then she stood erect and waved at her; it was Felicia. Instantly she shouted to everybody that the mistress of the land had arrived. They all stopped working and watched as Rosita approached. Anna and Felicia went over to greet her, all bubbly and joyous at this surprise visit.

Papa Joe signalled everybody to gather around, as Rosita went straight over to Mama Bimpe and Papa Joe and embraced both of them together. Once everybody was gathered around, Papa Joe said, 'Brothers and sisters, I introduce you to the owner of this hacienda.'

Rosita looked around at everybody, and then she said, 'Hello to you all and thank you for your hard work. You're very welcome to stay on this land.' As she said this, two men approached her. One Italian and the other French. The Italian man addressed Rosita.

'As the people's spokesman,' he began, 'we would like to thank you and we promise to do our best to have this hacienda ready and working as soon as possible. We're at your disposal for anything you may need.'

'On the contrary,' said Rosita, 'I should be the one to thank you all for being here to help me in my time of need. You know I cannot pay you for your work just yet?' she finished.

She was then interrupted by a woman.

'We don't want your money. Right now all we need is a safe and tranquil place to stay, a little shack where we can settle, instead of being kicked around from place to place,' the woman said. She could have been about thirty, but she looked forty-five. Tears were rolling down her tired and sweaty face.

'Then my good woman, if you believe in God, pray for us all. Pray for us to succeed in our cause. Be honest with each other, respect one another, and you will see that one day very soon I hope, you will have a permanent place of your own, and lots of work for all of you,' finished Rosita. Then she went back to Papa Joe and said, looking back at all of them. 'Obey Papa Joe, Vittorio, Stefano and Mariano. Papa Joe will run the hacienda for me when I'm not here. I think he will be a good father figure to all of you.'

Then she turned and led the two old people she loved so much, away from the crowd, to talk with them in private.

'Tomorrow,' she began, 'I'm going into Tucuman City. I want you to know that when the house is finished, I would like very much, if you and your family live in it.'

'What are you saying, Mistress Francesca?' exclaimed Mama Bimpe. 'The house is for you to live in!' Rosita just smiled at her. 'When do you think you will return from Tucuman? Is this trip really necessary?'

'Yes,' replied Rosita, 'it's very important for all of us. Nunziato, Jon Chian, Chen, and Manuel will stay behind, and they will make sure that no harm comes to anyone. I also want to thank you two very much for clearing up my grandparent's graves' this morning. I cannot tell you how much this means to me.' She hugged them both simultaneously again, and then turned away from them saying, 'And now I must go, I will see you later.'

Rosita made her way over to her horse, mounted it and headed back towards the others. She had hardly gone ten metres when she saw Stefano sitting under a tree with his hat over his eyes and a cigarette in his mouth. He was pretending he hadn't seen Rosita. She was not fooled by this façade though, so she led her horse toward him and stopped at his feet without saying a word. He looked up, pretending he was surprised, and said.

'Francesca, I didn't hear you arrive, I was just having a nap.'

'Really Stefano? You came all the way out here to have a nap, and on Angelo's horse too,' asked Rosita. Stefano just shrugged his shoulders and smiled. 'Come on,' she said, obviously amused, 'let's catch up with the others.'

Stefano got up, dusted himself down and went over to Angelo's horse, which was contentedly eating grass at the edge of the track, and mounted it. Rosita was just watching him as if waiting for an answer, but suddenly they heard gunshots, nearby. They both looked around to where the shots had come from but they saw nothing. They both galloped towards where Papa Joe and the others were, and they stood there with the others. There was no sign of any disturbance, but a couple of people were pointing towards where they thought the gunshots came from.

Rosita couldn't wait any longer, she had to go and see what was happening. So she drew her rifle from its holster and ordered Stefano to go back and get the others. Stefano looked at her sternly. He wanted to say that he should go to find out what was going on, and she should go and get help. But he reluctantly obeyed her, after all she was his boss and so he rode off as fast as he could to get help.

Rosita told Papa Joe to get all the people away from the area and into the house and then galloped towards the trees in the distance. Once there she stopped and listened, she heard someone running through the undergrowth, she dismounted and got her horse to lay down behind some bushes. She fed the first bullet into the chamber of her rifle, and bought the rifle up to her shoulder ready to fire. The running sounds got closer and she could now hear that there was more than one person. She imagined that somebody was running for his life. Her heart was pounding, as she didn't know what was ahead, but it was something she had to do. It was her land, and nobody had the right to make trouble in it.

All of sudden a native American woman and three young children burst out of the bush and stopped dead at the sight of Rosita holding a rifle up in their direction. The children quickly hid behind their mother.

'Go on running that way, you'll be safe there,' said Rosita quietly pointing behind her to the right.

The woman pushed her children in the direction Rosita had pointed to and said, 'My husband! He's wounded back there.'

'Don't worry, you get going, I'll find him,' ordered Rosita as she started walking slowly into the wooded area. She kept on listening and was moving the rifle back and forth in an arc across the horizon of her field of vision. She'd only got about fifteen metres when she spotted the wounded man, he was on his knees cradling his upper left arm. He heard Rosita approaching and looked up startled; he thought it was his pursuers. She quickly walked over to him and put her arm out to help him up. But suddenly she heard horses approaching; they sounded as if they were spread out. She signalled him not to move and crept backwards to hide behind a bush. The sound of horses came closer. Then she spotted three men on horseback.

One of them shouted, 'Hey! Over here, there is blood on the ground.'

The three men followed the trail of blood together. This was ideal for Rosita as she wouldn't have to worry about someone coming up behind her. It didn't take long for the three men to find the injured man now lying on the ground. One of them said to the injured man, 'So! You thought you could get away, aye?'

'Leave me alone, I have done nothing wrong,' said the poor man on the ground.

'I tell you what is wrong, you're an Indian, that's what is wrong.'

With that comment, the three troublemakers started to laugh in unison. One of them drew his handgun and pointed it at the Native American sprawled on the floor who curled up into a ball to try to protect himself as best he could. Luckily for Rosita, the three men were positioned at a forty-five degree angle to her, with one of the men hidden behind the man with the pistol drawn.

She couldn't delay any longer so she jumped up and shouted. 'Hey I'm here,' as she shot the man with the gun between the eyes and then the older of the three, who was positioned just behind the first, in the chest. The third man turned and rode off at a gallop, Rosita took aim and let off another shot, but didn't know whether she'd hit him or not. She ran over to the two she had shot, to make sure they were dead. She pointed the rifle at the head of a man she had shot in the chest. He was lying face down. She slowly turned him over by pulling at his arm. He was dead and there was no need to check the other one, as the back of his head was missing.

'Their bullying days are over,' she thought to herself.

Rosita heard more horses arriving from behind her, she guessed it was Angelo and the rest of her gang arriving. She went over to the Indian and helped him up, whilst still looking out for the third man in case he returned. She walked in the direction that Angelo and the others were coming from. There were ten of them altogether, and they rode towards Rosita guns at the ready.

Angelo, Manuel and Vincenzo stopped to help the wounded native Indian. The others rode in the direction of the third bandit after

Rosita had told them about him. The Indian man was obviously worried about how and where his wife and children were. So Vincenzo assured him.

'Don't worry, they are safe.'

Rosita gently removed his shirt to inspect his wound; she could not help him much standing here as it was quite a bad wound. Angelo pulled out a handkerchief from his pocket and tied it tightly above the man's wound, which made the man groan in pain, but he had to try to stop the bleeding. He wrapped another kerchief that Manuel had handed him to place over the open wound and put his arm up in a sling using the Indian's own shirt.

'We must get him to the barn and get the doctor for him quickly,' said Vincenzo.

Angelo and Manuel helped the poor man onto Vincenzo's horse. Then Vincenzo and Manuel left with the wounded man. Rosita looked towards where the third gunman had fled and wondered whether he had been captured.

Angelo took a hold of her arm, and said, 'Oh no you don't. From now on let others deal with these sorts of things. Now let's get back to the barn, so we can reassure Papa Joe and Mama Bimpe that everything is fine. Dear God, Francesca,' he said, and pulled her to him, in a strong embrace. 'Couldn't you have just waited for us?'

'I'm sorry, Angelo. Yes I could have, but if I had, the poor Indian lady and her children would now be without a husband and a father and those bandits would still be alive to cause even more trouble for others,' she answered.

'You always have an answer for everything, and that is why I love you so much, Francesca. But in future could you please be a little less reckless, please, just for me,' pleaded Angelo lovingly as he embraced her again, and then kissed her passionately. Rosita returned his kisses with equal passion, which helped her to shake off the adrenalin tremors which had started to take effect on her.

They then mounted their horses and headed back towards the barn. As they passed the field where Papa Joe had been working, they saw the old couple holding one another and Mama Bimpe was crying because she was worried for Rosita. After dismounting her horse whilst it was still trotting, Rosita ran over to them.

She flung her arms around them and said, 'Everything is going to be fine, come back with us to the hacienda. You two can take my horse.'

'No, we'll walk,' answered Papa Joe.

'Nonsense, take my horse, I'll go with Angelo.'

Reluctantly, Papa Joe mounted Rosita's horse, and with a helping hand from Angelo, Mama Bimpe sat side saddle in front of her husband.

When they all arrived at the barn, they saw that someone was tending to the poor Indian man who had been shot. They were preparing to take out the bullet which had lodged itself in the man's shoulder. They had all the medication and equipment they needed, as the doctor had left them during his last visit. The doctor had been called and was on his way, just in case of any complication. Angelo stayed in the barn to help out. Rosita sat outside on a log with her head in her hands thinking things through. The two sisters-in-law, Anna and Felicia come over and sat by her.

'Are you all right, you're not hurt, are you?' Anna asked.

'No Anna, I'm fine,' answered Rosita reassuringly.

'Are you worried about something then?' This time it was Felicia enquiring.

'No,' replied Rosita through a weak smile and then she went on to say, 'You see, my two dear friends, in a situation like I was in today, one shouldn't be afraid, one should only think about defending yourself. Especially when you come across ignorant, arrogant men like that, you have to think and act quickly. It's either you or them and I will not stop until I have finished off every last one of Don Camillo's thugs, whatever hole they may crawl into or stone they may hide under.'

Of course the two women knew why she was really upset. Rosita had been heavily reprimanded by her whole family; she had worried them all, family and friends very deeply. Rosita had heard the distress in Angelo's voice when he'd told her she should have waited for them. Of course Angelo and the others knew how capable she was at defending herself, but one person on their own was always riskier than when you're with others who can back you up.

'With the help of all the people around you here, I'm sure you will succeed at dispatching all of Don Camillo's bullies. But you must not put your life at risk, without you, mistress, we are all lost,' said Felicia.

'Hold on,' said Rosita, 'you two seem to think I'm putting myself in danger without a second thought?'

'Oh no, mistress, we just don't want anything bad to happen to you, that's all.'

'You don't have to worry about me, girls, I'm always careful and anyway, I have God on my side.' Getting up from the log and positioning herself between the two women, Rosita placed an arm over each of them and speaking very calmly said. 'Anna, Felicia, tomorrow I'll be going away for a couple of days or maybe longer. I want you to watch carefully over Papa Joe and Mama Bimpe. I want you to tell them that I said they shouldn't work so hard, there are plenty of young people to do the heavy work that is necessary. Your parents are in charge of the hacienda while I am not here, so they should just manage the place.'

'It's not easy to stop Mother and Father working hard, that's what they have done all of their lives,' Anna said. Then she asked, 'Mistress where are you going?'

'I just need to sort out some business.'

'You don't want to tell us the truth, do you? You're not going to choose your wedding dress, are you?' insisted Felicia, excitedly.

'No, my friends, I don't think we have the time to do that. But I promise I will bring back some good material, so you can make some winter dresses for yourselves. Which one of you can make dresses?'

'We both can,' Anna answered. 'But my sister-in-law here is very good, she makes lovely clothes.'

The three young women continued talking for another half hour about materials and colours that were in fashion at the moment, whilst waiting for someone to come out from the barn with some news of how the injured man was doing. Finally, Angelo came out. Rosita quickly got up and went over to him. Angelo wrapped an arm around her shoulders and squeezed her to him.

'How is he?' she asked Angelo.

'They got the bullet out, and I think he will be fine with a little rest. His name is Paco and he wants to see you, so he can thank you personally for saving his life and that of his family.'

All four went in to see Paco. Rosita knelt down by him and took hold of his hand.

'Angelo told me your name is Paco,' she said

He nodded in response. He looked rather weak as if he were about to faint at any moment. But he found the strength to lift his head and said, 'I am in your obligation for the rest of my life, Lady boss, muchas gracias,' Rosita blushed, at Paco's praise.

'It was nothing Paco, you just rest now and get better and look after your family.' Paco closed his eyes. Rosita looked up at the man who had pulled out the bullet from Paco's shoulder, with a worried look on her face.

'Don't you worry, miss, it's the sleeping drug I gave him,' said the young man. 'He will sleep for a while and feel no pain. We have sent for Doctor Pedrazza, he will give him some other medication if required.'

Rosita shook hands with the young man and thanked him. She saw how professional the bandage was that bound Paco's shoulder, this young man must have had some training in doctoring.

'I'm sure you have done a good job here.' she said, and with that she exited with Angelo, Vincenzo and the two sisters-in-law.

Angelo and his father walked off to carry on checking the work that was going on at the old hacienda, whilst Rosita, Anna and Topey went to see Paco's wife and children to give them the good news.

When they arrived at the shack, they saw Paco's wife, Cecilia, and the children sat on the floor drinking some hot soup. The woman looked up and saw Rosita. She immediately put down her bowl and approached her, knelt down at Rosita's feet, took hold of Rosita's hands and kissed them both, saying thank you repeatedly.

Rosita knelt down in front of Cecilia and embraced her, saying, 'Don't be silly, this is not necessary. We've come to tell you that your husband is out of danger, he's sleeping and he will be well very soon. If you wish you can go to see him over in the barn.'

Anna approached Cecilia and helped her up and then escorted her and her children over to the barn. Rosita instead went out and stood by Mama Bimpe who was cooking.

'What a lovely smell, what are you cooking?' she asked.

'I'm cooking stewed rabbit,' answered Mama Bimpe.

'Are you cooking for many?'

'I'm cooking for us, for your lot, and for the newcomers. Someone has to look after them until they can fend for themselves.'

'Thank you Mama Bimpe for everything,' said Rosita, as the sound of approaching horses drew her attention across to the barn. She excused herself and headed towards them. It was the men who had gone after the third bandit. Rosita approached Nunziato and asked if they'd managed to capture him.

'Oh yes, we found him, with one of your bullets in him,' said Nunziato.

'Was he dead when you found him?' she asked.

'No, we tried to make him talk, but he was too badly injured. Before he died he managed to splutter a warning that other men would come and get us. Anyway we buried him and his companions together, they can keep each other company forever. We then sent their horses back off the land.'

'And now what?' Rosita asked her father.

'Well, while you're away with Angelo, we have to stay here and protect these people. And we have to build a fence around the land. You and Angelo go to Tucuman, and I hope that your trip is not wasted.'

'Father, please don't worry, you'll see, everything will work out just fine. The families I'm going to see will help us, I'm sure of it. And anyway, don't you think that people like them who have a lot to lose, would already have someone around here to find out exactly what is going on?'

'Yes, darling,' replied Nunziato, 'I also think this could be true, especially after what happen at Donna Teresa's house. And from what my brother Vincenzo tells me, I'm sure that they know by now that Don Camillo has other enemies.'

'Of course,' said Rosita, 'that's why they haven't attacked the Hacienda Antigua yet, I think they are waiting to see what happens next. Well, yes, I think it will be easy talking to the four families knowing all this.'

The two Chinamen, father and son approached. Jon asked if everything was okay.

'Yes, everything is fine,' answered Nunziato as he started to yawn.

'Oh, it seems as if you're tired,' said Chen.

'Yes, a little, and I'm also a bit hungry, after all it is after two clock,' replied Nunziato.

'Very well then. Let's see what you and Francesca put in the nap sack for lunch,' said Jon.

'You can eat that later, or tomorrow. Mama Bimpe is cooking lunch for us as we speak,' interrupted Rosita. They all headed towards where Mama Bimpe was cooking. Stefano, Mariano, Vittorio and Manuel were already at the makeshift table, which was put together by placing planks of wood on top of short thirty centimetre diameter tree trunks, with a plain white cloth over it.

They were chewing on bread and tomatoes and as they approached Chen then said jokingly, 'That's charming, starting to eat without me.'

Vittorio made space beside him to let Chen sit down. And handed him half a loaf of bread, saying to him, 'Our stomachs were rumbling like mad, if we hadn't started eating the rumbles would have been heard in Las Cejias.'

Angelo made space for Rosita and himself, at the table too. And looking over to Vittorio said jokingly, 'Are you sure it was your stomach that was rumbling?'

'Not only do I have to share a table with a white man, but he insults me too!'

Mama Bimpe came over and handed a dish of stew to Angelo.

'Thank you Mama Bimpe' said Angelo with a smirk on his face.

'Excuse me, Mother,' interjected Vittorio, 'I'm your son, can't you see? You should be serving me first.'

'Leave me out of this you silly boy,' replied his mother joining in with the banter. Angelo passed on the dish of stew and bread roll he'd been given, to Rosita and burst out laughing at Vittorio being verbally slapped down by his mother.

Topey, Vittorio's wife and his sister, Anna, arrived with the cauldron of stew and more plates and straightaway began to help Mama Bimpe to dish out the rest of the stew. They both joined in with the infectious laughter not really knowing what the joke was about. They all continued laughing and chatting over lunch which took them just over an hour. At the end they all thanked and congratulated Mama Bimpe for the delicious rabbit stew she had prepared. The men got up and discussed what they were to do next. Rosita insisted on helping Mama Bimpe and the two sisters-in-law to clear up.

Rosita started to feel really content now after the drama from earlier. The smell in the air of freshly cut grass and the loosened soil from the fields that had been hoed that morning made her feel very light-headed in a euphoric way. Her spirit felt as if it were floating in the air. Everything seemed to be going the right way. Up until now, the people around her were busy and tranquil. They were not thinking about the inevitable trouble that lay ahead, but were just happy to have a safe place to stop for a while with their children and rest their minds. To work in peace without the constant threat of being bullied by nasty people pushing them about and abusing them. Their souls felt as if they had lived here for ages.

Rosita also felt some sort of spiritual force surrounding them, as if something was guiding everybody's mind. In the background of her thoughts she could hear the happy cries of children playing nearby. This was really like putting the icing on the cake for her. For they were her future, the future young people who would in a handful of years be working her land.

Her thoughts and plans were coming to her clearly and abundantly, fliting from place to place. She was thinking about the acre of land to the front of the old house, which in Rosita's imagination was once a beautiful English style garden. She could picture flowers and trees all around the house, a mini maze made from low cut bushes in a circular pattern to the front and the colourful beauty of garden plants filling all the way around to the back of the house.

Not very far from the left wing of the house, some young people had found a gazebo, built in the same Spanish style, overgrown with weeds and shrubs. She could picture it finished with Angelo and herself sitting under it with their young children playing nearby. A couple of kilometres away from the house, behind a small hill, not far from where Rosita had rescued the Indian family, there is a waste piece of land, that once was an apple and pears orchard, her mind was seeing this in full bloom.

During Rosita's last visit to the old hacienda, Stefano, along with a few of his friends, were out looking for food, and in doing so discovered a row of barracks where the workers once used to stay while they were working for her grandparents. She was planning in her head what to do with those when her thoughts were interrupted.

'Well, my good friends,' said Vittorio to Angelo and others, 'let's go for a walk or maybe we can go for some light exercise, it'll help our digestion.'

'What type of exercise are you talking about?' asked Angelo, 'my stomach is so full.'

At that, Stefano suggested they go knife throwing and to practise archery. Then he added, 'We shouldn't do anything too strenuous straight after lunch.'

'Excellent idea Stefano,' said Rosita, 'I'll come along too.' All the others agreed. So, they went off leaving the older men smoking and dozing in the shade. And Mama Bimpe with her daughters and daughter-in-law went in to catch a little siesta, after they had finished clearing away the pots and pans.

***

It was about six o'clock in the evening when they returned from their archery and knife throwing practice. They were bantering with each other about Rosita's luck in the archery, as Chen and Angelo had come joint second in their competition. They felt taken aback because they thought that their aim was good, but Rosita had beaten them both. The old men woke up to the sound of the bantering, and as the younger men approached Angelo said to them.

'Well, did you enjoy your sleep, old boys?'

The older men, looked at each other blankly, as if to say, what are they on about, we weren't asleep. But before anybody could comment everybody burst out laughing.

'At least, we have not been beaten by a woman,' said Nunziato stretching, as he and his brother got up and walked towards the barn, still laughing.

'Oh, I see,' said Angelo, 'let's follow them and see what they're up to, I'd like to see if the two brothers are still as good as they were.'

'What do you mean?' asked Rosita.

'Martial arts, have you not heard of it?' replied Angelo jokingly. Rosita was surprised at this. She knew that Nunziato could fight, but she had never seen Vincenzo in action.

'Hang on a moment. You never told me your father knew martial arts too.'

'You never asked me.' retorted Angelo, smiling down at her.

They all entered the barn, Jon turned to the group of men and said, 'We don't want any spectators here; if you want to stay you must take off your shoes and socks and join in with us.'

Angelo was the first to take off his shoes and socks then bowed to the centre of the barn and entered into the fighting area. The others followed directly. Everybody got into position facing Jon and Nunziato who had put themselves at the front and started to give instruction. Word got around quickly and pretty soon the barn filled up with others including youngsters who joined in with the class.

Rosita stood behind Angelo, so she could assess his abilities. His style was formidable, she thought to herself. Why had he never told her that he had learnt martial arts? Maybe he wanted to keep it a secret. She was glad though that there was more to him than he showed. They all stopped for a few minutes, after they had finished a half hour sparing session of Kung Fu. Rosita took this opportunity to step forward and stand by Angelo, but she didn't say anything because Jon was about to demonstrate another exercise.

This time Jon Chian asked them if they knew about Hap Ga self-defences. Most of them knew little or nothing about it, so were happy to try it and pick up some new techniques. Jon, briefly explained that the origins of this style of Hap Ga, goes back to the Qing Dynasty in the 1600s and used to be known as 'lion's Roar!' Rosita turned her head towards Angelo and smiled. They continued learning for another hour before Jon bought the lesson to an end. He was elated that he had so many people to teach.

Now while Jon Chian was answering questions fired at him by the crowd of youngsters that had formed around him, Rosita took Angelo by the arm and led him outside without a word. Angelo allowed himself to be led behind the barn. Once there Rosita embraced him and gave him a long passionate kiss.

'Well, well,' said Angelo licking his lips. Rosita had woken the sleeping dragon in Angelo. He had wanted to do this all day, but being surrounded by people all the time had managed to control himself.

'What have I done to deserve this?' asked Angelo, getting aroused very quickly.

'It's not what you have done. It's what you are. Every day that passes I love you more and more. You have some beautiful qualities, and I think I am the luckiest woman on the earth to have you by my side. I hope it lasts forever.'

'I hope so too. I know, with your love and the help of God, everything will work out just fine. And now I think we'd better get back.' he said, looking at her longingly and holding her gently to him, 'because we have to get home and pack. You know where we have to go tomorrow?'

That was what his brain had told him to say. But his heart was fighting this, urging him to do the opposite. His heart won the battle, because before he knew it he had wrapped Rosita tightly in his arms and had begun to kiss her like a hungry wolf devouring his prey, forgetting where he was, lost in the whirlwind of passion. Some children passed by but they didn't notice them; they were too busy running around chasing one another, frightening the chickens, and other animals that were tied to some trees.

When Angelo lifted his head away from Rosita, she still had her eyes shut and he was out of breath, in fact they both were.

'You, my beautiful witch, make me forget my manners sometimes. I almost made love to you, here in front of all these children, and anybody else who may have passed by.'

'Yes, darling, I'm sorry I couldn't help it either. We'd better get back, before they send out a search party to find us.' She said, still gasping for air, and they headed back to the barn.

Not long after, Angelo and Rosita said their goodbyes to Papa Joe and his family. To Nunziato and the rest of her closer friends who were staying behind to watch over the old hacienda for Rosita, until the big day arrived. They said a few quick words to Stefano, Mariano and the others, before they made their way back home. Rosita gave one more longer hug to the man who had been her father and protector for the last fifteen years, Nunziato.

'Be very careful Father, look after yourself,' she said, sad that she had to leave him behind, but she knew he would do a good job here with the help of all the others.

'Don't worry about us, darling,' he replied, 'we will have this place guarded day and night. No harm will come to us here. You just have a good trip and let's hope it won't be wasted. Go now and God be with you two.'

Angelo and Vincenzo were already on their horses. Rosita now mounted her horse and they rode off, waving as they went.

The horses were trotting at a low pace as the track they were travelling through was only wide enough for two horses at a squeeze; the three of them were riding in single file, one behind the other. Rosita was at the back. They moved in complete silence each of them deep in their thoughts. Rosita's body suddenly shivered, it wasn't because she was afraid, but as it was the beginning of autumn the evening air was becoming fresh, probably cooler than she'd expected. The beautiful summer days were over, making way for the rainy season. The leaves were changing colour and falling from the many trees dominating the landscape. As if she'd just woken from a dream, Rosita noticed that the trees around her had only a few sparse rust coloured leaves, the really cold weather was on its way. The coldest part of the year, May to August was almost upon them.

CHAPTER TWENTY

The next morning, the sun began glowing faintly through the clouds, but as the mist cleared away, the sun became brighter in the sky. The weather turned out to be warm. At Las-Cejias railway station, Rosita and Angelo waited for their train, Vincenzo and Juan had accompanied them. They didn't have to wait long, as the ten a.m. train arrived bang on time. Juan and Angelo put the bags on board the train, while Rosita hugged Vincenzo and assured him that all would go smoothly.

'Oh don't worry about me, Francesca; I know everything will work out just fine, just make sure you two have a good time.'

'Goodbye Uncle, we'll see you soon,' she said, and she quickly stepped up onto the train. Angelo and Juan jumped down from the train, Angelo embraced his father and Juan. He then turned to his father again and said.

'Father, I don't like the idea of you being alone while I'm away.'

'Don't worry, son, we have already worked something out. I'll be at the old hacienda working for most of the days, and at night Juan will sleep over at our house until you return.'

The train driver sounded his whistled, the train was about to leave. Angelo quickly jumped aboard, closed the door behind him and leaned out of the window with Rosita. There was a slight jolt and the train started to move off slowly. Rosita's heart began to beat faster into her chest, through both excitement and uncertainty of what was to come. They were on their way to meet some influential and powerful people that they had never met before but knew by reputation, and not always a good reputation. And even though she felt apprehensive, somehow deep inside her she knew that everything would go just fine.

'Bye Father, bye, Juan, and thanks for all your help,' shouted Angelo as the train began to move further away from where Vincenzo and Juan were stood on the platform. Rosita waved her handkerchief from the window until the train had disappeared into the distance. Angelo noticed that Rosita looked a little sad; her eyes were glistening as they filled with tears. Leaving her uncle and stepfather behind like this disturbed her, probably more than if it were Angelo she was leaving behind.

'Come on, darling, let's find our seats, we have a long trip ahead of us.' He tried to soften the mood a little by making a suggestive statement. 'We'd better find something to do to kill a little time,' he said, raising an eyebrow once or twice. It didn't work, so as soon as they'd found an empty compartment, Angelo closed the door behind them, took Rosita's hand in his and started to kiss it gently. He needed to see her smile, so he said with a wry smile.

'Just think, my darling, of all the interesting things that we can do all alone in this compartment, in the time it takes to get from here to Tucuman!' Angelo was looking into Rosita's eyes intently and was just about to kiss Rosita when the door to the compartment opened abruptly.

In walked a bearded man dressed in a long black robe and a big black hat. He was holding a book and a string of beads with a Star of David on it; he was a rabbi.

Rosita looked at him for a long moment, and then looked at Angelo, thinking to herself, 'bang goes your idea for interesting things to do!' He knew exactly what she was thinking and they couldn't help themselves from bursting out in laughter.

The man looked at them quite sternly thinking that they were laughing at him. He continued to fiddle with his beads and to pray. Angelo noticed his look, so he stood up, apologised to the man and introduced Rosita as Francesca and himself. He then led Rosita out of the compartment and into the corridor of the carriage for them to have a few moments alone and to compose themselves again.

The journey went well; they conversed with the rabbi on various subjects, on all of which the rabbi was very knowledgeable. They shared and exchanged food with him and played cards with him to pass the time. Not quite as Angelo had hoped and planned, but the time seemed to pass quickly. At about nine p.m. the train steward passed by to turn the seats up into bunks and hand out the sheets and blankets. By ten p.m. they were all tucked up in their separate bunks and the lights were turned down. The rabbi was already snoring.

Angelo looked at Rosita knowingly, slipped out of his bunk to join her for a quick hug before going to sleep themselves. They felt like a couple of naughty teenagers stealing a cheeky moment whilst the rabbi was sleeping. As usual, the quick kiss turned into a fight of passion against common decency. So after a few minutes of heated emotional kissing, Rosita was strong enough to pushed Angelo away, placing her forefinger on his lips and guiding him back to his bunk.

'Sweet dreams,' she whispered to him with a radiant smile spread across her face.

They arrived in Tucuman City early the next morning, a little tired and cramped after sleeping on the uncomfortable bunks for such long time. They were relieved to have arrived here, because they now had about a week to spend alone together, to do some sight-seeing as well as sort out their business. Rosita was looking forward to exploring this town, which was new to her. Yet she seemed to find it familiar. Maybe she had dreamed about it, or her father could have brought her here when she was young. She would soon find out one way or the other.

Angelo picked up the large bag whilst Rosita took her handbag and a small travel bag. They stepped off the train. Angelo took her by the hand and escorted her towards the taxi rank. A driver approached them from his cab and helped put the baggage in the boot and then opened the door for them. Once back in his seat, the driver started the engine and asked where the couple wanted to go.

'Can you recommend a good hotel?' asked Angelo.

"Certainly Sir. I will take you to the Grand Hotel, you won't be disappointed, I promise." Replied the driver. Neither of them said a word, they were both taking in the views from the window on their side of the taxi.

Within ten minutes the driver pulled up outside the hotel. The driver quickly got out and opened the doors for them and then he went to the back of the car to get the bags out of the boot. He even helped to carry them into the hotel entrance where a hotel porter took the bags to the reception desk. Angelo paid the driver his fare and gave him a large tip on top. The driver went off thanking Angelo and smiling at his good fortune. Then Angelo went to the reception desk and asked the receptionist if they had two single rooms available.

'I'm sorry, Señor, but we only have two double rooms available, would you like one of those?'

'That will be fine, my dear,' interrupted Rosita, 'but we're not married, we don't want to get into trouble with the management. What if the manager asks for a marriage certificate?'

The receptionist was a middle-aged but very attractive woman. Her face was clear and lightly made up, her mousy brown hair with a hint of grey appearing scraped back into a bun. Her green eyes were smiling, dancing with mischief.

'That will not be necessary young lady. My name is Mrs Laura Caruso and I am the owner of this hotel. I just require your signatures on the register.'

'Thank you, madam,' replied Angelo, 'that's very kind of you.' He blushed a little. They both signed the register, the lady behind the desk rang a bell and a porter came straight over. Mrs Caruso handed the room key to the porter and he picked up their bags and accompanied them to their room. The porter placed the bags in their room, and turned to go. Angelo followed him to the door and discreetly slipped a folded twenty peso note into the young man's hand, who in return thanked him whilst backing out of the door.

Rosita threw herself backwards onto the bed and said, 'Tonight at least we will sleep well, without the noise of the train rattling in our ears and through our bones.'

'Or the rabbi's snoring.' added Angelo as he moved towards her and lay down on his side beside her and suggested they had a little nap before they went out anywhere. He put his arm around her shoulders, to cuddle up with her.

'I think I will have a bath first. I will be able to sleep better afterwards, but you go ahead and sleep, darling,' said Rosita, turning towards Angelo. She took his face in her hands and pecked him gently on his lips a few times. He responded by kissing her a little more firmly, resting his lips on hers and exploring the softness of her mouth. One kiss led to another and Rosita forgot all about the bath she was going to take. She was lost in the heady haze of lovemaking. Angelo interrupted her dream state to whisper.

'Darling, your bath will have to wait now,' he pulled her tightly to him; Rosita tried to escape his grip and started to giggle. She knew she wouldn't get away now.

'Oh no you don't,' he said. She could feel his arousal pressing against her stomach. 'You started this. I tried very hard to be considerate and resist you, thinking how tired you must be after that long uncomfortable journey.'

Even though Rosita struggled a little, she was just playing the game. What she really wanted was to stay in the arms of the man she loved so much. They spiralled into such an intense passion, that not even a steam train passing through their room would have disturbed them. Eventually, they both fell asleep, naked in each other's arms. Angelo and Rosita slept so deeply it was late evening by the time they woke. It was a knock at the door that stirred them both.

'Who is it?' asked Angelo, with a sleepy voice.

'My name is Armando, Señor. I am the waiter,' came the reply from behind the door. 'I hope I am not disturbing you, but if you would like something to eat, the kitchen will be closing shortly.'

'One moment, Armando' said Angelo as he quickly dressed.

'Goodness, what time is it?' asked Rosita. She pulled the blankets up to cover her naked body. Just in time for Angelo to open the door.

'Good evening Señor,' said the waiter. 'I'm sorry waking you up, but my boss wants to know if you would like to eat downstairs or in your room.'

'One minute,' said Angelo, and asked Rosita if she was hungry and if she wanted to eat in the restaurant.

'Yes, darling, a little and it would be nice to eat in the restaurant. It won't take long to get ready. I'll eat anything.'

'Fine. Then we'll be down in ten minutes, Armando.'

'Thank you, Señor,' the waiter replied and turned to go back to his duty.

Angelo quickly closed the door, Rosita jumped up and put on a dressing gown and went into the bathroom. In a short while they were both ready to go down for dinner.

'I'm ready,' said Rosita.

'So am I, sweetheart, it's time to go down. We don't want to keep them waiting longer than necessary.'

Angelo quickly picked up his wallet; they looked at each other and smiled as if to say, yes, we both look okay. They walked down the staircase holding hands, both feeling quite relaxed after their lovemaking and much needed sleep. They looked like a couple on their honeymoon. They entered the restaurant, Rosita walking slightly in front of Angelo with his arm on her shoulder. They looked around the room. As expected there were a lot of people in the restaurant.

Armando, the waiter who had called on them earlier, saw them enter and immediately walked over to them with a smile, and said, 'This way please, I will take you to your table.'

'Thank you.' They both replied, and they followed him to a beautifully laid table. All the cutlery and glassware were sparkling clean, and there were flowers too. Armando helped Rosita with her chair. Every pair of eyes in the room were on them, they were obviously visitors. Rosita was dressed plainly but elegantly, with a brown pair of trousers and a white blouse with puffy sleeves, with ten little buttons on the cuffs. Her hair was bunched up at the top and cascading down the sides. Angelo wore a light brown linen suit over a light blue shirt. The waiter asked what they wanted to drink. Rosita ordered a martini on the rocks and Angelo a beer. The owner then approached the table.

'Good evening, Miss and Mr Curro' she said.

'Good evening Mrs Caruso,' replied Angelo and Rosita in unison. Angelo got up to greet her.

'Please don't get up,' said Mrs Caruso. 'Are you two well rested now?'

'Yes, thank you, very well rested,' replied Rosita, looking at Angelo.

'Good,' said Mrs Caruso. 'I hope your stay in our hotel will be comfortable. I must excuse myself now, I have some people waiting for me over there by the window. Your meal won't be long, I hope you enjoy it. And if you need anything, please don't hesitate to call me.'

'Thank you, Mrs Caruso, we will bear that in mind,' replied Angelo.

The waiter appeared with their meals on a trolley as soon as the owner had left. He served them their dinner and some wine, and then left them with a bow of his head and a smile. Angelo and Rosita started to eat, they were very hungry by now, much hungrier than they thought. During the meal they looked over towards Mrs Caruso a few times. Mrs Caruso also looked over at them occasionally.

Rosita said to Angelo, 'I have the feeling that Mrs Caruso is talking about us.'

'Don't worry dear, what could she be saying about us? Only that we are strangers in town.' he assured her, and continued to eat. As the evening went by, they noticed that people slowly started to leave, each one saying goodbye to Mrs Caruso as they left. Rosita looked at Angelo and said, 'She seems to be quite popular, doesn't she?'

'She must be, maybe people eat here regularly and have got to know her,' he replied. Nearing the end of their meal, a waiter approached their table and told them that Mrs Caruso had invited them to join her at her table for coffee, with her and her friends.

Angelo looked at Rosita questioningly. She looked at the waiter and said, 'Yes we would love to, thank you.'

Rosita quickly went to the bathroom to freshen up. When she returned, Angelo got up and they slowly walked over to Mrs Caruso's table together. As they approached the table, the two men who were sat at the table got up to greet them, the ladies with them just smiled at Rosita and Angelo. Mrs Caruso introduced everybody and they all shook hands. When Rosita and Angelo heard the names of the people, they looked at each other very surprised. But they continued to chat and laugh with their new acquaintances, Francesco Maiorana and Salvatore Ruvolo and their wives. Both Angelo and Rosita were wondering how it was possible for the people they had come to see in Tucuman City already know that they were here. Mrs Caruso interrupted Rosita's train of thought.

'How do you take your coffee, black, white, with or without sugar?'

'Black, with one teaspoon full of sugar please,' replied Rosita.

'And you, Mr Curro?'

'Please call me Angelo. I take two full teaspoons please and a drop of milk.'

They both drank their coffees slowly, whilst weighing up Mr Maiorana and Mr Ruvolo. When they had finished, both complimented Mrs Caruso on the coffee. Mrs Maiorana never moved her eyes from Rosita.

'Where do you come from, Francesca, or is it a secret?' she finally asked.

For a moment Rosita felt as if she was under interrogation, and she looked at Angelo for moral support.

'Of course we can tell you, Mrs Maiorana, it is no secret,' he responded. He took Rosita's hand and winked at her. 'We come from a village called Las Cejias.'

'Las Cejias,' exclaimed Mrs Ruvolo. 'I think I've heard of this village before. Yes, of course.' She proceeded, turning to her husband. 'I think you have been there before, darling, many years ago.'

'Yes, that's right my dear, I have been there before,' replied Mr Ruvolo. He then turned to look at Angelo. 'And are you two here on business or pleasure?'

'A bit of both really,' Rosita answered.

'Good, I hope everything goes well for you,' interrupted Mrs Caruso.

'We hope so too,' said Angelo.

There was a little pause in their conversation, then Mrs Caruso spoke up again, saying, 'What have you two got planned for tonight? It would be a shame to lock yourselves in your room again? The night is still young; you could go out and take in a few of the sights.'

'Thanks for the advice,' Angelo said. 'It sounds like a lovely idea.' He finished, and looked at Rosita for her view.

'Yes, darling, I agree, we've had enough sleep today. But we don't really know where to go. What is there to see in Tucuman?'

'My dear,' said Mrs Laura Caruso laughing, 'there are plenty of places to go. But I'll tell you all the places of interest tomorrow. Tonight though, it would be an honour for you to be our guests, and come out with us.'

'Thank you, you're most kind,' said Rosita, casting a quick glance at Angelo, who was talking to Mr Maiorana, 'but we can't go out anywhere too smart, because we're not dressed for the occasion and we don't have any formal wear. Tomorrow we need to go out to buy some clothes.'

'Ah, but you don't need to worry, my dear,' said Mrs Caruso waving one hand in the air. 'There's no need to dress formally where we're going. It's a casual place and you're both dressed smartly enough.'

'Very well,' Rosita answered. 'In that case, please excuse us for a couple of minutes, while Angelo and I go up to fetch a jacket. We will not be long.'

'Of course, please take your time, my dear, no need to rush.'

So, Rosita and Angelo left the table and headed for their room. When they reached it, they shut the door behind them and both sighed deeply falling into each other's arms.

'What do you think, Angelo? I have the feeling that they knew of our visit to Tucuman.'

'I'm not sure, darling,' he said. 'It seems impossible to me that they could have known, after all we never booked the hotel in advance or the train. And it has only been a few days since we decided we were going to come here and only a few people knew of our trip. But I know what you mean, I also had the impression they knew something about our trip. It's too big of a coincidence.'

'Well, what shall we do? Are we to go out with them, or shall we make an excuse and stay in? We must decide quickly,' said Rosita. For the first time she felt a bit helpless.

'Well, my dear, they are waiting for us now, we should go really. They have been very kind to us, and we could find out whether they knew about our trip or not and if they know why we're here,' finished Angelo, trying to convince himself that everything would be all right.

'Yes, my darling, you're right. Fine, I'll just be a minute; I'll brush my teeth and get my jacket.'

'Good, I'll get some more money, so we can pay our own way. And we should take our identification papers too, because you never know if we may need them.'

Eventually, Angelo and Rosita went back downstairs and into the lobby, where the others were waiting for them.

'I hope we haven't kept you waiting too long?' said Angelo.

'Not at all,' replied Mrs Caruso 'we have only just got here.'

'Good, then we can leave now,' said Mr Maiorana. 'And Mr Curro and his lovely lady can come with me in my car.'

'Thank you,' said Rosita.

'I'll go with Mr and Mrs Ruvolo, we'll see you there,' added Mrs Caruso.

They got into their respective cars and drove off. Angelo and Rosita were both in the back of Mr Maiorana's car, there had not been a great deal of conversation. Rosita squeezed Angelo's knee, and he knew that she was letting him know that she was uncomfortable about all of this. Curiosity as to where they were being taken was forming part of her nervousness. Angelo took a hold of Rosita's hand, raised it to his lips and kissed it gently to help reassure her. Then he put his arm around her shoulders and squeezed her gently. Angelo had noticed that Mr Maiorana had been occasionally looking back at them through his rear view mirror. Mrs Maiorana at one point asked if they were comfortable in the back. She had done this to break the awkward silence, as she could feel the tension and wanted to make them feel more relaxed.

'Yes, thank you,' answered Rosita confidently and then went on to ask, 'is it far, this place we're going to?'

'No, we are about to arrive now,' Mr Maiorana answered. Only seconds later the car slowed down and pulled up into the drive of a very large stately looking building. It had four steps leading up to the entrance, which had two columns one either side of the door.

'Here we are,' said Mrs Maiorana smiling as her husband brought the car to a halt and switched off the engine. They all began to get out of the car. At the front door of the building were two men and one of them walked towards the car.

'Good evening, Mr Maiorana, ladies,' he said bowing his head to them.

'Good evening, Pablo,' answered Mr Maiorana. He handed the car keys over to him, as the other car carrying Mr and Mrs Ruvolo and Mrs Caruso pulled up beside them. The trio were laughing at something as they were getting out of their car.

Mrs Caruso slipped between Rosita and Angelo, interlocked her arms with theirs and walked them into the luxurious building, saying, 'Well my friends, I hope you are in a dancing mood.'

'I think we could manage a few dances,' answered Mrs Ruvolo, 'as we are too old to dance all night anymore.' At this they all laughed.

'Speak for yourself,' said Mr Ruvolo, in a joking way, then Mrs Caruso asked Angelo and Rosita if they could dance.

'Well, we manage.' they answered, both in unison.

A very smart looking man came up and took their coats and hats, after which they all walked up the wide palatial stairs together and entered a large ballroom. There were a lot of people in the room, dressed casually but smartly and it had a friendly atmosphere about it. To the left as they walked in was a casino area, where people were playing card games and roulette. To their right there was a band playing and a dance floor full of people. They walked onto a slightly raised area which was cordoned off by a fancy rope and sat at a large table with four nameplates in the centre. They were F. Maiorana, S. Ruvolo, R. Mendoza, and M. Mendoza. As they sat down, a waiter appeared almost immediately and asked what everybody wanted to drink. Mr Ruvolo took the initiative.

'For us the usual please.' Then he turned to address Angelo and Rosita asking, 'What would you two like?'

Rosita asked for a glass of martini on the rocks and Angelo a glass of red wine. Rosita sat down beside Angelo, with Mr Maiorana on her other side, they were both a bit nervous, but tried not to show it too much. Rosita had to say something to distract herself from her nerves, even though she had Angelo beside her she felt like a fish out of water.

'This place is very nice, how long have you been coming here?' she asked Mr Maiorana.

'I'm glad you like it, we try to keep it nice and tidy. We don't let any riff raff in, so we seldom get any trouble. People come here to enjoy themselves. We have been coming here since we bought it.'

'Oh, it's your place, that's very nice,' she said, addressing Mr Maiorana. One surprise after another, she thought. 'I'm glad to see that there are still places like this for people to come to,' she proceeded, 'and it seems like all races of people can come and enjoy each others' company, without any trouble.'

Angelo had been conversing with the others but was keeping an ear open as to what Mr Maiorana was saying to Rosita. He didn't think she was afraid of them, but she was surprised at the way they had met with these people; the very people they had come to Tucuman City to see.

'This place is jointly owned by Mr Ruvolo, myself and two other families,' said Mr Maiorana. He then proceeded by adding, 'We also have a gymnasium downstairs, would you and your fiancé care to see it?'

'It would be a great pleasure,' said Rosita, turning to Angelo. 'Darling,' she said, smiling at him, showing Angelo that she felt a bit more relaxed, 'Mr Maiorana has invited us to look around his club; they have a gymnasium downstairs.'

'Yes, that would be nice,' said Angelo. He winked at her to show her he was relaxed too.

'Good,' said Mr Maiorana, 'let us go.'

Angelo and Rosita rose and followed Mr Maiorana, excusing themselves to the others. They walked into a long hallway. At the end of the hall, there was a very large painting; it was about seven-foot tall and started from the floor which seemed a little odd to Rosita and Angelo. To the left of the painting, by a window, stood two men who were in mid -conversation. As they were approached, the two men greeted Mr Maiorana. One of them went over to a panel of light switches, he pulled a lever, which was just to the right of the light switch and the painting glided to its left revealing a doorway. This led into a passageway which in turn led down some stairs. The lighting in this passageway was dull. Rosita shivered a bit, she saw something like this once in a horror movie. The three of them stepped through the doorway and the door closed behind them.

Rosita showed no hesitation or anxiety, even though it was truly spooky. Angelo felt proud of her, he admired her spunk. He took hold of Rosita's hand and they followed Mr Maiorana down the stairs.

When they reached the bottom of the stairwell they saw two very big men, who looked as if they were guarding a large doorway. The two men greeted their boss and then Rosita and Angelo. One of the men quickly opened the door for them. As they were about to walk through the door, they heard a very loud hissing sound followed immediately by a louder slapping sound. Both Angelo and Rosita recognised these sounds, and as they walked into the very large room they saw at least fifty young men, in rows practising martial arts.

Their arrival instigated an impressive reaction from the class, all the men, in unison stopped what they were doing, turned towards the visitors and acknowledged them with a bow. Mr Maiorana bowed back at the class, as did Angelo and Rosita out of habit as well as respect for fellow martial artists. Mr Maiorana then raised his hand to greet them all and asked the class leader how everything was going.

Rosita and Angelo noticed the attitude of their host towards the people who worked for him. They all had a great respect for him, which meant he was not a bad person to work for. They had imagined he could be just over sixty years old. But he looked and moved like a younger man, his body looked firm and strong, more like a man in his forties. And that must be the result of practising martial arts for many years, his hair was mostly grey but it was immaculately cut so made him look more distinguished.

'Very well thank you, Mr Maiorana,' the class leader replied.

'I have a few friends with me as you can see; would you give them a little demonstration of your skills?'

His men obediently bowed their heads again and got into position. Rosita and Angelo were guided to seats at the front of the class, and the demonstration began. Angelo and Rosita were riveted. The demonstration consisted of mock fights, high flying kicks, and use of weapons like long sticks, short sticks and knives. Breaking of boards and very impressive disarming techniques. These young men were really very good. One in particular had caught Angelo's eyes. The demonstration lasted about five minutes and when it came to an end the three spectators applauded. Rosita noticed that Angelo was still looking at the one young man who had stood out to him. He had a very stern look on his face.

As a second demonstration started, Rosita took the opportunity to whisper into Angelo's ear, 'What's wrong Angelo, you look worried. Do you think we're in any sort of trouble?'

'No, my love, if they wanted to harm us, do you think they would have brought us here. Too many people have seen us come in,' replied Angelo.

'Well, what's wrong then?'

'I think I recognise that young man over there, the one with long brown hair, standing next to the two tall Negroes. I think… no, I'm sure I've seen him at the hacienda, one of the casual work people who comes for just a few weeks at a time.'

'Are you absolutely sure?'

'Yes, I really do think so, I'm sure I saw him on Saturday, when we helped pack the vegetables. I caught him looking at us a few times.' Angelo finished.

'Then it wasn't a coincidence meeting them at the hotel. They knew we were coming. Should we sit and wait to see what happens next.' whispered Rosita.

Then she turned towards Mr Maiorana, she smiled at him sweetly whilst contemplating her next move. She couldn't wait any longer to find out what these powerful people were planning. Angelo was right, if they had wanted to harm them, they wouldn't have been brought here. She'd decided to take the first step.

'Mr Maiorana, your young men have put on a marvellous demonstration,' she said. 'They have shown a very high level of skill and they could be very useful to me in the not too distant future.'

'In what way could they be useful?' There was a short pause as he looked Rosita in the eye and then he said, 'Maybe at the Hacienda Antigua, Miss Rosita Miserendino.'

Rosita was taken aback by this comment, but in her surprised state she smiled at this strange but powerful man. Nothing more was said until the second demonstration was over. They again applauded the men. Mr Maiorana rose and bowed again to the class as did Angelo and Rosita.

'Let me introduce you to my men,' Mr Maiorana said. So, the three of them walked into the centre of the crowd of men who were all whispering to one another and focussed on Rosita and Angelo. Mr Maiorana stood in front of his men and said, 'Well my boys, this beautiful young lady thinks you're very good, and she also said she could use your skills back in her town.' When their boss had finished his speech, they all bowed their heads, thanking her for the compliment. 'And I have more news for you boys,' said Mr Maiorana, turning to face Angelo and Rosita, then proceeding. 'I have immense pleasure in presenting to you to Miss. Rosita Miserendino and Mr Angelo Curro. They are responsible for our delayed visit to the Hacienda Antigua.'

Suddenly from a complete silence, all the young men began to applaud the two respected visitors, who could only look at each other with bemusement. Then they faced the young men and bowed their heads. Angelo and Rosita both felt elated. They didn't know if they should laugh or cry. As the cheers and applause died down, the instructor of the class approached the two visitors and shook their hands.

He said to them, 'We manage to hear just about everything that happens at the Hacienda Antigua. And we have heard that you two are more than proficient at martial arts to a high standard. It would be an honour for us, if you would spar with two of our men, before you return to the hacienda.'

'It would be a pleasure,' said Angelo, 'but I must say, that we're not as good as your men.'

The instructor laughed, and then replied, 'There is no need to be so modest Mr Curro. I must leave now, I hope to see you soon, goodbye for now.' He backed up two steps, bowed his head, turned and walked away.

'It's time we left too,' said Mr Maiorana.

The three of them turned and headed back up, but just before they left the gym Angelo turned to look at the young man he'd recognised. Angelo smiled at him and nodded his head, as if to say, 'Yes I do know you.'

Once the three of them were back in the ballroom, they approached their table to find nobody there. They were all dancing to a lively waltz. Mr Maiorana excused himself, and left the table too. He walked over to a crowd of men, tapped one on his shoulder and they both went over to the bar. The other man was about fifty years old; they started talking and occasionally looked over at Angelo and Rosita. She in turn looked at Angelo with a questioning expression on her face.

'Yes,' he said, 'they are talking about us, but at least now we don't have to worry about it.'

'Yes, I know, Angelo, but I've had enough surprises for one night, I'm quiet tired now.'

'As a matter of fact, so am I,' replied Angelo. 'I would prefer spending this time in bed with you. When Mr Maiorana comes back over we'll tell him we're ready to leave.'

'Thank you, darling,' she said, smiling at him for his suggestive comment, and trying to conceal a yawn with her hand.

After a few minutes the others came back to the table and Mr Ruvolo said, 'Oh, you two are back, did you like our gymnasium?'

'Yes, we're impressed,' answered Rosita, 'both with the gym and the students.'

'Yes,' added Angelo. 'And I would like to thank you all for being so hospitable to us, it has been a pleasure meeting you, and I hope our friendship is a lasting one.'

'The pleasure is ours,' the women answered in unison. 'And you won't get rid of us so easily.' proceeded Mrs Maiorana jovially. 'I hope you will have time to have dinner at our house one evening, before you two return to Las Cejias.'

'We would like that very much, Mrs Maiorana. But please excuse us now, we hope you're not offended but I think we'd better get back to the hotel, we're feeling a little tired,' said Angelo.

'Offended? Dear God, of course not, don't even think about it. I can imagine you are very tired, actually I should apologise to you for taking you out so late, after all you had a long journey,' answered Mr Maiorana.

'Please, don't apologise,' intervened Rosita, 'you have made it incredibly easy for us to find you. Which reminds me to ask you, when you have a little time to spare Angelo and I would like to come and talk business with you. After all, that is the reason we came here to Tucuman.'

'When you're ready, just call on me and I will make time to see you,' said Mr Maiorana. At that, Mrs Maiorana spoke to her husband.

'Darling,' she said, 'why don't you ask these two nice young people to come to dinner tomorrow night? They can meet the rest of the family, and you can have a talk then.'

'That's fine by me, Veronica, but I don't want to impose on them. Maybe they would like some time to themselves.' answered Mr Maiorana.

'Well, how about it then?' insisted Mrs Maiorana, looking at Rosita, then at Angelo 'Will you come over tomorrow night? We'll eat about nine p.m.. That way you have all day together for sightseeing.'

'Very well,' said Rosita laughing, 'you have convinced us. We will be there by eight forty-five, could we have your address please?'

'If you want it, but your chauffeur knows the way,'

'Our chauffeur?' exclaimed Angelo, as Mr Maiorana pointed over to the bar, where the man who he was talking to earlier was standing.

'He will be your chauffeur for the duration of your stay in Tucuman.'

'I don't know what to say,' said Angelo. He'd not expected such kindness. They came to Tucuman only with the hope that they could talk to Mr Maiorana and the other families, but Rosita and he never expected such hospitality. This was surely because of Rosita's sincerity, charm, and charitable heart.

'There is nothing to say, he's waiting for you. When you're ready, he will take you back.'

'Thank you, Mr Maiorana, we're ready now,' said Rosita, getting up. So, they said their goodbyes to everyone at the table. Rosita started to feel very emotional, the long journey and all the surprises of the day had suddenly caught up with her. One day for sure she would indeed have plenty to tell her children, and her grandchildren.

'If you don't mind, I think I'll come back with you if I can, I'm feeling tired too, and I must be up early tomorrow,' said Mrs Caruso.

'But of course,' replied Angelo.

Mr Maiorana took them over to Pablo, the chauffeur, and introduced them to him.

The three of then left directly after their introduction to Pablo and followed him to the entrance steps.

'Please wait here while I get the car, said Pablo courteously. He then ran the twenty metres to the car and quickly drove it to the front of the club. He stepped out to open the doors for them. Mrs Caruso climbed into the front next to Pablo, whilst Angelo and Rosita got in the back. During the return journey to the hotel, they all felt their tiredness coming on and few words were exchanged. At the hotel they got out yawning and thanked Pablo for driving them back.

'It's my duty,' he answered. 'At what time would you like to be picked up in the morning?'

Rosita looked at Angelo for an answer, he held his hands up as if to say, as you wish.

'I don't really know, Pablo, as we have no set plans for tomorrow morning, but…'

'I have your number, Pablo,' interrupted Mrs Caruso. 'I'll telephone you when they are ready if that is acceptable.'

'As you wish, Mrs Caruso,' said Pablo smiling. 'Goodnight then, I'll see you tomorrow.'

Angelo and Rosita liked him the instant they had met him. He seemed a good, trustworthy and efficient young man.

'Good night,' they all replied, turning towards the door. Mrs Caruso went in first, and headed straight for the stairs leading to their room. They climbed the stairs together, and stopped on the landing outside their room.

'Goodnight, Mama Caruso,' Rosita said endearingly and kissed her on both cheeks. This was very touching for Mrs Caruso.

Angelo also kissed her hand and added, 'Rosita meant that most sincerely from the two of us.' Then he turned and followed Rosita into their room. Within minutes they had both undressed, brushed their teeth and slipped into bed, they were both very tired. They cuddled up together and fell asleep almost immediately, sleeping solidly until morning. Rosita was the first one to wake. She rubbed her eyes lazily, and stretched wondering what time it was.

She reached over to grab her watch, when she saw the time, she said loudly, 'Goodness, have we slept all that time?'

Angelo woke up to her voice, and said, 'What was that you said, mi amour?' reaching for her.

'Good morning, darling,' she said, kissing his forehead, 'I said, we've slept too long, it's nearly midday.' The only light in the room was coming through the gap in the curtains, and even in this dim light she still could see and admire his beautifully chiselled naked body. At once and shamelessly, her body was on fire. He must have sensed it, or heard her breathing heavily.

'No, it can't be,' he said jokingly, and pulled her on top of him.

'Oh no you don't, you rascal, we've got to get up, we have work to do.'

'Why?' he asked still holding her tightly, and manoeuvred her body in order for her to feel his arousal against her lower stomach.

'I tell you why,' she began, trying in vain to ignore his advances. She suddenly felt a tingle all over her body, and took a deep breath to gain control, but it was too late, she was sexually aroused. 'We've slept for too many hours,' she said hoarsely.

'Well, I think we should sleep a bit longer, after all I'm in no hurry to get up, what I need is right here on top of me.'

He began to kiss her with fervent passion, and she was powerless to stop him, her emotions ran away with her, and they made love with such ardent force, clutching at each other as if they were fighting for the last breath.

It was just after one o'clock by the time they were ready to go down. They found Mrs Caruso at the reception desk, greeting two new guests. As Angelo and Rosita approached, Mrs Caruso rang a bell and a porter arrived immediately. The porter took the new guests bags, and led them off.

'Good day, Mrs Caruso,' they said in unison.

'Hello,' she answered smiling up at them, 'did you two sleep well?'

'Yes thanks, fantastically well,' they replied.

Mrs Caruso summoned a waiter who had been standing at the restaurant door. He approached and stopped beside them.

'Is the table for Mr and Miss Curro ready?' Mrs Caruso asked the waiter.

'Yes Madam, it's ready,' he answered, smiling at the couple.

'Good, please show them to their table,' she said, turning to Angelo and Rosita. 'Do you mind if I join you for lunch?'

'Not at all, Mrs Caruso, we would enjoy your company,' answered Angelo.

'Fine, if you would like to take your seats, I'll join you in a minute,' she said, pointing her arm towards the dining room. The waiter showed them to their table and asked what they would like to drink. Both of them ordered coffee. After a few minutes, the waiter brought over three cups and saucers. He knew that Mrs Caruso never refuses a cup of coffee. He then fetched the freshly percolated coffee and started to pour it just as Mrs Caruso returned. She sat down without saying anything, took a sip of the hot black liquid and let out a long sigh.

'I do love a cup of coffee, it perks me up,' she said. 'What are you two having to eat? Have you ordered yet?'

'No, we haven't, we were waiting for you,' said Angelo.

'Thank you, my dears. Well let's order then, what will you have?'

'We'll leave it to you to recommend something, if you don't mind,' suggested Rosita.

'My pleasure. In that case, how would you like some homemade pasta with tomato sauce? My chef makes me fresh macheroni once a week,'

'I think it was a very clever idea of Francesca to let you decide,' said Angelo jovially.

Mrs Caruso called over a waiter and ordered three starters of honey melon and Parma ham, three home made pasta dishes and some red wine. The waiter left and they conversed among themselves about places to visit and the likes.

Twenty minutes later, the three of them were still chatting and eating. A waiter approached their table, and whispered something in Mrs Caruso's ear.

'Tell him to come over,' she said to the waiter, 'we have almost finished, but he can join us for a drink.'

Rosita and Angelo of course understood who it was Mrs Caruso was talking about. It was Pablo, the chauffeur. Mrs Caruso had telephoned him before she sat down to lunch. Pablo approached them and sat down with them and ordered an iced tea. Ten minutes later they had all finished their meals and drinks so Angelo and Rosita got up and thanked Mrs Caruso for the lovely lunch.

They left with Pablo and went for a ride around Tucuman, taking in the sights. Pablo looked after them as if they were his own family. The visiting couple had already bought lots of things; their arms were loaded with parcels and bags. Rosita was in her element and really enjoying herself, she loved looking in all the clothes shops, shoe shops, restaurants and bars with the lovely little cakes in the window, which seemed to be crying out to her, 'Eat me, eat me.' Pablo noticed the delight in their faces as they looked at the cakes and pastries. He glanced at his watch and noticed it was just past six pm. So he made a suggestion to Angelo and Rosita.

'Let's drop these parcels in the car; it is just around the corner. We can then come back to this bar and sample a cake or two, and a cup of coffee. What do you say?'

'What a great idea,' said Rosita, looking back at the window display full of delicious cakes. So they went back to the car and dropped everything off in the boot.

Back at the bar, they found themselves a table and sat down, relieved to take the load off their feet. It was a lovely clean and tidy place, and the smell of freshly baked pasties and buns was wafting around the place. Pablo called over the man who was standing behind the counter. He came straight over to the table. Pablo asked Angelo and Rosita what they desired. Both of them ordered a cappuccino, Pablo asked the man to bring over three cappuccinos and a selection of cakes on a tray.

'Very well, Señor, your order will be with you in only a few minutes,' said the barman stepping back slightly and giving a small bow, accompanied by a flourish of his right hand, before he returned behind the counter to prepare their order. He was so full of energy and whistling to himself. Rosita and Angelo smiled at one another and imagined he was the owner.

Just as the man had said, the order arrived within minutes. Two waiters accompanied by the man who had taken Pablo's order, brought over the cappuccino and cakes.

'Here they are,' said one of the waiters with pride. 'Enjoy them, Señorita, Señors.'

Pablo, thanked them. The little mini cakes looked almost too good to eat, there were about twenty assorted golf ball sized gastronomic works of art, delicately placed on a two tier platter. The three of them took a moment to savour the delights with their eyes before Pablo interrupted their thoughts.

'Please, señorita, take the first cake before we fight over the best ones.'

They all laughed at Pablo's joke, then Rosita took the cake that had caught her eye. It was a puff pastry roll covered with two types of chocolate, milk on one side and coffee flavoured on the other. The whipped cream was oozing out from the sides and chopped pistachio nuts were sprinkled on top. She took a delicate bite from the cake with her eyes closed to heighten the sensation. The two men were watching her with saliva accumulating in their mouths and their eyes wide open. After chewing the morsel three or four times Rosita let out a small groan of pleasure and opened her eyes. She looked at the two men who were still staring at her, she swallowed the last of the cake and licked her lips slowly and purposefully. The two men unconsciously licked their own lips watching Rosita, she then verbalised her verdict to the boys.

'They are really horrible, you won't like them.'

They all laughed again and tucked into the rest of the cakes. In between mouthfuls of cakes and sips of their cappuccinos they chatted idly about their plans for where to go later.

'Oh, look, we've finished the lot, how are we going to eat a full meal tonight at Mrs Maiorana's house?' commented Rosita.

'Well,' said Angelo, laughing, 'It's not every day we get to sit and devour such a delightful selection of delicious cakes.' The three of them all nodded in agreement, then Angelo proceeded. 'Don't worry my dear, we won't be eating till ten or maybe eleven o'clock tonight, I'm sure you will be hungry again by then.'

'You can be sure of that,' said Pablo. He then asked, 'Is this your first visit to Tucuman City?'

'Yes Pablo, it is, and we love it. Your town is beautiful and we're so glad to have met Mr and Mrs Maiorana, Mr and Mrs Ruvolo, Mrs Caruso and yourself of course. We also hope with a bit of luck, to meet the other influential families before we leave,' said Angelo.

'Oh, you'll meet them soon enough. As matter of fact, I think they will be at Mr Maiorana's place tonight.'

'Really!' exclaimed Francesca 'Well it looks as if our business here will be over sooner than we had hoped, so we can get back to Las Cejias. I can't help worrying that something is going to happen while we're away. I would never forgive myself if it does.'

'Don't worry about it so much, dear. With the help of our fathers and the others, everything will run smoothly, I'm sure,' said Angelo smiling at her to reassure her.

Having heard the anxiety in Rosita's voice Pablo decided to try to put her mind at rest, so he said, 'Mr Curro, I assure you...' but was cut off in mid-sentence by Angelo.

'Please, Pablo, use our Christian names, it make it a less formal atmosphere, and we prefer it.'

'Thank you, Angelo, Francesca. As I was saying there's no need to worry. I shouldn't be telling you this really, but I feel I can trust you. This morning we got news from the Hacienda Antigua and everything has calmed down a little after what happened at Don Camillo's house on Saturday. He has all his men guarding his place now. He sure is afraid for his life.'

Rosita figured that if Pablo knew this information, he must be totally trusted by his employer, so she decided to vocalise her thoughts to let him know how she felt and who she was. He, of course, knew who she really was. He had called her Francesca earlier because they were within earshot of others outside of the family connection and out of respect.

'Well,' began Rosita, seriously, 'he has good reason to be afraid, I suspect he is expecting something to happen very soon, he doesn't know exactly what or who to expect, but he knows that his end is near. I only hope that nobody beats me to it because I want Don Camillo to know by whom and why he is being stopped. I want to see his face when I announce my name, and I want to see my mother's face when I slay her lover before her as he had done to me all those years ago.'

It was obvious that Rosita had played this scene out in her head thousands of times and she was working herself up into a rage, her cheeks were flushed. Her heart was back at the Hacienda Antigua. Even though in some ways, she was content to be where she was with the man she loved. But she had waited so long for the time when she could reclaim what was hers by birth right. Her inheritance.

'Shall we go back now or would you like to stay a little longer my dear,' interrupted Angelo. It was plain to see she was getting herself worked up.

'Yes, I'm a little tired, but I would like to stop for another cappuccino, if Pablo is in no hurry to get back,' she replied.

'No hurry,' said Paolo, 'It's up to you, whatever you want to do. As you know my orders are to accompany you both anywhere, anytime, I am totally at your disposal.'

Pablo then called over the waiter and ordered three more cappuccinos. Between the two of them they tried to keep Rosita's mind busy by talking about exclusive clothes and shoe shops in a rich part of town, in order to calm her down. After they finished their cappuccinos, they made their way back to the car and headed back to the hotel.

It was about nine p.m. after Rosita and Angelo had rested a while, and freshened up, Angelo put on a black silk suit, with a white shirt and a black bow tie. He also wore his gold cufflinks with diamond studs, which Rosita had bought him. She put on a long white silk dress, with gold buttons fastening up the front from the waist to the neck. The sleeves were three quarter length with ruffled cuffs; she wore her two stringed white pearl necklace, which Angelo had bought for her.

They were ready and waiting in the lobby at nine thirty p.m. for Mrs Caruso, Pablo was in the car waiting for them all. As soon as Mrs Caruso arrived, they all got into the waiting car. Mrs Caruso sat in the back with Rosita, so she could chat with her without twisting around in her seat. On the way, Pablo asked Angelo if he and Rosita would like to go to the theatre at some point in the week, as *The Barber of Seville* was showing, with the famous singer, Victor Gui. Mrs Caruso overheard Pablo's suggestion to Angelo, and felt compelled to comment.

'Oh, Francesca, you really must go to see this production, it's really well done. I saw it in Buenos Ares, it's marvellous.'

Rosita was digesting the suggestion, but before she could answer Mrs Caruso, Angelo turned to face Pablo.

'Thank you, Pablo, that's an excellent idea.' Then turning to the back seats he said, 'We should go tomorrow night my dear, if Mrs Caruso said it's good, we must go to see it.'

'That's a lovely idea,' answered Rosita. 'I think it would be nice though if Mrs Caruso and Pablo came with us, don't you think?'

'Ha, this sounds like an invitation to me. Pablo, what you think?' said Mrs Caruso.

'Well yes! With pleasure, I would love to go,' Pablo answered happily.

'That's settled then,' said Rosita. 'Pablo, you could invite any member of your family or your wife to join us if you like.'

Pablo hesitated for a few long seconds and then replied, 'I have no wife; she left me many years ago.'

Rosita didn't know what to say to that, she was stunned at this revelation.

Angelo quickly intervened, and said, 'I'm really sorry to hear that, Pablo.'

'Don't be,' answered Pablo. 'Believe me it's probably for the best, anyway. She had her reasons; we hardly ever saw each other, because I was too involved with my work. She was tired of being alone, so she got together with a man she worked with. He was her type, he never went away.'

'I'm sorry I reminded you, and for being so presumptuous,' said Rosita. 'But I hope the two of you will still join us tomorrow,' she said. They all laughed at this comment.

'Francesca, not only would I be honoured to be escorted by Pablo, but I wouldn't dream of coming without him,' replied Mrs Caruso.

At that moment they pulled up outside Mr Maiorana's luxurious house. Pablo escorted them all into the house and straight into the drawing room and announced their arrival. Mrs Maiorana was the first one to get up and greet them by the door.

'Welcome, welcome, my friends, come in,' she said, and kissed Rosita's and Mrs Caruso's cheeks. She then slipped between Rosita and Angelo, intertwining her arms into theirs and she led them to the centre of the room facing the rest of her family. 'Angelo, Francesca, first of all, please let me introduce you to my daughter, Giuseppina and her fiancé, Miquiel.'

Meanwhile Mrs Caruso approached Rosario Mendoza and his family, while Pablo went over to Mr Maiorana. Approaching a large sofa to the left, Rosita and Angelo were shaking hand with Giuseppina and her fiancé.

Giuseppina said., 'I'm honoured to meet you at last, to see you face to face. My father has been talking about you two non-stop.'

'I hope he has been speaking well of us, Miss Maiorana,' said Rosita, as she felt herself going a little red in the face.

'Please no formalities, call me Giuseppina,' she replied waving a hand in the air. Giuseppina then introduced Miquiel her fiancé, who then in turn took Angelo and Rosita to his brother Rosario Mendoza, and the rest of his family. Over the next twenty minutes everybody had had a chance to chat to Rosita and Angelo. A maid then came into the room and told Mrs Maiorana that dinner was ready.

Mrs Maiorana then turned to her guests and invited them into the dining room. She took Angelo by the arm and led him through into the dining room, while Mr Maiorana offered his arm to Rosita and escorted her through and the others guests followed them in. They all sat down at a very large table, there was an air of relaxed jovial banter while everybody settled in their seats and waited for their feast to begin.

Mr Maiorana sat at the head of the table with his wife to his right and Rosita to his left, Angelo was placed the other side of Mrs Maiorana. Within a minute the maids started to bring in the starters, which were artichoke hearts in oil dressing with salami, ham and smoked salmon.

An hour and a half went by to complete the five course meal, which had a nice amount of time in between courses for a drink and more idle banter. There were many merry faces around the table as the wine was flowing freely. Because Rosita and Angelo didn't know many of the other guests very well their main conversations were with Mr and Mrs Maiorana and the few others they did know. They did though discreetly keep an eye and an ear on everybody at the table. As their coffee was being served, Mr Maiorana got up and asked Rosita and Angelo if they would like to get a breath of fresh air on the terrace. This of course was only an excuse to get them on their own, because he knew that they wanted to talk to him privately. The three of them picked up their coffees, so they could finish drinking them outside in the fresh night air. The three of them sat down at the table that was set up for them. Rosita looked up into the sky, she noticed how bright the stars looked and took a deep breath. Yes, she felt good, this was the first time since she'd arrived in Tucuman, that she felt truly happy. Angelo looked at her and saw how happy his Rosita looked, which in turn relaxed him. He took a sip of his coffee and spoke.

'Mr Maiorana,' he began. 'Firstly I'd like to thank you on behalf of us both, for your hospitality, your time and the opportunity for us to talk to you.' He stopped and looked at Rosita, but she didn't say anything. 'As you probably know, we have a bit of a situation going on at home, and we would like to end it as soon as possible. It would be a great satisfaction for us, but more so for my fiancée, because it is her battle. We're all trying to protect her and assist her in her quest.

I think you know that this is not only to do with revenge here, but what's also involved is the freedom of a lot of people back at the Hacienda Antigua.'

Mr Maiorana was nodding his head while listening to Angelo, then he stretched his arm out to pick his cup up, and he took a couple of sips and put the small cup back on the table.

'I know, Angelo,' he said, hesitating for a few long seconds before continuing. 'In fact we know all about what is going on at the Hacienda Antigua. We know the new and the old story, and you have all our admiration and support for your endeavours. We've been waiting for your word, and we will be only too happy to help in any way we can, you just have to let us know what you need from us and when, then rest assured it will be done.'

'Mr Maiorana, it is very pleasing to hear your offer of help and much appreciated,' said Angelo hesitating to look at Rosita again. 'But for any details about what we may need you for, will need to be discussed with Francesca, as she is the one who knows what is needed to be done first and when it is to be executed.'

Mrs Maiorana at that moment walked out onto the terrace and very politely interrupted them.

'Here you are, you crafty people. Couldn't you take the pace in there with all those gossips?'

Angelo quickly got up and walked toward her, saying, 'We only come out to get a breath of fresh air Mrs Maiorana, but now I would love another cup of your lovely coffee.'

'Of course,' she replied cheerily, 'I'll go and get it for you.'

'Thank you, you're very kind,' said Angelo, 'but I'll come in with you and collect it myself.'

He did this so that Rosita could be alone with Mr Maiorana to talk business. This could be the only time that she had to speak with this powerful man, alone. So Angelo took full advantage of his hostess' hospitality and sat inside drinking his coffee and chatting to other guests for about half an hour. Mrs Caruso then suggested that they all have a game of cards to pass some time away.

She is something else, thought Angelo to himself, as she made fun of all the young men and boasted about her prowess and card playing skills. They of course all laughed at her banter and gave her back as good as she was dishing out and after a few minutes everybody filed out into the sitting room and sat at the large table that occupied the centre of the room.

It didn't take long before nobody could hear what the other was saying, as an infernal hubbub of backchat was rumbling on. Each time the maid brought in another bottle of wine, it disappeared in no time. And even though all the windows were open, the cigarette smoke remained like a floating curtain in the room.

They had been playing for about one hour, when Rosita and Mr Maiorana walked into the room and walked over to the table.

'I think we did well to spend so much time on the terrace,' said Mr Maiorana to Rosita. 'They seem to be gambling heavily in here, the rogues. Can we join in, then?' he bellowed at the top of his voice. They all shuffled round and made room for them to play.

It wasn't until three o'clock in the morning when people started to slow down a bit. They had had so much fun playing game after game of cards, betting only one sweet at the time, but enjoying every minute. The game came to a natural end and all of the guests got up to leave at the same time. Mr and Mrs Maiorana showing their guests to the door. They all filed out saying their goodbyes. Mrs Caruso skipped down the stone steps leaving only Angelo and Rosita to say their good nights. Rosita verbalised a special thanks to Mrs Maiorana for the delicious dinner and for the enjoyable evening's entertainment. She glanced at Mr Maiorana and nodded her head.

'It was a great pleasure for us,' said Mrs Maiorana in response, 'I hope you enjoy yourselves at the theatre tonight.'

All the guests drove off, leaving their hosts at the doorstep waving them off.

CHAPTER TWENTY-ONE

The next day Angelo stirred and opened his eyes. The first thing he saw in the dim light of the room was Rosita lying asleep, stretched out to his right. He took a moment to savour this beautiful sight. She was on her back with her left arm above her head, her face directed at him. Her lower body was covered diagonally by the sheet, which hid her left hip and leg. Her right leg was bent at right angles and flopped out like a butterfly wing to her right. He slowly studied her curvaceous form from bottom to top. His eyes followed her exposed leg up to where her leg met her knicker line. He hesitated over this area taking in the beauty of the black lacy slips, the undulation of her half-covered pubic mound and the flatness of her lower abdomen accentuating the hip bones.

His eyes were on the move again, past her belly button up over the ribcage and onto the outstanding cleavage created by her sumptuous breasts. The matching black lacy bra was holding her in place perfectly, it was like the bra and Rosita were made for one another. He watched her chest heave up and down for a few minutes, utterly hypnotised by the slow steady swell and wane of her breasts. He slowly moved his eyes away from her chest to look at her elegant collar bones, neck and lower jaw.

She was beautiful in every way and at this moment he was the happiest man in the world. He moved closer to her resting on his elbow to get a better view, and then glanced over to the clock on the wall. It was exactly, three p.m.

Looking down to her feet again to take another sweeping look over her stunning form, planning on how he was going to wake her up by laying butterfly kisses over her chest and neck and finally un-cupping her right breast from its keeper and gently teasing her nipple.

But by the time his eyes reached her jawline again, he noticed that she was smiling and her brilliant deep dark intense were fixed on him in a mischievous way.

'Are you enjoying the view?' she enquired provocatively.

'Good afternoon, my love, I trust you slept well?' he replied changing the subject to try to hide his guilty schoolboy feeling.

'I believe I did,' she replied, rubbing her eyes with one hand, and with the other she was caressing Angelo's thigh, as it happened to lie on top of hers. 'My head feels a little heavy though; I think I may have to stay here for another little while yet.'

'What?' Angelo exclaimed, devouring her with his hungry brown eyes. Rosita looked irresistible in her perfectly fitting underwear, her long wavy dark hair falling loosely over her pillow. Angelo noticed her cheeks were slightly rosy, which was a sign to him that she was in a semi-state of arousal. 'You, beautiful lady, have already had eleven hours sleep,' he said as his left hand automatically traced across her flat stomach and onto the beautifully formed mound that was Rosita's right breast. He gently squeezed her breast, whilst looking her in the eye. He slipped his middle and index fingers inside her bra and teased her already erect nipple. His eyes lowered slightly to take in her alluring lips, which seemed to draw him subconsciously towards her. His lips rested on hers gently and started to glide from side to side, sensuously tickling her full pout. Instantly his entire body was aroused, and wanted her.

'Yes, I know my dear,' she said, breathing deeply as her heart raced, 'that's why I don't want to get up yet! Because I'm not as tired as I was when we climbed into bed at four a.m. this morning.' With a cheeky look on her face, she pushed him backwards and rolled on top of Angelo.

He pretended to struggle a little and called out jokingly, 'Help me Mrs Caruso! Francesca has gone mad!' Then he clasped her close to him and continued. 'So you tried to surprise me, eh? Well you cannot, because my guard is always up. So now I have you, what shall I do with you?'

In answer, Rosita kissed him passionately and wildly for a few seconds and then said to Angelo, 'I know what you can do my darling, you can finish what you started this morning when we got into bed, before we both fell asleep.'

Angelo didn't give her a chance to finish her sentence. He began to kiss her wildly, and hungrily. She'd teased him for too long for him to make love to her patiently. They both rolled around on the bed in a wild passionate frenzy, teasing each other sensually, and ending up taking one another completely in the act of lovemaking.

It was late afternoon by the time they were ready to go downstairs to meet Pablo. They were both in good spirits as they walked down the stairs, poking fun at one another. Armando the waiter met them as they walked into the lobby.

'Good afternoon,' he said smiling at them. 'Did you sleep well?'

'Yes, very well thank you,' Angelo replied. 'Have you seen Mrs Caruso around?'

'Yes, Mr Curro. You'll find her at the bar; she's having a drink with Pablo.'

'Thank you, Armando,' said Angelo.

'Not at all,' replied Armando, 'Pablo was right!'

'What about?' asked Rosita blushing a bit, imagining what they could have said.

'That you two would be down at five p.m.' he said quickly and then he turned and walked off smiling. Angelo and Rosita looked at each other and burst out laughing again, then both walked towards the bar and approached Pablo and Mrs Caruso.

'What would you two like to drink, something hot or cold?' asked Pablo.

'Coffee please,' they both answered in unison.

'Are you hungry?' asked Mrs Caruso. 'I can get the chef to cook you something or maybe a sandwich?'

'No thank you,' said Rosita, 'not for me, a coffee will be enough and then I would like to go out for a while.'

'Yes, just coffee for me too, thank you,' said Angelo. 'If we get hungry while we're out, we'll get a snack in some bar somewhere.'

They sat for a while, drinking their coffee and discussing the previous night's activities. Pablo looked at his watch and was aware of the limited time they would have before going to the theatre. So addressing Angelo said.

'Whenever you want to go out, I'm ready.'

'Yes, we're ready, Pablo,' answered Angelo, and both he and Rosita stood and bid Mrs Caruso a good day. She in turn reminded them not to forget they were going to the theatre tonight.

'Don't worry about that, we won't forget,' said Angelo, 'we're only going for a short jaunt, we'll be back in a few hours.'

They only had time for a short sight-seeing tour on this occasion, so they skipped the shopping areas and concentrated on monuments and places of beauty. Pablo firstly took them to see the cathedral in the Piazza Principal in Tucuman. Inside the cathedral they saw a beautiful statue of the Madonna Del Carmen, which was draped with a cape full of gold pendants of all shapes and sizes, which people had pinned there as donations to the Madonna for miracles she had performed. They also saw a bronze statue of an angel, which had been donated by the council of Tucuman in 1897.

Angelo and Rosita were taken aback by the beauty of the architecture and sculpting.

'The people of Tucuman are very religious,' said Pablo.

'I'm glad to hear it,' answered Rosita. 'I'm religious myself, but I hope to became a better Christian yet, just like my father was when he was alive.'

'Please don't judge yourself,' said Pablo. 'A person that loves God, and helps others in their plight for freedom, in my eyes, is a very good Christian.'

'Thank you,' Rosita said modestly. 'If you don't mind, when we finish here, could we go to get something to eat, I'm famished all of a sudden.'

'Of course, there is a great place around here that does amazing pizzas and delicious king sized hot dogs,' said Pablo.

'Please you two, stop talking about food, my taste buds are buzzing,' interrupted Angelo. 'I can almost smell the pizza.'

'The reason you can smell it,' began Pablo laughing, 'is that the place is literally around the corner.'

Rosita whispered into Angelo ear. 'You know Angelo, it's so quiet and peacefully in here, it's like being in Paradise.'

'I feel exactly the same, my love. At this moment, we're in Paradise,' said Angelo, as he looked into Rosita's eyes lovingly. That made her feel loved and secure.

She turned and looked at the counter with all the post cards and souvenirs of the cathedral. There was also a collection box. First she went over to the counter, and thinking of her friends at home, who were probably too poor to ever be able to visit Tucuman City, she bought a handful of postcards of the cathedral and some of the city. She then put some money into the collection box and headed towards the altar. Angelo and Pablo followed a little way behind. When they caught up with Rosita, she knelt at the altar and made the sign of the cross to pray. Angelo and Pablo stood back to give her space and admired another sculpture. When Rosita had finished her prayer, she got up and went over to the two men waiting for her.

'Would you like to stay a while longer or shall we go?' asked Pablo. Angelo looked at Rosita; she nodded yes with her head. Angelo placed one arm over her shoulder and said to Pablo that they were ready to go. The three of them crossed themselves facing the altar, and left the cathedral, moving straight towards the pizzeria which was called, 'La Cocina' They were almost being led by the smell of the pizzas.

They walked into the place laughing. A waiter came straight over to them, and took them over to a table. It was a small place, but very clean. They ordered a metre of pizza to share and something to drink. From their table they could see the chef prepare the pizza out on the counter. Francesca watched him in surprise, not believing what she was seeing. He was swirling the dough in the air, and singing away, it was as good as cabaret. As she had never seen anything like this before, she laughed to herself at what she was thinking.

'No wonder my mother's wrists ache when she makes pizza,' she said.

'Why?' asked Angelo and Paolo in unison.

'Because my mother works the dough on the table, by kneading it with her fists.'

The three of them laughed, as the waiter brought over the drinks. He said.

'Your beers, Señors, Señorita, the pizza won't be long.'

True to his word, the pizzas arrived within five minutes. They all tucked in hungrily and finished in record time because there was little conversation. Being so big and filling, they decided to skip dessert and went straight to coffee. After that Rosita asked Pablo to take them back to the hotel, so they could have plenty of time to get ready for the evening's entertainment.

Back at the hotel, Angelo knew they had plenty of time before Pablo returned to take them to the theatre. What Rosita didn't know, was that he wanted to spend at least one good hour in bed with her. With a bit of gentle persuasion Angelo could express his desires to her. The desire he'd kept under wraps all afternoon, the desire to make love to her again.

Rosita was under the shower, when Angelo crept in and caught hold of her, his strong hands burrowing through her long hair. His mouth came down on hers, speaking silently, of his love for her. She acquiesced to his kisses, feeling as though the earth had suddenly given way beneath her and she was now floating, as he moulded her to him. His hands tightened in her hair as he danced his lips over hers. His tongue tracing the outline of her lips before parting them, thrusting inside, deepening the intensity of his kiss, and exploring the warm velvet of her mouth.

Deep inside her, the passion went from a flicker to flaring quickly and uncontrollably into a roaring flame that swept through her like wildfire, consuming her.

'Angelo, please take me…' she cried, 'I can't wait any more.'

'Your wish is my command,' he whispered. He turned off the shower and while he was kissing her again, picked her up still dripping wet, and without Rosita realising it, she found herself laid on the bed.

Her arms crept up his muscular chest, fingers splayed and trembling with the onslaught of passion. She moaned low in her throat as his hands slid down her back, provocatively stimulating her spine before cupping her buttocks, pressing her against him so she could feel the heat and the strength of his arousal. Rosita felt as though she was melting, trickling down into a pool of conscious-less sensation. Rosita's head thrashed from side to side as her body arched against him.

'Oh, Angelo, that's so good...' There was a long silence except for the rustling of their bodies on the bed, their strained breathing and exclamations of ecstasy. He carried her to the heights of fulfilment, beyond anything she had dreamed possible. She cried out her love for him and him for her, while they made love with abandon.

They got to the theatre by five minutes to nine, and went straight to their seats as the show was about to start shortly. The four friends all enjoyed the opera very much. After the show, on their way out, Mrs Caruso met up with some friends of hers, and proudly she introduced Angelo and Rosita to them. After a little chit chat, her friends suggested that they all go to a bar and have a few drinks. Of course this would have changed their plans, because they were going to go straight back to the hotel.

Mrs Caruso looked at Rosita and said, 'What do you think, are you up to going on to a bar for a drink?'

'No, thank you,' said Rosita, 'I hope we don't offend you, but I'm a little tired tonight and would like to get to bed early. We have a lot to do tomorrow, maybe another night. But you stay with your friends Mrs Caruso, if you wish. We'll go back by ourselves.'

'I have to say no, too, I'm afraid,' said Mrs Caruso to her friends apologetically. 'I've had too many late nights just lately, way past my usual bed time, so I need to rest too. Maybe next time.'

So, they all said their goodbyes and the four of them went back to the hotel. Once Angelo and Rosita were in their room, they undressed and got ready for bed. Rosita sat at the dresser brushing her hair slowly and methodically, taking her time, knowing that Angelo was already in bed, waiting impatiently for her to join him.

She eventually turned away from the mirror and looked at him, put down the brush, went to the bed, and sat down on the edge.

'Come on sweetheart, get into bed, you need to sleep,' he said, grinning and patting the mattress.

'Sleep?' she questioned, lying beside him, 'I had something else in mind.'

'Oh yes?' he teased, 'I wonder what that could be?'

'Shall I show you?' she asked, leaning over him.

'Would you?' he played along. 'And the slower the better,' he said, with one of his devilish smiles. His mouth took hers in a wild, hungry exchange, before he helped Rosita off with her silk night-gown. He switched off the bedside light, putting the room in a low, romantic glow, coming from the moon light oozing through the balcony window. The dim light shimmered over her naked and beautiful body. His fingers and lips caressed her body gently, and her desire soon demanded satisfaction. Angelo moved over her, and she welcomed him. They clung tightly, and their passion lifted them onto an undulating sea of sensation, their love for each other soared strongly.

She whispered in Angelo's ear, 'I love you Angelo, more than anything in this world.' By now, Rosita was trembling with longing as he moved between her thighs, and she slid her legs about his waist. He penetrated her, sending exquisite sensual shocks cursing through them both. These waves of pleasure kept coming time and time again until gloriously they reached their climax together, with breath-taking fulfilment. When their breathing had come back to normal, they exchanged a couple of gently kisses before Angelo withdrew to lie by her side, and switched the bedside light on again.

'Do you think you're up to going to the gymnasium tomorrow?' he asked jokingly.

'Yes, of course I am, what makes you think I wouldn't?' she replied. 'I think it will be fun, and I miss the training. And don't forget that you were asked along too, so you have got to do something towards a demonstration.'

'I haven't forgotten,' he said. He then switched off the light and kissed her again. They very soon fell asleep in each other's arms.

It was Thursday morning about eleven o'clock, when Angelo woke up. Breathing in deeply with his eyes still closed and smiling in a satisfied way, he caught a waft of the aroma of coffee; he looked up and saw Rosita looking down at him with a tray of coffee, and biscuits.

'Good morning, darling,' she said, smiling down at him; she knew it would surprise him. 'Are you ready for coffee and freshly baked biscuits? They have just come out of the oven.'

Angelo smiled and without saying anything got onto his knees and looked at Rosita. She imagined what was going on in his mind, and she barely had time to put the tray down, as he pulled her down onto the bed and started to kiss her.

'Hold on, what do you think you are doing?' she said laughing.

'Nothing out of hand, just want to prove to you that I am awake enough for you.'

'But the coffee will get cold and those lovely biscuits, that are saying, "eat me, eat me." And don't forget, that you will need all the energy you can muster this afternoon.'

'OK I give in, where are the biscuits,' he said.

'They are on the tray, can you see them?' She had to laugh.

'Yes, well, I have changed my mind, I think I'll eat you instead,' and he started to nibble at her neck and shoulders. Rosita was laughing so much that she had no strength to push him away. As they were playing around on the bed, somebody knocked at the door, but they were making so much noise that they didn't hear it. Mrs Caruso was worried something must have happened for them not to answer because she knew that Rosita was already up, so she let herself in and walked into the room and they heard her say with a stern voice.

'And what's going on in here? I'm sorry, but I don't allow this sort of thing to go on in my hotel.' Mrs Caruso then couldn't contain herself any more, so she burst out laughing.

Angelo looked up at once and he was dumb-struck, he couldn't say anything, but after a few seconds, he covered his face with both hands. She had caught him almost naked, luckily he had his private parts covered. Mrs Caruso's eyes were having a feast looking at his gorgeous masculine brown, firm body, and she didn't even conceal her pleasure. Rosita continued laughing; she laughed so hard that she was almost out of breath, and had tears running down her face. She pointed to the chair in the corner of the room, inviting Mrs Caruso to sit down.

'No, thank you, my dear. I haven't got time to sit down, as I've got a lot to do today. I'll be out all day, so I'll see you tomorrow. Enjoy yourselves at the gym, I'm just sorry I can't be there to watch you two in action,' said Mrs Caruso.

'We're sorry you can't be there too,' said Angelo, 'We're getting used to having you around, along with your warm hospitality.'

Rosita got up off the bed, after having calmed down from her laughing fit and walked over to Mrs Caruso. She kissed her on both cheeks and said. 'We'll see you tomorrow then, I hope all goes well.'

'Oh, thank you my dear, I'm sure everything will be fine. Oh, I nearly forgot to tell you, Pablo is waiting downstairs. Also, I should tell you, you will have many friends and admirers at the gym this afternoon.' She then turned and made her way to the door. Angelo quickly threw on his dressing gown and ran over to Mrs Caruso.

'Wait a minute,' he said. She stopped at the door, he hugged her saying, 'I hope that one day you can come to Las Cejias, and stay with us for a while. Our house isn't as grand as your hotel, but you will be most welcome.'

'I would love to come down to see you too, maybe when things calm down a bit. Then I'll come with a friend,' she said.

'I see, a friend, say no more. Have a good day,' said Rosita.

Mrs Caruso shook her head tutting jokingly and then she turned and left the room laughing. She felt as though she was leaving her own children behind in that room.

After Mrs Caruso's intervention, Rosita and Angelo's passion had cooled down, so they decided to get ready for their day in a calm and collected fashion. They drank their coffee and got dressed quickly. When they got downstairs, Pablo was sitting in the lobby reading a newspaper.

Good morning, Pablo,' they both chanted. He looked up from his paper and smiled.

'Good afternoon,' he replied, 'I'm as hungry as a wolf, how about you two?'

'A little,' they answered.

'Would you like to eat something here, or out somewhere?' he asked, admiring the way this couple were subliminally radiating love to one another. It made him wish he was young again, so he could amend all the mistakes he'd made when he was younger. He would probably still be together with his wife today if he had made some different decisions.

'I think it would be better to eat here, don't you?' Angelo said, looking at Rosita for her approval. 'Then we can go out for a ride later, before we go to the gymnasium.'

'Yes, I agree. Will you join us Pablo?' she asked.

'Yes, thank you, I will.'

She stood between the two men, entwined her arms into theirs and led them to the restaurant.

CHAPTER TWENTY-TWO

When they arrived at the gym, Rosita and Angelo were not as nervous entering as they had been on their first visit with Mr Maiorana. They both walked in proudly, because they'd been invited to this place to do a martial arts demonstration. Pablo escorted them down to the changing rooms where they found everything they needed laid out ready for them. These included traditional black Chinese sahm suits in their sizes, sashes for their waist and padded sparring gloves. Once ready they followed Pablo to the gym, where there were already lots of people waiting for their arrival. They could feel the charged atmosphere, Angelo and Rosita were starting to feel fired up and excited, that they could feel the adrenaline pumping through their bodies. Both hesitated outside the open door for a few seconds.

Rosita looked at Angelo and said, 'You look great, Mr Curro,'

'You don't look bad yourself, Miss Miserendino,' he replied, and kissed her on her forehead. They bowed in unison before walking through the door into the gym and to their delight, everybody welcomed them with applause. Mr Maiorana got up from his chair and walked over to them. He greeted them with a shake of the hands; he then asked them if they'd had a good time in Tucuman and if Pablo had taken good care of them.

'Yes thank you, Mr Maiorana,' said Angelo, 'he is not only a good guide but a good friend too.'

Good, good,' said Mr Maiorana, 'I'm glad to hear that. Anyway, are you two ready for your demonstrations? These young people here can't wait to see you two in action.'

'Yes we are,' they both said, and went over to join the rest of the class to start the warm up. After fifteen minutes or so, they did some tai-chi type exercises in silent meditation, this lasted about ten minutes. Angelo then said to the men standing by him.

'Please take it easy on me when we start the sparring, as I'm not as good as you lot.'

'Neither am I,' said Rosita, 'so please don't laugh at me.'

'We know how good you two are,' said one of the other young men. 'Don't try to kid us; one of our men saw you in action that night at Don Camillo's house. The night you fought with those two bullies, the two ruffians you killed at the hacienda.'

Rosita looked at him in surprise and then said to him, smiling.

'I didn't know Mr Maiorana had a mole right there in the wolf's den.'

'We don't have anyone in there, it was me. I was outside the mansion snooping around. I wanted to get in but I didn't know how. Then I saw you go in and I followed you. I saw what you did, and there was a moment when I thought I should help you, but I found you didn't need my help. So, I just enjoyed the show.'

'Thank you, brother,' replied Rosita. 'I thought I had been careful not to let anyone follow me. You could have been one of them; I need to be more careful next time.'

The class was now ready to start a new exercise. They lined up in rows of ten and moving forward in precision movements, they kicked and punched and blocked imaginary blows. Angelo was not used to this type of class but was soon getting into it and feeling at home. Rosita and the others were more used to this regimented form of training and it showed, because they were very accurate and sure of their movements. After ten minutes of this they had a break. Some people went to the bathroom and some just sat around chatting, taking a drink and towelling the sweat off their faces and necks.

Angelo and Rosita went to sit down by their friend and protector. He looked at them admiringly and applauded them as they sat down. A man came over straightaway and gave them a drink. As they drank, another man came over and whispered something into Mr Maiorana's ear.

When the man had finished what he was saying, Mr Maiorana chuckled and said, 'That's a good idea; I'll ask them if they want to participate.'

The man walked off and Mr Maiorana turned to Angelo and Rosita with a sly look on his face.

'These young men would like to see you in combat with a few of them. But only if you would like to that is. Don't feel as if you are obliged to. They won't be offended.'

Angelo looked at Rosita and nodded at her, she responded with a nod too.

'It would be a pleasure,' Angelo said to Mr Maiorana. The old man was very pleased, he had a glint in his eyes, and he looked over to the young man who had put the question to him and nodded. The young man smiled and spread the word. They all got ready for the sparring; Angelo was picked to fight against the young man who had asked for them to fight.

They met in the centre of the floor, shook hands and Angelo said, 'My name is Angelo.'

'I am Pepe.' the young man replied.

Rosita was drawn against the young man who saw her fight at Don Camillo's Mansion. He shook her hand.

'I'm Pasquale.' His smile spread across both sides of his face. 'It is an honour for me to be fighting, sparring against you.'

Rosita acknowledged his compliment with a shy nod, and the sparring began. Everybody else sat around the hall in concentrated silence, watching every move the four in combat made. Every now and again, when a punch or kick got through, they broke into applause. Mr Ruvolo and Mr Mendoza walked in during the sparring session. They walked straight over to where Mr Maiorana was sitting and they sat down next to him without saying a word, so as not to disturb the concentration of the fighters, or of the audience, as they had been waiting for a long time to see Rosita fight. Their first sparring exercise was defence against club attack and overhead traditional knife attack forms. The audience were surprised at the style of defence Rosita was using, and they all wondered who the teacher could be who'd taught her. She was quicker and more precise than anything they had seen before. Some of them were also wondering if she had any fencing or sword skill to speak of.

Angelo and Pepe stood aside now as Rosita and Pasquale were now going to fight with two-metre long staffs. Her opponent was happy because he had found a worthy adversary, someone who could fight to his standard. Rosita was holding back though, she still had a couple of tricks up her sleeve.

Pasquale thought at one moment that he had her beat, but he was wrong. As he went for her, she somersaulted over his head and disappeared from his field of vision. The second she landed, with lightning speed she spun round to face his back and struck out for his neck with the staff, missing him by one centimetre. Everybody stood up and clapped in awe at this. Pasquale turned his head quickly and saw Rosita behind him. He smiled, and nodded his head in defeat, admiration and respect.

He then counter attacked and started to throw blows from all angles at Rosita, but she managed to parry all of them. She moved around with the speed and elegance of a cat, and jumped as if she had springs on her feet. Pasquale was good too but he wasn't as fast as Rosita. They came to the end of their routine, and it was time for

Angelo and Rosita to leave. The four fighters bowed to each other and left the floor, everybody applauding as they did so.

Mr Maiorana stood up and applauded. He then turned to his two friends who had come in a few minutes previously and said, 'Would you not be proud to have a daughter like her? Not that I'm not proud of my daughter, but Rosita has a great quality about her. She and Angelo make a lovely couple.' He then walked over to Angelo and Rosita.

'Bravo,' he said to them, 'I will wait for you two upstairs where I will buy you both a well-deserved drink.'

'Thank you,' replied Angelo, 'we won't be long.'

When Mr Maiorana and the others left, Pasquale came over to them and said.

'Well, my friend, I must say goodbye for now.'

'Why?' asked Angelo. 'Aren't you coming for a drink with us?'

'He's offended with me,' said Rosita jokingly.

'No! You know that's not true,' Pasquale pleaded.

'Of course we know, I was only joking. Maybe your girlfriend is waiting for you?' suggested Rosita.

'That's the truth. I'll see her in a couple of days, in Las Cejias,'

'What?' exclaimed Rosita.

'He's teasing you,' interrupted Angelo.

'Oh no, my friend's, it's true, I leave tomorrow morning. Do you have any messages you would like me to deliver to anybody?'

'Yes please,' said Angelo, 'for my father and my uncle. Would you tell them that all is going well and as planned, and that we will see them God willing, on Monday?' They shook each other's hands, and before Pasquale left, Rosita asked if she could send her regards to Papa Joe and family.

'That goes without saying,' replied Pasquale.

'God be with you.' they said to him as he left. Angelo and Rosita then went to take a shower before going upstairs to have a drink with Mr Maiorana and the other family heads. The six of them had a long, frank and detailed discussion regarding their common problem. When they'd all agreed the plan of action of how they were going to bring Don Camillo down off his pedestal, along with all the scum around him, they had one more drink to seal the agreement.

Friday morning, Rosita was stretching her arms up and forcing her eyes to open. The first thing she saw was Angelo's gorgeous naked body sprawled across the bed. She feasted her eyes for a few long moments, and then she leaned over and kissed him on his forehead, whispering, thinking he was still asleep.

'I love you so much, Angelo, what would I do without you?'

'Why? Are you thinking of leaving me?' he said looking at her with one eye still closed. ' I wouldn't try it if I were you, or you'll pay for the consequences.'

'Oh, you're awake!' she exclaimed.

'Yes, I have been awake for a while, and I've been watching you sleep. Oh boy, you look so angelic when you're asleep. You must have been very tired last night.'

'Why do you say that?' she asked, caressing his face, then his manly chest covered with light brown hair. It tickled her hand. A shiver of excitement ran through her body, he didn't miss that, which made him gasp with pleasure.

'Well,' he said in low voice, 'you worked hard yesterday, and very well too. I couldn't find the right moment, but I thought you were fabulous.'

'Thank you, darling,' she said, her hand tormenting him non-stop, sending tingling sensations all through his body. 'You didn't do too badly yourself.'

'When we retired last night I didn't get a chance to say goodnight, because you went straight to sleep,' he said, breathing deeply.

'I'm sorry, please forgive me, I didn't mean to,' she pleaded, with a concealed smile. She knew what she was doing to him.

'You're forgiven,' he said to her as he pulled her to him in a tight embrace. 'Do you know what I was thinking when I woke up?'

'No,' she said, moving on top of him, feeling his arousal, and nibbling on his ear.

'Well, we have had so much fun while we have been here I was just thinking that we won't ever forget the memories we made here. We will probably tell our grandchildren one day,' he said.

'Stop sweet-talking me, what are you really trying to say?'

'After you went to sleep last night I got to thinking about our conversations with the four family heads. The situation at home is getting tense and I am getting a little worried, as I think are you. So I was going to suggest going back home tomorrow. What do you think?' he asked. He felt a bit guilty suggesting cutting their break short, but he was hoping she agreed.

'You're right, I am worried,' she responded. 'But for now I think we should get up, because we have a lot to do if we are to leave tomorrow. We have a few more presents to buy yet, and we have people to say goodbye to. Maybe a meal with Mrs Caruso tonight and then we have to pack our cases.' She paused and kissed him tenderly on his lips. 'And! We have to have an early night tonight; otherwise we won't get up in time tomorrow morning.'

'Yes, my sweet, sweet witch,' he said, kissing her neck. 'One thing we will do for sure tonight is to get an early night,' he said with a smirk on his face. 'But we won't be going to sleep straightaway either,' he finished, still pecking at her neck.

'Oh Angelo, tell me, are all Italian men the same? Do they all have a one-track mind?' she asked, trying to distract him, so she could get away from him. If not they would spend all day in bed.

The day went quite quickly for them. They had finished dinner and were sitting having coffee with Mrs Caruso when Angelo looked at his watch for the second time. Rosita noticed this and said.

'Well Mrs Caruso, the dinner was exquisite, thank you again, but now you must excuse us, we must really get to bed early tonight. We'll see you in the morning before we leave.'

'I understand my friends, but wait a minute; I have a little something for you two. I'll give it to you now so you can pack it in your cases,' said Mrs Caruso, as she called over a waiter. He came over with two parcels in his arms; they were bound beautifully with a velvet bow. Mrs Caruso passed one over to each of them.

'Thank you very much Mrs Caruso.' said Rosita. 'You shouldn't have, you've already done more than enough for us.'

'Nonsense my dear, it has been a real pleasure for me having you stay here. You have fitted into my life as if you were my very own family. I won't forget that very easily,' she said, with tears welling up in her eyes. 'Anyway, enough of this sentimental paraphernalia. Please don't open these parcels yet, I don't want to see your reactions when you see them, just in case you don't like what you see. Now run along,' she said, trying to hurry them along because she could feel her emotions bubble up again.

'I'm sure they are lovely, whatever they are,' said Rosita feeling a little emotional herself. She kissed Mrs Caruso on the cheek wishing her a good night, and Angelo did the same. They walked off leaving Mrs Caruso clutching her cup of coffee, and watching them as they disappeared around the corner.

Angelo made sure that Rosita didn't go straight to sleep, as he had promised, but neither slept well anyway. They were both a little anxious as well as excited about going back home. They wondered what problems lay waiting for them at the Hacienda Antigua.

The sun had only just risen and Angelo awoke. He gently got up and went over to the bathroom quietly, so as not to disturb Rosita. When he got back, he sat on the bed with his back to the headboard. He watched Rosita sleeping and thought to himself how lucky he was to have her back after all these years, and how after all this time major changes were about to take place at Las Cejias. He would then be able to call her by her real name, Rosita Miserendino. Thinking she was asleep; Angelo reached out and gently caressed her cheek.

In fact Rosita was only dozing, she opened her eyes and said to Angelo, 'What's the matter darling, can't you sleep either? We're in the same boat, I hardly slept a wink last night. I wonder, what time is it?'

'It's just turned five o'clock, darling.'

'Oh, dear, still so early,' sighed Rosita.

'Yes it is,' replied Angelo, 'I think it would be a good idea if we try to get some sleep for another hour or so.'

He lay down on his side of the bed and took hold of Rosita's hand, and he pressed it against his chest. They both fell asleep instantly and slept, not for one hour, but for three more hours, which they had needed because of the restless night. Both woke at eight o'clock and quickly did their ablutions and got dressed. They had packed their suitcases the night before, so they were ready to leave. They had their breakfast for the last time with Mrs Caruso and Pablo. By the time they had had a chat and their breakfast it was nearly ten o'clock. Mrs Caruso arranged for a couple of porters to collect the suitcases from their room, and to take them down to Pablo's car. They all left the breakfast table together and headed for the lobby.

Rosita was arm in arm with Mrs Caruso, Angelo and Pablo walked along behind them. When they got to the car, they found both the Maiorana and the Ruvolo families waiting to see them off. Rosita and Angelo were surprised to see them here, as they had already said their farewells the night before.

Rosita walked over to Mrs Maiorana and gave her a hug. Mrs Ruvolo joined them in a group hug, then Rosita returned to Mrs Caruso again and hugged her tightly.

The old woman said, 'Go on, get going before I change my mind and keep you here.'

Lastly, Mr Maiorana embraced Rosita and kissed her on both cheeks, saying, 'Be careful my dear, very careful. I won't tell you to stay away from trouble, and to let your friends do the job for you, because I know I would be wasting my breath.' He then shook Angelo's hand, and gave him a quick hug, and said to him, 'Look after our Rosita, she has no fear, and this could get her into trouble. We wouldn't want anything to happen to her.'

'I know,' replied Angelo, 'but don't worry, everything will go well.'

'I have my reasons for worrying,' said Mr Maiorana. 'Every day Don Camillo feels more and more under pressure, and things could get very dangerous out there. Anyway I hope we will meet again soon, so I can give you a hand.'

'I beg of you Mr Maiorana,' Angelo interrupted, 'do not put your life in danger; you have done enough to help us already.'

'It's never enough to help people that fight for the right causes. I would like this ordeal sorted out as soon as possible. The people of the Hacienda Antigua have suffered long enough under the hands of Don Camillo. Now you'd better get going, the train will not wait for you.'

Angelo and Rosita quickly got into the car, and Pablo drove off leaving everybody else standing at the hotel entrance waving goodbye. Angelo took Rosita's hand and kissed it. He looked at her, but not saying anything, their eyes met and they smiled at each other.

'I'm fine, don't worry about me, darling,' she said. There was silence for a while and then Pablo said something that neither of them heard, because they were both deep in thought about they're visit here and how well it had gone.

'Sorry, Pablo,' apologised Angelo, 'what did you say?'

'I said that you have both captured the hearts of many people here in Tucuman.'

'Thank you,' said Rosita in a low voice, as she squeezed Pablo's shoulder gently. 'We came here to ask for help from people we didn't know, and we thought we were wasting our time, but instead we've found true friendship and support from everybody.'

Pablo drove very quickly to the station so as not to be late. They got there in no time at all, they were lucky the police didn't stop them. Pablo helped them onto the train with their cases, of which Angelo and Rosita had two extra for their return journey. Pablo embraced them both and said to them.

'I wish you both the best of luck in your venture.' He then quickly got off of the train and walked back to the window out of which they were leaning. The train started off slowly and they waved until the train disappeared into the distance.

CHAPTER TWENTY-THREE

The train started to slow down as it approached Las Cejias. Angelo put all the bags by the window. As the train pulled into the station they noticed that there weren't many people about, apart from a handful of armed men. They saw four serious faces looking at the train as if they were waiting for someone.

Rosita let out a yelp and said, 'Angelo look!'

'Yes, my darling, I know,' he said, squeezing her shoulder. 'I knew someone would be here to greet us.' The train stopped and the four men walked up to the carriage. Angelo handed down the cases and greeted them all with. 'Am I glad to see some familiar faces. Father, Uncle Nunziato what's the matter, couldn't you sleep, or were you all having nightmares?' he said, jokingly, as it was very early morning.

'Welcome back, amigo,' said Juan and Chen in unison.

They climbed down the steps of the train, Angelo embraced his father, and Rosita flung her arms around Nunziato.

'How are you, my dear father?'

'I'm very well, my dear, and yourself?' he replied in a whisper. He felt emotional, even though Rosita wasn't his real daughter; he loved her as if she was.

'I'm very tired of being sat down all those hours, and of all the dust I've swallowed on this trip, but apart from that I'm fine thank you.' Then one by one she embraced everybody else, as did Angelo. They all walked towards their cart, and were soon on their way, very happy to be back home and all together again.

Rosita asked Vincenzo how everything was at home and if anything had happened in their absence.

'Everything's just fine,' he replied, 'and everybody is anxious to see you two again. But the tension and the atmosphere is still strong, as if a time bomb was about to explode at any time.'

Nunziato, Juan and Chen were riding ahead of Angelo on their horses, Rosita and Vincenzo out front on the large cart. They looked round occasionally to check on them, glad to have them back. The cart moved noisily along and seemed louder than normal as there was nobody around at this hour of the morning. As they passed the front of the church, Rosita noticed that the door was open.

'Would you mind stopping here for a moment?' she asked. 'I would like to see Don Saverio?'

Angelo dismounted his horse and Rosita climbed down from the cart and they both walked into the church. Inside, there were only two old ladies that attended the church every morning as soon as the priest opened the door. Don Saverio was at the altar, on his knees praying. Angelo and Rosita walked quietly along the centre isle and sat on the front bench directly behind him. As they sat down he was finishing his prayer. He got up and turned to see who the newcomers were.

'Angelo! Francesca! My dears, how are you!' he exclaimed, as he gave them both a hug. 'I was just praying for you two; I heard that you were returning today.'

'We are fine, Don Saverio,' they assured him, 'and how about you? We've had a good trip, and our trip to Tucuman was a very successful one, everything went as planned. Even better than planned actually.'

'I'm very happy for you,' said Don Saverio. 'Tell me, who came to meet you at the station?'

'My father, Uncle Nunziato, Juan and Chen,' replied Angelo, 'and they are waiting for us outside so we'd better go now.'

'Good, fine, I'm glad to see your two ugly faces again,' he joked. 'You must be very tired, and grubby with all the dust that flies around those trains,' said the priest. He accompanied them outside and greeted the others who were waiting patiently. He then embraced Angelo and Rosita again and said to them, 'Go home and have a rest, you must be tired. I'll be over later for a coffee.'

'Good, we'll be expecting you, see you later,' Angelo replied and then they left.

It was seven o'clock and the sun had fully risen now bringing a comfortable heat. It was the end of March now and the air had cooled down a bit. As they approached the hacienda gates, they noticed that the place was heavily guarded. There were at least six armed men guarding the front of the hacienda. Rosita gave a worried look to her uncle Vincenzo.

'This is nothing my dear,' he said, 'wait until you see the fortress they have made of Don Camillo's mansion.'

They had to stop at the gates, as two of the guards approached them.

'Oh! You four have returned,' said one of the guards. They didn't answer him.

'What have you got in the cases?' asked the second man. He was scruffily dressed, and he smelt strongly of tobacco and alcohol. Angelo had the impression that the men at the gates were deeply under the influence of alcohol.

'Just my daughter's and nephew's clothes,' replied Nunziato, trying to keep calm.

'Homecomer's clothes eh? I think you have weapons in these cases,' shouted the second guard as he slammed his rifle butt down onto one of the cases. They all remained calm so as not to provoke

Don Camillo's thugs. But Rosita couldn't resist the challenge. She jumped down off the cart and stood face to face with the man with a subtle smile on her face.

'Listen to me carefully señor,' she said calmly to him. 'I have been travelling all night, I'm tired and I don't want to repeat myself. We won't open the cases, because we have nothing to hide from you. My father and uncle have come to collect us from the station, and that is all you need to know. I will only open my cases if Don Camillo comes here himself so please don't make anything out of this situation.'

'We won't call anyone out here; we're in charge of this entrance.' the man said to her, with a very loud laugh.

Rosita smiled coldly to herself and stepped closer to the man. Their eyes met and so did her knee, very sharply with his groin. He groaned and froze in a cold sweat, instantly dropping his rifle which Rosita snatched up. She shot one round into the air and then pointed the rifle to his head.

'Open the gate and let us pass or I'll blow your head off,' she ordered. The other guards were all taken by surprise. They had their rifles trained at the travellers, but were all looking at one another at a loss as to what to do next. The guard at Rosita's feet shouted in panic.

'Open the gate, for God's sake, open the gate.'

Just then more men rode up to find out what the commotion was about. Some of the new arrivals recognised Rosita, Angelo and the others.

One of them said, to the guard at the gate, 'Let them pass, they are residents of the hacienda.'

He then noticed the man on his knees still clutching his groin in pain, and started laughing heartily. He then taunted the man by saying, 'I'm sorry amigo, I forgot to warn you that this urchin kicks like a mule.'

Rosita calmly threw the rifle to the ground, and climbed back onto the cart, keeping her eyes on the bunch of guards. The gate was opened and Angelo led their party through the gate. As they did, Rosita noticed one of the guards ride quickly toward Don Camillo's Mansion, obviously to report what had happened here.

On arrival at Vincenzo's house, they all dismounted. The men started unloading the cart and sorting the horses out whilst Rosita headed straight towards the front door.

'Mmm, what a lovely smell,' she exclaimed. 'Can you smell anything, Uncle, what have you cooked this morning?' And just as she was saying that, Mama Bimpe appeared at the doorway.

'Mama Bimpe!' Rosita shouted as she rushed up to her and flung her arms around her. 'I've missed you so much.'

'Welcome back,' Mama Bimpe replied, emotionally. 'I'm so happy that you are both back safe and sound.'

Rosita sat outside on the bench with Mamma Bimpe and told the old woman what a wonderful time they had had in Tucuman City, that their thoughts were with them all the time they were away and how she and Angelo were happy to be back home where they belonged.

'Hey, what's happening here, aren't there any cuddles for me?'

'Angelo, my dear boy,' said the old woman, 'of course there's a cuddle for you and a hearty breakfast too. You must be famished after all that travelling.'

'Thank you, Mama Bimpe, I'm really happy to see you,' he said, putting his nose to the air and sniffing. 'Can I smell fresh corn bread?'

'Yes, Angelo, made especially for you and Rosita,' said the old woman, smiling from ear to ear. They all entered the house. Juan,

Chen and Angelo took the cases upstairs, while Rosita splashed some cold water on her face to freshen up. Angelo did the same when he came back downstairs, and they all sat down together for breakfast. They filled their plates with all the wonderful food Mama Bimpe had prepared for them. For a while there was silence, everybody was too busy enjoying their food.

Rosita broke the silence by saying, 'Home, sweet home! You can go to all the greatest places in the world, but your home is always the best.'

Angelo took her hand and kissed it gently saying, 'My dearest Angel, you couldn't have put it better.'

They all smiled at her, then continued to eat in silence for a while. Until Angelo interrupted the silence.

'I don't really understand,' he said. 'How can you all be so calm? Aren't you all dying to know what we accomplished in Tucuman this last week?' he finished, looking at everybody.

'Yes, but at the moment we're eating,' said Juan, looking at Chen with a grin on his face.

Vincenzo stopped eating, turned to Angelo and said, 'You know, I met a young man at the old hacienda, and he told me he was still very tired from his long journey on Friday. He also passed on your regards.'

At this Angelo put his hand on his forehead and said, 'Of course, he must have told you everything. I didn't think of that, excuse me.'

'But of course you're excused,' said his uncle Nunziato. 'You're tired. As soon as you two finish breakfast, I suggest you go and have a rest, after all today is Sunday, a day of rest. What do you say?'

'I say that you're right,' suggested Rosita. 'We've plenty of time to talk tonight. Well, I've finished eating so I'll go up and see you all later,' she said, getting up from the table. 'Please Mama Bimpe, don't let me sleep too long, a couple of hours are plenty for me,' she ended, and kissed the old woman on her forehead. Rosita waved to all and went up to sleep.

As she left the room Angelo slowly got up from his chair, yawning.

'Well I'm ready to go to sleep too. So excuse me all, and thank you for coming to fetch us and for cooking my favourite breakfast, Mamma Bimpe.'

They all said 'sleep well' in unison. Angelo went up and lay down next to Rosita, and within minutes they had both drifted into a deep sleep, curled up against each other. Angelo was the first to wake up, he rubbed his eyes and looked around the room, he was momentarily disoriented and wondered where he was. He finally realised it was his room, and then thought to himself, was the trip to Tucuman a dream. But he noticed the suitcases in the corner of the room and remembered being picked up from the station in the morning.

Angelo was still wearing the same clothes he'd travelled in. He turned to look at Rosita but she was not there. Wondering where she could be, he went to look for her, starting in her room. She was asleep on her bed; she too hadn't got out of her travel clothes. Angelo wondered how he hadn't heard her move from his room. He closed the door behind him and left Rosita sleeping, he headed onto the landing to go down and to his surprise found Chen asleep at the foot of the stairs.

'Hey, amigo. Que. passa?' Angelo said to him as he shook Chen's shoulder gently.

Chen looked up with a surprised look on his face looking bleary eyed at Angelo. Then he said to him, 'Oh, you're up, I didn't hear you come down the stairs.'

'That doesn't matter, Chen,' said Angelo, 'but if you were tired why didn't you come up to my room, or my dad's room? We have beds for you to sleep in.'

Chen smiled and rubbed his face. 'I didn't think I was that tired, I just dropped off,' he answered. 'I'm actually here on guard.'

'What for?' asked Angelo. 'Are things that bad?'

'Oh no, it's not that, but your father and uncle Nunziato asked me to make sure Francesca didn't go out by herself.'

'Listen, Chen,' Angelo said, and began to laugh, 'I think my father and my uncle Nunziato know Francesca better than we do, but if she really wanted to go out alone, she wouldn't have let you stop her. She would have sneaked past you without waking you like I did. Anyway, where is everybody?'

'Out, to buy a few things, then they will go to the church. They said they wouldn't be long. Did you sleep well?'

'Very well, thank you. What time is it?' asked Angelo.

Chen checked his watch. 'It's almost one o'clock,' he exclaimed. 'They should have been back a while go,' he said a little worried now.

'Don't worry, Chen, I'm sure my uncle and father stopped off to have a chat with the priest, and Juan has probably gone to have a chat with his brother at the bar.'

'I'm sorry, Angelo, I don't want to worry you, but I just have a funny feeling about this. I wanted to go with them but they insisted I stay here.'

'I tell you what, Chen, you stay here and wait for Francesca to wake while I go and look for them, how's that? Anyway, I think it will be easier for me to go in and out of the gates now that they are being guarded so rigorously. Especially as they only need a small excuse to start any trouble,' he finished. He too was feeling a little anxious now about what could have happened. 'If it is okay for you,

I'll go and saddle up my horse. Meanwhile you make yourself a strong pot of coffee, so you can stay awake for a while. Try to keep Francesca here if she gets up before I get back.'

Angelo set off on his way to find his father and uncle. He didn't like the heavy hearted sensation he was feeling, but he tried to ignore it. Halfway to the village, Angelo crossed paths with Don Camillo and Donna Teresa in a cart, accompanied by a few of Don Camillo's ugly thugs riding behind them. Both parties stopped, and he didn't like the cold look he was receiving from the group in front of him, especial from Don Camillo's bodyguards. The atmosphere was so cold that he felt as if he'd just had a cold shower. From that instant, he knew that something terrible had happen. He took a deep breath and kept his cool.

'Buenos tardes, Donna Teresa, Don Camillo,' said Angelo. He couldn't even crack a smile at them.

'Buenos tardes, Angelo,' said Donna Teresa. 'Welcome back.' She seemed a little sad. Again Angelo felt that unmistakeable wave of coldness come over him, even though the hot sun was shining down on them. He knew he had to watch what he said next, until he'd clarified what was behind this frosty reception.

Don Camillo said to Angelo in a cold manner, 'I'm sorry about what happened to your father Angelo, it shouldn't have happened. But nobody asked him to get involved in somebody else's business.'

That was enough to confirm Angelo's feelings of dread and without waiting for any other explanation. Angelo kicked his horse into an instant gallop. His heart felt as if it was in his throat, his mind working overtime. Was he dead? Dear God, don't let it be that he thought to himself. Like the wind, he rode into the village. He had tears in his eyes and was still wondering whether his father has been killed or what. As he rode into the village he saw a large crowd around Doctor Pedrazza's house. He jumped off his horse before it had completely stopped and pushed his way through the crowd.

'Oh poor boy!' he heard someone say.

Angelo burst into the house and went straight to the lodge where he knew the doctor saw his patients. There were more people crowded in the room. Then he saw Mama Bimpe sat down by his father holding his hand. As he entered the room, the priest Don Saverio Scalabrini, saw him come in, and went straight over to intercept him. He took him firmly by the arm and led him to one side, away from his father. Angelo was furious. He demanded to know who was responsible for hurting his father.

Father Scalabrini told Angelo to calm down and then said, 'It was one of Don Camillo's men that went for him. It happened so quickly that nobody could do anything to prevent it happening. Listen to me,' he whispered. 'Your father is in great pain, but Doctor Pedrazza has given him a sedative. I'm sorry to have to tell you, he is in a bad way. He has two broken ribs, we don't know if his lung is affected yet, a broken collar bone and bad bruising to his face. Please don't let him know yet, we wouldn't want him to worry too much in his condition.' proceeded the priest, 'We all feel for you and for your father, we're all behind you one hundred percent. I promise you, the person responsible will pay dearly for what they have done to your father, as will all his thugs.'

The priest's emotions got the better of him, tears started to roll down his face and then added. 'Your father is more than a brother to me,' and then he embraced Angelo, who was also choked up with emotion.

After a few long seconds, Angelo was able to speak.

'Thank you, Don Saverio,' he said, and he took out a handkerchief and wiped his eyes dry. He then went over to his father, and knelt down beside him, he kissed him on his forehead gently and said.

'Father, it's Angelo.'

Vincenzo opened his eyes and looked at his son, but didn't have the strength to say anything. Tears appeared in his eyes and started to roll down his cheek.

Angelo took his father's hand and held it, saying to him, 'Father, I'm going to take you home now, you wait and see, you'll get better really quickly.'

Vincenzo found the strength to smile at Angelo just to reassure him.

Doctor Pedrazza and a few others were organising a cart with lots of blankets and cushions in it. While this was happening, Manuel, Nunziato and Juan arrived; they looked possessed, with pallid complexions and distorted facial features. For an instant Angelo wanted to ask where the three of them had been while his father was being beaten nearly to death, but it wasn't the moment to find out. Manuel had obviously been crying, he felt so guilty because he had been with Vincenzo when it had happened, but couldn't do anything about it.

The atmosphere in that room was so tense one could cut it with a knife. Nunziato and Angelo embraced in silence, they couldn't say anything and there was no need to. They just looked at one another as if to say, 'this is the last time that Don Camillo interferes with our lives.'

They all congregated around Vincenzo and with great care and gentleness the four of them, Juan, Manuel, Nunziato and Angelo picked Vincenzo up on a stretcher and took him to the cart.

Back at the house Rosita had got up, and Chen was trying to keep her occupied by offering her some food, coffee and asking her to tell him all about the trip to Tucuman. For a while it seemed to be working. Rosita told him of the places they had visited and how they had met the four families, as well as their hotel and their hostess. By then she'd finished the snack and the coffee that Chen had made for her. Then she started to ask questions.

'Chen, you said that Angelo and the others would be back soon, that was nearly an hour ago. What's happened, are you telling me the truth? It's strange that they are taking so long, I have a bad feeling about this, Chen.'

'Francesca, please don't make me feel any worse than I already do. I was ordered first by your father and uncle Vincenzo, then by Angelo to make sure you stay put until their return. Please don't get me into trouble,' he pleaded.

'Don't worry Chen, you're like a brother to me, I won't do anything to make you more worried than you are at the moment,' she said reassuringly. Just then there was a knock at the door. 'Come in, the door is open,' invited Rosita. As the door opened slowly, Rosita instantly recognised the person. 'Maria, come in,' she exclaimed. 'What can I do for you?'

Maria looked at Rosita with sorrow in her eyes, she wanted to say something but couldn't.

'Chen, this is Maria, Donna Teresa's maid. Maria, this is Chen a very close friend from home,' said Rosita not moving her eyes from Maria's face; she looked really scared. 'Come over here and sit down Maria,' suggested Rosita, taking a chair from under the table. 'Tell me what's wrong, are you hurt?'

'No,' answered the old woman. 'I'm fine,' she said looking at Chen worriedly. She was not sure if she could talk in front of the young man.

'Don't worry, Chen is like one of the family,' encouraged Rosita as she began to tremble a bit. She somehow knew that behind this troubled face, there was definitely some very bad news waiting to be divulged. Maria could still not talk; she began to cry, then started to sob and covered her face with both hands. Rosita, placed her arm around the woman's shoulder, she was for once speechless, seeing the old woman in such distress. All at once the woman regained her composure; she dried her eyes with her white apron and looked at Rosita.

'Something terrible has happened to Don Vincenzo Curro.'

'What?' exclaimed Rosita jumping to her feet in a shocked reaction, her whole body tensed as if she were ready for battle.

'It happened this morning,' began Maria, 'when they got to the church. There were a few of Don Camillo's men hanging around and they were drunk. They insulted Mama Bimpe and they wouldn't let her go into the church. Vincenzo tried to stop them, telling them that she was with him and his family. The men jumped onto him and they were punching and kicking him, and one of them hit Vincenzo with the butt of his rifle. It happened so quickly, the others jumped down to help but it was too late.'

'What do you mean, too late? Is, is he…' Rosita couldn't say the word at first, but controlled her emotions and continued. 'Where is he now, is he still alive?' Rosita asked calmly, but she was crying, without releasing it.

'I don't know, I just heard Donna Teresa shouting at Don Camillo and his men. She said to them that she had reached her limit, this time they had gone too far and not to be surprised if there were any repercussions.'

'Tell me Maria, who sent you here?'

'Nobody, I slipped out when I could, but I'm afraid in case somebody saw me,' she replied.

'Well, if someone saw you come here, you can just say that you have come to visit me,' said Rosita.

'You don't understand. As things stand at the moment, Don Camillo and his men are suspicious of everybody and you are one of their main suspects, so please watch out for yourself. I must go now before someone catches me here.'

'Wait a minute Maria,' said Rosita grabbing her arm to stop her from leaving. 'If you know the risks involved, why did you come here?'

The old woman looked at Rosita for few long intense seconds, and then she said., 'You won't remember, but I held you in my arms, many times when you were young. I virtually brought you up, Rosita.'

'I'm sorry Maria, but I don't know what you are talking about,' Rosita said, a little shocked at Maria calling her by her real name, but at the same time keeping her cool.

'Wait a minute,' interrupted Chen stopping Maria from going out of the door. 'If you really came here of your own accord, you could do something else for us. It's very important but it could be a little dangerous for you.'

'Hold on, Chen,' ordered Rosita. 'What are you going to ask of Maria?'

'Don't worry Francesca, I just want Maria to deliver this news to the old hacienda.' Turning to Maria he continued. 'Well, will you do it Maria? It would be very dangerous for me to go and also I need to stay and watch over Francesca.' Maria hesitated for a several seconds, first looking at Rosita then back to Chen.

'I'll do my best,' she said eventually. 'I think I know someone there who I can trust. Goodbye for now,' finished the old woman and then she turned to walk out of the door.

'Goodbye, Maria, and thank you, I won't forget this,' said Rosita, Maria put a scarf over her head and walked out cautiously.

'What are we to do now, Francesca?' asked Chen.

'Not a lot, we can only wait until the others return and we can pray that my uncle is still alive. I know exactly how you're feeling at this moment Chen, it's like somebody is churning your stomach around. Now I understand why nobody came to warn me, they thought I would retaliate without thinking, but we are so close now that I can think straight and I know that when the time comes they will pay dearly for all their injustices.'

They heard something outside. It was a horse and a cart. Both Chen and Rosita quickly ran to the door and they saw it was their family returning. Rosita ran to the back of the cart to see if her uncle was there. Angelo jumped down from the cart and stood by her. She looked at her uncle who was sleeping and then back to Angelo with a questioning expression.

Angelo embraced her firmly and whispered into her ear, 'I don't know Rosita! I don't know.' There was desperation in his voice. They all rallied round and took Vincenzo from the cart. Rosita walked round to Mama Bimpe, who was still sitting the other side of the cart, and helped her down. They all headed up to Vincenzo's bedroom and laid him down carefully. Rosita knelt down beside him. She kissed his forehead and took his hand into hers holding it to her chest.

'Forgive me, Uncle, it's entirely my fault,' she said, as she started crying uncontrollably like a child. Nunziato took her by the shoulders and pulled her away. 'Father,' she said sobbing on his shoulder, 'if he dies I'll never forgive myself.'

'No, Francesca, you must not blame yourself, it's nobody's fault, it would have happened anyway,' he reassured her. Maybe he was trying to reassure himself too.

'Please, tell me father, what did the doctor say, and why is he not here?'

'Doctor Pedrazza did all he could my dear, we can only wait now.'

'Wait, for what, Father?'

'A miracle. A miracle from God. The doctor will come over later with the priest and some others. We have to sit down now and plan an attack before tomorrow morning. We must strike soon, because even Don Camillo is disturbed by what happened today. Somebody has to go to warn the people at the old hacienda, none of us can go because we're being watched where ever we go.'

'Maybe they will know by now, Father,' Rosita said, half as an answer and half as a thought out loud. For an instant her mind was transported back to the past. Fifteen years back, when she saw her real father stabbed to death. And now she may lose Vincenzo too. Not him as well she was thinking.

'How can they know by now?' asked Nunziato, interrupting her thoughts and bringing her back to the present.

So, she told him that a while ago, Maria, Donna Teresa's maid, had paid her a visit and told her all about what had happened and what she had heard Don Camillo and Donna Teresa say. Warning Rosita to take care, because she was in great danger.

'What do you think, Father. Did she come to find something out or not?'

'I truly don't know, darling,' he replied 'I can only say that God's day of justice is near and the tyrant knows it. I want to be there on the day, to watch the suffering in Don Camillo's face as he goes down knowing who has done this to him,' finished Nunziato, with his eyes fixed in a trance as he was recalling all the atrocities Don Camillo has caused over the years.

Mama Bimpe interrupted Nunziato's thoughts and said, 'Please everybody; let's go downstairs and let Vincenzo rest in peace and quiet. We can all get something to eat and you can talk your plans through.'

Angelo was sat on the bed next to his father.

Rosita looked at Nunziato and motioned her head towards Angelo and said to him in a soft voice, 'Father, take him downstairs, I'll stay with Uncle in case he needs anything.'

Nunziato did as Rosita had suggested, he and Angelo followed everybody downstairs. Mama Bimpe cut some bread, cheese, salami and ham and placed the food in the middle of the table. She also put some wine on the table, but nobody seemed interested in eating. The atmosphere was thick, Mama Bimpe burst into tears, and Angelo who was sitting next to her put his arm around her to comfort her. He didn't say anything; he just took out his white handkerchief and handed to her.

She dried her tears and said, 'Angelo, you can't imagine how happy he was this morning when you two got back. We had organised a party for tonight at the old hacienda, as it was the eve of Palm Sunday.'

Just then Rosita entered the kitchen and walked straight over to Angelo. She touched his shoulder and told him that his father was awake and he wanted to see him. Angelo quickly got up and went straight upstairs, and Nunziato followed him. Rosita sat down where Angelo had been sat.

'Please eat something,' urged Mama Bimpe to Rosita.

'No, thank you, Mama Bimpe, I can't. But I will have a cup of strong black coffee please,' she answered, gazing over the table at nothing in particular.

Chen got up in an impatient manner and said, 'I'm sorry Francesca but I can't just sit here and wait, I must go to the old hacienda to find out if they have heard anything.'

'Please sit down Chen, and listen,' said Rosita trying to calm him down. But who was she kidding? She felt as mad as he did, she felt as if someone was twisting a knife inside her. 'I'm sure someone will arrive very soon to confirm that they have heard the news.' She hesitated and took a deep breath to calm herself down. 'And if they don't come, we will go in a couple of hours, when it is dark. You, Manuel and I can walk there, as it will be easier to get past the checkpoints on foot,' she suggested. Another thought crossed her mind. That at the old hacienda, they were probably busy organising an assault by now.

'OK. Francesca, we will wait for another couple of hours, we'll do as you say,' said Chen, looking over at Manuel and winking. 'I'm going to sit outside for a while.'

'Me too,' said Manuel, following Chen out. Rosita was too preoccupied to see what the two boys were up to. Rosita was left alone with the old woman and her thoughts. After a minute or two, she asked Mama Bimpe if she could make up some camomile tea for Vincenzo, which she would take up herself.

'Yes my dear, but before may I give you a word of advice?'

Rosita nodded yes, she already knew what Mama Bimpe was about to say.

'Don't even think about going out after all that has happened, unless you're with Angelo, Nunziato and the others. One injury in the family is enough.'

'Yes Mama Bimpe, you're right. I'll try to be sensible,' she said, and left the kitchen. When Rosita arrived in Vincenzo's room, he was awake. Angelo and Nunziato were seated beside the bed.

Rosita walked straight over to them and kissed Vincenzo's cheek, and said to him, 'Mama Bimpe is preparing you some camomile tea, Uncle; do you feel up to drinking some?'

'I don't know my dear, but I'll try some,' he answered very faintly.

'Good, that's the spirit Uncle, you wait and see, you'll be up and about in no time.' They all chatted about other things rather than the tension which was rising in all parts of the hacienda. Vincenzo was joining in when he could, as he was slipping in and out of a shallow doze. His body was tired due to the internal repairing going on.

After a while the tea arrived, Angelo gently helped his father sit up, while Nunziato placed two pillows behind him to support his back. Rosita fed the camomile tea to Vincenzo a spoonful at a time.

After about a half-hour or so they all heard a cart arriving outside the house. Rosita looked at her adoptive father Nunziato with a serious look on her face. He nodded to her, as if to say, yes, go check who it is. She quickly got up and ran down the stairs two steps at a time. When she arrived outside, Chen and Manuel were greeting Stefano, and she saw Mariano, Luigi, Vittorio and Pasquale getting down from the back of the cart. She knew that the time had arrived to pay back all the atrocities Don Camillo Ferrero had subjected everybody to over the past fifteen years.

Her whole body was buzzing with adrenaline and her brain was working clearly and rapidly. On the cart there were some palms and a few baskets of bread and tortillas, which had been prepared at the old hacienda. But of course these were only decoys so that this trip looked authentic.

Vittorio, walked straight over to Rosita and embraced her with tears in his eyes. She noticed this and realised he had been crying. He asked her how Vincenzo was. Rosita informed him that Vincenzo was still alive, but they didn't know exactly how badly he was hurt and that the doctor was due anytime now, and they had to wait to see what he had to say.

'We were all so shocked this morning, when we heard the news,' said Vittorio. 'I wanted to come over, as soon I heard, but my father and the others wouldn't let me. They said it was more important to start to plan things for tonight. And we prayed that nobody here would do anything silly that would finish up with even more trouble.'

'It was the only and best thing you could have done,' interrupted Angelo. He had followed Rosita down just in case there was any trouble and was right behind her. 'We could only sit and wait for you to arrive. Anyway, let's go in now,' suggested Angelo.

'I'll stay outside!' put in Chen. Angelo nodded to Chen, and with that they all went upstairs to see Vincenzo. The newcomers piled into Vincenzo's room and greeted him.

Pasquale said jokingly to Vincenzo, 'What are you doing in bed? That's typical, just when we needed you!'

Vittorio came near Vincenzo and sat by him on the bed and kissed his hand. He asked him how he was feeling, trying to fight back the tears accumulating in the back of his eyes, but failing miserably. The hot tears rolled down his cheeks, leaving little wet trails leading down to his chin where the tears seemed to leap from his face. Vincenzo had always been like a father to Vittorio, and a very good friend to his family.

Seeing Vittorio so emotional, Vincenzo forced out a few words, 'Please, don't cry for me, Vittorio, I'll be fine very soon, wait and see. Right now I need you to stay strong and help Angelo and Francesca. That's the most important thing at this moment. Even if I already know that you and your family will do just that. Of course Vincenzo knew that Vittorio would die for them, as would hundreds of other Negroes, Chinese, and many from other races.

'Don't worry, Don Vincenzo, we're all ready and waiting to fight alongside Angelo and Francesca,' said Vittorio looking into

Vincenzo's eyes. Vincenzo nodded as if to acknowledge Vittorio's last comment but was drifting off again into unconsciousness.

Angelo now leaned over to his father and whispered, 'Father, we will all go downstairs now, so you can sleep for a while. We must plan out our next move.'

Mama Bimpe, had no interest in conversations about fighting, so as soon as everybody was downstairs again, she disappeared upstairs to keep an eye on Vincenzo. But not before telling everybody that if they needed anything to call her. The old woman dimmed the light right down in Vincenzo's room, because she not only wanted to keep an eye on Vincenzo as he slept, but she also wanted to keep an eye out of the window just in case anybody who didn't belong here approached the house. Not that the house wasn't already being watched over by Vincenzo's friends. As Mama Bimpe looked out from the window, the air was thick with tension; she could almost taste the trouble. The spilt blood of people wasted on the battlefield, she had seen this all before.

Downstairs, they had been busy talking and planning for about an hour. They had finally agreed on how they were going to attack the guards at their end of the perimeter to the hacienda. This was to act as a decoy for the main attack on the mansion, which Rosita had arranged back in Tucuman City with Mr Maiorana. The plan was that as soon as darkness fell over Argentina, Mr Maiorana's men would be ready to attack the scattered men that Don Camillo had placed all around the hacienda's perimeter. Whilst here, they would assault the main mansion early in the morning, so that the guards were either half asleep or in a drunken stupor, and the relief guards still asleep in their bunks.

'Right,' said Angelo, 'I advise you all to get a few hours' sleep now, we will have a busy night ahead of us.'

'Agreed,' said Vittorio. 'What about you two, when are you two going to get some rest?' Vittorio asked Angelo and Rosita. She looked washed out, thought Vittorio, but he had to admit to himself, that it was very rare to meet a girl like her. She really was her father's daughter, may God help her. She was a natural born leader. Even though this time she had let Angelo decide what the best thing was to do first. She probably couldn't get the thought out of her mind, that Vincenzo was nearly killed because of her, even though that wasn't the case. They had patiently and methodically put their heads together to work out the best solution. Their planned efforts were for the people in the old hacienda not to be in any more danger, ever again. In order for this to happen, all these bandits and thugs must be eliminated including the king pin, Don Camillo, and the sooner the better.

'We will wait up for the priest, the doctor and Juan. There is also someone else coming with them,' said Angelo. He knew that the rest of his friends would arrive soon and there would be more planning to be done.

'Fine, we will see you in a few hours then,' replied Vittorio. They all headed upstairs to rest. Vittorio was about to leave the kitchen, when Rosita called him back.

'Wait a minute, Vittorio. A quick word,' she said. She raked one hand through her dark hair, and rubbed the top of her head. 'Did somebody come to the old hacienda today to tell you what had happened this morning?'

'Yes, somebody did come, she spoke to my father. I only heard my father thanking her for coming to inform us, and that she had taken a big risk doing so, but that we had already been informed. Why did you ask me this question?'

'I'll tell you later, I just needed to know, so I could stop thinking about it. You go now and have some rest,' said Rosita with a faint smile. So, old Maria was telling the truth. Rosita was now wondering why she'd never come forward before. Maybe the old woman was biding her time, to make it seem to Don Camillo and his wife that she was loyal to them. Rosita now hoped that Maria had made it back to the mansion without being caught or questioned, or that maybe she had stayed at the old hacienda, where she would be safer anyway.

CHAPTER TWENTY-FOUR

Back at the old hacienda, there was a lot of activity. Everybody, young and old, anyone who could fight, were getting ready for the assault. Chickens, turkeys and geese were running round all-over in the yard, making such a racket. They knew, they sensed that something was going to happen, animals always do.

Jon Chian, had his group gathered around him while he gave them last minute tips on how to move about stealthily, so as not to let their enemies hear them arriving. Going over again how to disarm opponents quickly and quietly, before they have a chance to warn others. These men wouldn't be using firearms.

Papa Joe was doing exactly the same with his men, but they all had guns, daggers and some swords; they all meant business and formed part of the morning attack team.

Most of the women were busy preparing food or sorting out bandages and other medical supplies. They were preparing themselves for the worst. Others were in the surrounding fields pretending to work but actually being lookouts. Pasquale, the young man who fought at the gym in Tucuman with Angelo and Rosita, was there too. He had a large group of men who had been congregating from Tucuman over the last few days, arriving from different directions so as not to be too obvious. They were ready to fight alongside Angelo and Rosita.

Meanwhile, more men were on their way from Tucuman, as Pasquale had sent a message to Mr Maiorana, as soon as he'd heard what had happened to Vincenzo. Hopefully they would arrive late evening or tonight, heavily armed and ready.

Everybody who was going to take part in the battle went to sleep for a few hours to be sure they would be fresh for the night ahead.

It was about two o'clock in the morning and Vincenzo's house was bustling with activity. They were making the last preparations before the assault, and people were coming and going like a well-oiled machine. The doctor and priest had arrived to check on Vincenzo and were now helping with some other chores.

Rosita and Angelo knew they had many friends, but they were still surprised to see all these people pulling together inside and outside of the house. They wondered how on earth they had all managed to get by Don Camillo's men without being detected, as they were all-over the place on this land. Mama Bimpe was preparing coffee and biscuits for them all, with a little help from some of the young men. They all took their refreshments on the move, because they didn't have much time to waste.

Rosita went up to her room and knelt down at her dressing table where she had a crucifix. She started to pray to God, to help all of them get through this ordeal. After her prayer she went into Vincenzo's room. She tiptoed over to him and kissed him on the forehead thinking he was asleep. She looked at him for a few long seconds lost in thought, when suddenly Angelo came into the room to let her know that everything was ready.

She moved away from the bed to go to Angelo when she heard Vincenzo's voice saying to them, 'Be careful my children, and return to me safe and in one piece.'

'Don't worry about us Father, you go back to sleep,' Angelo replied, going over to him. He took one of his hands in his. Angelo of course knew that his father was in great pain physically but on top of that he was scared for his son's and Rosita's life.

'God bless you and protect you both in your crusade. Have the doctor and the priest left yet?' asked Vincenzo.

'No Father, they are still downstairs. The doctor is going to come up and give you some more medication soon, but the priest is coming with us,' Angelo replied. 'Now please rest, Father, and don't worry, everything will work out just fine. We will be on our way now.'

Angelo and Rosita met the others downstairs and for a long moment not a word was spoken. They were all concentrated on making sure they had everything they needed in place, then looked at each other and nodded, as if to say, all set, let's go. Everybody except Angelo, Rosita and the priest put on a balaclava, and one by one moved off in the direction of their designated positions.

Angelo, Rosita, Chen and the priest Don Saverio Scalabrini, headed straight to Don Camillo's residence on horseback. They headed out across country, off the main tracks, so as not to be spotted by the lookouts. As they got closer to the mansion, they dismounted and tied their horses to a tree. They walked carefully the last five hundred metres until they stopped around the corner from the entrance to the main house.

Angelo looked around the corner to see how many guards were posted out front. Chen was counting the seconds away, they had to give the others time to get into position, and hopefully they wouldn't encounter too much trouble on the way. The priest got ready to make his move, with a cross in one hand and a walking stick in the other. The time had finally come. The moment in Rosita's life that she had been waiting for, for fifteen long years.

Chen stopped counting, saying. 'It's time, my friends, good luck to all of us,' and gave the signal.

At the go ahead, the priest, with a relaxed attitude as if he was going out on a picnic, walked confidently towards the front door of the mansion. The guards spotted him, he walked slowly with the walking stick, the small cross he had hanging around his neck on a chain in his hand. With his eyes down he looked as if he was praying; one of the guards moved towards him.

'Halt! Who's there? Stop I said,' he commanded.

'Hey wait,' said the other guard, 'it's the priest. What are you doing here at this time?'

'Good morning, my children, I'm here to talk to Donna Teresa,' said the priest calmly with authority in his tone. 'It's very important.'

'Padre Scalabrini, what could you want to talk to Donna Teresa about at this hour?' enquired the guard who'd spotted the priest first.

'I've come as requested to offer her confession, now please open the door and let me in,' the priest shouted. 'Otherwise you will have Donna Teresa to answer to,' as he struck the floor with his cane. Without saying any more one of the guard's knocked on the large wooden door three times and the door opened a few seconds later. A huge man with a moustache appeared at the door, he was the size of an ox. He said in a deep gruff voice.

'Che passa, compadre? It's too early to change the guards yet.'

'I know it's too early for that,' said the guard outside the door, sounding very annoyed. 'But the priest is here to see Donna Teresa.'

'The priest must be crazy,' the big man roared. 'OK. Come on in.'

The plan went smoothly. While Don Scalabrini was complaining about being called crazy and slowly following the human ox into the wolves den, the guards were distracted by laughing at the priests rants. Angelo, Rosita and Chen jumped the three guards outside by placing their right hands over the mouths and jaws, their left hands behind the heads and simultaneously kicking the backs of the guards knees from under them and twisting their heads round to the right sharply, instantly breaking their necks. At the same time the priest took out the concealed stiletto sword from inside his cane and ran it through the big man's chest. He shoved him as he went down so that he couldn't fall near the door. The priest quickly crossed himself, asking God to forgive him.

Meanwhile the guards outside having been dispatched were being dragged inside and hidden. Once inside, the priest bolted the door behind them, so that they only had to face any guards inside the building. They all knew what they had to do now, so without a word they moved silently and swiftly to their next objective. Rosita went to the far left to listen at the inner door, to see if any movement may be occurring in the corridor leading to the kitchen. Angelo went to listen at the door immediately to their left leading to the lounge. Whilst Chen and the priest went to the far right towards the staircase and the door to the library, they looked up to check the landing and saw nothing. Don Scalabrini then looked over to Angelo and he signalled with his hand that there was some activity in the library.

Rosita also signalled activity in the corridor that led to the kitchen. Angelo noticed a big heavy chair by the staircase and he signalled Chen and the priest to fetch it and prop the chair behind the door to the library, in order to trap the men in temporarily, at least to give them some time to go check upstairs. As they were placing the chair, they heard some footsteps approaching along the corridor from the kitchen. Angelo and Rosita tiptoed to the hinged side of the door, while Chen and the priest quickly made their way up the stairs taking the steps two at a time and crouching at the same time making themselves a smaller target to see or fire at.

The door to the corridor opened slowly and a man appeared at the mouth of the door. He hesitated, stretching his arms up and yawned saying, 'I could do with at least another hour of sleep.'

The other man behind him said, 'That's all you ever want to do, sleep.'

The two men had hardly finished talking, as Angelo jumped out in front of the first man and said.

'I'll be happy to put you to sleep, my compadre!'

Angelo then swiftly kicked the man in the stomach and karate chopped his neck to knock him out. Rosita took the second man before he could reach for his gun. She kicked him in the face and knocked him out, then took hold of his head and twisted it sharply, and broke his neck.

'This is for my uncle,' she said.

And to her and others surprise, they weren't the only men coming through the corridor, another four of Don Camillo's men were following. They started to fight and the noise attracted the other men in the library downstairs, who tried to investigate the commotion, but found they couldn't get through the door.

At the same time, more of Don Camillo's men who had been circling the property had noticed that there were no guards at the main door and went over to check. Once they realised there was a commotion coming from the inside of the house, they proceeded to try to kick the front door down. Meanwhile, as Angelo and Rosita were putting everything into taking care of the four newcomers into the lobby, Chen and the priest made their way along the landing towards the study. They knocked at the door to check if anybody was in the room, and then stood either side of the door. The door opened and two men appeared in the frame of the door. As soon as they had opened the door they'd heard the shouts and grunts coming from downstairs; their focus was instantly diverted to the hullabaloo in the lobby, forgetting the knock that had bought them to the door in the first place. One of them had hardly enough time to say.

'What is going on?' When Chen with his knife and the priest with his sword, showed them exactly what was going on downstairs by running them through in the doorway before they had even had the chance to draw their pistols. Then Chen quickly looked around the study to see if there were any more surprises inside. But the coast was clear.

Chen said, 'Padre, the coast is clear; you know what to do here. I'll go downstairs and give Angelo and Rosita a hand.'

Chen got down into the lobby just in time, because even though Angelo and Rosita had just finished dispatching the four men in the lobby, eleven more men from the library had just managed to break through the door sending the heavy chair flying. As they filtered out they split into two groups. Six of these nasty looking men went for Angelo, Rosita and Chen, whilst the other five headed up the stairs to check if other enemies were snooping around. For a second, things were looking quite desperate, but not for long as Pasquale, Stefano, Luigi and Mariano appeared at the top of the stairs. They were a couple of minutes late, because they had met with lot of opposition outside before Pasquale's team had managed to enter from the secret passage way in Donna Teresa's bedroom. Pasquale instantly took care of the first two men heading up the stairs; by throwing two well-aimed knifes flying into their throats. The other three men were shot down by Stefano and Luigi while Mariano was watching their backs. Within seconds Pasquale and the others were on their way down to help in the lobby.

Outside the noise had started to get louder, it seemed that their plan was working. Rosita's followers and some people from the nearby Ranches had joined in with this crusade; they were all determinate to get rid of Don Camillo and his men. There were screams and gun shots going off left, right and centre, obviously more help had arrived.

As soon as Rosita had a chance she went upstairs in search of Don Camillo. She went straight to Don Camillo's room, but there was nobody in there. She rushed back onto the landing and saw the priest as he poked his head out of the study doorway.

She went quickly over to him and said, panting, 'Padre, Don Camillo isn't here,'

'But your mother is,' he replied. Rosita walked into the study and looked around. She saw Donna Teresa sitting in the corner of the room with her maid, Maria.

Donna Teresa was sobbing, saying, 'What's going on here? Can somebody explain to me what's happening?'

At that moment, the shelving panel, which hid the entrance to the secret passage opened and an army of men from Tucuman poured into the room. Rosita pointed towards the door and the men filed out of the room and down the stairs towards the action out front. Rosita now turned slowly and moved deliberately toward Donna Teresa, and with venom looked her straight in the eyes and asked.

'Where have you hidden that snake of a man who killed my father? Where is he?' she shouted in the face of Donna Teresa.

'What do you want from me? Who are you? Why are you doing this to us? After all we have given and done for you, and the hospitality we showed you. What's happened here?' Donna Teresa kept repeating, hysterically. The sight of the shelving panel opening, and all those men coming through, had taken her completely by surprise and finished her mentally, it was as if she was living a nightmare.

'It's a pity, Mother, you didn't know me when I was young, other people brought me up so how can you possibly know me now,' said Rosita with tears in her eyes. 'And what you say you gave to me was already mine. There isn't a hole deep enough for Don Camillo to hide from me, I'm going to find him and I am going to kill him.'

As soon as she'd said that, Rosita swung round on her heels and ran towards to door. She looked back at the priest who threw his sword to her, as he would now stay and do his duty as a priest and console Donna Teresa.

Angelo, Pasquale's team of four and Chen were still fighting back Don Camillo's men from the base of the stairs, they seemed never to stop coming. The more they put down, the more came running in. Angelo's mind was on Rosita, he wanted to go upstairs to make sure she was safe. This strong desire to know how she was doing made him glance quickly up the stairs behind him. This was a mistake, as one of Don Camillo's bandits nicked his arm with a knife.

Rosita had searched all the rooms upstairs and was on her way back down. She saw Angelo's arm being cut and flew down the stairs to help him and the others fight back the last handful of men that had entered to defend Don Camillo's house. Much to Angelo's delight, his mind was at rest now that he had the love of his life beside him. At last they finished off the men in the lobby and headed on out into the courtyard. As they got there they saw the two brothers, Manuel, and Juan back to back, fighting off a few more of Don Camillo's thugs.

'Oh! There you are, you two!' shouted Manuel as he managed to slay another rogue. 'Thank God, we thought you were in trouble. These bastards are coming out from everywhere like ants, but tonight we will triumph over them and squash them all.'

'Thank you my friend,' shouted Angelo, as he struck a bandit who had tried to hit Manuel in the back. Rosita was positioned with her back to Angelo, ready for anybody who came for them. At the same time she was looking round for any sight of Don Camillo. Suddenly she saw a group of men running through the gate at the entrance to the drive. Leading the group, was a familiar old man, a Negro holding a pistol in one hand and a sword in the other hand. It was Papa Joe.

'They made it?' she said aloud, so Angelo could hear. Manuel now moved to her side. 'The nest is empty, Don Camillo must be hiding outside somewhere,' shouted Rosita.

Manuel noticed Angelo's arm was bleeding, as it was daylight by now, and he said, 'Angelo you're injured! Let me take a quick look at it.'

'It's nothing Manuel, leave it, let's go to find that bastard,' said Angelo. 'Talk of the Devil and he shall appear.' He had noticed Don Camillo along with his personal bodyguards and other men pouring in through the gate. They were fighting as they moved towards the house, surrounded by Nunziato, Jon Chian, Pasquale and about twenty of their Negro friends and colleagues. The four of them rushed forward to help and fought their way through the ruck towards the centre where Don Camillo was being shielded by his personal guards. Rosita was frantically swinging the sword and kicking her legs to make a path to her objective, as she wanted to get to Don Camillo first, but his men surrounded him well.

As she approached the wall of men, she saw Pasquale, Chen and a few of the others acrobatically somersaulting into Don Camillo's men and clearing a space where they landed. This was very dangerous, but the only way to get to the centre where the head of these demons was standing. As Rosita finished off another assailant, she noticed Nunziato and Jon Chian either side of her. She signalled to Jon Chian to give her a boost. He immediately got into position in front of her, lunging forward with his right knee bent, his left leg straight behind him and his hands interlocked on his thigh. Rosita took two fast steps towards him, put her right foot onto his hands and with his boost took off in an acrobatic triple somersault, landing by her friends fighting their way through Don Camillo's personal guards.

'Hey!' she said, 'I thought you were my friends! Save some of the fun for me!'

She snapped a kick into the stomach of the man in front of her and smashed the handle of her sword down onto his head.

'Sorry, I didn't have time to send you an invitation, but I'm glad you could make it,' said Pasquale wittily.

'Thank you Pasquale, but don't forget Camillo is mine,' she replied aloud.

Chen then interrupted with, 'Francesca my dear, don't forget that you're not the only one who wants a piece of that bastard.'

By now, Don Camillo realised that things were getting out of his control. He ordered his men to retreat towards the mansion, thinking that he would be safe once inside, not knowing what surprises lay in store for him in the study. Some of the men from Tucuman had stayed with Donna Teresa.

Don Camillo's scrum had worked their way up to the front door now and Rosita shouted over the din of the skirmish to Angelo.

'We can't get to him from this side, but we could from the back of the house.'

She lashed her adversary across the face with her sword and kicked him in the groin. His fight was over for today as he was too busy curled up on the ground holding his nether region. Rosita then stepped towards Angelo, who was in combat with someone, but not for long, because Rosita did a flying kick to the centre of his back and finished him off. Angelo thanked her with a nod of his head, and she said to him.

'Would you like to accompany me to the back of the house so we can surprise our elusive friend?'

'Yes, of course, I'm sure our compatriots have things in hand here,' he replied, while they both ran around the back of the building, kicking and punching their way through. Chen, Jon and Manuel followed them round, knowing what they were up to. They helped Rosita and Angelo get up onto the roof without any trouble or being followed by any of Don Camillo's men. While Angelo and Rosita found their way to the secret entrance of Donna Teresa's bedroom,

Don Camillo and six of his men managed to enter the lobby bolting the door behind them.

Don Camillo sighed with exhaustion and fear, he put his hand to his head and said, 'Where have all these people come from? Even some of my people are turning against me. They will pay with their lives,' he hissed. He then noticed the bodies of the guards that he had left to protect his wife and the mansion, scattered around the floor. He exclaimed, 'Teresa my wife, where is Teresa?' At once he started to run up the stairs, with two of his men following him. The other four stayed behind to guard the windows and the door. He was furious knowing that his own people were turning against him, that his house had obviously been attacked and his wife may be in danger.

Halfway up the stairs he stopped in his tracks, looking up to the top he saw Rosita standing at the top of the stairs, with one hand on her hip and the other resting on her sword.

'You!' he hissed. 'Then I was right to suspect you, I knew you would be a trouble maker.'

As he said this, the two men with him placed themselves between Rosita and their boss, to protect him.

Rosita ignored them and said to him, 'You can stop hiding behind your men Don Camillo, because your day of judgement has arrived, and there is no place to hide.'

'You bitch!' he said spitting at her. 'How did you get in?' His eyes were out on stalks like a madman.

'You seem to forget that other people lived here before you did.'

Don Camillo's men were holding two knives each and were wearing confident smirks on their ugly faces, thinking to themselves that it would be a piece of cake to get rid of this girl. They moved slowly towards her, she didn't move until they reached the penultimate step. That is when she stepped back sharply and much to their surprise, Angelo and a gang of men from Tucuman sprung out in front of them on the landing. The two bandits hesitated for a second but then jumped towards Rosita. They hadn't a chance as Mr Maiorana's men, like lightning, disarmed and knocked them out before they got to the last step. Meanwhile Don Camillo ran back downstairs and ordered the rest of his men to open the door and let some more of his men in. He then went to lock himself in the lounge.

As soon as she had a chance, Rosita ran downstairs after Don Camillo, but as they got to the bottom of the stairs, many of Don Camillo's men were trying to come in through the front door. Two of the men from Tucuman were shot down straight away and a great battle started in the lobby. Don Camillo came out of the lounge again at the sound of the fighting and by skulking around the edges of the lobby, slowly made his way up the stairs again, followed by a few of his men. Rosita saw him in her peripheral vision, which took her concentration for a second, and she was stabbed in her shoulder. She stumbled and fell to the floor, but got up quickly.

Angelo's heart felt as if it had stopped beating for a long second, as he'd seen what had happened. With the help of a few of the men from Tucuman City, Angelo surrounded Rosita to protect her. Nunziato and Jon Chian entered the lobby and saw Rosita and Angelo still fighting for their lives. Although this was stressful it was also a relief and a weight off their minds to see that they were both still alive. Rosita started to edge her way back up the stairs, she was determined to catch up with Don Camillo, even though she knew he was not going to get away upstairs with Mr Maiorana's men waiting for him.

'Wait a minute, Rosita,' called Angelo, 'I want to tend to your shoulder.' He tried to put a handkerchief over her wound to try to stop the bleeding. But she ignored his efforts and made her way up the stairs. The adrenalin, emotions and sheer determination were driving her to her objective of confronting Don Camillo face to face.

Angelo followed two steps behind her and Nunziato with a few of the others behind them.

She stopped at the top step, she had to take a few deep breaths as she felt a little faint and she was now beginning to feel the pain from her wound. After a second or two, she continued towards the study and came across two men from Tucuman. They knew what she was after and signalled to her that her objective was in the study. She staggered into the room still feeling a little faint, Angelo right behind her in case she fell. Once in the room she saw Mr Maiorana who was sat casually in an armchair. As soon as he saw Rosita was injured he got up and went over to her.

There were a lot of people in the room, but she could only focus on Don Camillo. He was on his knees with his hands tied behind his back, looking very sorry for himself. She walked over to him slowly, there was no rush now. Her prey was trapped; he had come to the end of the line. She pointed the tip of her sword to the indent in his lower neck between his collar bones.

'Say your prayers you vermin, before I kill you, like I watched you kill my father, in cold blood fifteen years ago in that corridor,' she said, pointing towards the corridor with her free hand.

Donna Teresa then shouted, 'But it's impossible; you're Francesca, daughter of Nunziato Curro. Why are you saying these things, it's not true.'

At this, Nunziato couldn't wait any longer, so he stepped forward and said.

'My daughter, Francesca, died the night of the assault on the hacienda, fifteen years ago. Rosita here and I saw Don Camillo kill Don Sebastiano Miserendino in cold blood. So I took her away with me, or he would have killed her too, as well as me.'

Donna Teresa looked at Don Camillo in utter shock.

'It's not true; tell me it's not true Camillo,' she pleaded.

Don Camillo turned his head away from her and looked at the ground, he could not answer her. The sudden realisation hit her like a train; Donna Teresa fell to her knees and buried her face in her hands letting out a primal scream. Everybody in the room was rooted to the spot at the sound. After a few long seconds she looked up at Rosita.

'Rosita! My Rosita. Please forgive me if you can, I never knew, I never knew. I have made many mistakes in my life without knowing it and I've been very selfish. I couldn't see what was going on around me.'

Rosita was trembling at the overload of feelings and emotions; but she couldn't help not feeling sorry for her mother, at that moment. She slowly turned her attention back to looking at Don Camillo and was psyching herself up to run him through with the sword, so as to end his wicked life.

Mr Francesco Maiorana stepped forward and gently rested his hand on Rosita's hand that was holding the sword.

'Wait a minute, Rosita Miserendino, just listen to me first. Then you can do what you will with him. You have every right to kill him and also every reason too. But think carefully, if you kill him here in cold blood, like he did to your father, you won't be any better than he is,' stated Mr Maiorana, feeling sorry for her. He knew how she felt. 'I have policemen from Tucuman here with me,' he continued. 'He will be arrested and charged along with his rabble, those that are left. So, you and the people of Las Cejias can live here in peace.'

Rosita just looked at Mr Maiorana, then back down at Don Camillo. She hesitated, remembering all those years of dreaming that one day she would kill Don Camillo to avenge her father. But she knew that what her friend had said was right and that it was the proper thing to do. The hand holding the sword to Don Camillo's throat was shaking now. The overload of emotion and exhaustion was showing. She then looked back to Mr Maiorana and nodded in agreement, dropping her sword to the ground in front of Don Camillo.

Rosita half turned away from Don Camillo slowly, and then, with lightning speed, using the back of her hand, she swung round and struck the tyrant across the face. He fell to the ground. There was silence.

She was so emotional she couldn't speak. Her vision started to blur with the pain and exhaustion and she fainted. Angelo and Nunziato caught her before she hit the ground.

Four men stepped forward and led Don Camillo away. The battle was over and the rest of Don Camillo's men, those that hadn't run away or had been killed, were also arrested.

Not long after the assault, Donna Teresa had a stroke, and ended up paralysed down her left side. She spent the rest of her days confined to her room through her own choice.

Rosita made a quick and full recovery and married Angelo. Vincenzo also recovered and lived long enough to see two beautiful grandchildren grow up, a boy and a girl. And all the people of Las-Cejias lived a peaceful and happy live, all united with no prejudice.